The Forever Tree

Rosanne Bittner

BANTAM BOOKS

New York Toronto London Sydney Auckland

THE FOREVER TREE
A Bantam Book / March 1995

ISBN 0-553-56473-0
Published simultaneously in the United States and Canada

Bantam Books are published by Bantam Books, a division of Bantam Doubleday Dell
Publishing Group, Inc. Its trademark, consisting of the words "Bantam Books" and
the portrayal of a rooster, is Registered in U.S. Patent and Trademark Office and in
other countries. Marca Registrada. Bantam Books, 1540 Broadway, New York, New
York 10036.

PRINTED IN THE UNITED STATES OF AMERICA

RAD   0 9 8 7 6 5 4 3 2 1

A special thanks to Barbara Keenan and Lousie Snead, publishers of *Affaire de Coeur* magazine in San Leandro, California, for helping me find author Nieves Lorenzo, a native of Caracas, Venezuela, currently living in Oregon. Nieves works as a teacher of conversational Spanish, and also as an interpreter. Her "Spanish Love Notes" in *Affaire de Coeur* magazine helped me with the Spanish I needed to use in my story. Nieves was also kind enough to answer some questions for me regarding Spanish customs. I have studied Spanish myself, and though I am far from fluent, I consider it a beautiful language, with poetic flow and a rich, romantic flavor. There is a beauty and richness in our Hispanic culture and language, and in the Hispanic history of our country, that I feel many Americans do not recognize or appreciate. I came to respect that culture and appreciate its gentle beauty as I researched and wrote this book.

Author's Note

The setting and historical background for this novel are real. Only the characters and their stories are fictitious.

For those readers unfamiliar with Spanish culture, it was (and still is, for many Spanish people) a custom to give all children two last names. The first last name is the first last name of the father; the second last name is the first last name of the mother. Therefore, the children do not carry the father's last name. They are identified with the father through their first last name. As an example, my heroine's name is Santana Maria *Chavez* Lopez. Her father's name is Dominic Fernando *Chavez* Alcala. It is the father's and the daughter's *first* last names that identify them as related. When the daughter marries, she drops her own last name (in this case, Lopez) and takes her husband's last name.

Don (and *Dona*, for the woman) before a name signifies a wealthier, high-born Spaniard, almost like a title, as opposed to *Senor* and *Senorita* or *Senora*, although wealthier Spaniards can also be addressed as *Senor* or *Senora*.

Estancia means "estate."

Carino mio means "my beloved."

Mi esposo means "my husband" (*esposa*—"wife").

Te quiero mucho means "I love you very much."

A *Californio* is a person of Spanish descent born in California before it became a part of the United States. *Californios* considered California a separate country of their own, apart from Mexico or Spain.

There was a time, when our nation was young, when virgin forests covered almost the entire East Coast. As America was settled and land was cleared for farms, trees were cut for homes and for heating, and a great deal of this forest land disappeared. Then came the discovery of gold in California, and people rushed to the West Coast by the hundreds of thousands, creating new needs—new settlers needing homes, new cities needing buildings for businesses, people needing wood for fires. Not only was it expensive to ship that wood from eastern forests, but those forests could not furnish enough wood to feed a thriving, hungry, growing West.

All along the West Coast, from Washington to central California, lay one of the richest supplies of timber in the world. The only problem was that most of those trees were bigger than anything any eastern logger had ever worked with. It was impossible for one man to fell a California redwood, and in those early years, there were few men who had the knowledge and expertise to log the world's tallest, heaviest trees. While men scrambled to realize their fleeting dreams of gold, paying dearly for precious eastern lumber, they ignored a product that would one day make some men, men of vision and determination, far more wealthy than those who struck gold—the vast forests that covered the hills and valleys of California, Oregon, and Washington.

Among the Sierra redwoods, Douglas firs, sugar pines,

and western red cedars was the skinny lodgepole pine, useful only for fence posts and telegraph poles. It was not just the wealthy logging empires of northern California that gave me the idea for this story, but also the lodgepole pine; for as I read about it, I saw it as a symbol of how people can pick up their lives and start over, no matter what adversities and disappointments they face. The cones of the lodgepole pine are so tightly clenched, they do not open to release their seeds until the intense heat of a forest fire forces them to. After a fire, the lodgepole pine is among the first species of trees to begin new growth, rising from the ashes and bringing forth new life and hope for the future. It is the lodgepole pine that can make a forest last forever.

Part One

One

"Keep her steady into the wind!"

Will Lassater was sure the captain's shouted order had been lost in the roaring storm. He clung to the rail of the *Dutchess Dianna* as the worsening tempest tossed the 300-ton vessel about like a rowboat. Although it was only early afternoon, the clouds had blackened the sky to near darkness, and the violent deluge had hit suddenly as the ship rounded the Horn. In spite of his powerful grip and logger's strength, Will could barely hang on enough to prevent himself from being tossed overboard.

Until now, the weather through the South American seas had been tranquil and delightful, and they'd reached the tip of the continent yesterday. Now Will was worried he would lose not only the precious cargo of lumber he had intended to sell in California, but also his life.

Back in New England he had experienced many howling storms, but nothing like this, and at least then he had been on dry land. How would his mother and brother take

the news of his death? Going to California to build a new
lumber mill had been his father's dream before his own
death a year earlier. Now it was up to Will to make that
dream come true. He could not disappoint his family.

Another spray of ocean water nearly sent him overboard, and his thoughts turned to his mother, gentle, loving Ruth Lassater, who had sent him off with tears and
prayers . . . and with the precious wooden box that represented all the strength and dreams of her late husband,
James Lassater. That little box was packed away in Will's
gear. He would carry it to California, God willing, and it
would be as though James Lassater were with him, helping
him build the family business in a new land. The stories
they had heard in Maine about the trees in California
seemed farfetched, that they were too big for one man to
fell. Will was going to find out if that was true.

For now, though, he would be lucky to survive this
storm. The rugged Dutch flute that carried his valuable
lumber and maple syrup was usually easy to manage, requir-
ing only a sparse crew. At the moment those men were
running in every direction, answering orders shouted into
the wind by the ship's captain, David Eastman. Eastman
had carried Lassater lumber to faraway ports for years. He
had been highly respected and trusted by James Lassater,
and now Will could only pray he was skilled enough to
keep this ship afloat through what Will was convinced had
to be the worst storm even the captain had experienced.

The wind roared in his ears, and salt water drenched
him with such force, he could hardly find a moment to take
a breath. He shivered from the cold, the wicked wind and
rain penetrating the rubber slicker and hat he wore over
his wool jacket. Somehow the rain had gotten down inside
his rubber boots, and his feet were sloshing in cold water.

The ship groaned and tossed, and Will expected the
lumber in its hull to burst through at any moment, break-

ing open a hole that would send them all to the bottom of the ocean. The biting wind numbed him; the rain that stung his face was mixed with snow and sleet. It was only by his own strength that he managed to hang on to the railing as another huge wave raised the ship's bow so high, he was sure it would flip over. Two sailors came sliding down the deck, screaming all the way, trying to grasp something to stop their descent. One was close enough for Will to reach out and grab.

"Hang on!" he shouted, clinging to the man's wrist. The second man kept sliding, and Will watched him roll up onto a stack of ropes, then fly over the top of the ship's railing and disappear. "Man overboard!" he screamed, still clinging to the first man, but his words were lost in the wind.

The ship crashed down, creaking and shaking as a wave passed under it, and the sailor Will had grabbed was flung forward. Will lost his grip, but the sailor had already grabbed hold of some rope that was wrapped around one of the masts. The ship tilted in the opposite direction, and Will began to slide past the sailor. This time it was the sailor who grabbed hold of Will, yelling at him not to let go. They grasped each other's wrists, and there was no time to wonder about the man who had gone overboard. It was impossible for any man to leave his post or let go of his security to try to go save another.

The rain continued to pour in windblown sheets, so violently that Will could not even see who he was holding on to. He guessed the sailor didn't know who he was either. The ship heaved again, and somewhere in the wind Will could hear Captain Eastman shouting more orders. He clung to the sailor, managing to crawl to the same rope and grab hold of it himself as the bow again crashed down.

By God's grace the ship held together, but it continued to pitch and roll, and Will closed his eyes and prayed.

It was bad enough his mother had lost their father. He did not want her to get the news of her son's death also. He silently begged God to save the *Dutchess Dianna* and its cargo, not for the sake of wealth or his own neck, but for his mother.

There came a rumbling sound above the howling wind. Only seconds later a heavy barrel rolled toward Will and the man beside him as the bow again rose. "Look out!" he yelled, throwing himself over the sailor. He grunted when the barrel glanced off his shoulder and rolled on past, smashing against a post at the stern and spilling its contents of maple syrup. The syrup was quickly washed away as another roaring wave battered the deck.

Will rolled off the sailor, agonizing pain in his left shoulder.

"You all right?" the sailor shouted.

"Don't know," Will groaned. "I can hardly move my left arm."

"It's you! Mr. Lassater. I didn't know. My God, sir, you might have just saved my life. That barrel would have smashed into my head for certain." The sailor put an arm around Will and clung to him as yet another wave washed over them. "Can you hang on, Mr. Lassater?" the sailor shouted. "Your barrels of syrup must be coming loose. I'll go try to secure them."

"I'm all right, but to hell with the damn syrup! It isn't worth risking your life over." Will could barely see the man for squinting against the freezing rain.

"All part of the job, Mr. Lassater. You've got cargo on board that's damn valuable in California."

The sailor left Will before he could answer. Will watched him stumble and crawl and grab on to things as he made his way toward the bow. He disappeared in another wave, and Will ducked his head against the pummeling water. When he looked up again, he could barely see the sailor maneuvering himself around the barrels tied at the bow. Will had had the cargo area of the *Dutchess Dianna* packed so solidly with lumber and even more syrup, there had been no place else to put the extra barrels.

"Damn!" he muttered. If the rest of the barrels broke loose, more men could be hurt. He struggled against the raging wind, making his way forward in spite of the wild heaving of the ship. Fierce pain shot through his left shoulder when the ship tossed him against a mast, and it took him a minute to recover his balance. The ship's quartermaster appeared out of nowhere then, grabbing hold of him.

"You should be down in your cabin, Mr. Lassater!"

"I'm not going to let the rest of you risk your lives for my cargo without helping!" Will shouted in answer. "Help me forward so I can help that sailor up there secure those barrels of syrup."

The quartermaster obeyed, and the two men hung on to each other as they made the precarious walk to the bow.

"I cannot stay with you!" the quartermaster shouted in his Scottish accent.

"Go ahead and do what you have to do! I'm all right!"

Both men's faces ran with rain, and Will could feel more rain trickling down his back inside his shirt. "Throw me that rope!" he shouted to the sailor who was already tying more ropes around the barrels.

The sailor obeyed, and Will ran it around the barrels. He handed it back to the sailor, who had crawled across the tops of the barrels to the other side. He had already managed to tie one rope with no help, but with Will there it could be done much faster. Will ignored the pain in his shoulder and grabbed yet another rope. The sailor climbed back to the left of the barrels and tied it securely to a huge eyebolt in the side of the ship. He crawled back over the barrels while Will wrapped the rope around them, then handed it back up to him. The ship heaved mightily again, and Will slipped, crying out when he landed on his injured shoulder. He slid back down toward the stern, but managed to grasp the corner of a secured storage chest. He clung to it, amazed by the power of the storm, even more amazed that the *Dutchess Dianna* still had not broken apart.

"You're going below whether you like it or not!" came a voice near him. He looked up to recognize the red jacket of the sailor who had helped secure the barrels. He wondered how the man could stand to be out in this cold rain without a slicker, but he figured he must be accustomed to such weather and predicaments. As for himself, Will was beginning to wish he had tried the jungles of Panama rather than sailing the Horn, and he decided that if he ever went back home, that was the route he would take. Or he would take a wagon across the American plains and risk being killed by Indians. Anything but this.

He tried to protest as the sailor steered him toward the door that led to the quarters below, but because of the pain in his shoulder, he couldn't do much struggling. "I want to stay up top and help!" he shouted.

"You're just distracting the rest of the men," the sailor told him. "They feel responsible to protect you. After all, it's your cargo we're carrying, Mr. Lassater. You might say we're protecting our wages."

They both clung to the railings as they half stumbled down the stairs. "And here I thought you were being a good samaritan," Will said.

The sailor laughed, something Will was surprised he could do in the midst of such anger. "Not on your life," he answered. He guided Will to his cabin, and by the light of a madly swinging oil lamp, Will could finally see the man's face. After three months of sailing with these men, he knew each one of them well, and had a pretty good idea which sailors were the best and most dependable. This was one of them.

"Derek Carlson," he said. "You big Swede. I wasn't even sure who was helping me out there."

The ship rolled again, and Will caught hold of a support post with his right arm. Derek let go of him and clung to the doorsill. "You stay put till the storm is over, Mr. Lassater."

"I think by now you can call me Will."

"No matter at the moment. I'm going back up top. Soon as this storm is over we'll take care of that shoulder."

Before Will could reply, the man disappeared. The ship pitched again. Will kept his arm wrapped tightly around the post as he slid to the floor to sit down and ride out the storm. He hoped California was as peaceful and warm and beautiful as others had told him it was. "And those trees had better be as big as they say," he muttered, "afer going through all of this to get there."

At the moment he wished he were back in Maine in his parents' mansion, sitting by the hearth in his father's study, drinking good whiskey with his brother Gerald and smoking his pipe. At twenty-nine, Gerald was four years older than Will. He looked just like their father with his dark hair and eyes. He stood six feet two inches tall, broad-shouldered from years of wielding axes and saws. Everyone told Will that he looked more like their mother, with his sandy hair and blue eyes, but he stood nearly six feet tall himself and was even burlier than Gerald, something he liked to tease his brother about. It was all in good fun, for they were very close, and had grown even closer since their father died and the running of the mill had fallen into their hands.

Will had planned to marry and settle in Maine once. It still hurt some to think of Helen. He had loved her, but she had drowned at sea on her way home from a trip to

Europe to visit relatives. Now he understood more than ever how awful it must have been for her. It had been equally awful for him and for her family, not having a body to bury. Would he die the same way? How ironic that would be, and how terrible for his brother and his mother.

He hung on for dear life as the ship rolled and pitched again, and water seeped under his door and dripped through the ceiling above.

Will awoke to the sight of a blue sky outside the tiny window of his cabin. He was lying on his cot, still fully dressed, even to his slicker and boots. It took him a moment to remember how he had gotten there and why he had slept so hard. He shifted on the cot, gasped at the pain in his left shoulder. The rest of his body also ached, especially his right arm, from hanging on to the post for hours until the storm finally abated. He had stumbled to his cot, managed some sleep.

He looked around the tiny room. Only three private cabins were available on the cargo ship—one for the captain, one for the first mate, and one for any guest of the captain or a special passenger. The rest of the men slept in three-tier bunks in the hole, and ate in shifts in the ship's small kitchen. Will and the captain and first mate took their meals in the captain's cabin, which was the largest.

Now Will felt guilty for having nicer quarters than the sailors, who had struggled so valiantly the night before to save the ship and his cargo of lumber and syrup. One man had lost his life, maybe more by now, for all he knew.

He winced as he sat up and rubbed his shoulder, then rather gingerly stretched and bent his left arm. In spite of the pain, he could raise it, and he determined he must have a bad bruise, but probably nothing was broken. He closed his eyes and breathed a prayer of thanks, then removed his boots and stood up to take off his slicker. Everything underneath was still wet, and although every movement hurt him, he knew he had to get into dry clothes. He stripped down and threw the wet clothes in a corner, then hung his wool jacket over the back of a chair to dry out. He shivered in his nakedness and quickly grabbed a pair of clean long johns from his bag and pulled them on.

After throwing some wood in the small heating stove, he poured lamp oil over it from a large bottle kept in a secured compartment on the wall. He was glad to see that the oil had stayed put in the storm, and that the stove had not fallen apart. He lit the oil and closed the door, opening the damper all the way so that the wood would burn hard at first and quickly create hot coals.

Just as he grabbed a flannel shirt from his bag, someone knocked at his door. He got his right arm in the sleeve and opened the door, grimacing as he put his left arm in the other sleeve. Captain Eastwood stood outside the door with Derek Carlson.

"My sailor here says you were hurt last night," the captain said. "I came to see how you were doing. Derek was also concerned."

Will studied their faces, seeing the terrible weariness in their eyes. "I think I'm okay. Just bruised."

Derek put out his right hand. "You saved my life, Mr. Lassater."

Will guessed the sailor was about the same age as himself. He was a few inches taller than Will, and he seemed as broad as he was tall. His white-blond hair spilled in long waves around his ruddy, rather homely face. Will shook his hand, noticing the strength in the man's grip.

"And you saved mine, as well as my barrels of syrup," he answered. "I'm grateful for that, and I do wish you would call me Will." He looked at the captain. "I wonder if I could have a minute alone with Derek."

"Just as long as you're sure you're all right, Mr. Lassater. I do have a lot of things to do this morning, lots of things to be repaired. We're in the clear now, and from here on the weather should be good. It won't be long before we come into some warm Pacific winds. We'll make good time then, and we'll be out of this cold."

"Sounds damn good to me," Will said.

The captain looked at Derek. "Don't be too long. There's a lot of cleaning up to do, sailor."

"Yes, sir," Derek answered.

The captain left, and Will ushered Derek inside. He sat down on his cot and offered Derek the only chair in the room. Derek had to bend his head a little to keep from bumping it on the low ceiling. He sat down, and Will noticed he still wore the red jacket, which was so wet that Will could smell the wool. "I want to thank you again, Derek, for helping me. And I want to ask you if you're completely happy working on a ship."

Derek frowned. "Why would you ask that, Mr.—I mean, Will?"

Will grinned. Derek was known to the crew as an open, honest man who simply did as he was told. He was big and strong and a hard worker, never complaining.

"I ask because I would think a man like you would hate being confined to that hole below part of the time, let alone being a kind of prisoner when you're on a ship. No way off, spending months at a time with the same men, not being able to eat right, putting up with the rats and insects that are found on any ship. Wouldn't you rather be on land, out in the open, in a big land full of big trees, solid ground under your feet?"

Derek ran a hand through his blond hair. "I don't know what you're getting at, Will."

Will took a moment to rummage through one of his bags, coming up with two cigars that he was relieved to discover were dry. He handed one to Derek. "Smoke?"

Derek took the cigar, and Will went to the heating stove and opened the feed door. He stuck a small stick of wood inside and lit it, then turned and held it to the end of Derek's cigar. Derek took a puff, then Will lit his own before throwing the stick into the stove and closing it again.

"I'm headed to California to start up a new sawmill, Derek. There won't be a lot of men out there with lumbering experience, but I can teach them. What I need are men who are big and strong and willing to work. The better they work and the more trees they log out for me, the more money they'll make. I have a lot to learn myself about the kind of trees that grow out there, so we can learn together. I'm going to San Francisco first to sell my cargo, and I'll look for some men to hire there. I'm hoping to find a few men who know a little bit about logging and who are tired of looking for gold."

Will puffed the cigar for a moment. "The real gold out there is green, as far as I'm concerned," he continued. "From what I hear, there are trees in the California hills and mountains three hundred feet high, with enough wood in them to make up ten of our biggest maples or walnuts in Maine. I intend to harvest them, if I can get some Spaniard to sell me some land, or at least rent it out to me. How would you like to try being a logger?"

Derek studied his cigar before answering. "I might. I've never known anything but sailing, though. Been working on ships ever since I was orphaned at ten."

"How old are you now?"

"Thirty, I think. I lost track a few years ago."

"No wife?"

"I've never stayed on land long enough to take one. Plenty of women in all the ports, though."

Both men laughed. "Well, I don't have a wife either," Will said. "I'm doing this as kind of a promise to my father, who died last year. We want to expand Lassater Mills, and I've heard lots of stories about the supply of lumber in the West."

"I've never gone far enough onto land when we're in California to see any of those trees," Derek said, "but I've heard about them too. I wouldn't mind having a look at them myself."

Will grinned. "I'm told one man can't bring one down. Being a logger myself, I find that hard to believe. Maybe you or I can prove them wrong."

Derek scratched his head. "I don't know. I might miss the sea. Gets in a man's blood, you know, just like logging is in yours."

"I suppose, but after yesterday, I'm not sure I could *ever* get used to this life. Seems to me a man your size would hate being confined to a ship, having to walk bent over half the time. Why don't you give it a try? One year. You can always re-sign with Captain Eastman when he returns next year."

Derek smoked the cigar thoughtfully. "I guess I could."

"I need strong, honest, dependable men, Derek. After yesterday, I can't think of a better man to help me get started than you. Besides, I've also heard tales about the Barbary Coast and the docks of San Francisco. Hell, I might need someone along to help keep me out of trouble when I go looking for more workers."

"That you will," Derek answered. "The wharves of that city are alive with thieves and murderers. You'd better watch yourself there. But then, there are plenty of pretty whores ready to please a man!" He laughed boisterously. "I'm well acquainted with many of them. If you're eager for a woman, I'll take you to see the best. And handsome and strong as you are, they'll be fighting over you."

Both men laughed again, and Will shook his head. "I just might take you up on your offer to introduce me," he joked.

"And there's bound to be a lot of men hanging out in saloons and working odd jobs along the docks who are looking for better-paying work," Derek said. "San Francisco is full of ex-prospectors who never found their gold but don't want to go back home." He leaned forward, resting his elbows on his knees. "You know, with California becoming a state, and with the gold and all, it's growing really fast. Every year when we go back there it seems San Francisco has doubled in size from the year before. That lumber below decks will bring you a fortune."

Will's eyes lit up. "That's what I'm banking on, and if I sell California lumber cheaper than what they're paying for lumber being brought in from the East and from other countries, I'll have a near monopoly on the product. It's like I told you, Derek, the real gold is in that lumber!"

Derek grinned. "I can see how excited you are."

Will nodded, sobering. "This means everything to me, Derek. The family fortune and lumbering business depend on it. This isn't just my or my brother's dream, but our father's. He had always wanted to come to California and see the big redwoods. As far as we know, there are very few sawmills in California. The only one of any importance was Sutter's, and he's about out of business, so we've heard, because of the gold rush. All his help left him, and prospectors supposedly overran his land and took off with his livestock, trampled his crops and such. If I'm successful, I intend to open more than one mill, maybe have all my own ships someday, send lumber all the way to China, Japan, India, Australia. I was picked to come out here first and get things started because I'm single and have no other responsibilities." Will turned and opened the small trunk he had brought along. "This is what it's all about, Derek," he said, taking out the wooden box his mother had given him.

Derek frowned and stuck the cigar between his teeth. "I don't understand."

"My dad worked his own sawmill for over thirty years. About twenty-five years ago there was a forest fire and everything burned down, the mill, all his equipment. Some really hard times followed, and he could have given up. Instead he went out and scooped up some of the ashes into a little cloth sack and put them in this box, kept them all those years because to him they were a kind of symbol. He believed that from the ashes would come something even better. He built his first mill from nothing. He was a big, strong, determined man with a dream, one of the best lumbermen in Maine, and he borrowed and worked to get his hands on more wooded land, rebuilt, paid off all his debts, left his family wealthy. But because of all the demand in the West, our supply of lumber back in Maine is running low. We could go out of business someday without a new source. If I build in California, Lassater Mills could be bigger and more successful than it ever was in Maine."

Will stopped to wipe away the tears misting his eyes. "That was our father's dream," he continued, "and now my brother and I will carry it out for him. Having this little box of ashes with me makes it seem as though my father is here with me, urging me on." He looked up at Derek. "Will you help me? I could make you a rich man someday, and the big, open woods would surely be more enjoyable for you than this smelly, creaking ship."

Derek drew in his breath and puffed out his broad chest, then reached out his right hand. "All right, Will, I'll give it a try. I owe it to you for what you did yesterday."

Will rose as he shook his hand. "You don't owe me a thing. I'm just grateful to find you."

Derek released his hand and took the cigar from his mouth. "I warn you, I don't know anything about cutting down trees."

"I'll teach you. Hell, I'll need some lessons myself on those big redwoods. I'm hoping to find someone who knows at least a little bit about it, someone who can give me a few pointers."

"We'll find him. I'll help you." Derek straightened and bumped his head on a beam. He winced, and Will laughed. "I suppose it will be nice to be out in those woods and be able to stand up my full height," Derek said, laughing with him. "I am six feet six inches, last time I got myself measured. Say, you should come above after you get dressed. It's a pretty day out there, and we've got good winds, strong but gentle."

"I'll come up. I guess you'd better get to your chores. What's the damage?"

"Not as bad as we thought." Derek patted the support post in the cabin. "She's a strong ship, the *Dutchess Dianna.*" He grew somber. "The biggest loss was Louie being washed out to sea. It was impossible to save him. We'll be having a little service for him in a bit."

"I'll be there. I'm sorry I couldn't have helped him too."

Derek nodded. "Out here at sea a man gets used to friends dying, or at least he thinks he does. I've worked with Louie for four years now. I will miss him. Actually, I think it will be good to get off this ship for a year or so. Maybe I won't want to come back."

Will put a hand on his shoulder as he walked to the door. "I'm predicting that logging will get into your blood just as strongly as the sea has."

Derek stopped in the doorway. "Maybe it will," he replied.

The man turned and left, and Will walked over to his bags to dig out a dry pair of pants. The cabin floor was damp from water washing over the decks and down the steps, and from cracks in the deck itself. He was grateful it had not reached his personal supplies, especially the trunk with its box of ashes. He was surprised he had so easily told Derek the story about his father. The big Swede was a good listener. He finished dressing, his pain more bearable with the thought that he had found at least one good man.

"Now I need about a dozen more," he said to himself, "and a lot more than that before I'm through." He hoped it would be smooth sailing from here on, with no trouble from pirates or more storms. He was more eager than ever to get to California, and he grinned as he recalled his brother's comment that California was full of beautiful señoritas curious about handsome *gringos*. He shook his head. With the work that lay ahead for him, he'd have no time for women, except perhaps the wild ones along the wharves of San Francisco.

Two

MAY 1854 . . .

Sixteen-year-old Santana Maria Chavez Lopez stood on the balcony of a guest room in the ornate San Francisco mansion belonging to Hugo Bolivar. She hated San Francisco, hated the mansion, and most of all she hated the man who owned this house. Hugo had been courting her for six months, but she still did not feel any desire, even any liking, for him. She despised being so far from her father and her brother, so far from the beautiful ranch north of San Francisco where she had grown up, La Estancia de Alcala.

This chaperoned visit to Hugo's San Francisco home was a requirement of her courtship, and she hated every minute of it. Hugo's mansion was not home to her. It could *never* be home, even though Hugo had told her that once they were married, after she turned eighteen, they would spend most of their time here, instead of on Hugo's own ranch, Rancho de Rosas, which bordered her father's land.

She wrapped her robe closer around herself against the

cool morning air. Hugo's house sat high on a hill, and she could see out over San Francisco and the bay in the distance. A morning mist hung over the water, but the rising sun was burning it off. In spite of the noise and stink and the dangers of the dock area, from here it looked pretty in the morning light, the tall masts of ships visible in the distance, sharply outlined by the brightening sun.

In contrast to the appealing view, Hugo's house was, in Santana's opinion, austere and forbidding. Made of brick, it was too big, with towers at the corners that made it seem more like a dungeon than a home, and no gardens outside.

A dungeon it was, a prison, as far as she was concerned. It did not have the warmth of her father's stucco home back at the ranch, which had thick wooden doors and big, warm rooms filled with plants and leather furniture trimmed in rich, dark wood. Bright braided rugs were scattered across the tile floors, and all around the outside of the house were *portals* where vines climbed latticed walls. Plants and flowers grew everywhere in scented splendor. In the front *portal* a fountain fed by a natural spring flowed at the center, running down a white marble statue of the Mother Mary holding Baby Jesus. Santana enjoyed the sound of the splashing water, and liked to sit on one of the white wrought-iron benches nearby and listen to it, hear the birds singing.

She ached to go home and ride her favorite Palomino to her secret hideaway, a little clearing in the deep woods where a scraggly lodgepole pine stood alone, separated from the rest of the forest. The tree seemed lonely, and she well knew that feeling. She considered the tree her friend, and in that place she could pray, cry, dream . . . dream of the handsome young man who would ride into her life, a man she would love with great passion. Now that dream could never come true.

How could her father do this to her? she wondered, brushing away the tears that came so easily and frequently these days. She still remembered vividly the night her father, Dominic, had told her she was to marry Hugo. It had been during dinner. Hugo had been there, along with Santana's older brother, Hernando, and his wife, Teresa. Santana's mother, Rosa, had passed away four years ago.

Dominic had begun by telling the story Santana knew well, of how he had escaped the war in Mexico nearly forty years ago.

"My parents were very wealthy," Dominic said. "They and my brother and sister were killed in the revolution. At sixteen I was forced to flee Mexico or risk being executed myself. Your mother was only four years old. Her family and my family had always been close. Your mother's family and I escaped Mexico together, and we did so only because of one man, Hugo's father, Julio Miguel Martinez Jauquin. He had been a good friend of both our families, and he had left Mexico years earlier to live in California. He came back to convince our families to leave, and he got caught up in the war. When he saw we had no choice but to flee, he helped us, hiding us in the bottom of a supply wagon he had purchased in Arizona, pretending to have come to Mexico to sell tobacco, cloth, even guns, to the revolutionaries. We escaped to California. Your mother's parents promised her to me because they had been so close to my own mother and father. Years later, when Rosa and I married, we were very happy. Your mother learned to love me, and I her. And it was all thanks to Julio Juaquin bringing us to this beautiful land."

Dominic then raised his glass in a toast and announced that his daughter, Santana, had been promised to Julio Juaquin's son, Hugo Bolivar, and that they would wed in two years. Santana stared in shock at Hugo—whom she had never liked—then at her father. His story about how her own mother's marriage had been arranged and that she had learned to love Dominic did not ease her dread in the least. After all, Hugo was nothing like her father.

Hugo Bolivar was a man who basked in his wealth and power. Her father, and Hugo's own father, who was now dead, were true *Californios*, gracious and mannerly, kind and considerate, men who did not flaunt their wealth. Her father treasured his friendships, and he had been a loving husband and father. Santana loved him, hated disappointing him or doing anything to hurt his pride and honor. Yet from the moment he had announced her betrothal, she had continually contemplated ways of backing out of this marriage to Hugo, even if it meant bringing shame to her father.

How she wished she had more say in leading her own life, but Don Dominic Alcala believed that a sixteen-year-old daughter's place was to tend to her Spanish and English lessons, learn how to manage the household staff, and spend her free time pursuing whatever hobbies interested her. For Santana, those hobbies were painting and horseback riding, but she wanted to do more, to play a bigger role in helping run her father's sprawling *hacienda*, not just the household. After all, it was her home too. But it seemed the men in her world had all the power.

And one man would soon have all power over her. She shivered, remembering the conversation over dinner the night before, the way Hugo's black gaze had raked over her as he spoke endlessly of business and money.

"You will see how much wealthier I become by the time we are married," he had said at one point, as though he thought he could win her trust and love with money. "I know how to take advantage of the *Americanos*, much as I despise them. They have much money in their pockets, and I know how to get that money. I do not like California being a state now, but it is to our advantage. And when we are husband and wife, with your father's produce, his fine Palomino horses, and his beef, there will be no limit to how wealthy we can become. Together with my own *ranchero* and my holdings, we will increase our fortune many times!"

I do not care if you become the richest man in the world, Santana thought. *I will never be happy being married to you.*

"My own father was afraid to try new things, but I am not," Hugo continued. "I will take advantage of being a part of the United States, and rob the stupid Americans who come here looking for gold and who pay ridiculous prices for beef and horses and potatoes. In some mining towns, men pay a whole dollar for one potato!" Hugo laughed, a deep, throaty laugh that always sounded wicked to Santana. He stabbed at a piece of meat he had just cut. "Your father should plant potatoes," he said, directing his dark gaze to Santana again. "I have tried to tell him that. Someday I will help him run La Estancia de Alcala, and he will see the mistakes he has made."

"Father has always done well. He is a very successful man," Santana argued. "He simply does not care about riches in the way that you do."

Hugo frowned, his eyes piercing her. "And what does that mean, my sweet?"

The words were said with a sneer that chilled her blood. She suspected that once they were married, Hugo would try to cheat her father and brother out of everything they owned—their beautiful *hacienda,* the thousands of acres of grazing land, the thick woods, the many magnificent Palominos raised by Dominic and Hernando.

"To you, riches are everything," she had answered boldly, "more important even than loved ones. I can see it in your eyes."

Santana could still remember Hugo's wicked smile, the way his gaze drifted over her, lingering on her breasts.

Santana had felt like covering her breasts with her hands, as though she were naked. She felt sick to her stomach, as she always did at the thought of Hugo having the right to take her to his bed. In her mind, he was an old man at thirty-five, but it was not his age that repulsed her. It was his overbearing attitude toward women, his arrogance. She knew in her heart he would not be gentle with her, in spite of her virginity and her ignorance of such matters.

"You do not know me so well yet, Santana," he had said. "I would never choose riches over you, my beloved."

The words were so hollow and obviously meaningless that Santana had almost laughed, but there was a warning in his dark eyes . . . a look that told her this man would not tolerate disrespect or insults from her once she was his wife. She supposed Hugo Bolivar was handsome enough to some older women, but his domineering manner made him ugly to her. And how dare he suggest he knew more about running a ranch than Dominic Fernando Chavez Alcala! Her father was known in Santa Rosa, Napa, even as far south as here in San Francisco, for his magnificent Palominos—and for the simple fact that he was one of the biggest landowners in the state to have survived having some of his land stolen away by the hated *Americanos* when they came and took California from them.

The discovery of gold five years earlier had made him even richer, from selling horses and food to miners. Hugo had also become richer from selling fruit, wheat, and potatoes from his ranch, but she could not respect him for his wealth. He had not worked hard for it like her father. He had inherited his wealth from his father, and he had no appreciation for what it took to build something from the ground up.

Sighing, Santana left the balcony and reentered the guest room. At least this day with Hugo should be more enjoyable than most. He was taking her to the docks again, which she had visited on her previous trip to San Francisco.

In spite of the near-terrifying experience that had been—Hugo always traveled there with mounted armed guards—it had also been exciting. The distraction of the wharves would at least help get her mind off how much she hated having to come here and put up with Hugo. She could even fantasize about boarding one of those ships and sailing away forever, never to set eyes on Hugo Bolivar again, never to have to marry the man. Maybe it would be better to be carried off by some pirate or drunken sailor than to be Hugo's wife.

Her maid, Louisa, came into her room then to help her get ready. Santana knew Louisa thought her the luckiest woman in California, and she had given up trying to explain to the older woman that she wanted nothing of this marriage.

"Come and sit down and I will fix your hair," Louisa said. "It must be an adventure going to the docks. There must be many *gringos* there, and I hear some bad men, and bad women."

Both of them laughed. "Yes, there are many *gringos*," Santana said. "It seems that California is filling up with them now, ever since that American navy man, John Fremont, invaded and claimed California for the United States." She pouted. "Everything has changed so. I have even seen some of those Orientals. They look strange. I was not aware of so many different kinds of people until I visited the docks that first time."

Louisa twisted and pinned Santana's thick black hair. "Why does Senor Bolivar go there?"

"To do business. He meets ships coming in to see if they have anything he wants to buy and store in his warehouses. He is very puffed up when he goes there, behaving as the important businessman. His arrogance embarrasses me, but I will put up with it because the sooner we do all the things Hugo has planned for us, the sooner I can go home again."

Louisa sighed. "You always miss La Estancia de Alcala, don't you?"

"Always. I never want to live here permanently, Louisa."

Louisa only shook her head, knowing it was useless to argue. She had to agree that Hugo Bolivar did not seem the most lovable man, but she could not help being impressed by his wealth and importance. She finished Santana's hair and helped her dress, then left the room. Santana decided to wait there until Hugo was ready leave, choosing not to join him for breakfast. She had no appetite; she seldom did until she was home again.

She walked back to the balcony to get another glimpse of the harbor far in the distance, trying to count the tall masts, wondering what she would see this time. One thing she had to admit, some of the strong-muscled *gringos* who arrived on those ships were indeed fascinating. Some were even quite handsome in a rugged sort of way, the younger ones certainly more attractive than Hugo. Again she considered what her fate might be if she simply ran off with one of them, but she knew that was a foolish thought. She was trapped in her father's promise, trapped in Hugo's possessive claim to her, and some day she would be trapped in this cold mansion.

Three

Will marveled at the packed bay area of San Francisco, where buyers from gold towns and local merchants swarmed to meet the new ships coming in. The *Dutchess Dianna* had landed just before dawn, and already he'd had offers from several prospective buyers without even having left the ship. The need for lumber was so desperate, and the hunger for real New England maple syrup so keen, he decided he would simply write down names and how to contact buyers and wait for the highest bid.

The harbors at Portland back in Maine were busy, but never had he seen anything like the chaos in this wild gold town. He had heard that before the gold rush, San Francisco was merely a small, quiet Spanish settlement. For as far as he could see, the city was now a sprawling mass of buildings—some made of stucco, a few of brick, most of wood—structures that rose upward from the docks along a series of steep hills. Practically everywhere he looked the hills were covered with buildings, most of them with graduated foundations to follow the inclines. It crossed his mind that none of them would be very safe in case of an earthquake, although he had never experienced such an act of nature. Apparently San Francisco was growing so fast, little considerations had been given to planning the city in any logical manner. The result was a confused maze of hastily built businesses and homes.

"It doesn't happen often," Derek had told him when Will asked about earthquakes. "I'm never here long enough to feel a thing. They say those who stay get used to it, like you get used to the snow and winter winds in Maine. Besides, the beautiful weather in California makes up for having to put up with the ground shaking once in a while. It is a paradise, except it's not so pretty here in San Francisco. This is a city growing too fast for its own good."

Will could see that now, and he thought of how easily he could make a fortune here if he could log the vast forests that supposedly lay in the mountains and hills to the north. Thousands of men had landed here in the past few years, streaming through the city on their way to those mountains to look for gold, and San Francisco had become the supply center for all those prospectors and the smaller gold towns they populated. Those who did the supplying surely made more money than anyone who went to the mountains. Captain Eastman had explained over supper the night before that the city was also becoming the financial center for the gold taken out of the mountains and for the men who owned the mines.

Will scanned the nearby hills, wondering which one was Nob Hill, where the captain had told him only the wealthiest lived. His biggest curiosity, though, was for the forests farther north. It was impossible to spot any of the enormous trees he'd been told about, but the prospect of finding and logging them excited him more than the activity at the docks or seeing this wild new city.

"Tonight we do some gambling and whoring, huh?" Derek said as he helped Will untie the ropes around the barrels of syrup. "We will celebrate walking on solid ground, and celebrate my new job."

Will grinned. "I don't know about the whoring. I don't want to get some dreaded disease and die before I can get my mill going."

Derek laughed heartily. "I can show you the clean whorehouses. They have the prettiest girls there anyway."

"I have a feeling after I'm through dealing today and helping unload this cargo, I'll be too tired for anything. I need to find someone to warehouse this stuff, so I can get it off Captain Eastman's ship and keep it somewhere until the buyers pick it up. I can't believe that in the six hours since we landed, I've had offers for every last board of lumber and barrel of syrup. It's only noon, and I haven't even been off the ship yet."

"I told you you would have no trouble selling your lumber, and for prices much higher than you would get anyplace else. The buyers from the mining towns are crazy. They're desperate for supplies, and their pockets are so full of gold, they will pay anything."

Will had to concentrate to hear everything the man said because of the noise. Horses, mules, supply wagons, and people of all colors mingled everywhere, with dogs, pigs, and chickens adding to the confusion. He could not help noticing the Orientals especially. He had never seen a Chinese person before, and was surprised at how small most of them were. He'd been told they were hard workers, but he could not imagine that any of them could be loggers. They simply were not built for it, but he supposed he could hire a few to cook and do laundry for his crew.

Derek helped him lift down a barrel of syrup. "I'll probably sell this to that last man who came by." Will pulled a piece of paper from the pocket of his black cotton pants. "His name was Hector Munoz. He claims to buy for a Hugo Bolivar. Supposed to be one of the richest Spanish merchants in San Francisco. At the least, Bolivar owns several warehouses, and I could store my lumber and syrup with him."

"I've heard of him." Derek took a pouch of tobacco tied to his belt and pulled a pipe from his shirt pocket. "There aren't many rich Spaniards. They don't understand American business. I don't doubt that in a few years San Francisco won't even be thought of as Spanish anymore. Americans will take it over. Already have, I'd say. I don't know much else about Bolivar, don't ever stay here long enough to learn about people living here. I guess now I'll have time to learn more than the hearsay on the docks."

Will stopped working to take in more of the sights and to study the constantly moving mass of people. As he did, he noticed a fancy carriage making its way along the docks, a carriage that looked much too elegant to be in such a place. He took a moment to light his own pipe while he watched, enjoying the feel of the California sun on his shoulders. It felt good to be warm and to have reached his destination at last. The trip here was one he would never forget, and one he did not care to repeat. He decided that when he wrote his brother, he would tell him that if and when the time was right for Gerald to sell everything in Maine and move his family to California, he'd better travel cross-country by wagon, or perhaps try Panama. Maybe the railroad that was being built across the isthmus would be finished by then.

"Say," Derek said, "look at that shiny black carriage and those fine white horses. No American would come down here in something that fancy. I'll bet it's one of those rich Spaniards we were talking about. They like to show off their wealth."

Will noticed that four other Spaniards wearing guns on their hips were trotting behind the carriage on sleek black horses. It was obvious someone important rode in the carriage, and he spotted the buyer, Hector Munoz, walking beside it, talking to someone inside. Munoz pointed to the *Dutchess Dianna* and to Will himself.

"Must be the man's boss," Will said. "Hugo Bolivar."

"I don't know why he would be down here himself," Derek said. "Most of the wealthy, Americans and Spaniards alike, send buyers in their place. They don't like mixing with the rabble."

Will frowned. "I'm not rabble."

"Not you." Derek chuckled. "But look at all those sailors out there, and the whores parading around, let alone the thieves who will pounce on any man for his watch and jewels."

"This man is prepared. He's brought his own guards."

Both men watched the carriage pull up and stop in front of the *Dutchess Dianna*. A tall, slender man with dark hair and a mustache emerged from the coach, then turned and held out his hand. The hand and arm of a woman appeared, then came the woman herself.

"Would you look at that," Will muttered. Even from up on deck he could see she was young and beautiful. She exited the carriage and looked around, her dark eyes wide at the sight of the *Dianna*'s rigging. The tall Spaniard, dressed in tight-fitting black pants with a gold embroidered design down the outside of the legs, and a short-waisted jacket that matched the pants, approached the plank leading up to the ship's deck. He wore a black hat, and Will thought how the man reminded him of pictures he had seen of bullfighters. There was an arrogant air about him, and he looked much older than the woman on his arm. Was she his daughter?

The moment he let his gaze rest on the young woman, Will was enamored with her. Back in New England, stories of Spanish life in California seemed a bit romantic and unreal, as did talk of how beautiful Spanish women were.

Those stories were no exaggeration when it came to this one's beauty. As far as he was concerned, there were no proper words to describe her. Her yellow ruffled lace dress fell just off her shoulders, shoulders that showed dark skin that reminded him of creamed coffee and looked as though they would feel like satin if touched. Her full lips perfectly fit the elegant lines of her face, and her most beautiful attribute was her wide-set dark eyes, eyes that were full of curiosity as she boarded the ship. Her near-black hair was worn in a pile of curls on top of her head, with some of it hanging in longer curls at the back. Yellow lace was entwined throughout her hair, and she carried a matching yellow-lace fan, which she opened across her face the moment she caught him staring at her. Only those dark eyes could be seen above the fan . . . eyes that held his own for several seconds before she looked away.

"Senor Lassater, I am told." The Spaniard was close now, holding out his hand, and Will realized another woman had come on board too. She was young and attractive, but not dressed as elegantly as the one in yellow, nor nearly as pretty. "I am Don Hugo Eduardo Martinez Bolivar. You have already met my buyer, Hector Munoz."

Will shook the man's hand, which felt thin and cold. "I have, but I haven't yet made up my mind to whom I will sell my lumber. I am interested, however, in getting it off this ship and storing it. I hear you have several warehouses nearby."

"That I do." The man turned to the young woman in yellow. "*Pardon, mi querida.* I should introduce you." He turned back to Will. "I would not ordinarily come to the docks myself, but my *novia*—I believe you Americans call your intended fiancée—she is getting to know the city, as she will live here once we are married. She is from a wealthy family that owns a *hacienda* next to my own northeast of San Francisco. She enjoys seeing the big ships, as

she does not see such things in the country. I have my
guards along because she is so beautiful and I want to give
her full protection. There are many men on these docks
who would try to make off with such a *mujer bella*. I am
sure that you agree she is the most beautiful senorita in all
of California."

He turned to the woman, smiling. "This is my bride to
be, Santana Maria Chavez Lopez. Her father is one of the
richest landowners in California. This fine woman with
Santana is her chaperon and tutor, Estella Joaquin."

Will nodded to both women, and he found himself
struggling not to stare at the one called Santana. *Fiancée?*
She looked so young. Was this one of those arranged marriages he had heard about? When Hugo Bolivar smiled at
her, she did not smile back. Her eyes shifted to Will again,
and she closed her fan and smiled when he nodded to her.
Then she quickly and demurely looked away, opening the
fan over her face again. Will turned back to Hugo, realizing
there was something about the Spaniard that he did not
like, but he couldn't figure what it was. It simply disturbed
him that the sweet young lady with him did not seem at all
happy with Hugo's attention.

"I am honored to meet you and your intended, Don
Bolivar," he answered, deciding the man's relationship
with his fiancée was not his business. He needed to remain
on friendly terms with such men for the present. "And you
are right. Senorita Lopez is indeed the most beautiful
woman in all of California." What did it matter that he
had not even been off the ship yet? He didn't need to see
the rest of the women in this state to know that none
could compare to Santana Lopez. He had a feeling that a
man like Hugo Bolivar would be offended if he stared at
the senorita for too long, so he forced himself to keep his
attention on Hugo. "And what brings you to speak personally with me?" he asked.

Hugo smiled rather arrogantly. "Senor Munoz tells me you have brought a fine supply of lumber from Maine. I thought that since I was close, I would come on board and see it for myself."

"And I in turn am happy to meet an honored *Californio*," Will answered. He felt Senorita Lopez watching him again, but he kept his eyes averted. "Your buyer has told me all about you, and he says you will give me fifty cents for every board of lumber below and five dollars a barrel for my maple syrup."

"*Si*, that is a fair price," Hugo answered. "And you would not have to pay a storage fee."

Will folded his arms. "And you know that I am fresh here from New England. You think that I am unfamiliar with what is going on in California."

Hugo frowned. "What do you mean?"

"I've been shipping lumber here from Maine for three years now, Don Bolivar," Will said. "I know damn well what it's worth, and I could pay *you* fifty cents a board to store my lumber in your warehouse and still make a profit when I sell it to someone else. Actually, I've already been offered more than a dollar a board. All I'm doing now is taking names and offers. I haven't decided yet where to sell my lumber. I can tell you one thing, though, it's some of the finest you'll ever see—nice and straight, good hardwood from Maine. I've been in the logging business all my life, and I know which lumber is the best you can get, and that's Lassater lumber. I also know that my syrup is worth ten times what your buyer offered me. Maple syrup is a rare treat out here."

Hugo appeared taken aback at being turned down, and Santana felt a secret joy at the disconcerted look on his face. It was not often any man stood up to Hugo. She liked this *gringo* with his sandy-colored hair and beautiful blue eyes. He had a handsome smile, and he looked very strong.

She had never seen a man with such powerful-looking arms.

Hugo's eyes narrowed. "Who has offered you more than a dollar a board?"

"I won't say his name. All I can say is it's a buyer from one of the gold towns that's growing fast and needs lumber for building homes."

Hugo stroked his mustache for a moment. "Let me see this lumber."

"Fine." Will turned to the side and let Hugo walk in front of him. He glanced at Senorita Lopez again, and she smiled bashfully. He took note that she was taller than most women, perhaps only four or five inches shorter than he, when most women he knew were closer to a foot shorter. There was an air of privilege and dignity about her, but not haughtiness. He could see she was full of questions, but it was probably considered too forward for her to speak to a stranger. He needed to learn more about Spanish ways so that he did not accidentally insult or offend people like Senorita Lopez or Don Bolivar.

He and Hugo descended into the ship's hold, which was rich with the sweet smell of fresh lumber. Some of it had gotten wet in the storm and had never completely dried. "A few boards at the bottom are probably warped from the dampness, but the rest are intact," he told Hugo.

"Hmmm." Hugo held his chin thoughtfully. "And why do you come all the way to California yourself this time, Senor Lassater?"

Will leaned against a post. "I intend to stay, open a mill here, try logging some of your California redwood. We're getting low on timber back east, and with the demand like it is out here and such a vast supply of wood, I figured I'd see how I could do in California. Apparently there isn't much logging going on here yet, what with everyone's attention on the gold and on supplying the gold towns with food and such. You're farming grain and fruit, and providing horses, mules, tools, clothing, and such to the miners. But no one is paying any attention to the millions of acres of forest you have out here."

Hugo nodded. "So, you want to open a mill." He studied the lumber a moment longer, realizing Will Lassater did indeed know good quality. He faced him then. "I will make you a deal," he said. "I will buy this lumber for ninety cents a board and there will be no charge for storage, since it will be in my own warehouses until I get my own best offer from the gold towns. I will also buy your syrup for fifty dollars a barrel. You will make a little less, but I will make up for it by telling you where you can find the finest trees in northern California. I can guarantee you will be allowed to rent the land for harvesting the trees."

"Your property?" Will asked.

"Some of it. I own a very big *rancho* in the hills, Senor Lassater, about three days' ride from here. My land adjoins the *hacienda* of Don Dominic Alcala, Senorita Lopez's father. He has much more timber than I. There is a river at the western edge of his land that runs to the ocean, where you could set up your sawmill and where flatboats could pick up the lumber and take it to San Francisco."

Will frowned. "Why are you so willing to help me find what I'm looking for?"

Hugo grinned. "For a profit, of course. Rental of my land and a piece of the profits. I happen to think you have a very good idea. I have often thought there is surely a great profit to be made lumbering our own timber, but there are not many men who know how to do it." He studied Will's muscled arms. "I like a shrewd businessman, and I can see that you are very capable. It will take a man of strength and experience to log our giant trees, and you apparently have both. My buyer has told me that your family has run a sawmill back in Maine for many years.

Much lumber has been shipped here from the East, but never has a true lumberman come with it." Hugo folded his arms. "So? What do you say? I have men who can get your lumber off this ship today, and the day after tomorrow I can come for you and you can follow us to La Estancia de Alcala. I have to take Senorita Lopez home then. I am presently courting her, getting to know her better, allowing her to know me and learn about my many holdings. I have a home here in San Francisco, built in your own American Gothic style. I own many businesses here, many warehouses. My own *rancho*, next to Don Alcala's, is called Rancho de Rosas. We can talk terms on the way."

"How do you know Don Alcala will go along with it?"

A look of pompous sureness came into Hugo's eyes. "I will take care of Don Alcala," he said. "He knows that I am a good businessman, and I am, after all, marrying his daughter. One day his *hacienda* will belong to me. Anything that helps La Estancia de Alcala now helps me in the future. And if you do business with me, you will make a fortune, which I am sure is what you came out here to do."

"That's right, but I won't be owned by any man," Will said. "I'll want a contract that gives me the freedom to log whatever parts of the land I see fit, and to conduct my business in my own way. The mill will be solely mine, and all profits will go first into my name, after which I'll pay out whatever percentage we agree to. I will have the final say in what is fair to pay."

Hugo's eyebrows arched. "You are no fool, Senor Lassater."

"That's right."

Their eyes held with a hint of challenge, then Hugo smiled. "Fine. I would suggest that if you want to stay away from the scum of the wharves and keep from being beaten and robbed, you should stay at the Golden Palace Hotel in the better part of San Francisco. Anyone can tell you how to get there. I will come for you there the day after tomorrow, around nine A.M. I will pay you then for your lumber and the syrup. I am sure you have come with much more money than what you will get for this shipload of lumber."

Will grinned. "Much more. I intend to spend the next couple of days looking for men I can train to help me, maybe find a few who already know about the lumber business. It won't be easy to get a good crew going, and I probably won't be able to start logging until next spring. I have a few things to learn myself, and a mill to build. I am eager, though, to see those trees. I've heard a lot about the redwoods, how big they are."

"The biggest in the world, some say. You will see for yourself soon enough."

Will put out his hand. "It's a deal, then. Ninety cents a board and fifty dollars for each barrel of syrup. How about throwing in free storage of the equipment I brought with me? Until I decide where to construct my mill, I'll have to put it somewhere. I have more equipment coming in about two months on another ship."

Hugo nodded. "I will store it for you. Tomorrow I will have Senor Munoz come to your hotel and show you my warehouses."

"I appreciate that." They shook hands, and Will told himself to be wary. Something in the man's eyes said Hugo Bolivar could not be trusted. He wondered about the man's remark that his fiancée was there to get to know him better. If she did not know him so well, why was she marrying him? Was it a marriage of convenience, one in which she had no choice? Or was she marrying him for his money? She seemed too young to care about such things. Girls that age usually married for love and passion; and besides, she apparently already had money.

He followed Hugo back up to the deck, where the man's intended wife and her escort were holding tin cups under a spigot on one of the barrels. Derek opened the spigot, and both women laughed with delight as syrup flowed into their cups. They tasted it and exclaimed over its sweetness.

Santana turned as they approached, and instead of greeting her fiancée, she looked at Will. "Your syrup is wonderful, Senor Lassater. I have never tasted anything like it." She looked at Hugo. "You must buy a barrel and take it back with us, Hugo. It is most delightful!" She handed him her cup, and Hugo took a taste of the syrup.

"*Si, es mucho delicioso,*" he said with a grin. "I will most certainly have my men bring a wagon along to haul a barrel back to La Estancia de Alcala for my beloved."

Will watched the smile leave Santana's face, as though the moment was spoiled by the reminder that she was to marry Hugo Bolivar. She handed the cup to Derek and covered her face with her fan again.

"I have made a deal with Senor Lassater," Hugo told her, "to allow him to come back with us to your father's *hacienda* and have a look at his many hundreds of acres of fine redwoods. He is here to stay. He wishes to build a sawmill and harvest the trees."

Santana glanced at Will, and he wondered if it was just wishful thinking that made him sure he saw a look of delight in her eyes. He reminded himself that this woman was the intended wife of one of the richest Spaniards in these parts, a man who could probably be very dangerous if crossed.

"Then we shall see you in two days when we return home," Santana said to him. "I will be glad for you to see La Estancia de Alcala. It is my home, and the most beautiful *hacienda* in northern California."

"Ah, you are forgetting Rancho de Rosas," Hugo reminded her. "One day it is *my* ranch you will call home.

You must learn to remove your attachment from La Estancia de Alcala, *mi querida.*"

Again a look of unhappiness clouded Santana's eyes, so much so that Will found himself feeling sorry for her. Hugo told Will he would have men there within the hour to unload the lumber, then he led Santana and her tutor back to the carriage. Santana glanced back at Will once before stepping inside.

"That's the most beautiful woman I have ever seen," Will said to Derek as the carriage rolled away.

Derek stuck his pipe between his teeth. "And she is promised to Hugo Bolivar, my friend. You had better remember that. It is not something to be taken lightly, not in Spanish culture, I'm told. Be careful not to let your eyes linger on her for too long."

"That will be a difficult task, especially since I have to travel with her for nearly three days back to her father's *hacienda.*" He looked at Derek. "You're coming, too, you know. I'm not letting you out of my sight. You might end up sailing away again, and I'll be out my best man."

Derek put a hand on his shoulder. "I made you a promise and I don't break promises. But I think it might be best if I stayed here. I can look for more men while you do business with Don Bolivar and Don Alcala. I know this place, know who to trust. Most of the men around here are a lot more likely to talk to a sailor than a businessman from Maine."

"All right. Bolivar suggested I stay at a place called the Golden Palace. I'll get you a room there too."

Derek's eyebrows arched. "The Golden Palace! Pretty fancy for a homeless sailor."

Will grinned. "Enjoy it while you can. A logger's life can be rough."

Derek put his hands on his hips. "I am ready to wield the ax. I'll learn fast enough. You'll see."

"I don't doubt that."

Derek's face lit up with excitement. "Tonight we will roam the saloons and whorehouses," he declared. "We will begin asking around, telling men you are looking for help. You had better put most of your money in a bank first, my friend. Never walk these docks with too much in your pockets."

Will nodded. "I'll remember that." He tried to see Hugo Bolivar's carriage once more, but it had disappeared around a corner, taking the beautiful Santana Lopez with it. He was secretly glad he would be seeing her again, in spite of the fact that she was betrothed to someone else. "She doesn't want to marry him, you know."

"What?"

"Senorita Lopez. She doesn't want to marry that pompous man. I can see it in her eyes. It's probably an arranged marriage."

Derek rolled his eyes. "That is not our business. It's not wise to interfere in something like that, Will."

"I didn't say I would interfere. I'm just saying she doesn't want to marry him." Will looked at Derek. "I'm going to get to know her better, my friend."

"She belongs to Hugo Bolivar."

Will just smiled. Maybe *not*, he thought. Something in the woman's eyes had stirred an ache deep in his loins. He had never seen such skin, such eyes, such hair. She was innocent yet sultry, and he had not missed the way she looked at him. She was as fascinated by him as he was by her. He turned away to untie another rope around the barrels, reminding himself of the real reason he had come here. He would have to try to keep his mind off Santana Lopez, but it was not going to be easy.

Four

Will slugged down another shot of whiskey, hoping with each drink that he would be able to forget about Santana Lopez, that those dark eyes of hers would quit haunting him, her full lips would quit tempting him. He puffed on his pipe while he studied his cards, then he asked for two more. An ace and two kings, with a ten and an eight. He made his bet, and all but one of the six men at the table, one of whom was Derek, stayed in the game. He was sure he'd lost, but miraculously, his kings took the pot.

The other men groaned and cussed as Will raked in his money and shouted for another drink. He looked around as he waited for the drink and for the man next to him to deal. The saloon was filled with men of all sorts—Spaniards, Americans, most of them sailors and fishermen, gamblers and traders. Prostitutes hung around the necks of some, offering themselves. Most of the women were Spanish, a few Chinese. All night he and Derek had been careful to watch their backs, staying away from alleys and dark places.

Will picked up his new hand, seeing nothing worth betting on.

"You Will Lassater?"

Will looked up at a powerfully built, dark-haired man who appeared to be in his late thirties. "I am."

The man folded his arms, as though to display his muscles even more. "They say you made an announcement in here earlier that you're looking for loggers, men who want to cut trees for you."

Will threw in his cards without even bothering to discard and get new ones. "I am. You looking for work?"

The man put out his hand. "Name's Noel Gray. I've got a wife and kids up north a ways. Came here to find work. I worked at a sawmill up there, but the owner didn't really know what he was doing and he ran out of money and closed up, took off for the gold fields."

Will shook his hand, rising to meet him. "You sound like just the kind of man I'm looking for. I guarantee you I know how to run a sawmill that will stay in business."

"Well, I came to California with a dream of gold, like a lot of other men, but I soon figured out that for every hundred men who come here, maybe one finds gold. Even those that find it usually don't have the means to mine it right and end up selling their claim for less than they're worth. Back in Pennsylvania I worked at a sawmill, so I decided to get back to what I know best. Just my luck that mill up near Santa Rosa went under."

Will grinned with excitement. "You know about cutting redwoods?"

"I know they're brittle as hell and have to be handled just right or they break apart when they fall. I know you can't cut them at the base like the hardwoods back home. The base is full of pitch and the wood is nothing but fiber from a couple hundred years of swaying. You don't bring down one of those trees by yourself. It takes two fallers, and the men have to climb up to the best cutting height. Those trees take two cuts, an undercut and a back cut, and one tree can take two men a couple of days, sometimes a week, to bring it down."

"Damn!" Will turned and scooped up his money, begging out of the card game. "We have to find a place to talk. What was your name again?"

"Noel Gray. I—"

"Hey, mister, you can't cut out of a game just because you're ahead. It ain't fair to the rest of us." One of the other card players, a drunken sailor, stood up and glared at Will. "Sit your ass back down, greenhorn. You ain't in some fancy saloon back east playin' with your rich friends."

"I need to talk to this man. I'll rejoin the game later." Will started to turn away, but the sailor grabbed his arm. Will jerked it away. "Why don't you go sleep it off somewhere?"

The sailor was obviously looking for an excuse for a brawl. "I don't take insults from strangers," he said, and took a swing at Will. Will dodged him and came up with a hard right to the man's jaw, sending him sprawling. One of the sailor's friends sprang out of his chair and lunged at Will, and the fight was on. Derek grabbed his money and shoved it into his pockets as another man pounced on Will. Derek dived in and pulled him off, and in seconds the entire saloon was filled with men fighting over nothing. Someone landed a fist into Noel Gray, who had no choice but to fight back. Drinks went flying, tables sprawling, cards and money scattered everywhere. Those who were not fighting crawled around among scuffling feet to try to grab up the loose money, while the women screamed and dodged bodies and fists.

Will knocked the first man flat, but he was quickly replaced by another. He was vaguely aware that Derek had pulled yet another man off his back. He picked up his opponent and literally hurled the man over the bar, his body smashing into the mirror behind it. The bartender began cussing and hitting men over the heads with whiskey bottles.

So many men came at him then, Will hardly knew who to swing at next. He took several blows, but landed just as many with his own big fists.

"Let's get out of here!" he heard Derek yell. "Work your way to the door!"

Will tried to do just that, noticing that Noel Gray was also caught in the melee. It seemed everyone in the saloon was against him, Derek, and Noel. They fought their way to the door amid fists and curses, and sent a couple of men sprawling outside.

"Run!" Derek told Will. "This way!"

Will was not a man to run from anything, but he figured in this situation, Derek knew best. He followed, and Noel Gray was right with him. Derek led them up the street, a few men on their heels. He charged into a house and slammed the door. "Save us, Rosy," he said to a woman standing right in front of them.

Will and Noel stood there panting, faces and knuckles bleeding, and it took a minute for Will to realize they were in a fancy whorehouse. He stared around at a roomful of buxom Spanish women who smiled seductively at him, one of them making a remark about the strong-looking *gringo*. The woman called Rosy opened the door again and ordered the men outside to go back to what they were doing. She threw a few choice curse words at them in Spanish, and they dispersed.

Will stared at her in surprise. Apparently this prostitute had a lot of influence. Rosy closed the door and faced Derek, and Will wondered if there was a woman alive who had a bigger bosom than Rosy. He had never seen anything quite like hers, and she was not even fat, just a little stout. She was short and not very pretty, and she had a stern look to her that made him understand why men obeyed her. She put her hand to Derek's crotch and rubbed it.

"Well, you big Swede, I see you've got yourself in trouble again. It's been a whole year since I've seen you. I wondered if you'd make it back."

"I didn't start the trouble this time. My friend here did, Will Lassater."

Will stood there panting and speechless as Rosy turned her dark eyes on him to size him up. "Well, well," she said, smiling. "You're a handsome one." She glanced at Noel Gray. "You're not so bad yourself."

"I'm married," Noel said. "I only came in here because my friends did."

Rosy studied his broad shoulders. "Too bad."

Will wiped at blood on his lip. "Look, ma'am, I appreciate your getting rid of those men. Is there a place where we can wash up?"

Rosy nodded toward a curtained doorway. "In the kitchen. If either of you wants a warm bed for the night, I can fix you up." She turned to Derek. "I *know* where Derek here will be sleeping."

Derek grinned. "Will, this is Rosy Hernandez. She runs a nice, clean place here." He wiped at blood near his eye. "I'm staying here tonight. You'd better do the same. Wait till morning to go to the hotel. I can guarantee there will be men waiting for you to come out of here tonight, and some of them will have knives and guns. You'll have to stay."

Will looked at Noel. "Sorry about this mess."

"It wasn't your fault." Noel turned to Rosy. "I'll stay too. I'll pay you for a room, but I have no interest in one of your girls. I have a wife."

Rosy shrugged. "Sure." She looked at Will. "What about you? I've got lots of girls to choose from."

Will glanced at the several women who sat staring at

him, most of them quite young. He thought about Santana Lopez, her satin skin and sweet smile. None of these prostitutes could compare, but he was beginning to understand how easily a man could get lost in the dark beauty of these Spanish women. It had been a long voyage here, months without a woman. He felt displaced, confused, and he was sure it was partly because of the whiskey he had drunk. Visions of Santana kept spinning in front of him.

"I'll take the girl over there," he said, pointing to one who reminded him most of the woman who had just that morning tasted his syrup with beautiful lips. "First I have to wash off this blood and talk to Noel."

He and Noel went into the kitchen, where Will pumped some water into a bowl and used it to rinse his face. He picked up a towel and dabbed at the cuts on his hands. "We need to talk more, Mr. Gray, but obviously this is not the time. Again, I'm sorry for this mess. I don't usually hang around saloons and get into brawls and sleep with whores. I just arrived here this morning, and I figured the docks would be full of men out of work. I need to build a crew before I can start my sawmill."

Noel pumped some clean water for himself. "I understand," he answered, washing his own hands and face. "I was only down here because I was about to give up finding decent work and was feeling sorry for myself. I couldn't believe it when somebody in that saloon told me you were looking for men to cut timber for you. That's what I do best."

Will sat down at the table. "You've already told me things I've never heard before, even though I've been in the logging business all my life. I need men who know a little something about these trees out here. I'm leaving day after tomorrow to go talk to a Spanish rancher north of here who might let me stump out his land. Will you come with me? I'd like you along when I get my first look at the big redwoods."

Noel nodded. "I'll come. My family also lives north of here, so it will be on my way home."

"I won't be able to get into logging right away," Will said. "I'm waiting for more equipment to arrive, and then I have to build the mill. I can give you a job helping me do that, and you and I and Derek can continue looking for more men to build a crew. Derek is the man out there who helped us escape. I met him on the ship coming here from Maine. He's really a sailor, but he agreed to stay in port this time and go to work for me. I figured with his size and all, he'd be perfect for the job, strong and unattached. I'll need you to teach him and others what to do. Will you be my camp foreman?"

Noel lowered the towel from his face, surprise in his eyes. "You hardly know me."

"I'm a pretty good judge of men."

Noel grinned. Will could see he had probably been a handsome man, but hard work and age were catching up with him, although neither seemed to have affected his strength. "Out here we call a camp foreman bull of the woods," he told Will.

"Will you do it?"

Noel walked over and put out his hand again. "You know I will."

Will shook his hand and said, "Tomorrow I'm getting a room at the Golden Palace. Come there with me and I'll get a room for you too. We can talk over supper tomorrow night." He looked around the room. "I guess for tonight we're relegated to this place. I promise never to tell your wife where you stayed."

Noel laughed. "I appreciate that. You're a real godsend, Mr. Lassater."

"Call me Will."

"Then you call me Noel. I'll do my best for you, Will."

"That's all a man can ask." Will looked toward the doorway. "I don't usually spend a lot of time in places like this, but it's been a long time, if you know what I mean."

Noel laughed again, a little blood still trickling from a cut on his lip. "Go do what you have to do. I'll see you in the morning."

Will walked through the curtained doorway to see the young Spanish girl waiting for him. She was nowhere near as pretty as Santana Lopez, but that did not matter at the moment. She smiled and opened her robe to show him her body, full breasts with dark nipples, shapely hips. As she led him up the stairs, Will could feel the long day catching up with him. The minute he saw the bed, he didn't even care about sex. He just wanted to sleep.

He woke in the wee hours of the morning to find he was completely naked, the Spanish girl sleeping beside him. He pulled the covers away and studied her voluptuous body. Running a big hand over her silken skin. He cupped a breast and leaned over to taste her nipple. She stirred awake.

"*Mi amante,*" she whispered.

He raised up to greet her lips with his own, quickly on fire for a woman. Her tongue snaked into his mouth, and he moved on top of her, sliding his throbbing shaft inside her. "Santana," he whispered. He buried himself deep, and too soon the life spilled out of him in his great need. "Just lie still," he told the girl. "We will do it again." In moments the life throbbed into his loins once more, for all he had to do was close his eyes and imagine the woman beneath him was Santana Maria Chavez Lopez. He could hardly believe that he had actually remembered her full name.

■　■　■　■

Santana watched from the balcony, her heartbeat quickening, as the *gringo*, Will Lassater, pulled up in front of Hugo's mansion in a wagon loaded with baggage and a myriad of axes and saws and other tools. An older man, also a *gringo*, was with him, but it was not the tall, rather homely blond-haired man she had met on the cargo ship. She watched Hugo step out of the house to greet them, and she quickly turned away so he would not see she had been watching for the American. Hugo had told her he'd asked Senor Lassater to come here, rather than their meeting him at his hotel. Hugo wanted to show off his house to the American.

Donning her hat and veil, Santana called to Louisa that she was ready. Her bags were already packed, and her happiest moments in life now were when it was time to leave San Francisco to go home again. She was even happier this time, knowing she did not have to travel the next three days with just Hugo. The handsome American would be along!

Louisa came from an adjoining room, wearing a little flowered hat and a plain blue dress. "You are happy to go back to La Estancia de Alcala," she said.

"Five days is too long in this place," Santana answered. "I long for the beauty and quiet of home, and I miss my father." She rushed out of the room and down the wide marble stairs, anxious to leave this cold house and its echoing halls. She hurried to the front door, knowing Hugo's carriage was already parked in front, packed and ready to go. She opened the door and walked into something broad and hard, realizing in a split second that it was a man's body. She gasped, embarrassed, and backed away. It was Will Lassater whom she had run into.

"I am so sorry, Senor Lassater!" she exclaimed. "I was coming outside—"

"And in quite a hurry!" Will said, all of his senses

awakened at the sight of her. She wore a lovely mint-green dress, again with hat and veil to match, as well as gloves. Her brown skin was beautiful against the green color, her arms slender, the cut of her bodice showing a hint of her full breasts.

Hugo stepped between them, taking Santana's arm and squeezing it just enough that it hurt. "Yes, what is your hurry, my dear?" he asked, his eyes blazing with anger. "You will make the American think you are anxious to leave the home of your intended. I did not even call for you yet."

Hugo had never before even hinted at hurting her, and Santana felt a sick fear. "I—I knew the carriage was packed and ready. When I heard Senor Lassater's wagon pull up, I assumed you were ready to go. I did not want to keep you waiting, Hugo."

He smiled, but there was a wickedness behind it that reminded Santana how easily this man could be displeased. "I understand," he said. "Go back to your room, Santana. I want to show Senor Lassater my home."

Will felt like yanking the man away from Santana. He could see Hugo was hurting her arm, and when he finally let go, deep white imprints showed where his fingers had squeezed too hard. He glimpsed tears of embarrassment and indignity in Santana's eyes, and he suspected she was a proud lady who was only holding her tongue because there were strangers present. She glanced at Will once more before turning and rushing up the stairs.

"The young ones are so impetuous," Hugo said. "I will tame her once she is my wife."

Will firmly controlled the keen urge to land a fist into the man. He had to stay calm. This was none of his business, and this man was about to lead him to what he claimed was some of the finest timber in California. Will had a premonition that the day would come when he could no longer bear the thought of the beautiful Santana being forced to marry such a hard, arrogant man as Hugo Bolivar, but he had not even met the woman's family yet. Maybe he was wrong about it being a forced marriage. What made it all harder was the fantasizing he had been doing about Santana. Try as he might, he could not stop thinking about her, and now that he had seen her again, smelled her lovely scent, realized she was even more beautiful than he remembered, it would be even more difficult to stay out of her life.

He followed Hugo around the mansion, thinking how it lacked warmth. It was designed similarly to some of the brick mansions back east, but it seemed out of place here in California. He thought how his parents' home was just about as big, yet it had always been cheerful and warm, full of love. That was what he suspected was lacking in this house. He could already see that Hugo Bolivar was a man who loved only one thing . . . money.

He glanced at Noel, who made the tour with him, and they both shook their heads. "Give me a little cabin in the woods any day," Noel said quietly when Hugo walked into another room.

"I agree," Will answered. Both men grudgingly followed Hugo around, listening to his bragging, pretending to be interested. Finally Hugo announced they must get underway, as it was a long trip.

"We will have plenty of time to talk business on the way," he said.

Will was relieved, for he was eager to see the trees at La Estancia de Alcala. He and Noel walked outside to their wagon to wait.

"Who was that pretty woman?" Noel asked.

"Bolivar's fiancée," Will answered.

"She looks pretty damn young for him."

"She's the daughter of the man who might let me

timber out his land. She comes from a wealthy family, and I think it's an arranged marriage. You probably know more about Spanish customs than I do. You've been out here longer. At any rate, I don't think she's very happy about the marriage."

Noel shrugged. "I don't think they necessarily arrange marriages or force them. I only know they're pretty strict in their ways, very protective of their daughters—at least the upper-class ones are. I imagine her father more or less expects her to marry a wealthy Spanish man, and this one might be a good friend of the family. Spanish daughters take great honor in pleasing their fathers." Noel nudged Will in the ribs. "Then, of course, there are the loose, wild women, like the one you were with two nights ago."

Will grinned. "I'd had too much whiskey and had gone too long without. I was still feeling a little off my feet that night. All I've ever known is Maine and working with my father. It's a whole different world out here."

"That it is. A very different life-style, very genteel among the upper-class Spanish. But then there's the craziness of this city. The gold rush has totally changed California. A lot of *Californios* haven't quite gotten used to it yet." He leaned against the wagon. "By the way, you seem a bit too concerned about the senorita. What's her name?"

"Santana Maria Chavez Lopez. How's that for a name?"

"All the Spanish girls have names like that. Something about taking the father's first last name and the mother's first last name. I don't know. I get confused. That's why the child's last name isn't the same as the father's. It's the first last name that matches the father's. She's Santana Chavez Lopez, and I believe you said her father's name is Dominic Chavez Alcala. See what I mean?"

"I think so. Takes some getting used to."

Noel laughed. "Well, my friend, what concerns me is the *way* you said her name, with a bit of worship in your voice. You aren't having romantic thoughts about the senorita, I hope."

Will shrugged. "She isn't anyone's wife yet."

"She's as good as married, Will. Let me tell you something. You don't get mixed up with the promised wife of a man like Hugo Bolivar. You'd better stick to what you came here for, to expand Lassater Mills. Stay away from Spanish women who are promised to someone else, especially the high-born ones."

Hugo reappeared then, holding Santana's arm. She wore a lace veil over her face so that Will could not see her eyes, but he felt her looking at him through that lace. She said nothing as Hugo led her to the carriage. Two women climbed in after her, one of whom Will recognized as Santana's tutor and chaperon. Hugo himself climbed inside then, and his driver snapped a whip. The two white horses pulling the carriage were off.

"Promised or not," Will said to Noel as they climbed on to their wagon, "it isn't right to force a woman to marry a man she doesn't love. And although I've only met that woman once, I can tell you she holds no love for Hugo Bolivar. She's afraid of him. I hope the marriage isn't taking place anytime soon. Once I get to know her father better, I intend to have a talk with the man."

"Stay out of it, Will."

Will snapped the reins to the four mules that pulled his wagon. Two more were tied behind. "We'll see," he answered. He followed after the carriage, heading away from the city and into the quiet foothills.

Five

Will walked to a hemlock tree outside the home of Enrique Valdez, a ranch hand who worked for Dominic Alcala. He breathed deeply of the smell of pine, enjoyed the sound of a soft wind whirring through the branches. Somewhere in the distant hills, wolves began to howl. He couldn't sleep for thinking about Santana. On their trip to La Estancia de Alcala, Hugo refused to make Santana camp outside and sleep in an uncomfortable bedroll. He'd timed the journey so that they stayed at people's homes each night. The first night it had been the home of a moderately wealthy Spaniard who owned a ranch, and who had practically stumbled over himself to be ingratiating to the much wealthier Hugo. Will suspected the man feared Hugo would force him to sell out if he offended him in any way. This night, like last night, they stayed at the humble home of a ranch hand. Will could tell neither man was pleased about having Hugo Bolivar in his house, lording his wealth and importance. But they worked for the father of the man's *novia*, and they were gracious because they knew Dominic Alcala would want them to be.

For the last two nights Will and Noel had been relegated to sleeping in barns because there was no room in the small stucco homes of the ranch hands. These were men who rode the outskirts of Dominic Alcala's vast holdings, men who did not own much but, Will guessed, were glad to have the work and a place to live.

He could hardly believe that for two days now they had been on land belonging to one man. Apparently Hugo Bolivar's ranch was not as big, but it was big enough, and he was wealthier than Dominic because of his other investments. From what Will could figure, Hugo had more open farmland and farmed more fruits and vegetables and grain, which had made him a very rich man when the thousands of gold seekers had come to California and started buying food at outrageous prices. Dominic had also made a great deal of money growing food for the gold towns, as well as selling horses and cattle, but much of his land was still forested. Now that Will realized just how much land the man owned, he was almost giddy with excitement that he might be able to secure the rights to Dominic's vast acreage of timber.

There was something else he wouldn't mind securing the rights to, but she belonged to someone else, and he felt like a fool for being so infatuated with a young Spanish girl he hardly knew. If he thought she was truly happy, maybe he wouldn't give Santana Lopez so much thought, but—

"I suppose you're planning that sawmill already," someone said.

Will turned to see a figure approaching him in the moonlight. He recognized Noel's voice and his stocky build. "Can't help it." He looked up at the scraggly pine on which he was leaning. "I do hope the trees you've been telling me about are bigger than this."

A speck of red glowed in the darkness as Noel drew on a cigar he had lit. "These sparse woods we're driving through now are nothing, just a few skinny hemlocks and white pine," he said. "Oh, they're tall and straight enough. White pine is easily worked, and it weathers well. I promise you, though, that you'll drop your jaw when you see the Sierra redwoods. According to Hugo, that's mostly what is on the northern section of the Alcala ranch. I've been through some of this area myself, and I know there's a lot of open, rolling hills between here and the redwoods. We have a way to go yet to reach them."

"Where is your family located?"

"I've got a little cabin northwest of here. Not too far. Hugo claims some of Alcala's land reaches nearly to the coast, which means you'll also be able to work with the coastal redwoods. The Sierras have the thickest trunks, but the coastal redwoods are almost as thick, and they're even taller, two to three hundred feet. They say some of the redwoods aren't just hundreds of years old, but *thousands* of years old. Hard to believe, isn't it?"

Will looked up through the branches of the hemlock under which he stood, studying the stars above it. "Sure is. Seems a shame even to cut them."

Noel laughed. "You could cut for a hundred years and never run out. The entire Northwest is covered with millions and millions of acres of forest. There's an almost endless supply—red cedar, western white pine, ponderosa pine, sugar pine, Sitka spruce, Douglas fir, redwoods. And most of it is damn good wood, easily worked, resistant to rot. If a man knows what he's doing, he can practically overtake the world market, put Australia, Chile, Norway, and the eastern United States out of business. I think you're that man, Will. You have the know-how and the backing . . . and the desire. You'll be as rich as the mine owners, maybe richer."

Will laughed. "You sure know how to encourage a man."

"I have to. The richer you get, the more you'll pay me."

Both men laughed, and Will took a puff on his pipe.

"By the way, be careful with your smoke," Noel said. "Back east you get more rain and dampness. Not out here. It's dry as a bone most of the time. California is basically pretty arid, you know. One little ember can wipe out hundreds of thousands of acres, especially if the wind is right. We're sandwiched here between the sea and the Sierras, and we get some pretty strange weather. Sometimes it's cold in July and hotter than hell in January."

Will breathed deeply again of the sweet-smelling air. "I love it already, now that we're away from the noise and bedlam of San Francisco. I kind of hate to have to go back there, but I've got to get more men. I hope Derek keeps his promise not to go sailing off on another ship."

Noel grinned. "I wonder if he's still with Rosy."

"That's quite possible." Will leaned his back against the tree. "Did you marry a Spanish woman?"

Noel walked over and sat down on a boulder he could see by the bright moonlight. "I was already married when I came out here in '49," he answered. "Brought my wife and two sons with me from Pennsylvania. Bernice is a good woman, left her own family to come with me. It's been hard on her. It wasn't long before I decided I didn't want to subject my family to the miserable life of living in a gold camp, so I came this way and found work at the sawmill I told you about. Then that fell through, so I went to San Francisco. Left Bernice and the kids at the cabin near the sawmill. The poor woman probably thinks I've left her for good. I've got to get back there. I'll probably leave you once we reach Alcala's place and go spend some time with her while you get things straight with Alcala."

"I'd like you to stay long enough to come out into the big timber with me, explain a few things. After that I'll go back to San Francisco and find more men, wait for the rest of my equipment."

"Sure." Noel rose, grunting a little. "I'll do my best for you, Will. I'm getting older, but I can still fell one of those giants, and I think I can teach other men to do it. I need this job. I took Bernice away from her family, and she deserves something better than I've been able to give her so far. I'd like to build a regular house for her, something with more room."

Will nodded. "If things work out the way I plan, you'll be making damn good money eventually. We'll get her and the kids set up proper. How old are your sons? Come to think of it, I don't even know how old you are."

Noel grinned. "I'm forty, but I didn't marry till I was thirty. Tommy is nine and Mark is six. Maybe someday I can get them into the business."

"I envy you, having a family and all. I was going to marry once, but my fiancée drowned at sea coming back from visiting relatives in England."

"I'm sorry to hear that," Noel answered, frowning.

"It was over two years ago. Maybe it was supposed to happen. I don't know. Maybe I was supposed to come out here and start over. My father died a year ago, and he'd been talking about sending me here anyway. He had big dreams about getting into logging out here. He'd heard stories about the redwoods too. I felt obligated to come in his memory, to realize his dream for him. But I'm doing it for myself as well. Someday my brother might join me, once our mother is gone. We might move the entire business out here. Depends on how things go. I guess for a while I won't have time to think about women and marriage. I'll be too busy. This would have been hard to do if I'd had to bring a wife and family with me."

"Well, as far as women go, about the only kind you'll find out here are Spanish," Noel said. "Before the gold rush there were almost no white women at all, and most of the men who came out here to look for gold were single, or they left their wives and families behind, so there still aren't many white women. When you come out here, you fall into a whole different way of life, and the basic culture here is Spanish. Wife or not, I have to admit some of these Spanish women are the most beautiful I've ever seen. And don't tell my wife I said that. And if she ever found out I spent the night at a whorehouse . . ."

Will laughed softly. "Quit worrying." He looked over at the house where Santana slept. "I do agree about their beauty. I find myself deeply fascinated by women like that one in there."

"Santana Lopez?" Noel shook his head. "You've got to get your mind off that girl, Will. She's untouchable, not just by a *gringo*, but by any man. Do you think Hugo Bolivar doesn't know you're enamored with her? Why do you think he hasn't given you one chance even to look at her since we left? He's either kept her hidden away in that carriage, or he's rushed inside a house with that veil over her face. He won't even let her dine with us. We haven't talked with her or even seen her face since we left San Francisco."

"It isn't just us. I think it's his way of punishing her for talking to me. He's been angry ever since that morning she came rushing outside to meet us. That bastard is making sure she understands her place as the future wife of Hugo Bolivar." Will walked a few feet away, sighing deeply. "The better I get to know Hugo, the more I can't stand him, and the more convinced I am that that poor girl doesn't want to marry him. She's terribly unhappy, and it just isn't right, Noel. Whatever the reason for promising her to Hugo, her father must know she detests the man and doesn't want to marry him."

"I'm telling you, you'd better stay out of it, Will," Noel

warned him. "You're asking for big trouble, and you could lose your chance at rights to that timber. Even if Santana didn't marry Hugo, her father would never allow his daughter to marry a *gringo*. I doubt *she'd* agree to it, even with his permission. A woman like that is expected to marry her own kind."

Will faced him. "I'm not saying I'm interested in her myself. It's just that she's so young and innocent, and anybody can guess what that sonofabitch would be like on their wedding night. Have you seen how he looks at her? He can hardly wait to get her in his bed. Thank God they can't marry until she's eighteen. I got that much out of Bolivar. That won't be for another year and a half. That gives me time."

"Gives *you* time?" Noel folded his arms and shook his head again. "Hugo Bolivar has a lot of power, Will, a lot of connections. He could find ways to ruin you and all your big dreams. Would you give up all of that for one little Spanish girl you hardly know and who probably isn't even interested in you?"

She's interested, all right, Will thought. He pictured her pretty smile, her satiny brown skin, and those big, innocent dark eyes. "Maybe."

"Sweet Jesus," Noel muttered.

"And maybe I won't have to give anything up if I handle things right. I'll get to know Santana's father better first. It's not that I'm interested in Santana herself, not romantically. I just don't want to see her forced into a marriage with a man who will mistreat her."

"Don't tell me you aren't interested romantically. Hell, I only saw her for a brief second that morning she ran into you, and I remember how pretty she was. I also saw how you looked at her."

Will ran a hand through his hair. "It all sounds ridiculous, doesn't it? I feel like a fool, a twenty-five-year-old man acting like he's sixteen himself. I've never met a woman who hit me so hard emotionally and physically the first moment I laid eyes on her. I feel like an idiot. It must be my own confusion at being so far from home. Everything is so different out here. I feel disoriented. I guess I'm just not thinking straight."

Noel walked up to him and put a hand on his shoulder. "Take it from me, you *aren't* thinking straight. I know how it feels to land here and be so far from everything familiar, from family, home. Give yourself some time, Will. Concentrate on the real reason you came here, building your father's dream. Forget about Santana Lopez. There's nothing you can do about her situation. You'll only make trouble, not just for yourself, but for her, her father, everyone involved. Hugo Bolivar is not a man to cross."

Will breathed deeply, telling himself that the way he felt made no sense at all, that Noel was completely right. He nodded. "I guess you're right at that." He turned and faced the man. "Late tomorrow we reach Don Alcala's home. I'll get things straight with him and we'll have one of his men take us into the big timber. Once I see those trees, I'll probably forget everything else."

"That's the way. We'd better get some sleep. Come on."

Will started after Noel, taking a moment to stop and look again at the house where Santana slept. Was she as disturbed with thoughts of him as he was with thoughts of her? Probably not. He was being a fool about this. Gerald hadn't sent him out there to fall in love with a forbidden Spanish woman who was too young for him to begin with, and whom he certainly didn't know well enough to have any feelings for at all. He'd let her beauty appeal to his baser needs, and that had led him to believe he was interested in her. How could he be such an idiot?

He followed Noel into the barn and set his pipe in a

tin plate, then plunked down on a blanket in the hay. He would forget about Santana and concentrate on those big trees. Two hundred to three hundred feet high? He still didn't believe it. This sure was different country out here, and in spite of the gold rush, it was still sparsely populated compared to the East. The people he had met seemed to have an easygoing life, quiet, relaxed, their hosts gracious and accommodating. The land was peaceful and soothing, and he realized there were hardly any insects, no mosquitoes buzzing and biting at night. Everywhere he looked he saw only beauty—flowers, rolling hills, the purple Sierras in the distance, their peaks covered with snow.

He even found the Spanish language beautiful, and the people he had met, other than Hugo Bolivar, left him feeling warm and welcome. The men were handsome, and the women, even the older ones, had a lovely grace about them. The young ones . . . like Santana . . .

He turned on his side. He had to quit thinking about her. He finally fell asleep to the call of the wolves.

The entourage of Hugo's carriage, his two guards, and Will and Noel in their supply wagon moved out of a stand of trees and into open foothills. According to Hugo, they would soon be at the Alcala home. On distant hills Will could see hundred of cattle grazing.

All was peaceful as the morning progressed, until men, horses, and wagon passed through an area where hills rose on each side of the road, boulders jutting out of the tops of them. Will caught the glint of steel to his right. He looked up just as a shot rang out; one of the guards fell from his horse. Almost instantly a second shot was fired, and the other guard's horse reared as its rider cried out. In response to the surprise gunshots, the driver of the carriage quickly drew the vehicle to a halt. Will's mules balked and brayed as he in turn yanked on his reins. He figured the carriage driver should probably have made a run for it with those two fine white horses rather than stop.

Apparently Hugo thought the same. "It is bandits, you fool!" he shouted. "Do not stop!"

By then two men were riding down the hill toward them, pistols pulled. A third galloped from the left side and rode up behind them. "Halt! Or we will kill all of you!" one of them shouted.

Will looked at Noel. Neither of them wore a gun, and they didn't dare reach for the rifles that lay under the wagon seat, now that they were in the sights of the outlaws. The three men rode close, ordering everyone out of the wagon and carriage. Will and Noel climbed down, as did Hugo's driver. The apparent leader of the bandits, a middle-aged Mexican, dismounted and yanked open the carriage door. "Out! Come out!" the Mexican shouted.

"You are lucky my pistols are packed in my luggage, or all three of you would be dead!" Hugo fumed, stepping out first. "Do you know who I am? You will all three hang for this! I will have you hunted down! How dare you ride onto Alcala land and —"

"Shut up," the Mexican told him, placing a pistol under Hugo's chin. "I *do* know who you are. I worked for you once, Don Bolivar, and you fired me for not properly polishing this grand carriage of yours." Fiery anger glinted in the man's dark eyes. "You had a guest with you, and you were trying to make an impression, just as you are *always* trying to do. Now it is *I* who order *you!*"

The man backed away as Santana and her tutor and personal maid exited the carriage. The other two outlaws dismounted. They appeared to be Americans, displaced miners, Will guessed, who had come out here and lost everything. Now they were reduced to robbery. They both sported several-days-old beards and wore floppy, soiled hats. Their shirts were sweat-stained, their trousers filthy.

One of them ordered Will and Noel to walk to the back of the supply wagon, then followed them, his pistol ready, while the other American moved to stand closer to the Mexican.

Will and Noel did as they were told, while Hugo cursed and shouted that the outlaws were riding stolen Bolivar horses. Will noted that all three men were indeed riding beautiful steeds, the Mexican's a white gelding, the other two golden Palominos. It mattered little to him that the horses were stolen. What was more important was that the men had dismounted, which would make them easier to tackle if the opportunity arose. He looked at Noel, and he could see by the man's eyes that he was thinking the same thing.

"*Sí*, Don Bolivar, these are very fine horses that we ride," their leader was saying. "I have come back to help myself to one of your fine *caballos*, as have my friends here. And we will help ourselves to something else that is yours." The Mexican turned to Santana, a wide grin on his face. He wore a large *sombrero* but was otherwise dressed plainly in shirt and pants, which were as soiled as the other two men's. He wore gunbelts strapped criss-cross over his shoulders; the other men wore gunbelts on their hips. Will watched them all carefully, worried about Santana.

"Just do like we say and you won't get hurt," the man standing near him and Noel ordered quietly. "This ain't your affair, so there's no sense riskin' your necks. This is between Juan and Hugo Bolivar."

All of Will's senses of protection came alert when the Mexican reached out and tore the veil from Santana's face. She gasped, stepping back.

"Leave her alone!" Estella begged.

The Mexican backhanded the woman so quickly, no one saw it coming. Santana screamed when Estella spun sideways and fell against the carriage. Louisa started crying, turning to put her arms around Estella.

"What do you think you are doing!" Hugo shouted in rage.

The Mexican pressed the barrel end of his pistol against the man's chest. "You do not even remember me, do you?" he asked, sneering. "You probably do not know the names of most of the people who work for you. You just order them about like slaves and think that they should feel lucky to work for the grand and glorious Hugo Bolivar!" He stepped back again. "I am Juan Fernandez, and three days ago I was visiting a man who works for Don Alcala. He told me that Senorita Lopez had gone to San Francisco with you and would be coming back today or tomorrow. I have been camped behind these hills, hiding from Alcala's men . . . waiting."

He looked at Santana again, his gaze moving over her hungrily. She wore a beautiful sky-blue dress, fitted tightly at her tiny waist, its soft cotton material gathered about her breasts, the hooped skirt decorated with tiers of ruffles. She wore no hat, but just the veil, which had been held in place by combs at either side of her head. Now it was ripped away, and locks of her hair had sprung free with the combs. She glared defiantly at the Mexican, and Will thought how beautiful she was when she had that proud look on her face.

"Waiting for what?" Hugo demanded.

Juan smiled, then he reached out and stuck his hand into the bodice of Santana's dress. He jerked hard, pulling her to him. Santana faced the man boldly, her chin held high, but Will could see how terrified she was. Louisa gasped and sobbed harder.

"Waiting for you to come by so that I could steal your woman!" Juan answered Hugo, keeping hold of Santana's dress while he waved his pistol at him. "You are to marry this pretty senorita, no? She is the daughter of Don Dominic Alcala. She is worth *mucho dinero* to the great and wealthy Hugo, so she will come with us. And until you send men to Black Horse Hill . . . alone . . . with ten thousand American dollars, you will not see your lovely intended again. I will take her away, and she will be mine!" The man rubbed at Santana's breasts with his hand, but his eyes were on Hugo. "And if you take too long, senor, then even if you pay to get her back, she will no longer be the fresh virgin you wish to have for a wife."

Santana pushed at the man's arm, forcing his hand away, and stepped back. "How dare you!" she exclaimed. "Surely you know the wealth and power of my father and of Hugo Bolivar! You will *die* for this!"

Juan laughed deep in his throat. "I do not think so. I think to get you back, they will both do exactly as they are told."

"You are a fool!" Hugo said. "You will never get away with this. My men will hunt you down like the animals that you are!"

As Juan started shouting at Hugo, Will glanced down at a small hatchet stuck into a metal ring at the back of the wagon gate. He'd won plenty of hatchet-throwing contests back home, and he wondered if there was a chance . . . He glanced at Noel, then looked down at the hatchet again, trying to tell him he intended to use it if he could. The attention of the bandits was on Hugo and Santana and the argument taking place. Louisa and Estella were cringing in each other's arms, and the carriage driver literally cowered behind the two women. One of the guards looked dead, and the other lay writhing and groaning on the ground, a bloody hole in his side.

Will slowly reached for the hatchet, trying not to draw any attention to himself. Managing to grasp it near the blade, he quietly slipped it from the ring. He held it against his right leg, out of sight of the American who was supposed to be watching him and Noel. The man stood to their left, but his eyes were on Santana, whose breasts were partially revealed from Juan yanking at the front of her dress. Will met Noel's eyes, and Noel shifted closer.

"I'll take the one on the left," Will said softly. "Get ready."

Hugo was screaming at Juan, cursing him in Spanish. Juan shouted back, using precious time to vent his anger at the man he apparently hated with great passion. Too soon, though, he ordered Santana onto his horse.

"I will not leave with you," she spat at him. "I would rather die!"

Juan grabbed her throat and squeezed. Planting his pistol against her cheek, he jerked her by the neck to his horse. "You will do as I say, you arrogant bitch! Get on my horse, or I will kill these other two women and the driver, and those two Americans over there! Is that what you want?"

Santana glanced at Will, and his heart ached at the fear and desperation in her beautiful eyes. It was obvious she could barely breathe. She looked back at Juan. "Do not hurt anyone else," she whispered, choking. "I will go with you." She turned and mounted the horse.

"Now!" Will told Noel.

Everything happened in a matter of seconds. Noel whirled and used his burly body like a battering ram, bending down and running at the gunman nearest him, putting his shoulder into the man's midsection. The man grunted as he flew backward, his arms flying up and his gun sailing out of his hand. At the same time Will raised the hatchet and hurled it. It sang through the air, spinning head over handle, and landed with a thud in Juan's right shoulder. He screamed in horror, his gun falling from his hand. The others just stared in shock. The third gunman whirled and shot at Will, then tried to mount his horse, but the animal reared and pranced sideways.

As Noel landed hard fists into the face of the man he had tackled, Hugo finally moved, grabbing the gunman who was having trouble mounting his horse. Juan lay writhing on the ground, holding on to his right arm, which was nearly severed. Will ran to help Hugo, who was smaller than the American he tangled with. With his powerful arms, Will pulled the American off Hugo, who in turn grabbed the horse to calm it while Will wrestled the gunman to the ground. He heard a gunshot, heard Santana scream, yet he felt nothing at first. He rolled the gunman onto his back, keeping a knee in his gut while he slammed the man's gun hand against the gravely earth, over and over, until the man let go of his pistol. The next thing he knew Hugo held the pistol to the man's head and fired.

"That will teach the bastard to steal horses from Hugo Bolivar!" he growled.

Will heard two more gunshots, and Juan's screams suddenly stopped. He heard the other American begging for his life, another gunshot. He witnessed none of the assassinations. He only knew vaguely, somewhere in a swiftly fading consciousness, what must be happening. Pain began to burn at his left side, and he saw the ground coming up to meet him.

"He's been shot!" Santana screamed. "Help him, Hugo! We must get him to my father's house!"

Those were the last words Will remembered.

Six

Will awoke to the sound of birds singing. For a moment he wondered if he had died and gone to heaven, for the bed in which he lay was wonderfully soft, and the room around him was lovely, with paintings of landscapes and a bullfighter on the stucco walls, the furnishings all in rich, dark mahogany. The window was made of stained glass, set in an iron frame. It was open, and a gentle breeze ruffled the leaves of a plant nearby. The wonderful smell of roses was carried on the breeze, and the birds' singing was soothing to the soul.

He lay still, gathering his thoughts. He remembered Santana screaming, "He's been shot!" Had she been talking about him? He didn't remember being shot, but when he tried to sit up to think more clearly, pain tore through his left side. He groaned and lay back down, realizing it was true, and wondered if he was dying. It all came back to him, the attempted abduction of Santana Lopez, his throwing the hatchet. Was Noel all right? The man had a wife and children. He would feel guilty and responsible if something had happened to Noel. And what of Santana? Had she been hurt in all the scuffling? Whose house was this? Hugo's? Santana's?

Will put a hand to his side, feeling bandages. He finally remembered an awful agony, someone working over him, pouring whiskey into him, a pain in his side as though someone were gouging mercilessly at him with a knife. Had someone removed a bullet? Did whoever it was know what the hell he was doing?

Will closed his eyes, thinking what a strange beginning his new life in California had been. There had been a run-in with pirates on the ocean voyage, but Captain Eastman had ended that with a cannon shot that had landed smack into the main mast of the pirate ship, sending the mast crashing down and leaving the pirates unable to raise their sails. Then had come the dangerous trip around the Horn . . . lives saved, a life lost. The San Francisco harbor was a place he would not soon forget—the wild melee of activity, the lawless wharves at night; the fight in the saloon, where he could have been killed; the Spanish woman with no name, with whom he had slept at Rosy's place.

Several times already his life had been at risk coming here, and now this, a gunshot wound from bandits who'd tried to abduct an innocent girl for money. This land was indeed a far cry from the settled civilization of Maine, the busy but calm docks of Portland. San Francisco didn't even have an organized law-enforcement agency, merely a group of citizens who'd banded together and called themselves *vigilantes*. Apparently it was even worse in the country, where there was no law but that of the landholder.

He remembered now. . . . Gunshots after he'd disarmed the outlaw he had tackled. Hugo had said something about teaching them not to steal horses from him. Had he killed those men point-blank? Was that how things were done out here? No trial? No mercy? Someone stole from a man, so he was shot. It began to sink in what Noel and Derek had both tried to tell him about the power of a man like Hugo Bolivar. If Will did take more interest in Santana Lopez and something came of it, would Hugo consider that stealing too? Could he shoot him for it?

Will tried again to sit up, but groaned at the pain in his side. His head began to ache too. This was a beautiful land, but so foreign that he suddenly missed home very much. He missed Gerald and his mother, the cool weather, the hardwood forests. Mostly he missed life being civilized and orderly. In Maine a man knew where he stood, what was right and wrong, what the laws were. Here it was apparently every man for himself, survival of the fittest. A man had to watch his back every minute, like at the docks, where thieves were ready to pounce and knife a man for whatever money he might be carrying, or perhaps just for a ring or a watch.

Will's thoughts were interrupted when the thick wooden door to his room opened a little and someone peeked inside. With great pleasure he saw that it was Santana. The moment she stepped inside, he forgot all the bad things that had happened on his journey to this lawless place. He forgot about pirates and storms, thieves and prostitutes. He forgot about bandits and *vigilantes*, and about the fact that he missed home. She walked closer, and he saw in her eyes all that was beautiful about California.

She was dressed plainly, wearing a soft yellow dress, no jewelry, no extra color on her lips or eyes. Her hair was brushed out long and loose, pulled up by combs at the sides. Some of it draped down her arm, and he saw it fell nearly to her wrist. Her complexion was flawless, a soft brown with a satin sheen. He realized that except for that morning in San Francisco, when she accidentally ran into him, this was the first time he had seen her unveiled since leaving San Francisco; and the first time he had ever been alone with her. Her beautiful dark eyes were studying him curiously, and she halted at the foot of his bed when she realized he was awake and watching her.

"Senor Lassater, you have finally awakened," she said softly, as though afraid someone might hear her and find her there. "How do you feel?"

He swallowed. "I don't know. I . . . tried to sit up, but . . . there was too much pain. Can I have some water?"

"*Si*, I will get you some." She came closer, lifting a pitcher that sat on a stand near the bed and pouring some water into a porcelain cup.

Will thought how beautiful she was even when she was completely natural, no fancy hairdo, no elegant dress, no powder or color on her face. She did look even younger than he knew she was, though, and he felt guilty for having thoughts about her that a man should hold only for a mature woman. She came to him and offered the cup of water, putting a hand under his head and helping him raise up enough to drink. She held the cup to his lips, and he thought how wonderful she smelled, but couldn't quite place the fragrance. He noticed the smoothness of her hand as he drank the water.

"I should not be in here alone with you," she told him. "My father would think it improper, as would Hugo, but I was so worried." She set the cup aside and pulled a wooden chair up beside the bed. Will noticed she sat very straight and prim in the chair. "Father and Hugo are out choosing some Palomino mares that Father wishes to mate with a stallion Hugo owns. My father raises some of the finest Palominos in the world." She smiled. "My brother helps him. He is also gone today, out rounding up some cattle. The only other people in the house are the servants, and they do not know I came in here."

She glanced down, then looked at him again. "I

wanted to thank you, Senor Lassater, for what you did. You and your friend risked your lives to save me from something worse than death. My father is also very grateful. I told him everything that happened."

Will looked her over once more. "You're all right, then?"

"*Si*, I am fine. But I was so afraid for you. One of Father's men, an American named Marcus Enders, he took the bullet from your side. He used to be a doctor in the East, then came here to look for gold." She giggled and covered her mouth. "Father says Senor Enders could not keep his job as a doctor in the East because he likes whiskey too much and was often too full of it to operate on people." Her eyes widened in apology. "Oh, but do not worry! He was not full of whiskey when he took the bullet from you. Actually, I feel sorry for him. His wife died back East, and he took it very hard. He blamed himself for not being able to save her. That is when he started drinking, Father says. He is actually a fine doctor, when he is sober. Father says he did a good job and that you should recover.

"I went to the chapel and prayed for you. We have our own chapel here on La Estancia de Alcala, even our own priest. Because we are so far from a city, we keep supplies here for all the help. It is almost like our own little town. Our priest, Father Miguel Fernandez Lorenzo, lives here so that we and the many men and their families who work for my father can keep up with mass and confession." She leaned closer. "Are you Catholic, Senor Lassater?"

Will was enraptured just watching her talk, listening to her soft Spanish accent. She spoke English very well, and he supposed a man like Dominic Alcala would make sure his children were well-educated. He enjoyed the innocence in her eyes, her youthful enthusiasm, and the passionate way she had of speaking. There was no way of hiding her feelings behind those dark eyes. Everything was right there, open, honest, alight with curiosity.

"No," he answered. "I'm Protestant . . . Methodist. Is that a terrible thing out here?"

She frowned. "Father has grown used to dealing with Protestants, but he says that all of you will surely never reach heaven."

Will wanted to laugh, but it hurt too much. "Well, I guess I almost found out yesterday, didn't I?"

"Yesterday?"

"When I was shot."

"Oh, that was two days ago, senor."

Will was surprised. "Two days?"

"*Si.* As I said, I told my father everything that happened. I also told him that you and your friend were much braver than Hugo. Of course, I did not tell him that in front of Hugo, but it is true. Hugo was more interested in saving his horses than saving me. He thinks that just because he shot those men after it was over, that made him the brave one. He tried to make himself look like an important man because of that, but I told Father it was you and Senor Gray who were the brave ones."

"What about Noel? Is he all right?"

"He is fine, senor. He is out riding, looking at some of my father's trees, waiting for you to recover so that you can both go deeper into the forest on my father's land and see the big trees for yourself."

Will sighed in frustration, irritated that any of this had happened. He had so much to do, was eager to get out and see those trees. "Hugo shot those men?"

He watched her eyes, saw the disgust and hatred there. "*Si.* It was a terrible thing to see." Her eyes teared, and she shivered. "Father is angry that he did not take the men to his ranch first, rather than shoot them right in front of us. I have had bad dreams from it. I know that they were bad men, but to shoot them that way . . ."

"It was wrong of him," Will said. "I agree with your father. Where I come from . . ." He shifted in bed, grimacing with pain. "Where I come from, people don't just shoot criminals on sight. They're arrested and allowed a trial. A jury decides what will be done with them."

"A jury?"

"A group of people who hear what happened and vote on what should be done. We have laws, jails, judges."

Santana shook her head. "It is not like that here. In the city there are only *vigilantes* to make the law and punish criminals. There are no trials. And out here, landowners make their own laws. If a man steals a horse, he is hanged for it . . . or shot. People would say Hugo had a right to do what he did. Even my father would agree. It is the fact that he did it in front of me and Louisa and Estella that he is upset about. But then, after all, those men did kill both of the guards, and they might have killed you and your friend and made off with me. I suppose it is best that they are dead."

"Maybe, but with the kind of law you have out here, innocent men could be hanged or shot before they have a chance to defend themselves. And men like your father and Hugo can use any excuse to kill any man they don't happen to like."

She stiffened. "My father would never—"

"No. But Hugo would, wouldn't he?"

She looked at her lap. "You do not like him."

"I don't think many people do, including you. Why are you marrying him?"

She quickly rose, putting on a defensive look. "You are practically a stranger, and an American, who does not understand our ways. It is expected of me. My father gave his word many years ago to Hugo's father, who saved my family's lives during the Mexican Revolution. It is Father's way of uniting the wealth of both our families." She glanced toward the doorway as though afraid someone might hear her talking about her marriage, then looked back at Will. "I did not come here to talk about personal things, Senor Lassater. Such matters are not your concern. I only wanted to see that you are getting better, and tell you I am grateful for what you did for me."

Will rubbed at his eyes. "I'm sorry. It is none of my business. I came here to build a sawmill and cut trees . . . if your father will let me." It was becoming an effort to talk. Already he was feeling tired. "I'll stay out of your personal lives. Once I get started logging, I'll be too busy to get involved anyway."

Santana stared at him a moment, wanting to ask him a thousand questions about what it was like where he came from. And she wanted to admit that she, too, hated Hugo and had no desire to marry him. Did this American know of a way she could get out of her father's promise? She was too embarrassed to ask a stranger something so personal, and perhaps it would be a betrayal of her father. He would be devastated if she discussed such a thing with a man like this.

He was so easy to talk to, though, this Will Lassater. She wished they had all day. She wanted to know about logging, wanted to see him cut down one of the big redwoods. What had brought him here? What was his family like? Was there a woman back in Maine . . . a woman he loved? He was so very handsome, and although she had no right looking upon his bare arms and shoulders, she could not help noticing them as he lay there, so muscled, his chest so broad and hard. His sandy hair was tousled, which only made him more handsome, and his eyes . . . so blue. When he looked at her she felt he knew her every thought.

She moved the chair back where it belonged. "Father

is very grateful to you," she told him. "Because of that, he has told Hugo he already agrees you should be allowed to rent his property. When you are better, he will take you out and show you all that he owns. It is very beautiful."

Just like you, Will thought. "I am grateful to your father in return." He gave her a reassuring smile. "And to you. I'm sure you had a lot of influence in his decision."

"I only told him the truth about how brave you were." Her eyes widened. "I have never seen a man throw a hatchet like that. You are as fast with the hatchet as some men are with guns!"

Will kept smiling in spite of the ache in his side. "I've worked with tools like that all my life. Back home we have contests . . . how fast a man can saw down a tree, how fast he can split a certain number of logs, hatchet-throwing contests, tree climbing, wrist wrestling, things like that. And back home we don't carry guns around all the time, unless we're going hunting. My skill isn't with guns, just with saws and hatchets . . . and sometimes my fists."

She laughed, and Will thought how musical it sounded, light and cheerful, like the birds outside his window.

"It must take very strong men to do the kind of work you do," she said. "I have never seen a man built quite like you and Senor Gray, with such powerful arms. I would like to see you chop down one of our redwoods. I think you will find it impossible for one man."

"Well then, you've given me a challenge. Do you ride?"

She lifted her chin. "I ride better than most of the men on La Estancia de Alcala. My father says so. I have my own horse, a Palomino called Estrella."

"Star."

Her eyebrows arched. "You know Spanish?"

"Not as well as I'd like, but enough to get by. I figured if I was coming to California, I'd better learn."

"Why did you ask if I ride?"

"Because you should ride with us when we go out to inspect the trees. You could learn more about logging."

She smiled softly, but her eyes held a disappointed look. "I do not think my father would let me. He—"

They both heard the sound of horses approaching. "My father and Hugo are back! I must go!" She hurried to the door, but after peeking around it, turned back inside. "Delores is at the end of the hall talking to Louisa," she whispered. "I cannot leave!" She looked around the room, then ran to a large wardrobe and opened the doors. Few clothes hung inside, since this room was reserved for guests. She climbed into the wardrobe, putting a finger to her lips and giggling before closing the doors to hide herself.

Moments later Will heard men talking as they came into the house. He recognized one of the voices as Hugo's. The voices came closer, and Hugo walked into the room with a stocky older man who was still quite handsome in spite of his graying hair and mustache. The man was shorter than Hugo, very dark complected, and was dressed in black pants, a white shirt with a string tie, and high black leather boots that came to his knees.

"Ah, Senor Lassater, you are finally awake!" Hugo exclaimed. "Dominic and I have been out choosing some mares to mate with a stud horse that I own. We decided to come here as soon as we got back to see how our American friend is doing."

"Much better, thank you." Will put out his hand toward the second man. "You must be Dominic Chavez Alcala."

"*Si*," Dominic answered, shaking Will's hand firmly but gently. "And I cannot thank you enough for what you did in protecting my daughter, senor. I will be forever grateful. I have already told Hugo that I will gladly allow you to inspect my timber and rent whatever parts of my forested land you feel you need."

"I'm extremely grateful, sir," Will answered, still holding the man's hand. "Getting started out here is a dream my father had, but he passed away before he could realize that dream. I've come here to do that for him. If things work out the way I think, I will make a lot of money for Lassater Mills . . . and for you in the process."

"We will *all* make money," Hugo put in. "When I marry Senorita Lopez, we will combine La Estancia de Alcala with Rancho de Rosas, and Dominic and I will be the biggest landholders in northern California. Together we own thousands of acres of the big trees, senor. The supply will be endless. As soon as you are able to ride, we will take you to see the trees, and you will see that California grows trees unlike anything you have ever seen back home. Together we took care of the outlaws, and together we will conquer the great redwoods!"

Will just looked at him, hardly able to believe the man was taking credit for stopping Santana's would-be abductors. *What a pompous ass you are*, he thought. He wanted to ask Hugo point-blank in front of Santana's father, if expanding his holdings was the only reason he was marrying Santana. He felt like shouting at Dominic Alcala, telling him he was wrong to hold his daughter to a promise made years ago and let her enter into such an unhappy marriage; but this was not the time or the place. Perhaps there never would be a proper time. He certainly did not dare offend the man at the moment. Alcala was offering him the dream of a lifetime. "I look forward to seeing those trees, sir," he told Dominic. "But it's going to be a few days yet. I'm pretty sore."

"Of course you are. You take all the time you need,

Senor Lassater. We have plenty to talk about in the meantime. I will bring you a map and show you the lay of my land, where the thickest forests are, show you my boundaries."

Kindness shone in Dominic Alcala's eyes, and Will took hope in that. Perhaps he could be reasoned with. Will would take his time, get to know him better before he interfered with Dominic's personal life. He looked at Hugo, seeing something different in his cold, dark eyes. The only thing the man was thinking was that this entire venture was going to make him richer. "What happened to the bandits?" he asked Hugo. "And to my friend Noel?"

"Your friend is fine, senor," Hugo answered, smiling. "And you will not have to worry about the bandits. They are dead. They stole my horses, so I shot them." There was a hideously proud look on his face, as though shooting the men were the same as shooting a wild animal on a hunt.

Will frowned, deciding to take advantage of the opportunity to embarrass this man he had learned to despise in only a matter of days. "I remember gunshots . . . just before I passed out. Surely you didn't shoot them in front of Senorita Lopez!"

Hugo lost his smile, glancing at Dominic, then back at Will. "It had to be done quickly," he said. "They were still armed and we were not."

"The one I landed a hatchet into was unable to do any harm. Noel had the other man under control, and the man I'd tackled lost his weapon. You could have just—"

"I did what was necessary, senor. Out here men must live by the law of Hugo Bolivar and Dominic Alcala! They quickly learn not to cross either of us. My intended wife knows this. Her father lives by the same law."

Will held Hugo's gaze, knowing full well what the man was telling him. It was Hugo's law by which men must live out here, including himself. And that meant staying away from Santana. At the moment, if he'd been in full health, he would have had trouble keeping himself from landing a fist into Hugo Bolivar's face and wiping that arrogant look off it.

"I agree with Senor Lassater," Dominic put in. "I wish that you had not killed those men in front of my daughter, Hugo, but what's done is done. They committed a wrong for which they had to die. They were foolish men who should have known what would happen to them."

Hugo folded his arms authoritatively. "It is best that Senor Lassater learns that we live a different way here in California and understands the laws and customs of the *Californios*. Out here a man is master on his land, and any man who tires to steal what he owns must suffer just punishment."

Will ignored Hugo, afraid that if he didn't, he would say something that would be considered an insult. He kept his gaze on Dominic Alcala, who, he surmised, was a much more reasonable and merciful man than Hugo. "I appreciate your willingness to do business with me, Senor Alcala, and your hospitality," he said. "I will try to get out of this bed and your house as soon as I can. I'll build my own place near the mill once I decide just where to locate it. I'll pay you whatever you think is reasonable rent, plus five percent of my profits from the lumber."

Dominic nodded. "I will give much thought to what is a fair price. For now you must rest, senor, and you must also eat to get your strength back. I will have our cook, Hester, make a mild beef soup for you. Anything else you need, you tell her or my house servant, Delores. They will see that you have everything you need. When you are rested and able to get up, we will talk more and settle our agreement on paper. I thank you again for what you did. When you are well, you must show me this talent you have for throwing a hatchet. My daughter told me you were almost as quick as a man with a gun."

Will grinned in spite of his growing weariness. The pain and his weakness were catching up with him. "I've been wielding hatchets since I was about five years old. My mother . . . used to chastise my father for letting such a small child handle . . . such a wicked instrument. She was always afraid I'd chop off my own foot or hand."

Dominic chuckled "Well, you certainly impressed my daughter and the others. I must tell you that if Santana should try to come in here and talk to you, you just shoo her away. She should not come into a guest's room and pester him with questions, but the child in her makes her do foolish things sometimes. She knows it is forbidden to talk alone with any man, especially one she hardly knows. She cannot even see Hugo alone until they are married. When you are able to join my family at the dinner table, however, you may speak with her and answer the many questions I know she has about what life is like where you come from, and about logging. Even I have many questions, but I know that you are too tired for them right now. Please do not take offense at my warnings. I only tell you these things so that you understand our customs and do nothing to offend me or my family."

"I understand," Will answered. "Your daughter is very sweet and very beautiful, Senor Alcala. Senor Bolivar is a lucky man." He turned his gaze to Hugo, who was watching him closely.

"*Si*, he is very lucky," Dominic answered. "The day they marry, it will be the biggest wedding anyone has ever seen."

"We will have a *fiesta* here and in San Francisco," Hugo added, lifting his chin proudly. "It will last for days, perhaps a week. All of the most important people in California will be invited to come and meet my beautiful new wife, and Santana will live a grand life, like a queen!"

And she'll be the unhappiest woman in northern California, Will thought. "I'm sure you'll both be very happy," he said aloud. "By then I should have my sawmill in full operation, so I doubt I'd be able to attend the grand event." His eyes drooped. "Right now I think I need to sleep some more," he added, wanting to get them both out of the room so poor Santana could come out of hiding.

"Of course," Dominic said. "I will have Delores and Hester look in on you often. As soon as you are awake enough again to eat, they will bring you the soup. And I must tell you, I have tasted the syrup you brought from the East. It is wonderful! I have never tasted anything so sweet. Hester is excited about the many ways she can use it in her cooking. You will have to share with us some of your own ways of using the syrup."

"I will be glad to."

Dominic nodded and left. Hugo followed, but he lingered at the doorway, waiting for Dominic to go on without him. He turned back to Will. "I would remember what Dominic told you about staying away from Santana," he said. "She is impetuous and strong-willed, and she has the curiosity of a child. I believe she thinks you a bit of a hero, and I have seen how you look at her, Senor Lassater. I will be leaving soon for San Francisco again, and I am trusting that you will honor the fact that I have helped you by introducing you to Don Alcala and have encouraged him to allow you to cut his timber. Timbering rights are hard to come by, as many of my people do not care to allow Americans to use their land. You may repay me by keeping in mind that Santana belongs to me, and remembering the rules Dominic told you about. And I will remind you that no one steals from Hugo Bolivar."

Will glanced at the wardrobe, suspecting that the "impetuous" Santana was having trouble hiding a giggle. *She is not your wife yet*, he wanted to tell Hugo, *and she is not an object you can possess. She is a beautiful, virtuous young woman who has feelings and who surely does not want to be owned like cattle, but rather, loved and cherished.* "I will remember," he said aloud. "And I am grateful for your bringing me here. As for the incident with the bandits, I only did what I had to do. I don't consider it heroic."

Hugo's eyes bored into him, and Will could easily see that he could be as cold and cruel as the worst outlaw. The fact that he had killed those three bandits in cold blood told him that. "Then we understand each other, senor," Hugo answered. He grinned. "I hope you are better soon. When you are ready for your equipment, it will be waiting for you in my warehouse."

Will caught the meaning in the words. The man could lock up his equipment and keep him from getting his hands on it if Will displeased him. Hugo obviously enjoyed having that kind of power, and Will decided he'd better get started as quickly as possible and get his things out of Bolivar's warehouse in San Francisco. "I'd like to settle what you owe me for my lumber and syrup before you leave again," he told Hugo.

"Certainly."

Their eyes held a moment longer, two men who were willing to do business together, in spite of a growing dislike for each other. Will reminded himself how dangerous Hugo Bolivar could be, and he forced himself to be polite. Still, he knew that if he got more chances to talk alone with Santana, he would take them, if for nothing more than to try to talk her out of her impending disastrous marriage. First, though, he had to get things settled and signed with Dominic Alcala, and get his equipment out of San Francisco.

"You can come out now," he said softly when Hugo was gone.

The doors to the wardrobe opened slowly, and Santana peeked out. She covered her mouth and laughed. "Thank you for not telling," she said. "If not for worrying that Hugo would banish you and never allow you to rent my father's land, I would have come out of hiding when he was so proudly telling you you must never speak to me alone. I would have loved to have seen the look on his face!" Her eyes danced with excitement and impishness. "When you are better, I will see you when you dine with us." She hurried to the door and looked out, then turned to smile at him once more. "And it *was* a very heroic thing that you did," she added before slipping out of the room.

Seven

Will watched Dominic Alcala as the man rode ahead of him, sitting straight and proud on a magnificent Palomino gelding. Will himself had been given a Palomino mare to ride, as he and Noel followed Dominic and his son, Hernando, into the forests on the northern end of La Estancia de Alcala.

This was the day Will had been waiting for, the day he would finally get to see the big trees everyone kept telling him about. It was obvious Dominic was eager to show him his trees. The man was quite friendly and affable, and he loved bragging about his land. In the two weeks he had been at La Estancia de Alcala, Will had come to understand the pride of these *Californios*, their lovely culture and quiet dignity. He'd learned that Dominic's family had been in California for two generations, having fled a revolution in Mexico. California was home for them, a place they considered their own; and it had been hard for them to accept the rush of Americans that had flooded their land when gold was found. Now they were a part of the United States. It had all happened so fast that men like Dominic still had trouble realizing that this land was no longer an extension of Mexico, owned and controlled by Spaniards.

On La Estancia de Alcala and the few other Spanish-owned tracts of land that were left, they could maintain their culture, their own private worlds, where nothing had changed. There was nothing American about anything on Dominic's ranch. To stay there was like living in old Spain or in Mexico. At least, that was how it seemed to Will. He had never been to either place, but he figured staying with the Alcalas was probably as close as a man could come. Everyone dressed in the bright colors and unique styles that Spaniards wore. The food they served was completely different from what he was used to, and in fact, Dominic had asked his cook to make special dishes just for Will, who was not accustomed to nor ready for the hot, spicy dishes the rest of the family ate. For now Will was satisfied with corn bread and potato or rice pancakes, and Hester had a wonderful way of making eggs. He also had come to love a dessert called _almendrado_, almond pudding.

He was fast becoming accustomed to the gentle culture of the _Californios_, their relaxed pace of living, their generous and gracious nature . . . their beautiful women. He had not had the opportunity to talk alone again with Santana, but he was able to enjoy her company at meals. There he allowed himself the pleasure of watching her every graceful move, listening to her lilting voice and enjoying the lovely Spanish accent. She often spoke only in Spanish with her family, and they were all helping him master the language himself, laughing with him when he made mistakes. Hernando had a beautiful wife and children, who often joined Dominic and Santana for meals. There was much love among them, and he knew that Santana herself had much love to give. He still could not help thinking what a waste it would be for such a gentle young woman to marry a man like Hugo Bolivar. Hugo had left for San Francisco again, and Will was glad he was gone.

The more he became used to this beautiful land, and the more fascinated he became with Santana, the less he missed Maine. Now he could hardly wait for Gerald to come and see the place for himself.

Will and Noel followed Dominic and Hernando into a magnificent forest full of wondrously huge, tall trees. Noel told Will they were mostly Ponderosa pine and western red cedar. As he listened to the man, Will was again grateful he'd met up with Noel.

Noel had taken the past two weeks while Will healed to go get his family, whom Dominic had permitted to live in a small cabin on his ranch until Will could decide where he would build his sawmill. Noel would then move his family to that location and help run the mill. Noel's wife, Bernice, was stoutly built, a woman strong in body and in spirit. She was quite pretty in the face, but was not a woman to care about being fancy. She wore her ash-blond hair pulled into a tight bun, and her clothes were plain and practical. She was stern with her two sons, nine and six years old, and the boys were mannerly and obedient.

"You have a fine family, Noel," Will told him. "You sure your wife won't mind living out at the mill, so far from other women's company?"

"Bernice is used to it. We lived the same way back east. Fact is, we could use the extra money if you let her do the cooking for your crew. She's done it before. She's a good cook."

Will nodded. "I'll sure need one if she wants to do it."

"The boys will help her. Eventually, when they get big enough, I'll have them work at the mill and learn to cut trees."

Will thanked God he'd found someone who could be

so much help. He just hoped Derek was still in San Francisco rounding up more men.

"It is about another mile before we reach the redwoods," Hernando called back to them. "The big ones are close to the coast."

"Big ones?" Will looked at Noel. "It's hard to believe there really are trees bigger than what we're looking at right now."

Noel laughed. "You'll see. Like I told you, out here teamwork is very important. No one man cuts down a tree. Fallers always work in pairs. Some of the trees are so big that when they come down, you'll think there's been an earthquake. And you have to prepare a bed of boughs along the area where the tree is going to fall. Redwood is brittle. If it's not handled right, some of the trunk can break into hundreds of useless splinters.

"Once it's down, it's too big around to saw through without wasting a lot of time," Noel continued. "You plant dynamite into the trunk, but you have to be very careful to set it right. Then you blow the length of the trunk in half. That's the only way to get it small enough that two men can saw through it and prepare the logs for the mill. Once in a while the dynamite shatters the trunk and the wood is all wasted, but there's no other way."

Will just shook his head, realizing he had gotten himself into quite a venture. It was strange to have been in this business all his life, yet suddenly feel as though he didn't know anything at all. He would have to learn an entirely new way of logging, but he was determined to make it work. After several more minutes of riding he noticed the trees were changing, fatter trunks, taller. To look up was to feel as though he were in some sacred place, where God surely dwelled when he was resting.

"We're getting into the redwoods now," Noel told him.

"I will show you our biggest tree," Dominic called back. They followed the man for perhaps another half-mile, and Will could barely guide his horse for wanting to look up rather than ahead. It was unlike anything he had ever witnessed, trunks so huge as to defy any man to try to cut through them.

"My God, they're magnificent," he said, speaking quietly, reverently.

"What did I tell you?" Noel replied with a grin.

Will watched Dominic dismount near a tree that dwarfed him. He halted his own horse and climbed down, for the moment forgetting the presence of the others. He was overwhelmed by the immensity of the trees around him, some with diameters he guessed to be between twenty and thirty feet, and standing so high he could not make out the tops of them. He walked up to one and touched it almost lovingly.

"It seems a shame even to cut them down," he said, noticing his voice sounded as though he were in a closed room.

"Are they not magnificent?" Dominic asked. He walked over to Will, Hernando at his side. "These are the coastal redwoods, *arbol magnifico!* The trunks are even bigger on the Sierra redwoods west of here. We will spend the rest of the day and tomorrow riding the boundaries of La Estancia de Alcala so that you know where you can and cannot cut. We will have to camp in the forest tonight. It is too long a ride to do it all in one day. So, what do you think, *mi amigo?*"

Will was still touching the tree, staring upward, slowly walking the tree's circumference. He turned and looked at Dominic. "I think they truly are *magnifico,*" he answered. "I feel as though I am in God's house, and these trees are the great pillars of that house." He stepped away, taking inventory of the trees around him. "This is truly a gold mine, Dominic. A greater wealth lies here on top of the ground than in California's mountains."

Dominic smiled proudly, as did Hernando. "I would like to learn how to cut these trees myself," Hernando said. "My father will be too busy with taking care of the ranch to get involved up here. To the west there is a river that can be used to float your logs to the ocean. You will probably want to set up your mill at the mouth of the river. I will oversee our share of this new partnership with you," he added, smiling.

Will met the man's eyes. He liked Hernando, who was as handsome as Santana was beautiful. He also trusted Hernando and Dominic much more than he trusted Hugo Bolivar. He did not like the idea that one day Bolivar would have some say in this venture, as Santana's husband and Dominic's son-in-law. He had already perceived that Hugo had a great deal of influence on Dominic and even seemed to intimidate the man. How overbearing would he be once he was Santana's husband, how difficult would he be to deal with? Will suspected there would be trouble down the road, with Hugo demanding a greater and greater share of the profits from the logging, while Will and his men did all the hard work. He would have to be sure to draw up a carefully worded contract that would make it indisputable what went to La Estancia de Alcala and what belonged to Lassater Mills.

"I will enjoy working with you, Hernando," he said. "Looking at all of this, I am honored to be allowed to lumber out this land. I'll be careful not to completely strip the hills."

"That is very important," Dominic said. "It is dry here, but when the rains do come, they are often heavy. Without the trees, they wash away the hills and create mud slides and flooding."

Will breathed deeply of the sweet smell of pine and

rich redwood. He was so excited he felt like jumping up and down and laughing. He could hardly wait to write home about this, to tell Gerald that the stories they had heard about these trees were not exaggerations at all. He turned to Noel. "Show me how you climb one of these, and where you usually start cutting."

Noel, grinning with delight himself, walked back to his horse to retrieve a double-edged hatchet and two boards about five feet long and eight inches wide. "Here is something you will have to learn, my friend," he said to Will. He walked up to one of the massive trunks and chopped a wedge into it, then rammed one of the boards into the wedge. "This is a springboard. We use them like steps to get to the height we need."

He picked up the second board and with one arm hoisted himself gingerly onto the first one. While he used the first board to stand on, he cut a notch above it, and shoved the second board into it. Securing the hatchet in a loop on his belt, he grabbed the second board with one arm, then reached down to yank out the first board. He climbed onto the second, cut a third notch, and kept working his way up until he was five notches up the tree, about twenty feet.

Will, Dominic, and Hernando watched in awe. "My God," Will muttered. There is so much to learn, so many preparations to make before he could even begin building his mill.

"Normally there would be another man coming up with me, facing me," Noel called down. "Up here we would begin the undercut with our hatchets. It would probably take a couple of days with two men chopping all day to get the proper undercut on this one. While we're doing that, other men would be preparing a bed of boughs where we expect the tree to fall. We would chop the undercut at a forty-five-degree angle about one-third of the way through the trunk, then move to the other side and make a flat cut just deep enough so that the tree no longer has any support.

"If we do our job right, the tree will fall toward the first undercut without twisting and breaking up, or snapping up and killing a man by coming back on him. As soon as she starts to go, the fallers literally have to jump for their lives. We either hurry down the springboards we've left in the trunk, or just plain jump to the ground." Noel grabbed the top board and lowered himself to the next one, then grabbed that one too. He hung there a moment before letting go and tumbling to the ground. He stood up grinning, then walked over to Will. "When do we start?"

Will's heart pounded with excitement. "As soon as I get my equipment up here from San Francisco, and the rest of my supplies arrive. We'll leave for San Francisco in a couple of days, see if Derek has hired any men." He put out his hand to Noel. "I'm glad I found you." They shook hands vigorously, then Will turned to Dominic, putting out his hand again. "And I am also glad that Hugo brought me here to meet you. I would like to sign a contract as soon as possible, Dominic."

Dominic shook his hand. "There are not many Americans that I trust, but I feel I can trust you, Will, and I owe you this chance, after what you did for my Santana."

Will felt his blood rush at the mere mention of her name. He had not given up the idea of trying to talk Dominic into not allowing Santana to marry Hugo. First, though, he had to secure this contract and get to know them all better, learn more about their customs so that he could approach the subject without insulting anyone.

"*Gracias, mi amigo,*" he said to Dominic. "This land truly is beautiful, and these trees are like nothing I have ever seen. I promise it won't be long before you are a much richer man from this venture."

Their eyes met in mutual understanding as they squeezed each other's hands. "I will show you the rest of my land now," Dominic said.

Will nodded. "I'd like to see that river Hernando told me about, get an idea how difficult it might be getting the logs to it, and if it's deep enough to float them. As soon as we get back from exploring your boundaries, I'll leave for San Francisco."

"Are you sure you are well enough, my friend?" Hernando asked.

"I'm too excited to care," Will said. "But yes, I'm well enough."

They all remounted their horses, and Will looked upward once more before following Dominic and Hernando. The forest became so thick that it was difficult to ride through the trees, and so dark from the cover above that one could hardly tell the sun was shining. Will guessed that these forests would yield three to five times more timber than the forests back East. Everything he had read and heard about this land told him there were hundreds of thousands of square miles of this kind of forest in the Northwest . . . an endless supply . . . and an endless fortune for the men who knew how to timber out the woodlands. He was as elated as if he had struck gold, and he knew that he was here to stay. Home was now California.

Will could not resist one more ride into the thick forest before leaving for San Francisco. After he, Dominic, Hernando, and Noel had returned to the ranch, Will had gone back into the forest near the house. He had spent two nights listening to the nocturnal sounds, wondering if a bear or a bobcat or wolves would decide to make a meal of him. Staying alone among the magnificent conifers, listening to the whirring sound of the wind humming through pine needles, to the constant cry of wolves or the roar of a bobcat, had done something to him. He could not quite name this feeling he had, but it was close to reverence. If a man wanted to feel close to God, Will decided, all he had to do was spend a night or two among the monarchs of California's wooded hills. For him it was heaven.

As the sun dropped low on the horizon, he headed back toward the main house. Everything was packed for his trip to San Francisco, and Noel would go along to help him find more men. He was so preoccupied with thoughts of everything he had to do that he did not notice a horse to the rear and right of him as he came over the crest of a hill.

"Senor Lassater!" a woman called.

Will turned to see Santana standing under a lone lodgepole pine, holding the reins of her horse. The tree was surrounded by woods, yet there was a clearing around the knoll on which it stood. Will looked around to see if anyone else was about, then turned his horse and rode toward Santana. "Senorita Lopez, what are you doing here alone?"

As he rode closer, Santana studied him, his powerful arms, his attractive face. She liked Will Lassater more each time she saw him, and she had not had another chance to talk alone with him since the day she had snuck into his room. She had worried he would go back to San Francisco before they could talk again, and she had come here to her favorite place to think of a way she could see him alone once more. Now here he was, as though God had brought him. Why did she feel all shivery when he dismounted and walked closer, those broad shoulders showing his strength, those blue eyes looking so intently into her own?

"I often come here," she answered. "*Mi padre* lets me go riding alone, as long as it is only to this place that he knows I love." She looked up at the lone pine tree. "I hope that you would never cut this tree, or those around it that protect and shelter it. I feel sorry for it. It seems so alone here, so I come to keep it company. I call it my forever tree."

"The forever tree. Why is that?"

She shrugged. "When I think about how old the California pines become, and how young this one still is, I know it will be here for a very long time, long after I die, even though I am only sixteen." He saw a shadow of sadness cross her face. "So many things in life change as we grow older, but a tree is forever, a sign that some things never have to change."

Will frowned, touched by the way she described the tree as something with a heart and soul. That was how he felt about trees himself, that they were a form of living poetry, something strong yet warm, something that gave so many things to man—shade, homes, paper, the warmth of a wood fire. . . . "I'm glad to know you love trees as much as I do," he answered. He was sure he was not supposed to be alone with her this way, but he didn't care. She wore no veil, no special jewelry. Like the day she had come to his room, she was simply dressed. She needed nothing to add to her beauty.

"I love trees very much, and the birds, the animals." She turned to her horse. "This is my horse, the one I told you about."

"Estrella," he answered.

"You remembered her name."

"Of course. And she does have a white star on her forehead. She is very beautiful." *Just as you are very beautiful*, he wanted to add.

"*Gracias*, senor. I love to ride. Do you?"

Will looked around again. "Yes, but I don't often get the chance to ride just for pleasure."

Their eyes held, each wanting to say things they knew were forbidden. Santana could see Will was anxious. "It is all right, senor. No one will see us talking here, and even if they did, now that we know you so well, my father would not be angry."

He smiled. "I wish you would just call me Will."

Santana felt a flush coming to her cheeks. "It is best that I do not," she said, smiling shyly. "Well, perhaps whenever I see you alone this way."

Will wondered if that meant she wanted to meet alone with him more often. That did not seem wise, but then, she was too young to be wise, and he was too enamored with her when she was near like this to care about doing the wise thing himself. "Good," he answered. "I have enjoyed getting to know you and your family, Santana. May I call you Santana?"

"*Si*, when we are alone."

Will looked her over, thinking how lovely her naked body must be under her dark riding habit. "I doubt that will happen very often."

She shrugged. "I suppose not. You will be very busy soon with building your mill, and I will be busy with my schooling, and with preparing myself for marriage."

He caught the hint of bitterness in her words. "We never finished talking about that the day you came to my room. Surely you don't really want to marry Hugo Bolivar."

She turned away. "That is a forbidden subject."

Will sighed. "All right then, what *can* we talk about?"

She faced him again, smiling. "Logging. Tell me all about how you will cut down such big trees, how a sawmill works. I am going to try to talk my father into bringing me with him to see the mill once you have it running."

"Well . . ."

"Come! Sit with me on the big rock here in front of my forever tree."

She tied her horse to a small bush nearby and walked to a rock that had a flat face angled just enough so that a person could sit on it. Will tied his own horse and followed, a little voice warning him that he should get on that horse and ride hell-bent out of there. A stronger force, though, made him stay. For more than two weeks now he had argued with himself that he should keep out of this woman's business, but every time he saw her at meals, listened to her talk, realized what a lovely and innocent woman-child she was, he felt anger and frustration at the thought of her becoming Hugo's wife.

"First tell me about the place called Maine," she urged, patting the rock with her hand, indicating he should sit beside her. "I have never been away from California, or even any farther from my father's ranch than San Francisco. What was the voyage like coming here? I want to know about your family, and how did you feel when you saw the big trees for the first time?"

"Whoa!" Will protested, putting out his hand. "One question at a time." He sat down and pulled his pipe from his pocket. "Do you mind if I smoke?"

"No," she answered, smiling eagerly. "I like to watch you smoke your pipe. My father smokes only cigars. I much prefer the smell of a pipe."

Will packed and lit the pipe, then turned to meet Santana's eyes. What was it that he saw there? he wondered. Admiration? A deep fondness? Did she see him as some kind of hero? Did she just want his friendship, or would she like him to be more than a friend?

He answered all her questions, telling her about his family's history in logging, how he was there to fulfill his father's dream. He told her about Maine and the winters there, and the wild, dangerous voyage to California.

"I guess I'm here to stay," he finished. "I don't relish ever having to go back, and a man can get used to this land real fast. It's beautiful here. And as far as how I felt about those trees the first time I saw them . . ." He shook his head. "I felt like I had stepped into God's private dwelling."

Santana watched him as he spoke, studying his firm jawline, the rugged lines of his handsome face, the way his sandy hair draped over his shirt collar in thick waves. So many times she had wondered how it would feel to be held in his arms. In spite of his obvious strength, he was surely a gentle man, and from what he had told her, he surely came from a loving, caring family. He was nothing like Hugo. Yes, he had come to California to get rich, but riches would never turn a man like Will Lassater into an arrogant pig like Hugo. She knew this man saw right through all of it, that she did not want to marry Hugo, the kind of man Hugo was. Still, she refused to talk to him about that. It just seemed too personal, and there was nothing this American could do about promises made between two Spanish gentlemen.

"That is how I feel also about the redwoods," she said, "as though God dwells there. I think a tree is a beautiful thing. A tree provides so many things for us. Our homes, wood for heat, sometimes even food—berries, your maple syrup. So many things come from trees. They are one of God's greatest gifts to us." She sighed, looking up at the tree under which they sat. "You did not answer my question. You must promise never to cut this tree or any of the trees close around it."

Will grinned. "I promise. If this is your favorite place to come to be alone, then I will never touch it. Everyone needs his or her own little hideaway."

Their eyes met. "*Gracias*," she said. "You are a very nice man, Will Lassater. I like talking with you. You make it easy. I can never find anything to talk about with Hugo. He only likes to talk about himself and his riches." She looked away, realizing she had said something she had not meant to say. "I suppose I will get used to him. Once he is my husband, we will have many things to talk about, and there will be children to share."

A pain stabbed through Will's gut at the thought of Bolivar bedding Santana. He had no doubt the man would be rough and demanding. "You don't really want to marry that man and have children by him, do you?"

Santana rose, walking a few feet away. "I told you I cannot talk about that. I should not have even mentioned him."

"Nobody knows we're talking about it. Something tells me you *need* to talk about it, Santana. Probably nobody else you know understands how much you detest marrying Hugo. They all think you should be honored and privileged to marry such a man. But you don't want to, do you?"

She faced him with tears in her eyes. "It is wrong of me to say such a thing to an American who has only known my family for such a short time. You must understand our ways, Senor Lass—I mean, Will. Father expects this marriage. I should be honored. For me to refuse to marry Hugo would be a disgrace to the Alcala name."

Will shook his head. "I would never put honor above my daughter's happiness. Surely your father knows the kind of man Hugo is. He's a bragging, cocky bastard who loves himself a thousand times more than he could ever love another human being. He won't be a good husband to you. He'll be cruel to you and will probably be unfaithful. He'll use you to bear his children and that's all you'll be good for."

"Please, stop! You must not talk that way. Let's talk about something else. We—" She stopped when she heard riders coming. "I must go."

"Santana, wait!" It was no use. She hurriedly climbed up on Estrella, sitting sidesaddle, and rode off. Moments later Hernando and two ranch hands rode into the clearing.

"Will!" Hernando called out. "Have you seen my sister? She is late in getting back. She often comes to this place."

Will glanced in the direction Santana had ridden. He doubted she would want her brother to know they had been sitting there talking for the last hour. "I stopped here myself to do some thinking. Santana rode by just minutes ago. She said a hello and went on." He pointed to where she had ridden. "That way. I'm sure she'll be heading home soon."

The two men studied each other, and Will suspected Hernando did not fully believe him. Will had noted that Hernando had shown a great dislike for Hugo himself. Maybe he could approach Santana's brother about the marriage, find out if there was any way Santana could get out of it. He guessed Hernando didn't want her marrying Hugo either.

Hernando nodded. "I will ride after her and make sure she comes home right away so Father will not worry." He tipped his hat and rode off with the two ranch hands, and Will walked to his horse. He mounted up, then took a moment to study the tree that Santana loved. Their talk had made him feel closer than ever to her, and it had awakened something deeper than friendship. He had to face the fact that he was beginning to look at Santana as more than an innocent girl. She was certainly a woman in body, and she had a beautiful, giving spirit. Was he falling in love? No, that was crazy. This feeling probably just stemmed from feeling sorry for her having to marry Hugo, and from being mesmerized by her dark beauty. Maybe once he got to San Francisco and then got busy building the mill, he would forget about her. It wouldn't be wise to interfere with the affairs of the very man whose land and forest he needed to fulfill his dream.

Perhaps the little talk he and Santana had had would

plant enough doubt in her mind that she would do something about the marriage herself . . . but she carried the same Spanish pride as her father, whom she loved very much. Would she allow herself to be given in marriage to a man she despised just to honor her father's name?

Damn! Of course she would. That's the way these people were, and he'd be damned if he'd stay out of it. There must be something he could do. Thank God the marriage wouldn't take place for more than a year. He had some time yet to think about it, and to learn what he could do to stop such a marriage without the Alcala name being dishonored.

Eight

Santana's heart quickened when the noise and sights of the mill struck her senses. For nearly a year an ambitious Will Lassater had been building his logging enterprise, which included a sawmill at this site, high in the mountains on the northern end of La Estancia de Alcala, as well as a finishing mill near the ocean. Since leaving for San Franciso to hire loggers and wait for more equipment to arrive, Will had visited her father only once, several months ago. To her disappointment, she had been gone, on another excursion to San Francisco with Hugo.

She could not help wondering if the visit had been deliberately timed. Since Will had been in San Francisco just before that, and was supposedly dealing with Hugo as a buyer for his lumber, he must have known she was going there. Had he chosen that time to visit her father purposely to avoid her? Her father had gone to watch Will's progress several times, but Will had not returned to the ranch. She had hoped he would, hoped they would find more occasions to talk, yet she did not fully understand why it mattered.

She had exhausted all ideas of how to avoid her marriage to Hugo without disappointing her father. The wedding was only three months away, and somewhere in the back of her mind she had hoped Will Lassater would come to her rescue as he had when she was nearly abducted by the *banditos*. Still, that one time they'd had a chance to talk, she had refused to discuss the matter. Why did she think he would bother with her problem any more since then? He was a busy man, and an American besides. To interfere with her people's customs could cost him the deal he had struck with her father, and like the other Americans who had come there to rape California for its gold, he was there to rape it for its trees. Americans loved riches, and those riches came before love and honor, did they not?

Her thoughts were interrupted by the screaming of a saw and the roar of some kind of engine. She reminded herself that she had decided not to think about Hugo today, or of the terror she felt at knowing he would soon be her husband. On her last visit to San Francisco, Hugo had brought in the most skilled and expensive dressmaker in town to measure her for a wedding gown. He was already planning a huge celebration, working on an invitation list that included all of San Francisco's most prominent businessmen. She had wanted the wedding to take place on her father's ranch, to celebrate with old friends of the family, but Hugo insisted it take place in a cathedral in San Francisco, determined it would be the event of the year.

With her wedding date fast approaching, she had finally convinced her father to let her come along with him on another of his visits to the logging site to see what kind of progress Will had made. She had reminded her father that it was 1855 already. In November she would be eighteen, and once she was married she would probably have to spend most of her time in San Francisco and would not see much of her father or La Estancia de Alcala. She wanted to spend some time with Dominic while she had the chance, so he had agreed to bring her with him.

She rode beside Dominic, and they were followed by several ranch hands, both for protection and for helping make camp at night, building fires and cooking their meals. It had been an exciting trip for her, a two-day journey deep into the big redwoods, listening to the owls and wolves at night. She loved the forest, loved the smell of it, the quiet. . . .

It certainly was not quiet at the mill, however. They broke through a stand of trees to a clearing that had been made near a small lake. The lake was packed with floating logs, and two men stood on top of a couple of the logs, poking at them with long poles, apparently trying to break up a jam. From somewhere inside a building across the lake came the screaming sound again, and the noise of what Santana figured must be the steam engines her father had told her about, used to run two gigantic saws that cut the huge redwood logs into lengths of board. Dominic was learning a great deal about the logging business, and his stories had stirred her own curiosity to the point where she simply had to see all of it for herself.

"Will is only just getting started," Dominic told her. "I do not believe he has even made his first shipment to San Francisco yet."

"How does he get the lumber to the ocean?" she asked.

"I will let him explain. Come. Let's see if we can find him."

They rode around the lake, and Santana could see that Will had built his own little town. Crude cabins were spread out all over the clearing, and in front of one of them a woman was scrubbing clothes on a washboard, two little children playing at her feet. Santana guessed that a larger log building in the distance was where the men gathered for meals. Her father had told her Will had brought in two cooks, a man and a woman, to feed the loggers, and a supply merchant from San Francisco had set up a store to provide the necessities of everyday living for the loggers and those who had families. Much of the food used there came from her father's own farm, so already Dominic was making money from the venture over and above what Will paid him to rent the land. Soon he would begin taking a percentage of the profits from the mill.

"Will wants to bring in a teacher and build a small school," Dominic said. "I had no idea what it takes to get into this business. Now I can see why the lumbermen before now have failed. It takes much money just to get started. Will told me that with the lumber and syrup he sold here last year, and more lumber his brother sent a few months later, he made seventy-five thousand American dollars! And he apparently had much money behind him to begin with. This *gringo* is a rich man already, but he says he has spent most of his money hiring men and building this mill, as well as the finishing mill on the coast. He is anxious to begin selling his lumber. I am sure Hugo has found many markets for it already."

And I will be married to Hugo, but secretly love Will Lassater, Santana thought. She drew in a quick breath, realizing it was the first time she had entertained the thought of loving Will. Up to now she had merely been fascinated with the man and thought of him as a hero. She was surprised at the sudden knowledge that perhaps she did love him. But how could that be? She had been with him so few times, had not even seen him for a year. Surely it was just her dread of marrying Hugo that brought such thoughts to mind.

The noise in camp was almost as bad as in San Francisco. Men shouted at one another, saws screamed, men, mules, and oxen were everywhere. One team of eight yoked oxen lumbered toward them pulling a string of logs that had the bark stripped from them. The animals and logs moved along a strange-looking roadbed made of partially buried logs, which Santana could tell made it easier to drag the fresh-cut logs to the lake. A young *gringo*, whom she guessed to be no more than fourteen or fifteen, walked in front of the oxen with a bucket and broom, stopping occasionally to swab something from the pail onto the roadbed, then spread it around with the broom.

"Father, what is he doing?" she asked.

Dominic scratched his head. "I do not know. That roadbed was not here when I visited last. It is something new Will has done. I see that it goes far up into the hills, probably to where the trees are being cut. Perhaps the boy there puts something on the logs in the road so that they are more slippery, which would make it easier to pull the big logs across them."

They made their way carefully around scrap lumber and piles of bark, the smell of fresh-cut wood so strong that it almost hurt Santana's nose. Suddenly she felt an odd tremble, and her horse reared at a popping noise that turned into a mighty roar, almost like an explosion. The earth shook, and Santana clung to Estrella's reins, patting her neck to keep her calm. Behind them one of the ranch hands' horses did rear up and throw its rider.

"Father, an earthquake!" Santana exclaimed.

Dominic laughed. "No, my child. That is simply the sound of one of the big redwoods coming down somewhere above us. I hope no one was hurt. Will has explained it is very dangerous work. The last time I was here one of his men had been badly injured."

Santana felt a sudden alarm that something could happen to Will. Why did it upset her to think he could be wounded or killed doing this work? Why did she care so much for a man she had not even seen for so long?

They continued toward the mill house, where the

painfully loud sawing was taking place, while behind them the man who had been thrown let out a spray of cuss words as he got up from a bed of bark and wood shavings and brushed himself off. Dominic ordered the men to find a decent place to make camp for the night. "We will stay here today and tonight," he told them before riding on with Santana.

Men who worked for Will glanced at them as they rode by, some nodding and smiling, each one staring at Santana. They were all burly, rugged-looking men, most of them American, although Santana did spot a few Mexicans and even a couple of Indians.

They rounded a corral where more oxen and mules were kept, along with a few horses. As they approached the sawmill, Will himself emerged to see them coming.

Santana's heart beat faster when she saw him, more handsome than she remembered, looking tired from working hard, but tanned and brawny. It was a hot August day, and he was sweaty, his hair full of sawdust, yet that did little to detract from his good looks and bright smile. She could see the surprise in his eyes at seeing her there, and yes, she saw pleasure. He seemed glad she had come. Had he missed her, thought about her even a little bit?

"Dominic!" he greeted them, brushing sawdust from his shirt and hair.

His shirt was open part of the way, and Santana could see hairs on his chest that trailed up to the dip in his throat. His shoulders and chest were even bigger than she had remembered, and she wondered if she was noticing these things because she was a year older. Lately she had given thought to things she had never considered before, like her own womanliness, noticing how men looked at her . . . how Will was looking at her now.

"*Buenos dias*, Senorita Lopez," he said "I am surprised and pleased to see you here."

"I wanted to come and see for myself," she said. *"Mi padre* has told me so much about what you are doing here. Can I see how you cut the logs with the big saw inside?"

Will looked at Dominic. "It's a little dangerous in there. She'll have to stand exactly where I tell her to stand. Fact is, this whole place is dangerous, from the buckers and cutting crews clear down to the finishing mill on the ocean. A lot of these men are still in training. I lost a man just last week."

"I am sorry to hear that, senor," Dominic answered as he dismounted. He walked around and helped Santana down from her horse. "My daughter will do whatever you tell her to do, but you had better let her see that saw or she will pester me to my dying day. All she has talked about is coming here to see all of this."

Will grinned, but Santana could see he was troubled that one of his men had been killed. "How did the man die?" she asked.

Will led her and Dominic toward the mill. "One of my fallers was smashed in the head by a huge trunk that walked across its stump when it was falling. He died instantly, thank God."

"Walked across a stump?" Santana stopped walking. "What does that mean?"

Will turned to look at her, fighting urges that he thought would have been buried after not seeing her for all this time. But she was more beautiful than ever, he realized. She was much more a woman, her figure more filled out, maybe even a little taller. He almost wished Dominic had not brought her, but it was good to see her at that. Her dark skin glowed against the white silk blouse she wore, beneath a suede vest. Her matching suede riding skirt fit her waist and slender hips fetchingly. Her eyes were wide with curiosity and concern, her nearly black hair was pulled back at the sides with combs, and she wore a wide-brimmed suede hat.

"Sometimes a tree doesn't fall just like it should," he told her. "Other trees get in the way, changing its direction and causing it to twist, or come back and move across its own trunk. Sometimes it springs up, whacking the faller if he doesn't make it down from his perch in time. The fallers have to make their way up a trunk by use of platforms or springboards, because we can't cut a tree right at the base. It's too brittle and fibrous there. So when it starts to come down, the fallers have to get out of the way. Sometimes they don't make it."

Santana frowned. "Do *you* ever do that yourself?"

He shrugged. "I figure I can't teach other men to do it if I don't learn it too. Back east we never had to climb up trees like that, although stump walking can happen with any tree. We've had our share of accidents back in Maine, but my father and brother and I have been lucky. A few minor accidents. My brother broke his arm once, and I got a deep cut in one leg from falling with a hatchet in my hand."

Will looked up at the steep hills that surrounded them and sighed. "Still, logging out here is a completely different thing. I've never seen trees that take two men a whole week to cut down. Some are up there so high in the hills that it's too much of a climb for the oxen, and too steep a pitch coming back down with tons of logs behind them that could overtake them and kill them. I'm working on ways to get them out of there, maybe by building more chutes and flumes."

"What are those?" Santana asked, excitement showing in her eyes.

Will could see that she liked all of this. Some women were so refined and pampered, they would not even want to come to a place like this—noisy, dangerous, dirty. But

Santana seemed interested, eager to learn. "Let's go inside and look at the band saw," he said, yelling as the saw began cutting again. He took hold of her arm and led her inside the mill, standing her against a wall so she could watch one of the huge band saws slice through a gigantic log.

Santana stared in wonder as the gigantic saw vibrated up and down by massive pulleys run by a deafening steam engine. The blade screamed when it met the wood, and steam poured from it as a man sitting on a scaffold above poured water over the blade to keep it cooled.

"That track the log is attached to is called a head rig, or log carrier," Will shouted. "It moves back and forth by steam power. That man riding the log is called a dogger. Each time the log shoots back after a cut, he has to operate the dogs, the big claws that hold the log in place. They have to be reset after each couple of cuts to keep pushing the log over for a new setting until the entire log is sliced up. That man's job is damn dangerous."

Santana's heart caught in her throat as she watched the dogger. He sat atop the log, clinging to it as it shot back and forth on the head rig. He was sweaty, his hair plastered to his head, and he looked weary, yet also strangely exhilarated. "A man must have to like his work very much to be willing to do that," she yelled back at Will.

Will grinned, then led her back outside. "You're right about these man having to like what they do," he said as she brushed sawdust from her skirt. "They're a rough bunch, let me tell you, but that's the only kind you can get up here for this, most of them with no families and no responsibilities, men who like to live dangerously and are proud of it."

"It cannot be easy to keep such men in line," Dominic said.

Will brushed more dust from his hair himself. "I pay

them well and feed them well, brought a couple of good cooks here from San Francisco. I've had to knock a couple of the men into line, fire a few, hire more. I'm working on building the best crew I can. Of course, with accidents constantly happening, I'm always having to replace someone. My friend Derek, who I met coming here on the ship from Maine, has become my official personnel man. He's in San Francisco or some other town more than he's here, always looking for men who need work. There seem to be plenty of them—men who came out here to get rich and found it wasn't so easy after all. But they like California so much they don't want to leave, so they'll jump at anything to earn a living."

Santana watched Will as he spoke, admiring his intelligence, his ability to handle such rough men and keep them in line. Will Lassater was sure of himself, but was not arrogant, like Hugo. Yes, he was probably rich and would become much richer, but he earned his way by hard work, not by hiring other men to do everything for him, as Hugo did. He could easily hire an overseer for the mill and sit back in San Francisco and rake in the money, but he was not that kind of man. Something told her that no matter how successful Will was, he would always be right there, working among his men, keeping an eye on everything that was going on.

She was still staring at him when he turned to look at her again, and something in his blue eyes told her he saw her as more than a child now.

"Back to your earlier question," he said. "Chutes are just what the word sounds like, rounded beds made of wood that are built down a steep mountain and used to shoot logs down to a mill pond. Logs from higher up sometimes travel up to ninety miles an hour coming down a chute, or so I'm told by Noel. I'm going to build my own chute next year higher up in these mountains. It's safer to use than letting oxen try to haul that much weight down a steep bank.

"Flumes are like chutes, only they're water fed. You cut the logs into boards first, then you float them down a flume. That's what we're doing here. Most of those boards we're cutting will be sent down a series of flumes to my finishing mill on the coast, where the finished lumber is stacked and stored. It'll be loaded onto ships that soon will come once every two weeks with orders from lumberyards in San Francisco." He looked at Dominic. "Eventually I intend to have my own lumberyard there, maybe even my own ships, so the whole thing, from cutting the trees to delivering finished lumber, will belong to Lassater Mills. That's where you make your best money, keeping your hands on every step of the project."

Will led Dominic and Santana away from the noisy mill and toward the larger log building Santana had noticed earlier. He kept hold of her arm, and her heart fluttered to think he was being so protective of her as she stepped gingerly over pieces of wood and around mud puddles. A fresh rain the night before had left the ground soft, and she had to lift her skirts with her free hand to avoid the worst mud.

"Hugo must be excited that you are finally in almost full operation," Dominic said. "He will no doubt find plenty of business for you and buy some of the lumber himself for resale."

Will stopped walking and faced Dominic, then glanced at Santana with a somewhat guilty look in his eyes. "I won't be dealing with Hugo," he said.

Dominic's eyebrows arched in surprise. "But why? It is Hugo who led you to me. He is my friend, and soon to be my son-in-law."

"I know what Hugo is to you, Dominic, but I have to tell you I don't like the man, nor do I trust him. I never made him any promises. He was willing to introduce me to you, so I took him up on it."

"But you led me to believe . . ."

"I never meant to lead you to believe anything more than the fact that I wanted to log your trees. I have dealt honestly and fairly with you, and I will continue to do so. I simply told Hugo when I saw him in San Francisco last month that I prefer not to have a middle man. I do all my own dealing and find my own customers. He wasn't too upset, considering he figures to get a piece of the pie anyway when he marries Santana."

Santana caught a hint of bitterness in his voice. So, he had thought about her over the months, and he still did not think it was right that she should marry Hugo. Had he said something to Hugo about it? Had they argued? Oh, what a brave man he was, to stand up against someone like Hugo. Hugo had many friends in San Francisco, men who could possibly put Will Lassater out of business before he even got started, but that did not worry Will!

"I hope you aren't too upset, Dominic," Will went on. "I mean no insult to you, but I prefer to do my own business dealing, and there's something about Hugo Bolivar that just rubs me the wrong way."

Dominic looked angry at first, frowning as he rubbed his chin. His anger faded to concern as he said, "I understand a man who wishes to handle his own affairs, and I know that Hugo can be a bit arrogant and overpowering, but his father was my very good friend. He saved my life, and my wife's family's lives, from the hands of death in Mexico, and for this I must always respect his son."

"I understand," Will said. "But I have no ties to the man and don't care to create any. It's you I'm contracted with, and you'll get your fair share when I start filling orders and figuring my profits. I won't cheat you, Dominic."

Their eyes held, and Dominic nodded. "Of this I have

no doubt. You have very honest eyes, Will Lassater, and I can see the quality of man that you are. I could be angry, but I cannot forget that you risked your life to save my daughter once."

Perhaps I will have to risk it again, to save her from Hugo Bolivar's clutches, Will thought. He had an idea how to prevent the marriage, though he told himself he was crazy. He had pushed Santana and thoughts of rescuing her from Hugo from his mind for months now. Seeing her again, however, brought it all back, the ache of wanting her for himself. "I'm glad you understand," he told Dominic, putting out his hand.

Dominic shook it and said, "We will stay the day and a night. I know that Santana has many more questions. I hope you will have time to answer them so that she will not bother me with them once I get her home again."

Will laughed. "I'll try. I've built my own small cabin not far from here. I'd like you and Santana to sleep there tonight. It's the best I can do. I'll bunk with one of the other men. In the meantime, we'll go over to the cookhouse and see if we can rustle up some tea or coffee. We can talk there, away from all the noise and mud.

"Tonight I want you and Santana to join me there for supper. We'll eat between crew shifts so that Santana doesn't have to put up with the crude manners of some of these men. I know you prefer Spanish food, and I guarantee that among the many dishes my cooks put out every night, you'll find a bit of everything. I have so many different nationalities of men working for me, I have to try to accommodate them all—Americans, Mexicans, Chinese, Indians, several Swedes, a couple of men from England. It makes for some pretty rowdy conversations sometimes, and not a few fistfights over differences in cultures and habits. It's been quite a challenge whipping these men into well-tuned crews. The Chinese work mostly at cleanup and laundry. Most of them just aren't built for what has to be done up at the logging site, but I have a few who make good bolt punchers—men who work down at the finishing mill using a pike pole to guide shingle bolts onto a conveyor belt that carries them to the mill to be cut into roofing shingles."

"You have such strange names for the different jobs these men do," Santana said. "Doggers, fallers, bolt punchers. What other jobs are there? What different things have to be done between cutting a tree and getting it to the finishing mill?"

"First things first," Will answered. "I'll take you to my cabin now so you can unload everything and freshen up. We'll meet for that cup of tea or coffee in a little while and"—he turned to Santana—"I'll answer all your questions."

As he stared into her dark eyes, he was surprised at how happy he was she had come. Should he tell her what had really happened between him and Hugo? That he had bluntly told the man he didn't think he had any right marrying her? He was already on Hugo Bolivar's blacklist, and things might get worse. Now that he had seen this beautiful young woman again, he just might have to have the same argument with Dominic . . . or perhaps do the unthinkable and act on his idea for getting her out of the marriage. It was probably a stupid thought, and he was too damn busy for this, but how could he let it go? There were only three months left.

Was she worth the risk he would be taking? Had the climate here in California, or perhaps a noseful of sawdust, affected his mind? To do what he was considering could mean risking his very life, but when Santana smiled at him the way she was smiling now, he knew he had to try. He had hoped that after all this time it wouldn't matter to him anymore, but now he knew otherwise. Still, he'd better tell her first and get her reaction. Maybe she had changed her own mind and was now willing to marry Hugo.

"Let's go get your horses and gear," he said to her and Dominic. As they walked back to the horses, Will wondered how, once he'd talked to Santana and obtained her permission to do what he had in mind, he was going to tell her father that a *gringo* wanted to marry his daughter.

Nine

"Watch yourself," Will called back to Santana. "I hope Estrella is surefooted. Sometimes there's a boulder hidden under the brush in places like this. Stay right behind me."

"I happen to be a very good rider, Will Lassater," Santana answered as they made their way on horseback up a steep bank, "and Estrella is as surefooted as any horse in California. She loves me. She would never let me fall."

Will grinned. He didn't have to turn around to know Santana had a pout on her beautiful face at his suggestion that she couldn't ride as well as he. He was glad Dominic had given in to her begging to let her come and see the cutting, and even gladder that Dominic himself had been too tired to come. The man had entrusted Santana to him, had even let her ride alone with him, which made Will realize how much Dominic Alcala had come to trust him. He might not have been so willing if he had known Will's true feelings for Santana.

They made it to the top of the bank, and the ground leveled off for several hundred yards. Not far away was a clearing, where several men stood atop a gigantic redwood log, scraping at the bark.

"Those are peelers," Will told Santana. "The bark on redwoods is so hard and thick, it's easier to transport the logs if you peel it off first. This is the tree you heard come down earlier today. It will be several days before another one is felled. It takes that long to cut through one and for these men to get this one out of here.

"When the peelers are done, the buckers come in with two-man bucking saws and cut the trunk into sections of various lengths, from sixteen to forty feet, before they're hauled by oxen down to the mill pond. The next tree will be cut into shorter sections for shingle bolts. Those will go down to the finishing mill to be shaved into roofing shingles.

"Overall, the most important men I have are the bull whackers. They handle the oxen, sometimes ten yokes of them. Between the weight of the logs and sometimes the orneriness of the oxen, it can be a dangerous job." He stopped his horse to watch the peelers for a minute, telling one of the men to inform the buckers he wanted this one cut into twenty-four-foot segments.

"I will never remember all of this," Santana said. She rode up beside him and looked at trees that towered overhead. "But it is fascinating."

Will smiled, appreciating her interest. "Well, there are some jobs you won't get to observe. There are flume herders, men who keep the boards moving through the flumes between the mill up here and the finishing mill below. Then there are the men who keep the logs from jamming up in the pond and keep them floating in the river farther below. They're called river pigs, or sometimes rollers. If you had more time, I'd take you and your father to the finishing mill, but it's over half a day's ride on horseback, through some pretty rugged country."

"You must have many men working for you."

"About fifty so far." As they talked Will noticed how

his men eyed Santana. Any man would appreciate her beauty, but some of these men came from the meanest quarters of San Francisco, and he had little doubt that the only women they were used to were the rough whores there. He hoped they knew they had better show some respect to the daughter of the man whose land they were using.

One thing Santana would *not* want to visit, he thought, was the bigger bunkhouses where the single men were housed together. She would probably faint dead away at the mixture of odors, damp wool shirts and socks hanging up to dry, smoke from wood-burning stoves, kerosene, spittoons, sweat. Plenty of these men didn't know the meaning of the word clean, but they were a hardy lot, most of them dependable. He was glad that so far no whores had followed them there. He wouldn't want Santana to see just how wicked a logging camp could get, and he had no doubt that eventually the inevitable would happen. As his little settlement grew, the whores and whiskey peddlers would follow. He had made it very clear to all the men, though, that anyone caught drinking on the job would be fired.

"We've all been learning together," he continued. "I don't know what I'd do without Noel. There are a few others here who've logged before, so I've had good help. Until coming here, I thought I knew all there was to know about logging, but it's a whole different undertaking out here. I've never seen trees like this. I've had to learn things I never needed to know or do back home."

"So, you still think of Maine as home?"

He turned to meet her eyes. "Wherever you're born and raised, it's always going to be home. But it's becoming dimmer in my mind. I love it here now. I don't think I could ever go back." *I don't think I could ever leave you, or this beautiful land.* "It would be dangerous to bring you here once we really get rolling. We try to cut new trees well away from where the buckers are working, but there's always the danger of a new fall coming too close and injuring someone. At any rate, we aren't at the pace of bringing down more than one tree every few days, so there's no worry about another fall nearby. My goal is to have crews working at different areas around the clock, start on a new tree every day so that eventually we fell a tree a day. That will take a lot of men, not just up here, but also down at the mills. More bull whackers, more everything, including money."

"And you will be a very busy man." Too busy to think about her, Santana thought.

He nodded. "Come on. I'll show you how the men do a back cut standing on springboards. Noel is my foreman up here. He's probably working on a cut himself. He likes the physical labor." Will rode on ahead of her again.

"You should tell Noel that his wife and children miss him. Let him go and see them more often, Will. I saw Mrs. Gray at her cabin at the ranch before we left. She said to tell you to unchain her husband for a while and let him come home."

Will laughed, glancing back at her. "I don't stop him from going to her. He's up here because he loves it. He's building a cabin for her. Should be done soon. Then she can come here and be with him. I'm even going to hire a schoolteacher for Noel's children and the children of other families up here." He led her on into a dense section of forest, where the sounds of men shouting and hatchets echoing through the trees seemed to disappear.

Santana could no longer hear the distant sound of the huge band saw below them, and she saw no one about. Will turned his horse and faced her. "It's pretty here," he said. "I found this place not long after I decided to start cutting in this area. I don't know why, but this particular spot seems special, the way the sun filters through the trees, the way all other sounds are shut out. I think I'll leave this spot just like it is."

"Like the special place where I go to be alone?"

He nodded. "Something like that."

Santana suddenly felt as though she had been brought here for a purpose. "I thought we were going to watch Noel chop down a tree."

Will smiled. "Believe me, the tree will still be there hours from now, days from now. There's no hurry."

She blushed, unable to think of anything to say. There was a strange look in Will's eyes, one that made her feel undressed, yet she did not mind the sensation. Why did she find that same look unbearable when she was with Hugo? "There is something you want to say?" She never thought she would find a *gringo* so appealing, but Will looked wonderful. He had bathed and shaved, and was wearing a clean plaid shirt and cotton pants that fit his hips in a way that stirred something in her she had never felt before. He was studying her intently, as though deciding if he should say anything at all. Finally he spoke up.

"Be honest with me, Santana. You're getting married in three months, but you still can't stand Hugo Bolivar. Am I right?"

She closed her eyes, part of her wishing he had not gotten into the subject again, yet another part of her glad that he had. Still, the situation was so hopeless. . . .

"All these months I have not seen you, and so quickly when we meet again you bring up my marriage to Hugo." She met his gaze again. "It is not your concern, Will Lassater. I only came here to see your logging camp, not to talk alone with you like this, not to discuss something so personal, something we have no right—"

"I think you damn well *did* hope we'd get another chance to talk alone," he interrupted. He dismounted, holding the reins of his horse as he walked closer to her. "I think the only reason you pestered your father to bring you this time is because the wedding *is* getting so close, and you're more frightened about it every day. You came to see if I still cared, if maybe I had come up with a way to get you out of it."

Santana's eyes widened in feigned disgust. She slid down from her horse and faced him. "That is ridiculous! Why on earth would I turn to a *gringo* to get me out of *any*thing? And in this case, it would be hard enough for even the most honorable *Californio* to try to stop this, let alone an American!" She folded her arms defiantly. "I am destined to marry Hugo Bolivar, and I simply must accept it. I will get used to him." She stood her ground, although she felt like running at the strange look that came into Will's eyes. He seemed almost angry with her, and as he stepped closer, his powerful frame made her feel like a child.

"Get *used* to him?" he almost growled. "You've had two years to get *used* to him! Tell me, Santana, has he kissed you yet?"

She held her chin high, refusing to show that the question embarrassed her. "Of course not! It would not be proper!"

His smile was hard, without humor or warmth. "So, you don't even know if you could stand the man's thin, probably cold, lips touching your mouth." He glared at her. "The thought is almost revolting to you, isn't it?"

"Stop it!" She turned away, blinking back tears.

Will grasped her shoulders and spun her back around. "Santana, once he's your husband he'll do a lot more than kiss you on the mouth with those lips. He's a cruel man. I can see it in his eyes. He won't be kind to you!"

She jerked away, folding her arms again, rubbing them nervously with her hands. "It is *you* who are the cruel one, talking to me this way when you have no right!" Her shoulders shook with a sob. "There is nothing . . . that can be done . . . and you hardly know me. To interfere could cost your life, and it could most certainly cost you the right to harvest my father's trees."

"We have a contract. He can't break that."

Santana frowned. "You say that as though . . . as though you are thinking about doing something that might anger my father."

"It might."

A thousand thoughts swept through Santana's mind. What on earth could he do? Other than get himself in terrible trouble. "I do not understand . . ."

He stepped closer, grasping her arms gently. "Understand this." He leaned down, and in spite of the warning voice that told her to run away, Santana stood still and watched his handsome face come near. His full lips met hers in a hungry but tender kiss unlike anything she had ever experienced. Until now she had only known the quick kisses of a father and brother, usually on the cheek. She had not been able to bear the thought of a kiss from Hugo, and thank God he had not tried. Yet here she was letting Will Lassater, an American, a *gringo*, kiss her lips, draw her close, enclose her in his arms and crush her breasts against his hard chest! She felt her own arms lift, wrap themselves around his neck as though they had a mind of their own, for surely she had not embraced him willingly. This was all wrong!

He finally released her mouth, and she wondered where her next breath would come from when he moved his warm lips down over her throat. "Crazy as it sounds," he murmured, "I think I love you, Santana Maria Chavez Lopez. See? I even remembered your full name, after all this time."

He put a hand to the back of her neck and pressed her head against his shoulder. "I know you have no idea how you feel about me yet. I only know I cannot let you marry Hugo. I want you to be free to choose, Santana. I kissed you to awaken the woman in you, the woman who should be allowed to give herself willingly to a man she truly wants and loves, not forced into a man's bed because of some long-ago promise or because of pride."

What comfort she felt in his arms! Santana marveled. So strong, yet so gentle. This man would never force her to do anything she didn't want to do. He understood how afraid she was. "There is nothing else I can do," she answered, feeling new tears fill her eyes.

"No, there isn't," he said. "But there is something *I* can do. I have given it a lot of thought."

She pulled away, wiping at the tears on her cheeks with her fingertips. "I do not understand."

Will stood a little straighter. "I am going to challenge Hugo for your hand."

Her eyes widened in shock. "What! You—you cannot do that! You would be risking your life! Hugo is very good with the pistol!"

"Don't worry about that. I have my own plans."

"But . . ." Her mind raced with uncertainty and fear. "I . . . well, I . . . if you win . . . it will mean that I must marry you. Father would never approve of me marrying a *gringo!* And I hardly know you!"

He smiled softly. "You know me well enough by that kiss." He touched her cheek with the back of his hand. "But it doesn't matter. If I win, I have the right to free you from your obligation to Hugo in an honorable way. I promise to do that, Santana. I want very much to marry you, but I would never force it. You would be free of Hugo, and free to do what you please and marry whomever you want."

She turned away, taken aback by his generous gesture. "I do not know what to say. I . . . I never thought that an American would care to become so involved." She shook her head. "I cannot let you do this."

"You have no control over the matter. The only choice you'll have to make is whether you want to marry me when it's over."

She looked back at him, astounded that she could have feelings of love for this man who was still like a stranger. He had apparently been thinking about this for the past year, even though he had not seen her. What an unusually honorable man he was, for an American. "If you lost, my agony at having to marry Hugo would be made worse by knowing you died trying to stop the marriage. I could not live with that."

"You won't have to. I happen to think I can win a match with Hugo Bolivar. I am a firm believer in fate, Santana. I think God brought me here with more in mind than helping me find his beautiful trees. He wanted me to find you, and to save you from a living death. That is what life would be like for you with Hugo. I also promise that someday I will be as rich or even richer than Hugo. I will be able to offer you all the things he offers you now, and more, because I will offer you love and gentleness, honor and respect. He won't offer those things."

Santana swallowed back a lump in her throat. "You are a good man, Will Lassater."

He stepped closer again. "And I happen to think you are a good woman, a young lady with a good heart, and with much love to give, to the right man. The few times I have talked with you, I have seen a love for life, a generous heart, and a youthful excitement that makes me all but worship you. Most well-bred women would never dream of coming here, but you have graced this place with your beauty, and you haven't once turned your nose up at anything noisy or dirty or unpleasant. You love the trees as much as I, and I think this is something we could share,

Santana. I want to settle, have children. I almost married someone, three years ago, but she was drowned at sea."

Santana gasped, putting a hand to her chest. "Oh, how terrible! I am sorry, Will."

He stepped closer again. "It's in the past. Now I'm here in California. It's like stepping into another world, and if I can marry the most beautiful Spanish woman in this state, then California will truly be home for me. I will never go back to Maine."

As they gazed at each other, Santana knew what her choice would be if Will won a duel with Hugo. He said she would have her freedom, but would she want it? No. She already knew she was falling in love with him. Perhaps it had started that first day she saw him standing on the deck of the *Dutchess Dianna*. His kiss had awakened something in her, something wonderful and stirring, something that made her feel warm and happy and more alive than ever before. She wanted to feel it again, and she did not resist when he took her into his arms once more, pressed her close, and met her mouth with another kiss, this one hotter, deeper, more searching.

She flung her arms around his neck, feeling desperate at the thought of Hugo shooting this man down in a duel. Surely God would not let such a thing happen. Fear and anxiety raced through her at the thought of it, yet she also felt an exhilarating pride that Will thought so much of her to do such a daring thing. Will Lassater truly was her hero.

Santana's heart beat so hard that it hurt. Just as Will had instructed her to do, she had secretly sent one of her father's men to the logging camp to tell Will that Hugo had come to visit again. Will did not know it yet, but Hugo had not come just to see her this time. He was enraged that Will had left him out of all business dealings. When he had arrived three days ago, he had gone directly to Dominic's study to tell Dominic what Will had done. Santana knew Hugo and her father had gotten into an argument, for she had listened at the door, having heard the shouting and wondering what it was about. What she heard had frightened her, for Hugo was already furious with Will. What would he do if Will came to tell the man he intended to challenge him for her hand?

Hugo's words still rang in her ears. "Then break the contract!" he had shouted. "This man betrayed me! I helped him find the land for logging, and he turns around and refuses to do business with me! I will not tolerate it!"

Dominic had managed to keep things relatively calm, answering Hugo in his usual steady voice. Her father was not one to yell. "Will says that he never promised you anything. You were willing to introduce us, and we struck a deal, Hugo. The man has been very fair with me, and he has spent everything he has building his mills. I cannot turn around and tell him he cannot cut the trees."

"It is your land! Your land! You can do whatever you want!" Hugo had practically screamed in reply.

"And I can also dismiss you from my home if you continue your shouting. I honor you, Hugo, as my best friend's son, but I do not have to stand here and let you yell at me. This is a matter between you and Will Lassater, not you and me."

Hugo had let out some kind of grunt, and there had followed a moment of silence.

"Let us have a cigar together, Hugo," Dominic had said then, "calm ourselves down before supper. Let us talk about how the farming has gone this year."

Santana smiled inwardly at how her father was always the diplomatic one. He sometimes seemed to cower a little with Hugo, but she knew it was his way of keeping the peace. He hated arguments, while Hugo seemed to thrive on them.

Now she was afraid for Will. With Hugo already angry, how would he react when Will announced his intentions toward her? Neither she nor Will had told her father, afraid that in order to avoid a confrontation, Dominic would send her to San Francisco and allow Hugo to marry her before her birthday.

She covertly glanced at Hugo. The whole family sat at supper, her brother and Teresa and their children, and Hugo. Now that the wedding was getting closer, the familiar look in Hugo's cold eyes was becoming even more frightening. It reminded her of the look she had seen in the eyes of a cat once, when it was stalking a small rabbit— stealthy, hungry, ready to pounce.

Will would surely come soon. The message had been sent three days ago, as soon as Hugo arrived. It took a day and a half to reach the logging site, so Will might not get there until tomorrow, unless he rode like a madman. Already Hugo was talking about leaving in the morning and taking her with him to try on her wedding gown and help him with arrangements for the grand *fiesta* he had planned for after the wedding. Will must come soon! She had lied to Enrique Lopez, her father's top man, when she'd told him to send someone for Will, saying that her father had requested it and that it was extremely urgent. The messenger must ride hard and fast and get Will back to the ranch quickly. Enrique had looked doubtful, but he had done as she had ordered.

She hoped when Will arrived they would find a chance to be alone again. Maybe if she rode to her forever tree, he could follow her there. She wanted to kiss him again, to feel those strong arms around her, arms that made her feel so warm and protected. New feelings surged through her every time she thought of him. She wanted to please the blue-eyed American who had a way of making it impossible for her to think straight. In case he should arrive that night, she had asked Louisa to pull her hair into a tumble of fancy curls, and she wore a coral-colored dress that was puffed at the shoulders and dipped to reveal a tempting bit of cleavage. Louisa had told her that the color was immensely flattering, and the woman obviously had thought she was dressing for Hugo. Considering the way he was looking at her, Hugo apparently thought the same. In spite of the danger to Will, she could hardly wait for the man to find out her primping had been for the *Americano*, not for the pompous Hugo Bolivar!

Hester came out of the kitchen to serve a dessert of *pudin de pina y coco*, Santana's favorite pineapple-and-co-conut pudding, but she could hardly touch it, her stomach hurt so much from worry. Finally she heard horses riding hard around the back of the house to the front door.

"Who could that be?" Dominic wondered aloud.

Hugo set down his spoon. "It sounds like someone is in a hurry. Perhaps something is wrong."

They waited a moment, looking from the dining room through the sprawling great room toward the double front doors, which stood open because of the warm night. "Take care of my horse, *por favor*," they heard the rider say as he strode toward the doors. "I'll come and get my gear later."

"That sounds like Will Lassater," Dominic said.

Immediately Hugo scowled and rose. "Why would he come here so late in the day, and in such a hurry?"

They all watched as Will entered the house, walking through the great room to the dining room. He looked tired and sweaty. He had apparently ridden very hard to get there, and Santana loved him all the more for it. He had kept his promise! Her heart pounded with both fear and admiration. He looked wonderful, in spite of the dirt and sweat. He glanced at her once, his blue eyes blazing with determination, and that look set her afire with pride and desire. Her hero had come to rescue her!

Dominic rose, and Hernando looked up at Will curiously.

"What is this all about, Will?" Dominic asked. "Has something happened at the mill?"

Hugo glared at him. "Yes, what is the meaning of this interruption?" he demanded rudely. "It is poor manners to come walking in on a family supper, especially looking as you do!" His gaze swept over Will scathingly, but Santana suspected he was jealous of Will's muscular build and *gringo* handsomeness.

Will looked as though he would like to hit the man, but he turned to Dominic. "Forgive me for the interruption," he said, holding his hat in his hand. "I came as fast as I could. I knew Hugo was here and I feared he would leave tomorrow before I had a chance to say what I came to say."

Dominic frowned. "How did you know he was here?"

Will glanced at Santana, then back at Dominic. "That doesn't matter. The point is I am here, and I have something to discuss with you and Hugo. Finish your supper first, if you like. I'll wait outside."

He turned to go, but Dominic told him to wait. "Come to my study now," he said. "This is apparently very urgent."

Will nodded. "Fine." He glanced at Santana again and gave her a faint, reassuring smile.

Hugo also looked at her, then at Will. The fierce glare he sent Santana warned her of his suspicion and his rage. She was relieved when he turned and followed Dominic to his study, Will walking behind. Tears suddenly filled her eyes, though, as she reminded herself of Hugo's power.

"What is that look in your eyes, my sister?" Hernando asked. "Do you know what this is about? Are you the one who told Will that Hugo was here?"

She looked at Hernando defiantly. "*Sí*, I sent for him." She rose and walked toward the hallway down which the three men had disappeared. "And you will find out soon enough what this is about." She headed down the hallway to listen at the door to her father's study.

Ten

Will entered Dominic's study and threw his hat onto a red leather chair. Hugo already stood in one corner with his arms folded, watching him warily, as Dominic walked over to a liquor cabinet and took out a bottle of whiskey.

"I would prefer some chilled wine," he said, "from my own vinyards. This seemed so urgent, however, that I didn't bother to tell Hester to bring us some." He poured three shots, turned and handed one to Hugo, then walked over to Will. "Drink this down, *mi amigo*. You look as though you need it."

Will took the tiny glass and downed the fine whiskey while Dominic moved behind his desk. "Now, Will, you may tell us why you are here."

Will took a deep breath. It was now or never. He faced Hugo with unflinching eyes. "I have decided that I wish to challenge Hugo Bolivar for the hand of Santana Maria Chavez Lopez." He watched Hugo's face darken, watched his eyes narrow to slivers of hatred. For several seconds Hugo said nothing, did not even move.

"Well, well," he finally said. "It is not enough that the

Americano betrayed my confidence by not doing business with me. Now he wishes to rob me of the woman I love!"

Will stepped toward the man. "You don't love Santana! You desire her for her youth and beauty. You want her for an ornament on your arm, to show off to all your rich friends. But you don't love her totally, unselfishly. You would not be kind to her, gentle with her. I have been around you enough to know the kind of husband you would be, and I don't think it's right that Dominic should feel obligated to hand his daughter over to you because of a promise made to your father, who apparently was a much better man than you have ever been!"

Hugo sucked in his breath and stepped closer himself. "With every word you speak, you give me even more reason to *kill* you!" he said between gritted teeth.

"And all I need to kill you is to think of how you would treat Santana on her wedding night!" Will shot back.

"Stop!" Dominic said, stepping between the two men. He faced Will. "When did you decide this? Why should I give my daughter to a *gringo*, who does not even share the same religion?"

"I'm willing to change my religion," Will answered, finally taking his eyes from Hugo. "I'll do whatever I have to do, follow any custom you require. You know me to be an honest man, Dominic, and hard-working. You know that one day I will attain great wealth from my mills, and I will be able to give Santana the sort of home and comforts she deserves.

"I can also promise you, Dominic, that when you leave this life, all of your land will remain intact. Hugo would most certainly find a way to cheat Hernando out of his inheritance. But I would be willing to let Hernando run the ranch and the farm. All I want is to continue harvesting the trees."

He looked beseechingly at Dominic. "I am telling you that you cannot trust Hugo Bolivar. He only wants Santana for his pleasure, and because through her he thinks he can double his land holdings. He will not be kind to your daughter. Her happiness should mean more to you than forcing her to marry another Spaniard because of custom or a promise."

"How dare you stand there and insult me right in front of my face!" Hugo shouted. He pushed Dominic out of the way and walked to within a foot of Will. "You did not answer Dominic's first question! When did this start? What does Santana think of this? Someone should ask her what *she* wants!"

Will's smile was hard as he stared down at the smaller man. "Fine. Ask her. As for me, it started when I met you and Santana and found out she was promised to you. I could see in her eyes that very first day that she can hardly abide you. I could see fear in her eyes, also. I have even seen doubt in Dominic's eyes, but he is a man of his word. Santana in turn respects her father. She would never insult him by backing out of this on her own. She needs help, and I'm giving it to her. I'm offering her a way to end her engagement to you without dishonoring her father. If you truly love her, you will be willing to duel for her, willing to risk your life for her."

Hugo literally trembled with rage. "You bastard!" he growled. "How much have you seen of Santana? What have you and she been doing behind my back?"

Before he could say another word, a fist slammed into Hugo's face. The blow sent him reeling backward. He landed against a chair, which toppled over from the force and sent him sprawling. Will headed for him again, but Dominic grabbed his arm.

"Enough! If it is going to come to this, let the fighting be done someplace else, not in my house!"

Will stepped back, flexing his fists, as Hugo rolled to his knees. Groaning, he managed to grasp the edge of Dominic's desk to help pull himself up. He held a hand to his lower lip, but it was bleeding so profusely that the blood trickled through his fingers and dripped onto his ruffled white shirt. Dominic quickly handed him a clean handkerchief, and Hugo pressed it to his lip. "I prefer to settle this here and now!" he said. "With fists!"

"No!" Dominic stepped between them again. "Will is much stronger and younger than you, Hugo. This way is not fair, but a duel would leave you an even match."

"I need no fancy duel to—"

"Are you afraid, Hugo?" Will taunted.

Hugo stiffened. "Duels are for *Americanos*, but if that is what you wish, I am not afraid of your uncivilized practices! You are a man with no honor!"

"I am honorable toward those who *deserve* honor. Your insult to Santana just now should show Dominic the low opinion you have of women. Santana is a chaste young lady. Dominic himself can testify that until last month, I hadn't even seen her for over a year."

Will turned to Dominic. "You recall that when you visited my logging camp last month, I took Santana to watch the cutters. We spoke then about my feelings toward her, and her fears of marrying Hugo. I knew then I had to do something to help her. Call her in here if you want. She will tell you she is willing to marry me if I win a duel for her hand."

Hugo spoke before Dominic could. "Why would any well-bred Spanish woman like Santana choose to marry the likes of you over Hugo Eduardo Martinez Bolivar?" His words were slurred because of the sore lip. "There are many women in San Francisco who would *pay* to be married to me!"

"Then marry one of them!" Will answered. "And leave Santana alone!"

Hugo stepped boldly closer, still holding the handkerchief to his lip. "Even if I no longer wanted her, I would not give you the satisfaction."

"The only reason you won't back down is pride," Will said. "You're afraid people will see you for the coward that you really are. You would lose honor if you refused to accept this challenge over the woman you're supposed to love!"

Hugo blinked, and Will could tell by the look in the man's eyes that he had hit on the truth. Hugo Bolivar did not want this. He was afraid to fight, and was looking for a way to get out of it by saying Santana had sullied her reputation and therefore did not deserve such honor as having her intended fight for her hand.

"Santana has done nothing wrong," Will said. "Dominic knows it. Everyone on this ranch knows I've been here only once since I left last year, and Santana was in San Francisco with you at the time. Even when I took her to watch the fallers last month, some of my men were around every place we went. She knows this is between you and me, Hugo, and you aren't going to back out of this. I won't allow you to give the impression to others that Santana is anything less than honorable. To refuse this challenge is an insult to her reputation, and to your own honor and courage."

Hugo lowered the handkerchief. "You are a dead man, Will Lassater. And when you are buried, Santana Lopez will be *mine!*"

"We shall see."

"I will go and get Santana," Dominic said. "I trust that the two of you will remain civil while I am gone. I will not have fighting inside my home!" He left them glaring at each other and opened the door to his study, only to look out and see Santana hurrying away. She had obviously been listening. "Santana!" he called.

She turned. "Yes, Father?"

He almost smiled at her attempt to look innocent. To be honest, he had not been totally surprised at Will's challenge to Hugo, not when he had seen how Will and Santana had looked at each other at the logging camp. Santana had been so insistent on going with Dominic, and he had suspected she was more interested in seeing Will Lassater than the camp. He had a high regard for Will himself, but he knew Hugo's power, and his ability with pistols. This was not going to be an easy thing for Will, and how would Hugo treat Santana if he was the victor? Dominic had had his own doubts about the marriage, but had not known how to stop it. He did not like the prospect of his daughter marrying a *gringo*, but he greatly respected Will Lassater. He was a hard-working man of bravery, honor, and wealth.

"Go and get your brother and come into the study," he told Santana.

"*Si, Padre.*" Santana hurried away, returning moments later with Hernando. They both came into the study, and Santana felt a secret glee at seeing Hugo's bleeding lip. Will had given him his proper dues for insulting her.

"What is it, Father?" Hernando asked.

Dominic took hold of Santana's arm and walked her around to face all three men. "Will has challenged Hugo for your sister's hand," he told Hernando.

Hernando's eyebrows arched in surprise, and he looked at Will. "I did not even know—"

"That I had an interest in Santana?" Will faced him. "I have had, for months. All that time I tried to stay out of it. I still might have if I thought she was marrying an honorable man who would be good to her. I don't like sticking my nose into family matters, Hernando, and I understand you and your father's insistence in keeping a promise to Hugo's father. But I've suspected all along that neither you nor Dominic truly wants Santana to marry this man, and I know for a fact that *Santana* doesn't want to marry him. She's *afraid* of him! I'm offering her and you a way out of this."

"This whole thing is outrageous!" Hugo exclaimed. "This family has been friends of my family for years! My father saved Dominic from the revolution!"

"That doesn't give you the right to take Santana as a wife!" Will shot back.

Hernando looked at his father in wonder, then at Santana. "You knew about this?"

"I already told you that I am the one who sent for Will." Santana faced Hugo proudly. "I am willing to marry whoever wins the duel."

Hugo glared at her. "You would marry an *Americano?*"

She turned her gaze to Will, desire suddenly pulsing through her. Yes, she would not mind this man making a full woman of her. "If he wins my hand honorably, *si*, I would marry him."

"Then it is done," Dominic said. "My daughter has expressed her willingness in the matter. The challenge has been made before me and Hernando, and it cannot now be changed. There is only the decision of when and where . . . and what weapons will be used."

Hugo straightened his shoulders, looking confident. "Pistols, of course."

Will nodded. "You may use a pistol. I, on the other hand, intend to use a hatchet."

Santana gasped, and Hugo's eyes widened in surprise.

"A hatchet!" Hernando exclaimed. "Against a pistol?"

"It worked once before, with the outlaws."

"That was different, you fool!" Hugo spat out the

words. "You caught the man off-guard. This is a duel! You could never—"

"I've chosen my weapon," Will interrupted. Hugo appeared unnerved, which was what Will wanted. If Hugo lost this duel, he would die hideously, and he knew it. Still, Will knew it was a great risk for himself.

"Then you most certainly are already a dead man," Hugo said. "And in two months Santana will be my wife." He turned his dark, menacing gaze on Santana. "Whether she likes it or not!" He looked at Dominic. "Why waste time? Tomorrow morning at sunrise, at the grove of oak trees near your family burial ground." He grinned. "It will be convenient."

Will returned the man's confident grin. "Have Dr. Enders there, too . . . and make sure he's sober. A hatchet wound can be a pretty horrible thing, especially if it doesn't land right and the victim lives." In spite of Hugo's dark complexion, Will could see him pale at the remark. He wanted Hugo to think about what could happen if he lost. He had already seen Will use a hatchet, so he knew that Will certainly had a chance of winning. If Hugo was nervous enough, he might miss his mark when he turned and fired.

Hugo dabbed at his still-bleeding lip again. "I am going to the chapel now. I will ask Father Lorenzo to bless me and to pray that tomorrow my bullet finds its proper mark, so that Santana will indeed marry the best man." He glanced at Santana before walking out.

Dominic looked at Will. "I will have Delores prepare a room for you. Hugo's room is on this end of the house. I will put you at the other end so you do not have to see him any more tonight."

"*Gracias*, Dominic. I am sorry to bring your family this disruption, but I have thought about this for many months, and I know I have to do this."

"I for one am glad," Hernando said. "I have said nothing all this time because I knew it was my father's decision, but I have never liked the thought of my sister marrying Hugo, nor of Hugo getting his hands on La Estancia de Alcala."

Dominic sighed resignedly. "I have watched Hugo grow from a spoiled, demanding little boy into a spoiled, demanding man. I did not want to see the kind of man he truly is, because I could not bear the thought of how he might treat Santana. So far he has been quite respectable, but his eyes tell me that once Santana is his wife, he would treat her very differently.

"I also do not like the thought that he would take her to San Francisco, away from those she loves and who love her. If you win this, Will, I would like your promise that you will not take my daughter away from here, that you would not take her to your home far in the East. I am an old man, and I love Santana. I would not like spending these last years of my life never seeing her again."

Will looked at Santana, an aching need stirred by the sight of her standing there so proud and brave, looking ravishing in her coral dress. It pleased him to realize she probably dressed so beautifully in the hope he would get there that night. He turned his gaze to Dominic. "I have no plans of ever leaving California. I have too much invested here. And it will take many years to harvest your forests. I have no reason to take Santana anywhere. And I have no intention of interfering with or trying to take anything that Hernando will inherit rightfully. The only thing I would want is full rights to the forest once you have passed away."

Dominic nodded. "It is a fair request, if you become my son-in-law."

Will looked at Santana again. "First your daughter has to agree to marry me. I have promised her that if I win this duel, she is a free woman. I will not demand her hand." He looked back at Dominic. "I don't want Hugo to know that. I am only telling you because I want to set your mind at ease. Santana hardly knows me. I won't demand anything of her. I am only doing this to keep her from Hugo's clutches."

Dominic nodded. "Then you are a more honorable man than I thought. I will go to the chapel later myself, to pray for you, not Hugo." He closed his eyes. "God forgive me. His father and I were very close."

"I will go to the chapel too, with Father," Santana said. She walked closer to Will. "I will also pray for you, Will Lassater," she said softly. "And if you win the duel, you need not make me a free woman. It is true I do not know you well, but I know enough to see what a fine husband you would make for any woman. *Gringo* you are, but I am telling you now that I will marry you if you are the victor."

Their eyes held, and Will could not imagine anything more glorious than having Santana's naked body pressed against his in bed. "I would find it a great honor to call you my wife," he answered, searching her eyes, seeing there a look that told him she had changed from child to woman. He longed to kiss her full lips again, to taste her mouth, her neck, her breasts, to claim her virginity. If not for the presence of Dominic and Hernando, he would grab her close and relish the feel of her in his arms. He forced himself to look past her at Dominic. "I rode pretty hard and fast to get here. I would like to go to my room and clean up, then maybe eat something. After that I intend to get some much-needed sleep."

"Of course. Hernando, go tell Delores to prepare a room."

Hernando left, and Dominic came from around his desk and reached out his right hand. Will shook it. "I do not fully approve of my daughter marrying an *Americano*, but I want only her happiness. Come. I will show you to your room." He took hold of Santana's arm and escorted her out. Will followed, watching the graceful flow of Santana's walk, her slender waist, her beautiful shoulders. What would Gerald think of his marrying a Spanish woman? He missed his brother, looked forward to the day when he and his family could join him in California. For the moment, though, nothing mattered but the fact that he had challenged Hugo Bolivar to a duel. After tomorrow he might not need to worry about Santana or Gerald or the mill. He might find himself lying in a grave next to Santana's mother.

Santana wrapped her shawl closer against the early-morning chill. She sat in the open buggy in which she, her father, and Hernando had ridden to the grove of oaks a half-mile east of the house. Teresa had stayed behind with the children. Dominic had tried to convince Santana she should not come, but she would not hear of it. Will Lassater was risking his life for her that morning. If he was wounded, she wanted to be with him. No matter what happened, he should know she cared.

Her stomach felt tight, and she had not eaten any breakfast. Nor, according to Dominic, had Will. He had left his room before sunup, and Hugo had proclaimed that he had backed out of the challenge and run off like a coward. Hugo had ridden alongside Dominic's buggy on his shiny black horse, maintaining a cocky pose as though he were some great Spanish warrior. His lower lip was swollen, but he pretended it did not bother him. He always traveled with several guards, and they were with him now, one of them carrying a case with a pair of fancy pistols inside. A man had been sent hightailing to Rancho de Rosas the night before to get the pistols from Hugo's gun collection.

To Santana's delight, Will was already at the dueling site when they arrived. She had taken pleasure in seeing a slight fear in Hugo's eyes when he saw Will practicing throwing his hatchet. With amazing speed and accuracy he landed it into the narrow trunk of a young oak. He walked up and yanked it out, walked back and threw it again, landing it in almost exactly the same spot. Hugo seemed to flinch at every thud. Will's Palomino was tied not far away, and now Hugo had dismounted and handed his own horse over to one of his guards. A few men from La Estancia de Alcala who had heard what was going to happen had already filtered in to watch, and now a sizable crowd was gathering. A cool mist still hung in the air, holding in it the scent of the ocean, even though the water was several miles away.

Santana had worn a mint-green dress with short sleeves and a scooped neckline, but the morning was so chilly she was glad for her white knit shawl. Her hair was wrapped in one thick braid around her head, for she felt she looked older that way, and what was happening here was not child's play. These two men were fighting over her hand, and one of them would most likely die. She did not see it as an act of love on Hugo's part. He was simply saving his pride, and had probably agreed to this duel only because he was sure no one could best him. It was Will who was taking the greater risk. He had instigated all of this just to keep her from having to marry Hugo, and she loved him all the more for what he was doing.

Yes, she loved him, in spite of his still being very much a stranger to her. If he was killed, a part of her would die with him, and the rest of her would die when Hugo Bolivar made her his wife. Will had to be the victor. She had prayed so hard that he would be.

Dominic called the two men together, and it seemed to Santana that even the birds knew the gravity of the situation. Usually in the early morning the air rang with their singing, but this morning all was silent. The sun was barely up over the mountains to the east, and it shone through the mist in a soft red color. There was no wind. An owl hooted somewhere nearby, then stirred the tree branches when it flew off.

Santana felt weak and tingly all over, her nerves stretched to their limit. None of this had seemed real until this moment, as her father explained how the duel would take place, and Will and Hugo watched each other with hatred in their eyes. Hugo had dressed in a black suit with a white ruffled shirt, rings on his fingers, knee-high black boots, the fine clothes of a Spanish gentleman. Will wore a simple plaid flannel shirt, cotton pants, and worn leather boots, a powerfully built, barrel-chested man who was obviously much stronger than Hugo. But this was not a duel of strength. It was a duel of skill, and Hugo was one of the best with a pistol. Still, Will had a skill of his own, with the wicked hatchet that he gripped tightly in his right hand.

"You will stand back-to-back and you will each take ten paces as I count them," Dominic was saying. "At the count of *diez* you will turn and fire." He glanced at Will. "Or in your case, throw the hatchet."

Santana watched Hugo's face. It seemed pale, and beads of sweat were showing. Surely he was terrified of taking a hatchet between his eyes, or in the middle of his chest. Or he could be maimed for life if Will's aim was slightly off. Her heart pounded with dread as Dominic had Hugo and Will stand back-to-back. Will had not looked at her once, and she knew it was because he was concentrating all thoughts and energy on the duel. His life hung in the balance. Dominic began counting, the men began walking, and Santana felt an odd pressure build in her head as the intensity heightened. Her ears were ringing from the dead silence in the air, and her father's voice sounded as though he were standing in a small, stuffy room.

"*Uno, dos, tres, cuatro, cinco, seis.*" Santana felt almost faint, and she scrunched a handkerchief in her now-sweaty hands. "*Siete, ocho, nueve—*"

Santana's heart stopped as, before her father reached the count of ten, Hugo turned and fired. Shouts rose from the small crowd that watched, and Santana stood up in the buggy as Will's body pitched forward, blood quickly staining his upper back. Hugo stood motionless, his smoking pistol still raised, while Dr. Enders rushed over to Will. Hugo glanced at Santana, an evil grin moving across his lips, then turned his gaze to Dominic.

"You did say *diez*, did you not?"

Enraged, Dominic glared at him, fists clenched. "You know that I did not! And this ends our agreement, Hugo. I will not allow my daughter to marry a *coward*."

Hugo's grin faded. "I heard the tenth count."

"You heard no such thing! You were afraid Will Lassater could throw that hatchet before—"

"Get away from me!" they heard Will say. Everyone's attention moved to him again as he struggled to his knees. He rested there a moment, then managed to get to his feet. Already the entire left side of the back of his shirt was soaked with blood, but he managed to turn around, still gripping his hatchet. Hugo's eyes widened in terror, and he slowly lowered the pistol, which by the rules had been loaded with only one shot.

"Your aim . . . was a little off, Hugo," Will said. "Maybe it was because . . . you were so nervous about feeling my hatchet . . . buried in your skull. Or maybe it's because you knew . . . you were doing a cowardly thing . . . to shoot before Dominic reached the count of ten." He took a deep breath, and it seemed to be a struggle for him just to stay on his feet. "I believe . . . I still have . . . my turn coming."

Santana could now see a hole and blood at the upper left part of his chest, where the ball from Hugo's pistol had apparently gone all the way through him.

"You have shown all of us," Will went on, though every word seemed an effort, "the coward that you . . . really are." His eyes blazed with bitter hatred. "Will you stand there now . . . and let me have a shot at you . . . to save your honor? Or will you . . . turn and run?"

Hugo straightened, his face bathed in sweat. Santana was almost certain she saw tears in his eyes.

"Go ahead, you stinking *Americano!* I will not run from you!"

Will raised the hatchet. "Take my advice, Hugo. Don't move . . . not even one inch. If you do, you risk being maimed for life . . . or dying a terribly slow death. Let it be quick."

Everyone watched in stunned silence. Hugo made no move. Will flung the hatchet, and it whirled with lightning speed through the mist. It all happened in less than two seconds. Hugo squeezed his eyes shut as the hatchet headed straight for his head; then he cried out and fell away as the weapon skimmed the left side of his head, taking off part of his ear and a bit of his scalp before landing in a tree behind him. Hugo dropped to his knees, shivering and holding his hand to the left side of his head. Blood poured through his fingers and down his arm onto the sleeve of his black silk jacket.

One of Hugo's men rushed to his side, calling for Dr. Enders, who ran over. He pulled some gauze from his bag and told Hugo to press it tightly against the side of his head, that he could do little for him until the bleeding slowed. Will half stumbled closer, refusing to let anyone help him walk. He stood over Hugo, and the others backed away.

"I could just as well . . . have put that between your eyes," he told Hugo, "but I like to think I am a better man than to do something so barbaric . . . even if you do deserve it. Consider yourself lucky today, Hugo . . . but also defeated. If you had not shot at me before I had a chance to turn . . . we could call this a draw . . . but your own cowardliness has made you . . . the loser. Get the hell off this ranch. Let your own men tend to your wound. I prefer . . . never to set eyes on you again!"

Hugo managed to get to his feet. "This is not over," he growled.

"It is for me," Will answered. "If you choose to keep it going, my hatchet will find its proper mark the next time."

Hugo glowered at him, but for the moment he was defeated. He looked over at Santana. "If you marry this *Americano*, you will be marrying beneath yourself. But it no longer matters to me. I want nothing to do with a woman who sells herself so cheaply!"

Will grasped the front of Hugo's shirt, yanking him forward with surprising strength, considering his injury. "You will not insult Santana, either here or in San Francisco. If I hear you have, you are a dead man. Every person here knows I have a right to kill you . . . whenever it pleases me. You don't play fair, Hugo, and in that case, neither do I. Now get the hell out of my sight . . . before I go get that hatchet and bury it in your skull!"

Hugo sneered. "Someday, I will find a way to destroy you!" He turned and ordered one of his men to help him to his horse, then told another guard to go to the Alcala home and get his belongings. Still holding blood-soaked gauze to the side of his head, he rode up to Dominic. "This is the end of our friendship. I am sorry to lose it, but if you

take this *Americano* as a son-in-law, there will never again
be any dealings between us."

"Even if Will Lassater does not marry Santana," Dominic said, "I would want no more dealings with you anyway,
Hugo. I will not do business with or be the friend of such a
coward. It is good that your father is dead and did not see
what happened here today!"

Hugo sniffed, then jerked his horse around, stopping
beside the buggy to glare at Santana. "Someday . . ." he
said, his dark gaze raking over her as though he were ripping off her clothes.

"Coward!" she spat at him.

He glared at her a moment longer, then rode off.
Santana turned to see that Will had finally sunk to his
knees, and she realized he was probably about to pass out
from loss of blood.

"Get him into the buggy and take him to the house!"
Dominic ordered. "Come with us, Dr. Enders. And no
drinking until you have tended to his wounds."

A bleary-eyed Marcus Enders, whose face was continually puffy and whose eyes were constantly bloodshot from
too much drink, followed the men who helped Will to the
buggy. He climbed in beside him, quickly ripping off more
gauze and stuffing it into the front and back of Will's shirt.
Santana climbed into the back of the buggy herself, sitting
down and placing Will's head in her lap. She leaned close,
stroking his hair.

"You must live now, *mi querido*, so that we can marry.
Please do not die. It is only this moment that I have realized how much I love you. *Te amo como jamas he amado.*"

Will opened his eyes to look into her beautiful face. "I
love you as I have never loved before," she had told him.

"*Te amo, carina mia,*" he answered.

Eleven

"Well, well, I don't believe my eyes." Noel Gray strolled into the room where Will lay resting. "When the messenger came and told me the real reason you left the mill four days ago, I figured you had completely lost your mind."

Will grinned, then grimaced as he used his right arm to brace himself so he could sit up straighter in bed. "I've been up and about a little. I'll be out of here in a couple of days. It's not that bad. The shot went right through me, apparently missing anything vital, and Dr. Enders does a pretty decent job as long as he's sober. I won't be chopping at a tree anytime soon, but I can run things otherwise. How's everything going at the mill?"

"Well, we brought another big one down with no mishaps, but some of the wood at the lower end shattered. I only came to verify that you're all right and see if everything I was told is true. I've got to get back to camp pretty quick."

Will ran a hand through his hair. "What would I do without you?"

Noel pulled up a chair. "Without me you probably

would have stayed put to run things because you're the only other one who can. Then you wouldn't have come here and gotten yourself in this mess. Then again, you probably would have come anyway, just closed down the mill first. Apparently you decided this was pretty damn important. I thought you had put Senorita Lopez out of your mind. You haven't mentioned her to me for months."

Will grinned rather sheepishly. "I had every intention of leaving it all alone, but as the day of her marriage to Hugo drew closer, I couldn't stand it. I don't even know if she really wants to marry me. I've told her she's free to do what she wants now. I just couldn't let that lecher get his hands on her. She's too sweet and innocent." He shook his head. "Before I left Maine to come here, I never would have dreamed of doing anything so crazy. It must be something about the air out here. It seems like a man loses himself to another world here, like nothing in his past is real anymore. In my wildest imagination, before I came here I never could have pictured myself getting into something as dramatic as a duel over a Spanish woman."

"Or as gallant," Noel added.

Will waved him off. "Stupid, maybe, but not gallant. I just felt sorry for her."

"You love her?"

Will met his eyes. "I guess maybe I do."

Noel rested his elbows on his knees. "Some women can cause a man to do some pretty strange things, especially when they look like the senorita. I can see how she'd be easy to love. She's not just beautiful, she's amazingly unspoiled, considering how she was raised, and she's spirited too. I think she might make a very good wife."

"You see it, too, then?"

Noel nodded. "I see it, and I guess I don't blame you. I just wish you'd told me what you were up to when you left."

Will reached over and picked up his pipe from an ashtray on a stand beside the bed. "Get me a light from over there by the fireplace, will you?" As he watched Noel cross the room, he thought again what a wonderfully sprawling, beautiful home this was, with big, airy rooms, wide hallways, slate floors. Every room had a fireplace and double glass doors that opened to gardens full of roses. He figured the great room was at least thirty feet square, and it was made more magnificent by a cathedral ceiling that was supported by huge pine beams. Plants decorated every corner, and the windows were nearly always open, letting in the sounds of birds and the smell of roses. "I'll have to build a home like this for Santana if I marry her. Maybe I'll build something even bigger and more beautiful, farther back on her father's land, where she'd be closer to the mill."

Noel lit a long match and cupped a hand around it to keep it lit as he carried it back to Will. Will puffed the pipe to get it burning, then closed his eyes for a moment to enjoy the rich tobacco. "There wasn't time to tell you what I had in mind," he said in response to Noel's earlier statement. "The messenger came and told me Hugo was here, and I had to get back fast before he could take Santana off to San Francisco again. You were up at the falling site, so I just left a few instructions with Derek and took off. I'm sorry about all that, and I'm very grateful for your taking over and keeping things going. I know it's a wild, rough lot of men we've got working up there."

"We're making it, but it would be best if you came back as soon as you can. What about this Hugo Bolivar? Do you think you're rid of him for good? He strikes me as someone who won't accept defeat lightly. He's a damn powerful man, you know."

Will puffed thoughtfully on the pipe before answering. "He'd be a damn fool and an even worse bastard than I figure him to be if he gives me any more trouble. He owes his life to me. After he shot me in the back, I had every right to plant my hatchet between his eyes, but I didn't do it. I just hope that doesn't prove to be the worst mistake of my life."

He exchanged a look of understanding with Noel, both men wary of what a man like Hugo might try. "I hope so, too, my friend," Noel said. "For now I'm just glad you're alive. So, when's the wedding?"

Will grinned again. "I don't know yet if there'll even be one. I haven't talked to Santana since this whole thing took place, although she was there when it happened. I wanted her to take a few days to think about everything. I don't want her to feel obligated to marry me, or to look at me as some kind of hero. I want her to make a clear decision. I'm getting out of this bed this evening, and I've asked Dominic to allow me a private talk with her out in one of the gardens. Soon as I'm well enough, I'll come back to the mill and let you know what I'm going to do."

"And if she decides not to marry you, you'll be as mean as a bear for the want of her."

Will took the pipe from his lips and studied it. "Could be. I didn't think it would matter that much, but I find myself hoping more and more that she'll take the chance. She's beautiful, gracious, loving . . . I see a lot of strength in her, Noel, and she loves the trees like I do. She finds my work exciting, wants to learn all about it. She's easy to talk to and—"

"You don't need to convince me, Will. I hope you get what you want. Like I said, I just came to make sure you're going to be all right."

Will sat up straighter, flexing his left arm a little. "Sore as hell, but otherwise all right. My biggest problem has been weakness from loss of blood, but it's been two days and I'm feeling a lot better."

"The news is already spreading, you know. Most of the

men at camp know about it, and I imagine if Hugo had some of his men there, word will get around San Francisco when he gets back. His reputation will suffer because of this, and that's going to make him an angry man with revenge on his mind. You watch yourself."

"I'm not afraid of Bolivar. If he does something to get back at me for this, I won't spare his life the next time."

Noel read the hatred in Will's eyes and knew he meant what he said. He put a hand on Will's arm. "You take care of yourself. I'll keep things running. Don't get up and around sooner than you should."

Will nodded. "You're a good man, Noel. Someday my brother will come and help me expand, but I promise you'll always have a top job with us. He'll be busy handling the shipping and finding new customers, so I'll always need a good man on the site. How soon will that house you're building for your family be finished?"

"Pretty quick. I'm anxious to get them moved in, tired of only seeing Bernice when I come here. She's eager for the move, even though she'll be living in a pretty remote area with few women for company. She's used to that. All she cares about is being closer to me. I'm glad to have found a solid job where I know I can stay put for a while. I'll never forgive myself for dragging Bernice out here in the first place, but we're here now, and maybe we can finally settle in one place, thanks to you."

"Well, thanks for coming. I'll be fine."

Noel rose. "That's all I need to know." He put out his hand and Will shook it. "I'll see you back at camp in a few days, then. Good luck with Santana. I hope there will be a wedding."

"Thanks." Will felt a surge of aching desire at the thought of it. Now that he had done what he had done, he was more sure than ever that Santana was the woman he wanted for a wife, the woman he wanted in his bed every night. He was a citizen of California now. Santana seemed to represent everything that was rich and beautiful about this land that so enchanted him, and he was even ready to give up his own religion and study Catholicism, just because it was what she would want. He nodded to Noel as the man left, but his thoughts were not on him or the mill. They were on a beautiful young woman with a curvaceous body that made a man ache. He would take up her religion, her customs, learn her language more thoroughly, build her whatever kind of home she wanted, wherever she wanted it. Whatever Santana Maria Chavez Lopez wanted, she would get, just as long as she would consent to be his wife.

Will walked out the front doors of the Alcala home and into the garden area. Trellises of roses graced both sides in two nearly solid walls of flowers, leading to the brick wall that braced yet another set of thick wooden double-doors that led outside the house. The garden formed an outdoor entranceway to the front of the house, a private area where one could sit outside and enjoy the air without actually leaving the house. A statue of the Mother Mary was at the center of the garden area, in the middle of a huge marble birdbath, and potted plants sat everywhere, an array of varieties. The whole setting was peaceful and comforting.

On one of the several benches he saw Santana waiting; on another bench against the opposite wall sat her tutor, Estella Joaquin, who smiled and nodded to him as he approached. He suddenly felt as nervous as a schoolboy at his first dance, and he realized he was more worried about this meeting with Santana than he had been about the duel with Hugo. As he came closer he realized she had worn what must have been one of her most magnificent dresses, a cascade of yellow lace over yellow satin. Her hair was pulled into a mass of curls on top of her head, with little yellow roses twisted into the curls, and she wore drop earrings that looked as though they contained real diamonds. She was staring down at her lap and twisting a linen handkerchief in her hands, which were covered by yellow lace gloves.

"Santana?"

She started at the sound of his voice, then rose. The puffy short sleeves of her dress revealed the milky brown skin of her arms, and its ruffled bodice beautifully outlined her full bosom. She reminded him of candy, and he wanted to taste her.

"My father must have explained why I was not at supper," she said softly.

"He did. He said you wanted to wait and see me when you had an answer for me." He glanced at Estella, then back at Santana. "He also said that now that we . . . well . . . now that I have asked you to be my wife, our meetings must be properly chaperoned."

"*Sí.*" She looked at him with concern. "You will be all right?"

"I will be. I'm leaving for the mill in a couple of days."

Her eyes teared. "I wish to apologize for what Hugo did. At first I thought he had killed you, and I wanted to take a gun and shoot him myself. Then you showed him up as the coward he really is. I am glad, more glad that I do not have to marry him."

He studied her eyes and was touched by the gratefulness he saw in them. "Nor do you have to marry *me,* Santana." The entire *portico* smelled of roses, and the air held the hush of twilight. Will felt lost in the beauty of it, and in the beauty of Santana Lopez.

"And what do *you* want, Will Lassater? Tell me truly."

He couldn't keep his gaze from sweeping over her, noting how perfectly formed she was. Her outer beauty was surpassed only by her inner beauty. A man couldn't do much better in choosing a wife than to have Santana to come home to every day. "I want you for my wife," he said. "You're beautiful, enchanting, gracious, intelligent, and generous. Perhaps it is too soon to say that I love you, but I know that I would love you very deeply in time. I honor you, respect you, and I would never abuse you or be unfaithful to you. I cannot think of a better woman to be a mother to my children, and I promise you that if you marry me, I will never force myself on you. I will let you decide when you are ready to be a wife. I will be the best husband I can be, and someday I am going to be one of the wealthiest men in California. You will live in as grand a style as any man in this state could offer."

Santana smiled softly. Will looked wonderful, standing there in his simple cotton pants and checkered shirt. He had come so quickly to challenge Hugo that he had brought little with him in the way of extra clothing, but she liked him this way, rugged, simple, so handsome with his thick sandy hair and those blue eyes that made her heart flutter.

"I in turn cannot think of any man who could make a better husband," she said. "You are handsome, successful, and you are a man of great honor. You are brave and strong, and with you I would feel safe and protected. And I, too, would find you easy to love. Perhaps we already love each other, but for the moment what we feel is enough to be husband and wife. Because of what you did, one thing I know that you are and always will be is my very good friend, who was willing to sacrifice his life for me when he hardly knew me, only to keep me from . . ." Her eyes teared again, and she dabbed at them with her handkerchief. "I cannot thank you enough for getting me away from Hugo in a way that saved my father's honor." She met his eyes again. "But you should know that is not the reason I would marry you. It is for all the other things that you are, and because I want no other woman to own you. I want you for myself."

Their eyes held, and Will reached out and touched her cheek with the back of his fingers. "You will marry me, then?"

"*Sí*. The first Saturday after my eighteenth birthday in November, if that is all right with you."

He smiled. "That's fine with me. I'll hire some men to start building a home for us, toward the northwest corner of La Estancia de Alcala, so you won't be far from your family, but also closer to the logging site. You tell me what kind of home you want. Money is no object."

"Just as long as there are many gardens as there are here. I would like it Spanish style, like my father's house. I do not want something big and cold like Hugo's home."

Will nodded. "One level then, stucco, something with a nice view." This was all so formal, he thought. He wanted to grab her close, taste her mouth, feel himself inside of her. Suddenly he burned with the want of her, and he realized the next two months were going to seem like an eternity. At least he knew he had plenty to keep him busy. "I don't think I could finish a house by the time we marry. You may have to live here for a while longer afterward."

"I understand." Santana could not look away from him. For the first time in her life she wanted a man to touch her in private places, wanted to feel her nakedness pressed against his. She knew what was expected of a wife in bed, for she had made Louisa tell her, and she was not afraid—except that she feared she might not please him. "Until we have our own home, we will use my father's guest house for privacy after we marry. Noel will have moved his family to their new home by then."

"You're sure, then?"

"I am sure." She blinked back more tears, tears of joy

for the wonderful change that had come into her life. *"Te amo, carino mio."*

"Te amo, mi querida," he answered. So, already they could say I love you, Will mused. Perhaps only a tentative love now, but a love that he knew would grow into something wonderful and binding. "Shall we go and tell your father of our decision?"

"Si." She offered her arm, and Will took it, glancing over at Estella. "We're going inside so that I can formally ask for Santana's hand in marriage."

Estella smiled with pleasure. "I am glad for both of you."

Will led Santana toward the front doors, which stood open. She felt numb, exhilarated, afraid, excited, anxious. Every emotion she could name was rushing through her, and she didn't know whether to laugh or cry. She was officially rid of Hugo Bolivar! She was going to marry the handsome *gringo* from that faraway place called Maine, a man who could cut down the mighty redwoods with his powerful arms . . . arms that would hold her in the night and make sure that Hugo Bolivar never came near her again.

It was a grand *fiesta*, with more than three hundred people attending. Some had come from from as far away as San Francisco to see the beautiful Santana Maria Chavez Lopez marry the *Americano* who had fought a duel to win her hand. The wedding ceremony was conducted by Father Lorenzo in the little chapel at La Estancia de Alcala, which was only big enough for family members and closest friends. Others stood outside, including Noel and his family, Derek, and several men from the mills, which Will had closed for one week. When it was announced that Santana and Will were man and wife, everyone cheered. Musicians hired out of Santa Rosa played guitars and trumpets, performing both Spanish love songs and faster-paced music, to which many danced.

Will hardly had time to think about his wedding night. The celebrating, drinking, dancing, games, gift giving, and eating lasted well into the night. The women took Santana to her own room in the wee hours of the morning to sleep, while Will himself drank so much that he passed out. When he awoke in his room in the main house the next morning, he heard laughing and more music. He had been told about wild Mexican celebrations that lasted for days, and now he understood it wasn't an exaggeration. By the time he cleaned up and went outside, blindfolded children were beating at a *pinata*, their parents shouting directions and cheering them on. A huge table was spread with breakfast food—scrambled eggs, pork, corn bread, rice, potato pancakes, tortillas, chicken, pastries, coffee. Some people were lined up to eat, and he noticed Santana was standing with several other women, helping to serve guests!

He smoothed his still-damp hair. He did not wear the fancy black silk suit made for his wedding by a seamstress Dominic had hired. He wore only a white shirt and black cotton pants. He noticed Santana was dressed in white again, but this time the dress was of simple cotton, not her lace wedding dress. He would never forget how she had looked the day before, in the most beautiful gown he had ever seen, cascading lace ruffles that led to a train several feet long.

He felt like a fool this morning. Yesterday he had married the most beautiful woman in California, but he had gotten so caught up in the celebrating that they had not even slept together last night, although he suspected that was how it was supposed to be. Women had whisked his wife away before he could carry her off himself, and considering the condition he'd been in by then, it was probably a good thing.

He hurried over to her side, putting a hand to her waist and pulling her away from the table, while others laughed and made teasing remarks about the groom finally being awake and ready to make her his wife. He held her close, ignoring their remarks.

"Santana, my beautiful *esposa,* to whom I pledged my life yesterday. Please forgive me. Your father and brothers and the other men—"

She put her fingers to his lips. "They kept you from me and got you so full of wine that we could not be together. That was deliberate, *carino mio.* Did you not understand that?" She smiled. "It is better the first night to stay away from each other, to relax and settle down from the excitement of the ceremony and the celebrating. Today we have all day to just be together, to greet everyone, to relax and take our time. Eat some breakfast with me, my love. We will walk and talk, and we will make plans for our home and our future. Later tonight we will go together to the guest house. We will be left alone then."

His gaze dropped to her bosom, much of its fullness revealed by the low cut of her dress. He understood now. This was the time for the female to strut before the male, to entice him, and yet to take her own time so that she was ready. Dominic and Hernando and the others had deliberately kept them apart last night so that in his inebriated state he would not be too forceful on his new young bride. It was all planned. He grinned. "May I at least kiss my wife?"

She smiled. "I have been waiting."

He leaned down and met her lips, parting them, searching her mouth hungrily. People around them cheered and called out more remarks, but Will did not care who watched. He pressed her tight against him, stretching out the kiss, on fire for her, wondering how he was going to get through the day. Finally he released her. "I promise not to drink one drop of wine today," he whispered in her ear. "I want to be perfectly sober tonight."

She kissed his cheek. "Perhaps it is I who should drink the wine today."

He frowned, touching her face. "Don't be afraid, Santana. Don't ever be afraid. I promise you that sharing bodies will be the most satisfying thing you will ever know."

Santana relished the feel of his strong arms, realizing he could easily break her in half if he wanted. But Will Lassater would never harm a hair on her head. "Tonight we will know, *mi esposo*," she whispered in reply. "Come, share some breakfast with your wife."

Will grinned, letting her lead him back to the table full of food. They spent the rest of the day meeting the many friends of Dominic Alcala—farmers, ranchers, miners, businessmen, customers, suppliers, ranch hands. He had met many of them the day before, but he had been too drunk to remember them. There followed more gift giving, games, music, and dancing. Never had Will known a people who could make so much out of celebrating something. Everyone was warm and friendly toward him, welcoming him into their world.

Morning moved into afternoon, and afternoon into night. Many of the men got drunk again on Dominic's endless supply of wine, but Will did not touch it. He wanted to be fully aware of this night, of every touch, every move, the glorious sight of Santana's body. A huge bonfire was lit, and Santana turned Will over to her father and brother. They sat him down on a log and told him to stay right there for a special treat. Moments later the musicians struck up a rhythmic song with a provocative, sultry beat. People let out a chorus of *aaahs* when a dark-haired woman appeared. She wore a brief red top that bared her middle and was also cut low to expose a good deal of her breasts. Her red ruffled skirt wrapped tightly around her hips, the waistline below her belly button.

The woman advanced toward Will, hips swaying enticingly to the rhythm of the music. She stood in front of him, whirled around so that the full skirt exposed her slender legs all the way to her thighs, then turned her back to him, gyrating her hips in a motion that had a hypnotizing effect on him. Men grinned and whistled, cheering her on, and Will found his lust for his new wife building at the suggestive movements of the Spanish dancer.

For several minutes she danced, finally reaching out to him. But as he reached to take her hand, she darted away. Then Santana appeared from out of the darkness, wearing a low-cut, form-fitting red dress, her hair brushed out long, her dark eyes showing desire.

"No other women for you now, my husband," she said. "Only Santana Maria Chavez de Lassater." She held his eyes boldly, putting her hands on his shoulders, and he rose. The music continued, and Santana moved with the rhythm, gradually coming closer to Will until her swaying body rubbed against him. Finally the music ended, and everyone clapped and whistled and made suggestive remarks to Will.

"I wish to go to the guest house now," Santana told him.

Will realized what a fabulously beautiful, hot-blooded woman he had married, and he suddenly felt nervous. It occurred to him that he might not be able to please her, but he was damn well ready to try. He picked her up in his arms and carried her off.

Twelve

Will walked inside the guest house and kicked the door closed, shutting out the cheers and sly remarks of those who had followed them there. He had carried Santana for the entire quarter-of-a-mile walk, but she was so light that it had not been a task. She had her arms wrapped around his neck, and her head rested on his shoulder. The way she was curled up, when he looked down at her he could see almost the entire fullness of her breasts, breasts he longed to touch, to taste, but that would depend on Santana.

"Here we are," he said, kissing her cheek. He started to put her down, but she protested.

"Wait. I like it here. I like feeling your strength, *carino mio*." Santana looked into his eyes, and in the next moment his lips met hers in a hot, hungry kiss. Something in her came alive, a youthful passion mixed with curiosity and an eagerness to please, and in turn to enjoy the pleasures of being a woman. Something in her ached fiercely, maddening desires welling up unexpectedly. She never dreamed she could feel like this, but she wanted Will Lassater to do terribly naughty things to her. She wanted him to touch secret places. Fiery needs swept through her, dulling her fear and apprehension. Perhaps it was the little bit of wine she had drunk, mixed with the desires she had awakened in herself when she danced for him and saw how his gaze raked her body.

"*Te amo, carino mio,*" she whispered between more kisses. "I did not think I was ready, but . . ." His lips moved down her neck, and she threw her head back, gasping when he kissed her breasts.

He carried her to the bedroom, paying no heed to the fact that the entire house was decorated with flowers and *pinatas* that they were supposed to break open to find money and other gifts. Nor did he pay much heed to the beautiful mahogany four-poster that Dominic had ordered from San Francisco as a gift for his daughter and her new husband. It was covered with red satin sheets and a red quilted spread. White silk was draped gracefully between the posts. Will kept hold of Santana in one arm while he leaned down to rip away the quilt and the top sheet, then he laid Santana on the bed.

She curled onto her side, watching him as he tore off his shirt to reveal a broad chest and beautifully muscled arms. There was still a fresh-looking scar on the upper left part of his chest from where Hugo's shot had torn through him from back to front. Another scar on his lower left side showed where he had been shot by the bandits that had threatened to kidnap her. Both times he had risked his life to save her from harm, and to her he was her brave hero, a man who deserved to take pleasure in her now. Hair the color of that on his head covered his chest, just enough to make him even more masculine and appealing. He bent down and removed his leather boots and his socks; he unbuckled his belt, unbuttoned his pants, and pulled them off. Now he wore only his knee-length underwear, and something bulged at the junction of his thighs, that mysterious part of a man that she only partly understood. Like a stud horse he would put that huge thing inside her tonight, and to her surprise she wanted him to do just that. She was afraid of the pain, but not of Will Lassater; and he had promised that she would learn to enjoy it.

He started to climb onto the bed, and she could see his blue eyes were dark with desire.

"Take them off," she told him. "I am not afraid. I want to see you."

Will felt on fire with the want of her. He was surprised at how she had suddenly awakened to the woman in her, and was delighted at her eagerness. He removed the underwear, and watched her eyes widen at the firm manhood that was presented to her. She sat up, meeting his eyes as she undid the bodice of her dress and pulled it down over her shoulders, then farther down, to her waist. She wore no undergarment. She was so beautiful that Will's head spun with the fierce need to be inside her.

"I want to do it quickly so that the pain will be over," she said. "Then we will sleep in each other's arms, and later in the night, you can teach me other things. We will go slower then, and we will learn about each other, and I will enjoy being your wife."

"Santana—"

"This is the way I want to do it." She got off the bed and stood beside him, removing her dress completely. She stood there naked, her arms folded over her breasts. Hesitantly, she looked up at him. "Do you like what you see, Will Lassater? Do I please you?"

Will was literally shaken by her boldness. He had not expected this, had thought she would protest at the last minute. Yet in spite of her boldness there was a lovely innocence about what she was doing, a child yearning to become a woman. He knew without question that this was her first time, that she would not do such things for just any man . . . only for him, her husband, her love.

He picked her up in his arms and laid her on the bed, then climbed up beside her. He watched her eyes as he ran a hand over her soft skin, her belly, cupping a breast, stroking his thumb over a taut nipple.

"You're so beautiful, Santana. How can you ask if I am pleased with what I see? There is no woman who can compare."

He met her mouth hungrily, then trailed his lips to her throat, and down to kiss each dark nipple. He lingered there, savoring the sweetness of her breasts, knowing by her whimpers that she liked what he was doing. She grasped his hair, and he took a breast more fully into his mouth, unable to control his desire as he sucked wildly, knowing it would help her if he brought out her wildest passions before entering her. He must make this as easy as possible for her.

He licked and kissed at her other breast, then met her mouth again in an intimate kiss, searching deep with his tongue while he massaged her breasts and teased her nipples. He ached to explore, to taste, to see every private inch of this dark beauty who was now his wife, but some things would have to wait, or he might frighten her. She wanted him to do this quickly, and he would gladly oblige.

He reached down and gently felt her, touching her in light circular movements, awakening the ripe womanhood waiting to be freed. She gasped his name when he stroked the little nub that he'd learned stirred a woman's desire. He could feel the slippery wetness that told him he could easily slide into her now, but he waited until she drew in her breath in a sweet climax. She looked almost surprised as she arched against his hand, and quickly he moved between her legs, smothering her gasps with kisses. He told himself it was best if he did this quickly. It would be easier for her.

He shoved hard, felt himself breaking through something. All his life he had only done this with whores or loose women who had already been with men. Santana was his first virgin, and it made him feel like a virgin himself. Her scream frightened him, yet he could not stop. No woman he'd ever been with had made him feel like this, and he groaned in his own ecstasy as he pushed over and over, unable to stop in spite of the tears he tasted on her cheeks, her cries of pain.

Santana knew she had no right to make him stop, but her fierce desire and excitement had turned to piercing pain. She dug her nails into the hard muscles of his arms, closed her eyes, and reminded herself that it would not always be like this. Pain tore through her insides like hot fire, consuming her privates, her belly, yet there was a strange pleasure in that pain, a tiny hint of how this might feel once the hurt was gone.

"I'll end this quickly," he whispered, just before she felt a surging pressure deep inside her. She knew instinctively that it was his seed spilling into her, seed that could make her pregnant with his child. She would like nothing more now than to give him a son. Finally he relaxed against her, remaining inside her for a moment. She sniffled back her tears, and he pushed himself up, resting on his elbows on either side of her. He leaned down and kissed her eyes, kissed away her tears.

"I'm sorry, Santana. I swear by Mother Mary that soon you will want this. You will enjoy it and take as much pleasure in it as I have had this moment."

She wiped the last of her tears away. "Do not be sorry. I told you I wanted it this way." She met his eyes. "I love you, Will Lassater, and now I belong to you. Our marriage is consummated, and there is nothing Hugo Bolivar can do now to change it. It is done, and I . . ."—new tears came —"I cannot imagine how horrible this would have been . . . to have Hugo doing such a thing to me." A sob shook her. "He would have laughed at me. He would not . . . have been sorry like you. He would not have been . . . willing to wait if I was not ready, but I know . . . that you would have." She flung her arms around his neck, loving him for the simple reason that she was not afraid of him. "I hope that quickly I will be with child. I want to give you many children, Will. And I want . . ." She kissed his cheek, his mouth. "Tell me that I pleased you. I do not want to disappoint you."

Will grinned. "There isn't a woman on earth who could please me more, not in looks and beauty, and not in the way it felt to be inside of you." He met her mouth in a gentle kiss. "Let's go and wash," he whispered. "Then we'll just lie in each other's arms for a while, maybe get a little sleep. When we wake up we'll eat, or maybe we'll just make love again. I could do this over and over all night, but maybe you aren't—"

She touched his lips. "The more we do it, the less the pain. Isn't that right?"

He nodded. "Something like that. I've never been with a virgin before. I suppose all women are different, but eventually it always becomes enjoyable."

She scowled. "I am jealous of all the other women you have been with. Promise me you will never again touch any woman but me."

He slid a big, callused hand over her, touching the hairs between her legs, massaging her soft belly. "I already promised that when I married you. Besides, why would I want anyone else, when I have the most wonderful wife in California?" He got up from the bed. "I'll see about getting some water to wash."

Will walked into the kitchen to get a bucket of water,

only then noticing how beautifully decorated the house was. The kitchen table was loaded with all sorts of food and wine. He smiled at how Santana's people seemed to think of everything, how supportive and friendly they had been, so happy for them, everyone celebrating the marriage. He had married into a good family, and he felt like the luckiest man alive. It struck him that he could never go back to the life he had known in Maine. He was becoming even more deeply enchanted with the Spanish culture, the magic that was California.

In some ways he and Santana were still strangers, yet it didn't matter. He had no doubt that they would find themselves totally compatible over the years, and he knew he had done the right thing. He would not change any of it. He carried the water into the bedroom, where some towels were stacked on a small table for them. They washed themselves, and he calmed Santana's alarm at the blood on her thighs, assuring her it was normal and she was not dying. He gently washed her himself, then carried her back to the bed. They pulled the covers over themselves and wrapped their naked bodies together, nestling into a pillow to sleep.

Santana relished the protective arms in which she rested, thinking what a night of horror this would have been with Hugo. "Thank God for my Will," she whispered. "You are like a gift from heaven."

"And you are like an angel," Will said.

They fell asleep, while outside the many friends and relatives continued to dance and eat and drink well into the night.

Will awoke facing the outside of the bed. He could see a hint of pink light coming through a crack in the curtains at a window, and all senses told him it was from a sunrise. It took him a moment to get his bearings, but then something moved against his back, and he was quickly reminded of where he was and who was with him. He turned over and pulled Santana into his arms. "You awake?"

"*Si, mi esposo*. And I am so happy this morning." She kissed his chest, his throat.

"Wait," he told her. He turned over to take two pieces of peppermint candy that had been placed in a dish beside the bed. Now he knew why. Newlyweds would not want to jump up and clean their teeth on their first morning together, but they would most certainly want to make love again. He put a piece of candy into his mouth, then rolled over and held one against Santana's lips. "Kissing in the morning will be more pleasant if you suck on this first," he told her with a wink.

She smiled and stuck out her tongue, and he placed the candy on it. He wondered if one day he could talk her into doing some of the wilder, arousing things with her tongue and lips that the whores did. There was plenty of time for such things, though. Today they would just enjoy each other, this newness, the thrill she would find in intercourse. While she chewed the candy, he gently rubbed the soft skin of her thighs, stroked his hand over her firm bottom, massaged her belly, slid his hands up to her breasts, cupping them, toying with her nipples.

"I like when you touch me," she said. She traced her own slender fingers over his chest, touching his nipples in return. "Does it excite you when I touch you here, as it does me?"

He grinned, looking down to watch her nipple grow hard at his caress. "Yes, I like it too." He quickly chewed and swallowed the candy so that he could savor a breast. He moved his hand down to her private places, feeling his way into the warm crevice between her legs to find the magical spot that would excite her. He wanted her to feel the least amount of pain possible when he loved her again, which he most certainly would do this morning, maybe more than once before they dressed and went back to the main house for breakfast. After that he intended to come right back here with her and spend the rest of the day in bed.

"Will," she whispered. "What is this you do to me?"

He kissed her other breast as he moved his finger in a circular motion. He felt her legs opening for him. "Just making love to you, *mi esposa*," he answered. "*Te quiero mucho*."

"Oh, Will . . ."

He covered her mouth in a sweet kiss, telling himself to be patient. If he could stir her to another climax before he moved inside her, it would help her relax. He wanted so much for her to enjoy it more this time. He slipped a finger inside her, and she gasped with delight. He returned to stroking the hard crown of her love nest until finally she shuddered, crying out softly. She reached around his neck and kissed him wildly, grasping his hair and begging him to make love to her again, to come inside her again.

He gladly obliged.

Santana never knew she could be stirred to near-painful ecstasy by being touched the way Will had touched her. He made her feel wild and wanton, bold and beautiful. He made her want to open herself to him, to envelop his hard shaft deep inside of her and make sure he never wanted to do this with any other woman. To her utter delight, it did not hurt as fiercely as it had the night before. This time a milder pain was mixed with a new feeling, a strange hunger to be filled by him, to feel him rubbing inside of her, to please him by meeting his rhythmic movements with her own arching motions, so that she could take every inch of him inside herself.

What a wondrous thing this lovemaking was! But she knew it was only this wonderful when it was with a man she loved and respected. If this were Hugo . . . No! She could not even bear to think of it! She focused on Will's face, on the pleasure she saw there. He closed his eyes then, groaning her name as he thrust hard. She felt his life spilling into her, and she knew that it was true that this act of love became more and more pleasurable after the initial pain was gone.

"Please do not stop," she whispered. "It feels so good this time."

He kissed her hair. "Just give me a minute."

They lay still, and within minutes Santana could feel him growing hard inside of her again. He raised up to his knees and looked down at her naked body, rubbing her slender thighs. Grasping her bottom, he brought her up to him and thrust himself hard and deep, glorying in the way she offered herself to him so boldly, her eyes closed in rapture as she held onto his forearms.

Again he released himself, and this time he felt almost weak from the sheer ecstasy of his first morning with his new wife. He kissed her gently, then rolled onto his back. "We should clean up and dress and go eat some breakfast. Some of your guests are leaving today. We should be there to thank them and tell them good-bye."

"I agree." Santana rolled up onto one elbow and looked down at him, her hair brushing across his chest. "But we will come back here afterward, no?"

Will grinned. "We will come back here, yes." He reached up and grasped some of her hair, fingering it. "In my whole life I have never awakened feeling this happy."

She smiled. "Nor have I. We truly belong to each other now . . . forever."

"We truly do. Right now I don't know if I'll ever be able to get enough of you."

"Nor I you."

He sat up and kissed her. The kiss deepened, and it was understood that they must make love again before rising. It was too warm and sweet and wonderful, wrapped together in the satin sheets. He rolled her onto her back, and this time there was no foreplay. She opened to him, and he buried himself inside her yet again. Will had never known the pleasure of taking a virgin, and he wondered how he was ever going to make himself go back to work, for it would mean leaving her for several days at a time. If he didn't need the mills to make his fortune and to give her all she deserved, he would give up his dream and spend the rest of his life right there in her bed.

He smothered her with kisses, moving in quick, pounding rhythm so that she cried out his name over and over in her own glorious fulfillment. Again she brought the life forth from him, and he wondered if he had already made her pregnant.

"This time we really do have to wash and dress," he said, rolling away from her.

"I agree."

They looked at each other and laughed, then Will rose and prepared the water. They quickly washed and put on clean clothes. Before they left the room, Santana glanced at the bed, noticing blood and remnants of lovemaking on the satin sheets. She blushed. "Oh, Will!"

He just grinned. "It happens." He tossed the quilt over the end of the bed, then pulled off the sheets and rolled them into a ball. "Delores will think nothing of it. I will tell her to please come over and change the bedding. Don't worry about it." He dropped the sheets in a corner and drew her close. "Are you all right?"

She slid her arms around his waist. "I have never been happier."

"You have a special glow today. You're going to be teased, you know."

"I know. I do not mind. I am proud to be the wife of William Glenn Lassater."

"And I am proud to be your husband."

He kept an arm around her as he led her outside and to the main house. A few people had gathered around a table of fresh breakfast food, and the air was full of the smell of frying sausages and fresh coffee. As predicted, they were greeted with hugs and jokes about how they were feeling. "So, you stop making love just long enough to eat, huh?" Hernando said, winking. He and Teresa and the children were sitting at a table, eating.

"I'll eat fast," Will joked.

Several people laughed, and Will put a few sausages on a plate. Almost instinctively, he looked toward the steep hills to the north, where, several miles distant, his mills were located. His smile faded as he thought he saw smoke in the vicinity of his logging camp. "Jesus," he muttered. He squinted, looking harder, praying.

Santana saw his expression and she turned to look. "Fire!" she cried.

A forest fire was something everyone in California dreaded, and it was quite windy that day. Even worse, the wind was coming in from the west, which would mean that if there was a fire up in the hills, it would be pushed deeper and deeper into the forest. It could burn for days and take millions of acres with it, including both of Will's mills.

Will threw down his plate. "Get my horse!" he shouted.

"Will, it's too dangerous!" Santana shouted, grabbing his arm.

"That could be my mill burning! Noel's home is up there! All those men!" He charged past her toward the stables, as word of the fire swept through the crowd. A few other men who lived east of where they saw the smoke also began looking for their horses, some hitching buggies. There was a general commotion as women herded their children together, and men shouted orders. Dominic had just come out of the house, and he made the sign of the cross when he saw the smoke.

At the stables Santana begged Will not to get too close to the fires. By then Noel and Derek had joined him. Santana knew about California forest fires, knew that often people were killed, thinking they could outrun the conflagration, but Will would not listen. He quickly saddled his horse and mounted up.

"Take me with you!" she begged.

"I can't. I may be too busy to keep track of you. You stay here with your father. And keep Noel's wife company. She'll be worried too. Thank God they hadn't already gone back."

"Will!" She grasped his leg, tears in her eyes. "I love you! I will pray it is not the mill. Please be careful, Will. Do not try to fight it. You cannot stop these fires! I do not want to lose my husband after only one day!"

Her tears tore at Will's heart. What a hell of a way to start a marriage. He'd had plans of doing nothing that day but lying in bed with his new wife. "I'll be back. It will be all right." He reached down and touched her hair, then rode off, followed by Noel and Derek and a few more men from the mill who had still been at the ranch celebrating the wedding.

"Will," Santana whispered, choking back tears. "Please, sweet Mary, Mother of God, protect him."

Thirteen

Will, Noel, and the others rode through the night, but once they reached the deeper forest, it was impossible to see any fire farther ahead because of the density of the trees. In spite of undergrowth and the dangers of running into branches and trees, they made their way through the night, mostly walking the horses. Will felt crazy with the need to reach the mill, but with stopping to rest the horses, it would still be more than a full day's ride, even if they rode at a breakneck pace and didn't stop to sleep.

By late afternoon the next day they reached the house Will was building for himself and Santana. His heart sank when he saw it was burned to the ground, only the stucco walls still standing. He had deliberately cut a clearing around the house to help save it in case of a forest fire, and he frowned at the realization that only the house was burned, not the trees around it. A deep, ugly suspicion began to form.

"The rest of you men ride on," he ordered. "There's still fire farther up near the mill. They'll need your help. Noel and I will catch up."

The men obeyed. "We'll do all we can, Will," Derek told him before riding off with the others.

Will dismounted. He walked around the burned ruins of his home before looking at Noel, who was still on his horse. "Something's not right about this," he said. "No forest fire jumps this far. I don't see a burned tree anywhere near."

Noel looked around. "Real suspicious, all right."

Will closed his eyes, feeling sick. "I can't look at this right now. Not after spending my first night with my new wife, promising her I'd bring her here soon. Let's go see what's happened at the mill."

He mounted up again and urged his horse forward, the smell of smoke and burned wood strong in his nostrils. Still, he saw no fire in the immediate area. He stopped for a moment, watching the sway of the tops of the trees.

"The wind has changed. Maybe that's a blessing."

"Going back to the west, out to sea," Noel said.

They rode on, men and horses weary from their long, hard ride. They had pushed the horses nearly to their limit, and Will felt bad about it, for he rode one of Dominic's finest Palominos. It was nearly another day's ride to the mill, and Will wondered how it was that none of the forest between there and his new home was burned. They rode into the night, catching up with the other men, who had stopped to rest. By early afternoon the next day they finally reached the clearing that led to the mill. To Will's relief, he saw no damage to the immediate area, but a wide strip of trees to the west of the mill were burned black, their branches sticking out like skeletons of the woods. A few men were still running about with buckets, dousing buildings, all of them black from smoke and looking weary.

"Boss!" one of them shouted. Will spotted one of his buckers, Shelby Seward, a middle-aged man with big shoulders and a huge belly. He had a thick beard that revealed almost nothing of his face but his nose and eyes. "We got lucky. She swept right up from the coast, almost reached the pond and the mill, and then, like a miracle, the wind changed, just like God bent right down and blew it the other way! Saved the cuttin' site and the roughin' mill. It turned late yesterday. We wondered if you could see the smoke from the Alcala ranch."

Will rubbed wearily at his eyes. "I saw it."

"What about my place?" Noel asked anxiously. His house was situated between the roughing mill there in the hills and the finishing mill on the coast.

Shelby frowned and shook his head. "I'm afraid your house is gone, Mr. Gray."

"Damn!" Will swore. "I'm sorry, Noel. I'll see that new accommodations are built right away, and I'll pay you extra for new clothing and furniture. Thank God your family was down at the ranch." He turned to Shelby. "Where did the fire start? There haven't been any storms, and all of you men know better than to be careless with your smokes."

Noel dismounted. "This whole thing stinks of arson, Will, and we both know who might have done it. You think about it. I'm going to head down to the finishing mill to check the damage, check my house."

He turned and walked away, and Will also dismounted. He asked one of the other men to take care of the horses, brush them down and water them. He turned to Shelby. "What do you think, Shelby? Was it set?"

Shelby fingered his beard. "Well, sir, it looks real suspicious. Started at the finishin' mill. 'Course you know how fast a fire moves through somethin' like that, all that wood dust and wood chips and such. The wind was just right. If it was set, whoever did it must have figured the wind would carry the flames right up the mountain to this mill and then the logging site. If it had, we would have lost all our buildings, the homes of the men who have families, all the valuable trees in this area, everything. It was pretty well planned, I'd say, except whoever did it didn't plan on the wind suddenly shiftin' like that."

Will put his hands on his hips, looking around. "Be honest with me, Shelby. Is there somebody among these men who has a grudge against me for something? Maybe thinks he's not being paid enough? Maybe somebody I fired?"

"I don't know of any of the men havin' any beef against you, sir. Far as them you fired, I've never seen any of them come back around here. 'Course anybody can sneak in of a night, I suppose. Whoever it was probably came up from along the shore durin' the night, set the fire in early morning. It had to be somebody who knew we were shut down and there wouldn't be a lot of men around."

Will looked toward the burned trees that led for three miles down to the shore. "Whoever it was snuck farther in and burned the home I was building for my wife."

"I'm sorry, sir. We didn't even know about that."

Will's jaw flexed in anger. "That only proves to me that it was deliberate, aimed directly at me. I have a damn good suspicion who was behind it." His hands clenched into fists, and he began to pace. "Hugo Bolivar. I should have killed him when I had the chance!"

"He's the man you fought with in order to marry Señorita Lopez, ain't he?"

Will threw his head back and breathed deeply. "The same. He wouldn't come here and do it himself, but there are plenty of men who would take the kind of money he can pay them to do it."

"I'm real sorry, Mr. Lassater. I know this'll set you back."

Will turned away. "Is the finishing mill completely destroyed?"

"I ain't been down there. I was too busy up here tryin' to keep buildings watered down until the wind changed. Them that came up from down there say it's gone. The building itself can be rebuilt in no time, and we can rebuild the flumes, but how long do you figure it will take to get new equipment?"

Will stooped down and picked up a piece of wood. "I'm not sure. I wrote my brother months ago to buy more of everything I need and ship it to me. My plan was to start up a second mill site. Now I'll just have to use some of it to rebuild the finishing mill. I'll go to San Francisco and talk to the man I contracted with to store my equipment. I'll have to warn him to take extra precautions. If Bolivar did this, he might try to burn down the man's warehouse once he knows my equipment is there. I just hope it arrives soon so I can get fully back into business."

He turned to look at Shelby. "Whoever did this figured this mill would burn, too, but by the grace of God it didn't, and I'm still in business! We'll do what we can right here, do some finishing work. It won't be easy, but it'll be enough to keep things going, and we can stockpile our shingle bolts. Some of the lumber can be cut by handsaw. I'll pay men extra to do it."

Shelby nodded. "They'll do it, Mr. Lassater. We'll all help keep you on your feet. Them that's been workin' on your new house, they can clean up there and start rebuildin'."

"No. I picked a place that's too remote. Santana will be there alone a lot. I wanted her closer, but after this . . . She's got to be closer to the family's main house where ranch hands can keep an eye on things. She won't like being so far away, but it's safer." With a violent motion Will flung the piece of wood he'd picked up. It landed far away in the pond. "That son of a bitch is going to pay for this! I've got to do something to let him know he'd better not ever try something like this again." He looked at Shelby. "I think I'll pay Don Bolivar a little visit when I go back to San Francisco to talk to my buyers."

From the look of fiery anger in his bloodshot eyes, Shelby was glad he was not the one Will Lassater was angry with. "You watch yourself, Mr. Lassater. That Bolivar, I've heard of him, mighty rich and powerful. You don't even know for sure he did this."

Will put his hands on his hips, pacing again, feeling the strong urge to hit someone. "If it weren't for the fact that my house was burned, I wouldn't be so sure myself. But that was a deliberate slap in the face. That house is something Santana and I would have shared together." He walked closer to Shelby. "I'm not afraid of Hugo Bolivar. I never have been and never will be. He's going to find out his little plan didn't work, because God is on *my* side, and I've still got my mill and my main camp. When I'm through with him, he's the one who will be shaking in his shiny black boots. You can bet on it!"

Shelby swallowed. "Yes, sir, I reckon maybe I can."

Will sighed, running a hand through his hair. "Get me a fresh horse, will you? I'm going to gather the men and have a talk, explain the situation. Noel can stay here and get things running again. Apparently we're going to have to post some guards at night." He rubbed at his tired eyes. "I'm going back to my wife. I don't relish telling her about our new home being burned."

"It's a real shame, Mr. Lassater, but at least you weren't all moved in. You didn't lose furniture and personals, or your lives."

Will's nostrils were beginning to burn from the strong smell of smoke and charred wood. "I guess I should be glad for that much." How he wished Hugo Bolivar were standing in front of him that minute. He'd wrap his hands around the man's skinny throat and squeeze until Hugo's dark, evil eyes bulged right out of his head! The worst part of this would be telling Santana, especially when he had to tell her she would have to live so far from the mill. He didn't relish only seeing her every six or seven days, but that was the way it would have to be, at least for a while.

He left Shelby to walk around the pond and several hundred yards farther on, to where the fire had turned back on itself. God was surely with him, for it was a miracle that the wind had changed. He looked up at the charred trees, and a hawk flew overhead. Suddenly he remembered the box full of ashes that his mother had given him. He still had it, kept it sitting in a windowsill in his cabin. He realized he had never shown it to Santana or told her of its origin. There were a lot of things she still didn't know about him. They were lovers, friends, husband and wife, yet in some ways still strangers. But one thing he knew for certain. Santana had the strength to help him through this.

He thought about what his mother had told him that his father had said. "From these ashes will come something better than we had before."

Will knelt down and scooped up a handful of blackened wood chips. "You're damn right, Dad," he muttered. "And I have a good woman to help me do it, just like you did."

Hernando left the table to answer a knock at the door, and Santana, who had been eating lunch with her brother and Teresa at their home, waited anxiously, hoping it was someone with news about Will. She didn't have much of an appetite, for her stomach was too upset from worrying. The day Will rode off, she and everyone else had noticed a shift in the wind several hours later, and had stared at the distant smoke for hours until it finally dissipated. None of them, though, had any way of knowing for sure if the fire was at the mill.

Santana waited, hearing voices at the door, and Hernando finally came back to the dining room. "That was Frederique, the stable cleaner. He ran here to tell you Will just rode in."

Santana breathed a sigh of relief. "Go to the main house and tell Father. I am going to the stables!" She ran out, her heart pounding. Was he all right? Had the mill burned? This was the fourth day since he had left, and oh, how she had missed him! She lifted her skirts and ran, and by the time she reached the stables, Will was already leaving them. She stopped, seeing how tired he looked, knowing by his eyes something dreadful had happened. Still, she could also tell that he was as glad to see her as she was to see him.

"Will!" She ran to him, and he enveloped her in his arms, gripping her almost desperately.

"The finishing mill is gone," he said, "but the wind changed by some miracle and the main camp didn't burn."

"It was my prayers," she answered. "After you left I went to the chapel and I prayed so hard, *carino mio.*" She kissed his cheek. "I am so glad you are all right."

He grasped her arms, pushing her away slightly and studying her, agony in his eyes. "Our new home burned. I'm sorry, Santana."

"Our home! But how? It is far from the campsite, and on the east side . . ."

"It was pretty damn obvious to me that it was deliberately set. Not just the house, but the mill fire too. Whoever set the fire at the finishing mill figured the wind would carry the flames all the way up to the main camp and the roughing mill, probably the cutting site as well. The wind saved us, but someone came on farther in and set the house on fire. There's no doubt in my mind that whoever it was, he was paid by Hugo Bolivar."

Santana's eyes widened in horror, and she stepped back from him, aching at the sight of her weary husband, who clearly had not slept much since he'd left. "Surely he wouldn't—"

"You know that he would, Santana. I can't prove it, but it all makes sense, the fire starting right after we marry, our new home burning." He shook his head. "I don't think we should rebuild there, Santana. It's too remote, too dangerous for you. We'll build closer to the main ranch."

"No, *mi esposo!* I would not see you for days at a time." She touched his chest. "Please do not decide this yet. We can talk about it."

Will sighed, too tired to argue. "Go on to the guest house and have Louisa prepare a bath for me, will you? I'm going to discuss this with your father and Hernando, see if they feel as I do that Bolivar could have done this, see what they think about where we should build."

He kissed her forehead and walked toward the main house. Santana felt her heart would break into a million pieces at the thought of being so far from her beloved, for that was how she thought of Will now. That first night and morning with him had been like a beautiful dream. She had felt so happy, so fulfilled. He had been as kind and tender as she had hoped, and she could not think of any man, Spanish or *gringo*, who would be a better husband.

"Hugo!" she muttered venomously. She stormed on to the guest house. How she hated him! She would not let him keep her and Will apart by forcing her to have to live closer to home. He would not spoil the wonderful, beautiful thing she had found with Will Lassater, and soon Hugo would discover he had not destroyed the mill after all! He could not stop a man like Will, and neither would he stop her own resolve to live closer to the mill so she could be with her husband.

She went inside and asked Louisa to prepare a bath for Will. The woman quickly began heating water on the large wood-burning cookstove in the kitchen. Coals that remained from heating water for Santana's own bath earlier were still hot. Louisa added more wood to the fire, and Santana went into the bedroom to lay out some clean clothes for Will. After setting out the copper bathtub, she checked that there was soap on the washstand, then took a clean towel from a dresser drawer and laid it on the stand. She turned to stare thoughtfully at the big mahogany bed where Will Lassater had made her a woman. She had slept alone in that bed the last three nights, and although she had slept alone all her life, she had felt lost and lonely. One night with Will beside her was all she'd needed to know she wanted him close every night.

She sat down on the bed and waited for what seemed forever. Finally Will came into the house. She heard him telling Louisa he would help her carry the water, and moments later he walked into the bedroom and poured two buckets into the tub. Louisa followed with another bucket. Will glanced at Santana, and she knew by his expression that her father and Hernando had agreed she should be closer to home. She wished she knew more about men, how to argue with a husband, convince him . . .

It came to her then. She said nothing as Louisa walked in with yet another bucket of hot water. The kitchen stove was big enough to hold six metal buckets, and it took all six to fill the tub, plus a couple of extra buckets to cool the water so that it was not too hot. As Will left to bring in the last two buckets of hot water, Santana quickly twisted her hair onto the top of her head and shoved in a couple of combs to hold it up.

Will returned with the last buckets, and Louisa walked

in behind him with the cold water. "I will set these beside the tub, senor," she said. "You may not need them. The heated water was not quite as hot as it should be." She turned and left, and Santana got up from the bed and followed her out, grabbing her arm.

"Whatever you do, don't come back into the bedroom," she whispered.

Louisa smiled, then giggled, and hurried to the kitchen. Santana went back into the bedroom to see Will was already stripped down to his underwear. She closed and bolted the door. His back was to her when he removed his underwear, then he stepped into the tub and slid down until the water met his chin.

"This is just right," he said, realizing Santana was in the room. "My God, I'm so damn tired."

"I can understand," she said, walking closer. She began unbuttoning her dress.

"What are you doing?"

"I am getting into the tub with you."

Will frowned, but the look of weariness and defeat in his eyes turned to desire as he watched her shed her clothes. "Santana, I'm too tired and upset to be a husband to you right now. And we have a lot to talk about."

"*Si*, we most certainly do, *mi esposo*." It felt strange to undress in front of a man in the daylight, but it was also exhilarating. She knew by his expression that Will liked what he saw, and she intended to remind him of what he would be missing if they lived far apart. She climbed into the tub. "Let me bathe you, *carino mio*."

"Santana . . ."

She leaned forward and let her breasts brush against his chest, then met his mouth in a suggestive kiss. "Do not speak," she said. She took the bar of soap and wet it, then began soaping his face and neck, shoulders and arms. "Later I will shave you," she told him. She rinsed his face and neck, then soaped her hands again and slid them down his body. She smiled with pleasure when she found that part of him that had made her feel such wondrous ecstasy. Her touch quickly brought the swelling hardness she had hoped for. She sat closer, spreading her legs on either side of him, and carefully eased herself down, burying his shaft inside of her. Will groaned her name as she moved up and down slowly, trying not to splash water out of the tub.

In only minutes she felt his life surge into her, and she smiled with delight at how easily she could stir her husband into making love. She straightened, still straddled over him. Taking his hands, she placed them on her breasts. "To make me live here, *mi esposo*, is to wait many days at a time to do this again. That is how it will have to be for now, until our new home is rebuilt, but I will not let it be like this forever. We will build exactly where we intended to build, so that we can be together. I will have Louisa with me, and we will hire a cook and a housekeeper, and we can hire men to watch the house. We will build stables so that I can have Estrella with me, and so that I can raise other horses, and I will often ride to the mill site to lunch with you."

"Santana—"

"I will not listen to any more talk about building anyplace else. To do so would be to let Hugo accomplish what he meant to accomplish—make it difficult for us to be together. Do you wish to let him win this time?"

Will studied her determined expression, then let his gaze fall to drink in the splendor of her nakedness, her slender body straddled over his own, her full breasts so firm and inviting, their brown nipples hard from excitement. How could he go for several nights at a time without his wife in his bed? Of course he could hire guards, and with a personal maid and a cook there, she would not really be alone. And she was right. He could not let Bolivar win this one. Bolivar . . . The thought of the man trying to spoil his happiness with Santana, the thought of him almost having this beauty for his own wife, stirred in Will a renewed determination not to let Bolivar spoil what he had found with Santana. "Let's get out of here and dry off," he said to Santana.

She moved off him, and they both washed themselves. After she got out of the tub, Santana ran to the dresser to get another towel for herself, while Will dried off with the one she had left on the washstand.

Will watched her bend over to get the towel, fire ripping through him at the sight of her firm bottom. He walked up behind her, took the towel from her, and rubbed it over her breasts. Turning her, he drew the towel down over her body, her belly, her bottom, her thighs and legs, then back up, pushing the towel between her thighs. He left his hand there and knelt, kissing the damp hairs between her legs.

Santana grasped his hair, whispering his name. This was something new, something she had never dreamed of letting a man do. He remained on his knees, gently parting her with his thumbs. She groaned and spread her legs, whimpering his name as his tongue caressed secret places, igniting a fire in her as hot and wild as the fires that sometimes raged through California's forests. She felt the wonderful, pulsating ecstasy he had brought out in her that first night when he toyed with the same spot with his fingers, only this time what he was doing was even more intimate. Somewhere deep inside she told herself she should feel ashamed, yet she did not. This was Will. This was her husband. He had a right to take his pleasure in whatever way he chose, and when it brought her this much pleasure in return, where was the wrong?

She cried out with an aching climax, and in the next moment Will was laying her back on the bed. They did not even bother to pull the quilt away. He entered her almost violently, his shaft hard and hot. He smothered her with kisses, and she could taste her own sweetness on his lips.

For Will, this was strangely like a victory over Hugo. Yes, this woman belonged to him. No other man had been this intimate with her, nor would any other man ever touch her this way, certainly not Hugo Bolivar! The thought of it brought out a fiery possessiveness that caused him to thrust in fast rhythm, making sure she knew to whom she belonged.

He wanted the lovemaking to last forever, but finally he could hold back no longer. He grasped her hips and raised up to his knees, gritting his teeth and burying himself deep, groaning as his release came almost painfully. He finally relaxed and stretched out beside her, pulling her against him so that her head rested on his shoulder.

"I'm so sorry about the house, Santana," he said when his breathing had slowed, his heartbeat returned to normal.

"It does not matter, as long as we can rebuild in the same place. Please say that you will." She toyed with the hairs on his chest as she leaned back to look at him. "I do not want to be apart from you."

"I suppose you think you have tricked me into making a decision."

She smiled. "Perhaps."

He kissed her forehead. "Well, it worked. You're a witch, Santana, a woman of magical powers. You have a way of affecting my mind so that I can't think logically."

She touched his lips with her fingers. "Nothing will happen. Whoever did it would be a fool to try it again."

Will's sensual ecstasy faded at the thought of Bolivar trying to burn him out and destroy him. "Yes, he would be a fool. And I intend to make sure he understands that."

Santana lost her smile, raising up on one elbow. "What do you mean?"

Will touched her face. "Don't worry about it. You just think about how you want to furnish our new home and start ordering things. I have to go to San Francisco to talk to some of my buyers and see if by some miracle the extra equipment I ordered from my brother has come in yet."

She frowned. "You will go to see Hugo, won't you?" She shook her head. "Please do not do that, Will."

He left the bed and walked over to the tub to wash himself. "That is one area over which you truly have no control, my love." He returned to the bed and pulled back the covers, crawling under them. "Right now I am going to sleep. We'll spend one more night together, then I have to leave for San Francisco. I have a lot to do, Santana. We won't see much of each other for the next several weeks, but when the house is finished and I have things straightened up at the mill, we can get around to living a halfway-normal married life." He kissed her cheek before settling down into bed. "I'm sorry it has to be this way, but I intend to make sure this never happens again."

He turned over and closed his eyes, and Santana knew he was too tired to get into an argument about it now. In fact, she supposed she could do nothing to stop him. His feelings about Hugo were not something she could trick him out of, as she had managed to change his mind about her having to live close to her father. He would take care of Hugo in his own way, and there was nothing she could do but pray for him. She could only hope this was the last trouble Hugo Bolivar would give them.

Hugo raised his wine glass to toast the several San Francisco businessmen and their wives who had joined him for dinner and to talk about investing in a railroad being discussed in Congress. "Some say it would be impossible to build a railroad all the way from the East to our beautiful state of California," he said. "But we all know what such a railroad would do for us. Our city would grow beyond our wildest dreams. If we make plans now, gentlemen, we could all end up much richer than we already are."

"I fully agree," one of the others said, raising his own wineglass.

They all toasted the railroad and their host. Hugo smiled, knowing that most of the men did not like him, but were eager to socialize and do business with him because of his money and power.

"I don't believe it's possible," said another. "I think that sometimes our Hugo has some rather farfetched ideas, but if it does happen, I don't want to be left out."

They all laughed.

"You will not be left out, *mi amigo*," Hugo said. "All you need to do is promise your investment. I will speak with the railroad representatives when they—"

His words were interrupted by shouts, someone yelling, "You can't go in there!" In the next moment Will Lassater barged into the elegant dining room, his eyes blazing, his complexion dark with rage. Everyone turned to stare, and when one of Hugo's butlers tried to grab his arm, Will turned, yanking a hatchet out of his belt and waving it at the man.

"Get the hell out of here!" he growled.

The wide-eyed butler turned and ran, and Will headed toward Hugo, hatchet in hand. Women gasped, and one screamed when Will suddenly flung the hatchet. It narrowly missed Hugo's head and landed in the ornately carved wooden mantle behind him.

"My God!" one man exclaimed. They all stepped back when Will reached Hugo, who stood there looking terrified and frozen in place. He dropped his wineglass as Will grabbed him around the throat and shoved him backward, knocking over his dining chair. He practically carried

Hugo by the neck with one hand as he forced him to the fireplace and pressed his back against its stones.

"You set those fires, didn't you!"

"What—what fires?" Hugo stammered. "I do not know—"

"You know damn well what I'm talking about!" Will ripped the hatchet from the mantle and laid it against Hugo's nose and forehead, his powerful hand still against Hugo's throat in a viselike grip. "Don't forget that I have every right to kill you." He flicked the razor-sharp edge of the hatchet just enough to nick the skin and draw blood on Hugo's forehead. The man whimpered, sweat breaking out on his brow, his eyes wide with terror. "You mess with me or Santana one more time, you arrogant bastard, and I'll not hesitate to put this blade right through your skull!" He grabbed Hugo's shirt and jerked him forward, pulling downward so that he sank to his knees. Blood ran down his face and onto his white shirt, and Hugo lifted a shaking hand to his wound.

Will turned to the others. "Sorry to interrupt your dinner, ladies and gentlemen, but if you're looking to do business with this man, you'd better think twice about it. He's a liar and a cheat, a coward and a back-shooter. He shot me in the back in a duel, before we reached the count to turn and fire. I spared his life, but apparently he didn't appreciate it. He hired someone to set fire to my logging mill and the new home I was building for myself and my wife. I can't prove it, but I know he did it. Hugo Bolivar is no man of honor and not a man to be trusted." He turned to Hugo. "And if he ever gives me trouble again, he'll be a *dead* man, even if I have to hang for it!"

He turned and walked out, and everyone looked at one another, embarrassed for Hugo but also suddenly ashamed to be his guest. "Who was that?" someone asked.

"Will Lassater," one man answered quietly. "He's

building a lumber mill up north of here. I've been buying lumber from him myself for my construction business. Seems like a pretty good man, been in the business all his life. I read in a newspaper a few days ago that he married Santana Lopez."

No one else spoke. They all just stood there awkwardly, not sure what to do. Hugo managed to get to his feet and walk to the table, his face and hand covered with blood. Several of the women looked away. Hugo knew many women were already repulsed by the scar on his head and his partially severed left ear, courtesy of Will Lassater. He picked up a linen napkin and held it to his forehead.

"You may all . . . leave," he said weakly. "I will understand."

Several of the men cleared their throats, all thinking the same thing as they helped their wives with their capes and found their top hats. It had been rumored that Hugo Bolivar had shot a man in the back in a duel over Hugo's then fiancée, Santana Lopez. Apparently, the rumors were true. Now there had been a fire at Lassater's lumber mill. If Hugo had had the fires set, how could the man be trusted?

"Listen, Hugo," said the man who knew Will, "we'll look into this railroad thing ourselves. There's plenty of time. Word is Congress is more concerned with growing trouble with the South over tariffs and such than with putting out money to build a railroad."

Hugo could feel the change in the air. The women whispered among themselves; the men appeared embarrassed and uncomfortable. By this one act, Will Lassater had gone a long way in destroying his business associations in San Francisco. It would take months, maybe even years, to regain the trust of many of these men. His guests left rather silently, and he stood there alone at the head of the elegantly set dining table. He took the blood-soaked napkin from his forehead and stared at it, still shaken over the feel of the big blade nicking his skin. He gritted his teeth, literally growling with rage.

"Someday," he swore. "Someday . . . Will Lassater and my sweet bitch, Santana, I will find a way to repay you both! I *will* find a way, and Santana, my little slut, you will wish you had married me after all!"

Part Two

Fourteen

MAY 1857 . . .

Will rode as fast as possible, worried he might already be too late for the birth of his first child. He was even more worried that something could happen to Santana. She had not carried the baby well, had started bleeding a month too soon and was forced to lie in bed these last four weeks. He had asked Marcus Enders to stay close the past month, putting him up in a small guest house he had built near his and Santana's new home. He just hoped the man was sober today. Enders was a good physician when he wasn't drinking. Will couldn't completely blame the man for drinking the way he did. He had never gotten over the fact that he hadn't been able to save his own wife, and Will supposed that if that happened to him, he might drink his life away too.

He had grown to love Santana much more deeply than he had thought possible. She was attentive, giving, a good helpmate, and smarter and better-schooled than he had realized when he married her. She had made a point to get involved in the lumber business, to learn how it operated, and had even begun helping him keep his books. It had upset her the past month that she couldn't get out of bed, but a child was more important than the business, and now the baby was finally coming. A messenger had come to get him that morning, having ridden all night. Now it was nightfall again. The baby had probably already been born.

He wasn't far from home now, and he did not intend to stop until he got there, even if it meant riding his horse until it dropped. He prayed all had gone well, and wished he had come home a few days earlier, as he'd originally planned. A breakdown of the steam engines that ran his band saws had created big problems with a backup of work, though, and there had been an accident up at the cutting site, a man badly injured.

The logging camp had grown into a small city, with the saloons and whores that naturally appeared in places where there were a lot of well-paid single men. Will knew Santana was very jealous of the way some of the prostitutes looked at him. "You are a rich and handsome gringo," she would say. "They want to know what you are like in bed. I can see it in their eyes, but you belong to Santana Maria Chavez de Lassater!" Yes, he belonged to her, and gladly. There wasn't a woman in that camp who could please him the way Santana did. The beautiful young woman he had married had blossomed into the best wife a man could ask for, and now she would be a mother.

He finally reached the house, a sprawling stucco home fashioned after the Alcala house. It was built exactly where they had originally planned, high on a hill that overlooked the valley far below. On a clear day they could see the Alcala spread several miles south of them. Besides the house itself, they had built stables, a guest house, and several other outbuildings. Santana insisted on having a number of horses, and Will knew she'd be eager to go riding again, now that the baby had been born.

He guided his horse around a rose garden to the front of the house, where he quickly dismounted and tied the animal to a hitching post. At Santana's insistence, the post was made from some of the burned wood from the fire that had destroyed the original house. To her it was a way of saying that nothing was going to stop them. He gave a passing thought to Bolivar, glad that there had been no more trouble from the man. Perhaps there never would be.

At the door Will stopped to brush remaining sawdust from his shirt and hair, wishing he'd had time to clean up a little. He was sweaty from the hard ride, and still wore his heavy work boots and cotton pants and shirt. He hurried inside the house, where the new cook, a heavyset, aging widow named Anna Martinez, greeted him anxiously. "She is very weak, Senor Lassater. She was in labor much too long. She keeps asking for you."

"The baby?"

"A healthy son, senor."

Will closed his eyes and said a quick prayer of thanksgiving. He hurried to the bedroom, one of four. He and Santana had dreamed of filling all three other bedrooms, perhaps even having to add more someday. Right now, though, he wasn't sure he wanted her or himself to go through this more than once. Knowing what she must have suffered made him feel guilty for making her pregnant. How strange that something so exotically pleasurable could lead to so much agony. It didn't seem fair that only the woman should suffer labor. He should be suffering some kind of pain too.

The housemaid they had hired, Ester James, met him at the door. "Mr. Lassater! You're here at last. The child was slow in coming, but he is a healthy boy. Dr. Enders is still with your wife." She patted his arm. She was an older woman whose children were already grown. Her husband, Harold, worked at the logging camp, and Will had built a small cabin near the main house where Ester and Harold could stay when Harold came to see her. "I think she will be fine now."

Will entered the room and stared at Santana, startled at how gray she looked. Her hair was stuck to her head from sweat. He felt awkward and helpless, wondering if Santana hated him for what she had suffered. Dr. Enders was washing his hands, and Santana lay quiet, looking too still, too ashen. When she opened her eyes and saw him, though, she managed a smile.

"Will," she whispered.

Enders turned to look at him. "At last you're here. The baby is fine, but Santana is pretty weak."

Will blinked, wondering when he would wake up from this strange dream. He walked over to kneel beside Santana, taking her hand. She looked at him with eyes that showed the struggle she had just endured. "It is a boy, a son for my Will."

He squeezed her hand. "Thank you, *carina mia*. I'm so proud, but I'm also so sorry I wasn't here."

"It is all right. He came . . . a little sooner than . . . we expected. I would like to call him Glenn . . . your second name . . . and Fernando, for my father's second name. Glenn Fernando Lassater Chavez. He must . . . have two last names . . . the Spanish way . . . his father's and . . . his mother's. All our children must be . . . named so . . . to show they are legal . . . children of honor."

Will grinned as he stroked a few strands of her damp hair away from her face. "You and your long names." He kissed her cheek. "Call him whatever you want. You're the one who went through hell bringing him into this world."

Santana swallowed, licking her dry lips. "We name our children . . . this way . . . so that not just the father's name is honored . . . but also the mother's."

"And I fully agree that's how it should be." He looked at Dr. Enders. "Are you sure she's going to be all right?"

"Yes. Why don't you go take a look at your son and let her rest?"

Will nodded, still feeling stunned. "Thanks, doctor."

The man shrugged. "I guess I'm good for something once in a while."

Their eyes held, and Will could see Enders's pain. He realized how hard it must have been for this man to lose his own wife when he felt he should have done something to save her. Enders nodded toward a cradle, and Will walked over to look at his new son. The boy started crying, healthy squalls coming from a furious little being that probably wanted to go back into the warmth of his mother's womb. Will had thought he could imagine how it would feel to be a father, but this was unlike any feeling he had ever known . . . pride, worship, awe, even a little fear. The boy was dark, like his mother, a shock of thick black hair making him look comical. His eyes were blue, and Will wondered if they would stay that way. Santana had often said that she hoped one of her babies would have his blue eyes.

"There is a letter for you on the dining table, Mr. Lassater," Ester said as she returned to the room. "A rider from the ranch brought it."

Will touched his son's cheek, marveling at its softness, relieved that the child looked so healthy. After telling Santana he would be right back, he walked out of the room to find the letter. It was from Gerald. He quickly opened it, and the first words tore at his heart.

Dear brother

I hate to have to write you with news like this, but our mother passed away . . .

His eyes quickly teared, and he couldn't even read the date. For as long as it would take a letter to get there, his mother had probably been dead for six months already. She had died without his even being aware of it, and he would never see her again.

He forced back the tears and finished the letter. Ruth Lassater had died October 28, 1856. Here it was May of '57. He had gone on all this time not realizing his mother had already left this life. If only he could go back to Maine once more, see the old home, see his mother one last time.

He finished the letter, his son's bawling filling the house. Gerald planned to sell everything and come to California . . . finish the dream. He wanted to invest in a fleet of ships, so they could transport their own lumber to distant ports, eliminating shipping fees and middlemen.

It would be damn good to have Gerald there, to see his brother again, all the family he had left. He hoped Gerald would take the overland route, as he had told him to do when he'd written him after first arriving in California. The voyage by ship was no trip for a woman and children.

He closed his eyes, memories flooding over him—of a loving father and mother, of things he'd done as a boy, of being tucked in at night by a woman with gentle hands and kind words. What a strange day this had been, new life, a new family in a new land; and now the news of his mother's death. Part of him wanted to laugh and rejoice over the birth of his son; another part of him needed to weep. His mother's death seemed to represent the cutting of the last tie to his past, and it hurt. He walked outside and sat down in a wicker chair on the *portico*, letting the tears come, feeling almost like a little boy needing to be held by his mother. But the little boy was a man now, and he had Santana . . . and a new son.

Ester's voice came from the doorway. "Your wife wants you to come back inside and visit with her and your son."

Will nodded without reply, pausing a moment to wipe his eyes. Taking a deep breath, he crunched the letter in his hand and shoved it into his pants pocket. He hurried back into the bedroom, suddenly needing Santana's love more than ever. In spite of her ordeal, she looked beautiful to him now, lying there with little Glenn wrapped in blankets and nestled in the crook of her arm. Everyone left the room so they could be alone, and Santana frowned when she saw his face.

"What is it, _mi esposo?_ There is great sorrow in your eyes."

He sat down on the edge of the bed and reached over to gently hold his son's tiny hand, thinking how big and calloused his looked next to it. "There was a letter waiting for me," he answered. "It's from Gerald." He closed his eyes. "My mother died, more than six months ago."

Santana drew in her breath. "I am so sorry. I know the feeling, but in your case, to be so far away . . ." She turned her head to kiss her baby's hair. "Yet this same day . . . a son is born to you. Life goes on, _carino mio._ Now you are the father instead of the son. You have a son of your own . . . and we both love you."

He smiled through tears, then turned and lay down on the bed beside her and little Glenn. "Thank God for both of you," he said, slipping an arm around them. "And in a few months my brother and his family will be here. Gerald is selling everything and coming to California. If he's coming overland, he's probably on his way right now."

Santana cuddled her baby closer. "Then we must pray for their safety. It will be good for you to be with your brother again."

Will raised up on one elbow, touching her face. "You're a good woman, Santana, and I know you'll be a wonderful mother. You're my family now, but it *will* be good to have Gerald here."

He pulled the baby's blanket away to study the infant, who was sucking on his own fist. "He's beautiful, Santana. This is a wonderful gift." He kissed her lightly. "I don't want you to go through this again too soon. I'd better sleep in a different room at night."

"You will do no such thing," she said. "I do not sleep well when you are not holding me. God will decide when another child comes, not us."

Will settled down beside them again. "We'll talk about it later. Right now I'm just glad you're both all right. You need to rest. We both do."

"*Si*, my love. Sleep with us for a little while . . . and be with those who love you. Through us, your mother is still with you."

The words were comforting. Will fell asleep remembering another life, another world, another time . . . gone forever.

Hugo read the short announcement, brought to his attention by his business partner, Marcos Parales.

BIRTHS: On May 28 a son was born to lumber baron William Lassater and his wife, Santana Maria Chavez de Lassater, daughter of wealthy landowner Dominic Fernando Chavez Alcala . . .

He did not finish the article. He tossed the paper to the floor and walked to a window that looked out over the fast-growing city of San Francisco. Its growth was helping make him richer, but that growth had come because of the

Americanos. Until Will Lassater had arrived, Hugo had always welcomed the *gringos* and their money; but he'd never thought he would lose a woman to one. Will and Santana had been married eighteen months, and still the embarrassment of the loss ate at him. Not just the duel and the shame of his scars, or what Will had done and said in front of his business associates, but also the mere fact that he had stolen Santana. For years he had watched her grow and mature into a deliciously beautiful woman. At night he would dream about how satisfying it would be to break her into womanhood, to own her, to have her on his arm and be the envy of other men. Lassater had destroyed those dreams.

What irked Hugo even more, though, was Lassater's success with his lumber mill. Already he was being called a lumber baron. Hugo sniffed. The man was far from matching his own wealth. Still, Hugo had not been able to discourage others from doing business with him, and secretly, ever since Lassater had disrupted his dinner party and threatened him with that damn hatchet, he had been afraid of Will Lassater.

The bastard! It should have been his own son to whom Santana had given birth, not the *Americano*'s! He still dreamed of getting his revenge on the two of them. He had almost succeeded when he'd had Will's mill and home set a fire, but he dared not try that again. It hadn't stopped the man anyhow. But he had to do something to show Will and Santana that he was not afraid, and to remind them that he was still there, still thought about them.

He grinned. Congratulations! That was what he would do. He would send them a note of congratulations on the birth of their son. It would be a friendly gesture that they could not argue, yet it would irritate Will and make Santana uneasy. They would see the real message, a little reminder that he was still there and still angry. He suspected that would particularly disturb Santana, who had always seemed afraid of him anyway.

He sat down at his desk, taking out a piece of his finest parchment. He dipped a pen in an inkwell and wrote the note neatly.

Permitame ser el primero en felicitarle. "Let me be the first to congratulate you," he repeated aloud, then kept writing, "on the birth of your son. May there be many more. Perhaps one day I will pay you a little visit." He smiled. That was enough to be friendly, but the last remark would unsettle Santana. He would send a gift with the note.

Will sat in the *portico* of his lovely Spanish home. He held six-month-old Glenn on his lap, and as he looked around at potted plants and a statue of the Mother Mary, he wondered if there was anything left of the *gringo* in him. Today was his and Santana's second anniversary, and he had taken the day off. The sad thing was, that was not the only reason he wasn't working. He had lost another man the day before, the sixth death since he had started up three years ago.

From what he heard from lumbermen who came to work for him from camps in Oregon and in Washington territory, his average of two deaths a year was far better than normal, but that did not ease the sorrow he felt each time he lost a man. This one had died horribly. He'd just topped off a tree when for some strange reason the trunk began to split apart. With his rigging rope tied around the entire trunk, when the tree split, the rope pinched him between it and the closest half of the tree, crushing the breath out of him long enough to kill him before the rope finally gave way. The men below had watched helplessly as he'd flailed futilely, pinned against the tree, then had gone limp. They'd buried him late the day before, and as always when a man died, Will had closed the mill for three days.

Most of the men would ease their minds about the death by drinking and whoring, pretending it could not happen to them, yet celebrating life in the wildest way possible, because they knew how close death was to them every day on the job. Will preferred to spend this time quietly with Santana and his son. He turned little Glenn around to face him, and the boy grinned and giggled when he tickled him. He kissed the baby's fat cheek, thinking what a handsome son he had, his hair and skin dark like Santana's, but miraculously, his eyes still blue. Against his dark skin and lashes, the blue was beautifully enhanced. He was going to be a handsome young man someday, Will was certain. With a mother like Santana, all his children would surely be beautiful.

His thoughts were interrupted when he saw a covered wagon approaching, lumbering up the roadway that led to their home. It was pulled by four oxen, and someone walked alongside them, driving them with a stick. He recognized one of Dominic's men riding ahead of the wagon, and watched as the man pointed toward the house. The man driving the oxen waved the stick.

"Hello, brother!" he shouted.

Will rose and walked out of the *portico*, staring, hardly able to believe his eyes. "Santana!" he called. "Come and get Glenn! I think my brother is here!"

Santana left the kitchen, where she had been directing the preparation of a special meal for their anniversary. "Are you sure?" she asked as she stepped onto the *portico*.

Without reply, Will shoved Glenn into her arms and ran out of the gardens and down the road leading to the house. Santana watched as the man driving the oxen handed his stick to a woman sitting in the wagon seat. He headed for Will, and in the next moment the two men embraced, laughing, hugging. Santana blinked back the tears in her eyes, glad for Will, who had missed his brother; glad for herself, for she had always carried a little fear that he would want to go back to that place called Maine. Now it was certain that would never happen. Maine had come to him, in the form of Gerald Lassater. At last Will would have more expert help at the mill, and his family would be together again.

She walked down to where the wagon had stopped, and there followed a barrage of introductions. Gerald's wife, Agatha, who Santana guessed was about Will's age, looked tired and a little confused. It had surely been a long and difficult journey. The children, however, looked none the worse for wear. James was nine, Suellen seven, and Dora three. Will had never seen Dora. She'd been born after he left.

Gerald looked tired and thin, like his wife, Santana thought, but it was obvious he was Will's brother. Gerald was a couple of years older and perhaps an inch taller. In spite of his loss of weight from the trip, one could tell he was well-muscled. He and Agatha marveled over everything, from Santana and their handsome, healthy baby boy, to California's weather and beauty, and the size of some of the trees they had seen on their way from the ranch to Will's house.

"Those are babies compared to what's up at the mill site," Will told them. "You'll both have to come and see them with your own eyes. It's the only way to make a believer out of someone who hasn't seen the big redwoods yet." His constant smile since greeting them finally faded. "Trouble is, logging here is one hell of a lot more dangerous than it was in Maine, and it was bad enough there. Handling these monsters is no easy feat. We lost a man four days ago."

"Damn," Gerald muttered. "So that's why you're here

and not at the mill. Dad always used to close down when someone was killed."

Will nodded, then put an arm around Santana. "But today is also our second anniversary."

Gerald put out his hand to shake Will's. "Congratulations!"

Will smiled again. "Your getting here today makes it an extra good day, in spite of the accident. We have a lot to talk about, brother. The mill is going full force. It's a regular little city up there, saloons and all. It's a rough lot of men, but I've got good help. One particularly good friend named Noel Gray has taught me a lot about how to fell and log these trees. I have another good man I met on the ship coming here, a big Swede named Derek Carlson. Noel has a home and a family up at the mill, but Derek isn't married." He shook his head. "My God, there's so much to tell you. We even had a fire that I think was deliberately set. I didn't let it stop me, though, and the equipment you sent last year really helped."

"Deliberately set?" Gerald said. "By whom?"

Will looked at Santana, both of them remembering the note of congratulations and the gift Hugo had sent when Glenn was born. They had returned the gift unopened, knowing full well the real reason Hugo had sent it. Will realized that Gerald didn't even know about the duel. He had not bothered to explain all that when he'd written to tell Gerald he was getting married. "It's a long story. Come inside. Santana was just having a royal meal planned for our anniversary, so you picked the right day to get here. Have supper with us. You can put yourselves up in the guest house. When you get straightened out, we'll see about building a home for you."

"A real house sounds wonderful," Agatha said. "Something without wheels."

Gerald put an arm around her waist while the children

ran off chasing one of the three dogs that roamed the Lassater homestead. "We have a lot to tell you too," he said to Will. "That is one trip we'll never forget. There were several times when I was afraid we wouldn't make it. So much death, the danger of Indian attacks, coming through the Nevada desert wondering if we'd ever reach fresh water again, then getting ourselves over the Sierras. At least now there are a few forts and little towns along the way. I can't imagine what it must have been like ten or fifteen years ago when people first started coming out here.

"We left Maine last February, cut over to the Great Lakes, fought snow and mud across Michigan and down through Illinois to St. Louis, where we took a riverboat to Independence and left from there by wagon. We had to leave in February in order to reach Independence in time to hook up with a wagon train that would get us over the Sierras before too much snow set in. Even then we cut it close. We got caught in one snowstorm that I was afraid would keep us up in those mountains the rest of the winter."

"It's hard to say which is worse," Will said as they all headed toward the house. "The trip by sea takes even longer and is just as miserable and probably more dangerous. I'm glad you came by land."

"Well, I'm here now and I've got big ideas, Will. Like we planned, I want to invest in a fleet of ships, do our own shipping, and deal directly with our own customers. And you know, there's talk of a railroad connecting all the way from Chicago to San Francisco. Some think it can't be done, but I think it can. If it does come to be, we can open whole new markets in the East for our lumber. The only thing holding up further progress on a railroad is that Congress is more concerned right now about trouble with the South over tariffs and slavery. You probably don't get much news out here about it, but things are looking real bad, civil war in Kansas and Missouri, some Southern states threatening to secede."

Will stopped walking. "Secede from the United States?"

Gerald nodded. "They're talking about splitting off and having their own country, their own laws. They don't like Washington telling them how to run their business and threatening to abolish slavery. We're supposed to be a free country, and owning slaves has become an embarrassing issue, let alone the way some of those Negroes are treated."

Glenn started to fuss, and Will took him from Santana and bounced him on his arm. "You're right. I didn't know it was that bad."

"Some think it could lead to all-out civil war."

Both men's eyes revealed deep concern for what that could mean. Santana watched and listened, a nameless fear settling deep in her soul at the way the two men looked at each other. She knew little about Gerald's world back in the East. To her it still seemed that California was removed from all that. She still had trouble thinking of it as part of the United States. There was another world on the other side of the Sierras that she knew nothing about, but Will did, and he still felt a connection to it. He probably always would.

Will took a deep breath. "Well, let's not get too deeply into those things today. Let's just celebrate the fact that you're here and you're safe. You and the family can bathe and eat and we'll visit. Tomorrow we'll go up to the mill, the whole bunch of us."

Santana put an arm around Agatha. "I am so happy to know you. Will has missed Gerald very much. I am glad that his brother is finally here."

"Yes. Gerald has been eager to come," Agatha answered, "but I am afraid I miss home very much. My own family is still in Maine. Living out here, so far away, will take some getting used to."

"I will help you. You will grow to love California as much as Will has," Santana promised. "And we will be good friends. There are many days and nights when we will have to keep each other company, when Will and Gerald go on business trips to San Francisco, or when they have to stay at the mill for one reason or another. But it is not too often. Will talks of building us a home near San Francisco, so that when he has to go there on business he can take us with him. We do not like being apart."

Agatha sighed. "I don't like it either. That's why I worry so about the trouble with the South. I'm afraid it will lead to war, and I'm not sure what Gerald will do. I know him like a book. He'll feel obligated to do his part in protecting Northern interests, not just for economic purposes, but out of a sense of duty."

Santana frowned. "Surely he would not go all the way back there to fight in a war!"

Agatha watched Will and Gerald enter the house arm in arm, Will still holding Glenn in his other arm. "I don't know."

The strange feeling of dread came over Santana again. No. Maybe Gerald would go back for such a thing, but not Will. There was too much holding him here now.

Fifteen

Will slid his arms around Santana, pulling her close so that their bodies moved against each other in the middle of the plush feather mattress on their pine four-poster. He and Gerald had built a large home on a hill overlooking San Francisco, big enough so that the two families could share the house, or either family could use it alone when just one of them had to be in the city.

He looked around the big, airy bedroom, thinking how the house reminded him of the one he had lived in back in Maine. The elegant two-story home had been built in charming Gothic Revival style to please Agatha, who missed living in a house that was more like what she had known back east. Santana did not mind living in a *gringo* house this time, because this one was warm and cheerful, made of wood and painted white, including the delicate-looking lacelike trim around all the gables and the top of the porch roof, a porch that wrapped around the entire house.

Both women enjoyed the house. When it was necessary to be in San Francisco, they spent their days tending the children and watching the growing city below, a city burgeoning, sprawling, spreading in every direction. The Chinese population was exploding, and other foreigners were also flowing in, some with dreams of a better life, many shipped there to work in the gold mines. The trouble was, there were more immigrants than there were jobs, and many of them arrived penniless and homeless and stayed that way.

In spite of the noisy city below them, it was relatively quiet on their hill, which was part of the reason Will and Gerald had chosen this spot to build. It was far removed from the noise and filth and danger below, especially the wild area around Pacific Avenue and Kearny Street, which had been nicknamed the Barbary Coast because it was so much like the ruthless pirate center on the coast of Africa that bore the same name. Santana hated it whenever Will had to go anywhere near there, but sometimes that was the only place to find hardy, unattached men who might be willing to work at the mills.

Santana snuggled against him and sighed. *"Buenos dias."*

Will kissed her hair. "Good morning, love."

Santana smiled sleepily, enjoying the quiet morning, the way the sun filtered through the lace curtains of the large bay window. Somewhere in another part of the house she could hear the families' two Chinese maids talking together in their own strange tongue. It made her wonder what had happened to the days when her beautiful California belonged only to the *Californios*, when it was quiet and peaceful and full of Spanish-speaking people who took life slowly and cared little for big cities. The discovery of gold had certainly changed this land she loved. Still, she could not exactly complain about the Americans coming there, for if they had not, she would be married to Hugo now.

"How would you like to go to the opera tonight?" Will asked her.

Santana took a moment to gather her thoughts, remembering then what an exciting day this would be. "I would love to go," she answered, kissing Will's neck, loving him for always being concerned about her happiness. They could have built their beautiful "city" home on Nob Hill, where all the other wealthy businessmen of San Francisco lived, but Hugo also lived there. She had not wanted to be anywhere near his ugly brick mansion, did not want to take the chance of running into him in the street.

At the thought of being married to Hugo, she pressed herself more tightly against Will. How naturally they fit together, she thought, how fulfilling their lovemaking still was, in spite of the fact that she had given birth to a second child, a daughter named Ruth, after Will's mother. Will insisted she was as slender and beautiful as ever, but Santana was sure she had become slightly thicker in the waist. Still, the pain of a second birth and filling out a little more had been worth it, for now she had the beautiful daughter she had wanted. Ruth Maria Lassater Chavez was just three months old, tiny and delicate and dark. She was not the chunky, robust baby Glenn had been when he was born, but she was healthy. She had her mother's dark eyes, a sweet personality, and was already sleeping through the night.

Santana turned onto her back, opening her eyes and thinking what a happy house this was. Every room had polished hardwood floors with colorful braided rugs scattered throughout. The parlor floor was covered with a plush Oriental rug, and green-velvet curtains graced the large bay window there. All the rooms downstairs had bay windows, and the entire house was decorated with lovely furnishings from the East, most made of cherry wood. She listened as a wonderfully huge grandfather clock in the parlor chimed seven o'clock, and she relaxed in the pleasure of this quiet moment with her husband. The children were still sleeping soundly, including Gerald and Agatha's four young ones. Agatha had given birth to another son six months earlier, and they had named him William. Between the two families there were six children, and when they were all awake, the house was lively.

Back at La Estancia de Alcala, Gerald had built a home only about a half-mile from her and Will's, but he had not built it in the Spanish style. It, too, was a two-story Gothic, except that it was made of brick because of the fire danger. Agatha had insisted on keeping things more like what she had known in Maine.

Thinking of her in-laws, Santana turned to her husband. "Will Gerald and Aggie go to the opera with us?"

"Sure they will. This will be a night of celebration, you know. This afternoon we christen our new fleet of ships, and tonight we'll go out on the town, dine at the best restaurant, go to the opera. It will be good for Aggie."

"She misses Maine and her family there. I think coming to the city helps her forget her loneliness, even though she does not like San Francisco so much. She loves your brother, but she still is not used to being so far from home. I think that if you took me all the way to the other side of the country, I, too, would be homesick, in spite of how much I love you."

"You would, would you? Even when we made love?" Will pulled her close again, pushing her satin nightgown up along her thigh, thinking how much she still pleased him after nearly four years of marriage. He kissed her tenderly. What a good four years these had been. The lumber business was booming. Just as he had predicted, his wealth was growing beyond his wildest imagination, prices prime for good lumber. Thanks to Gerald's help, they now owned a second sawmill farther north. Noel was in charge of that mill and was now a very well-paid man.

Today he and Gerald would christen their fleet of six ships, all owned by Lassater Mills, ships that would carry Lassater lumber to China, South America, Japan, the East Coast, and even Europe. Buyers from many parts of the world seemed to find their way to San Francisco, lured first by the gold that backed the city's banks, second by the fact that so many thousands of people had flocked there and merchants of every sort had businesses in the city.

San Francisco was fast becoming the center of finance and supply not just for nearby mining towns, but for many distant ones. More and more such towns were springing up all over the West, as gold finds spread far beyond California. Clever businessmen, forward-thinking men like himself, were building factories that produced mining equipment. They realized that the real wealth lay in supplying the miners and residents, rather than in panning for gold. More people and goods arrived in the city just about every day, and the docks were so packed that there weren't enough warehouses to hold everything.

Will figured that probably made Hugo Bolivar very happy. So far on his business trips to the city, he had managed to avoid running into the man. They had no business connections, but some of the men Will dealt with also did business with Bolivar. Will was glad he'd been able to avoid him.

"I will be happy to get home again," Santana said, interrupting his thoughts. "I miss the quiet of the forest, and our home there reminds me that most of this land still belongs to people like my father, the true *Californios*."

Will grinned, moving a hand between her legs. "Oh? Would you like all us *gringos* to leave?"

She met his eyes boldly, opening herself to him and

taking a deep breath as his fingers toyed with secret parts that only Will Lassater knew intimately. She had never quite gotten over the thrill of his magical touch. Sometimes he stirred her to a pulsating climax this way, and sometimes it happened while his magnificent manhood was buried inside of her, filling her, taking her on another journey into ecstasy.

Each time was a little different, and she never grew tired of pleasing her man and taking her own pleasure in return. She closed her eyes now, relishing the circular movements he made with his fingers that brought out a wicked wantonness in her soul. "The children could wake at any time," she whispered.

He leaned down and kissed her throat. "They'll keep." His mouth slid down to kiss her breasts, and she pulled away the thin straps of her satin gown, pushing it away from her breasts to bare them for him. Will wondered why it was so pleasant for a grown man to suckle like his baby daughter still did. He could taste Santana's milk, for her breasts were full, ready to nourish little Ruth when she awakened. But first they would share this sweet moment in the quiet of early morning.

"There is much to do, *mi vida*," Santana said. "Do we have time for this?"

"When have we not had time for making love?" He nuzzled at her neck and moved on top of her, not bothering to remove her gown. He slept naked himself, and was already swollen hard with need. He thought how that need would not even be there if not for sharing a bed with his beautiful Santana. It was Santana he needed, not the sex. He needed to give her pleasure, to show his love in the ultimate demonstration of devotion. Making love with Santana was almost like an act of worship. She brought forth feelings he'd never known he was capable of experiencing. He loved her more than his own life, and he had not regretted one day of his marriage to her.

All good sense told him they should not do this so often. He hated the thought of getting her pregnant again, hated the fear of what could happen to her every time she gave birth. Little Ruth had been easy enough, but he didn't think he would ever get used to Santana's cries of pain or the realization that many women died in childbirth. Yet here he was again, unable to control the need to feel her hot wetness caressing his shaft in welcoming pulsations.

She never refused him, and she did not fear having more children. "Whatever children we have will be God's will," she would always say. "They are his gift to us. If he thinks it is time for another baby, he will see that we get one, so it does not matter how often or how few times we do this. We could do it once a month, and if God says it is time for another child, that will be when he is conceived."

Will wasn't so sure that made sense. Prostitutes had ways of preventing pregnancy, but Santana would have none of it. Her religion did not allow prevention methods, and he had taken that religion for himself. Besides, his better sense never prevailed when her firm, curved body was fitted against his own on a quiet morning like this, especially when he was in a mood of celebration for how well things were going.

"*Te amo como jamas he amado,*" he groaned, moving in sweet rhythm, glad to know that after two children he could still give her such pleasure. Her only reply to his words of love was to arch against him in a climax that pulled at him in rhythmic spasms, driving him wild with ecstasy, so that he thrust hard, holding back for as long as possible so she could get maximum pleasure before he finally was unable to control his own release. His life spilled into her, and as Santana would say, he would let God's will be.

He kissed her several times, then lay down beside her. After a few minutes of content silence, he said, "You were right. We have a big day ahead of us. Reporters from a couple of different newspapers will be there. Having our own fleet of ships has brought us up in status among the elite of San Francisco."

Santana stroked the stubble on his chin. "I do not care about being a part of San Francisco's elite, except that it will show Hugo Bolivar that my *gringo* husband is indeed becoming as rich and important as he. I prefer to be back at our home on La Estancia de Alcala."

"We'll go back in a couple of days." He raised up on one elbow. "As for today, my beautiful wife, I want you to wear your finest. I've invited many prominent men and their wives to the christening. I want them all to envy me my Spanish beauty. Today we announce to all of California that Lassater Mills is an established lumbering business that is here to stay." He stroked some damp strands of hair away from her face. "I'll have some extra men there to keep an eye on you and Aggie. There are a lot of scurvy characters down at the docks, but we picked a place at the northern end of the bay area. It's not so bad there."

He recalled when he'd first arrived in San Francisco, how wild and unruly the dock area was then, how he had nearly lost his life that first night. It was much worse now in many places, but it would be relatively safe where they were going, especially if he had armed men along. He had promised his guests there would be no problem.

Little Ruth, who slept in a bassinet near the bed, began to fuss.

"Time to get back to reality," he told Santana. "I'll wash up and tell Louisa to start preparing a bath for you. I'll bathe myself when you're finished."

He kissed her nose and got up, and Santana thought how happy he was that day. She was glad for her beloved.

He had worked so hard for this, he and Gerald both. Even Noel and Derek would be there. Everything was perfect—except for all the talk about the strong possibility that the Southern states back in the eastern part of the country might declare war against the Union. That troubled Will deeply.

Santana still felt no particular allegiance to the United States. She just hoped the troubles in the East would not lead to war, for she was not sure she could keep her precious husband from getting involved.

Will shook hands with Captain David Eastman, thanking him for his long association with Lassater Mills back in Maine, an association that would continue now with Eastman as captain of one of the new cargo ships, as well as master of the entire fleet of six ships. Eastman had worked independently for years, his *Dutchess Dianna* hauling products for other businesses as well as Lassater Mills. But the *Dianna* was getting old and beginning to leak, and Eastman was ready to hand over the responsibility of actual ownership to someone else.

"We've come a long way," Will told him. "My father trusted you, and I know Gerald and I can also trust you to ship our lumber and come back with the profits. And I know you will hire men to captain the rest of these ships who are as trustworthy as you have been, my friend."

"I'll do my best, Will."

Flash powder exploded as they shook hands again. Business associates who had been invited watched the proceedings with interest, all of them seeing in Will a man capable of immense success, one whose friendship could be valuable in the future.

A small crowd of riffraff had also gathered to watch. The men Will and Gerald had hired to stave off trouble mingled at the back of the crowd of invited guests, keeping others from getting too close.

Santana watched proudly as Will and Gerald took turns telling those present about the progress of Lassater Mills, and the fact that their new ships were also available for hauling other trade goods for anyone interested in using them. Gerald then asked Agatha to come and stand beside him on the dock platform, and Will did the same with Santana, reaching for her to join him. The children all sat in the two open carriages that had brought them there, three-month-old Ruth in Louisa's arms. Santana hoped the ceremony would be done in time for her to get Ruth back to the house for her three-o'clock feeding. Agatha had the same concern for six-month-old William, who sat in the lap of his nanny.

Santana glanced at the carriage, and she smiled at her sweet and handsome son, Glenn, nearly two and a half years old now. He grinned the warm smile that reminded her of Will, and even from this distance she could see his marvelous blue eyes. He was a stocky, robust boy who was going to be built like his father.

Gerald's other three children sat watching quietly, eleven-year-old James, who was eager to start learning the logging business; nine-year-old Suellen; and little Dora, now five. All but Dora had Gerald's sandy hair and blue eyes. Dora was a natural blond like her mother, with hazel eyes.

Santana moved to stand beside Agatha, feeling sorry again that this quiet woman still had not acclimated herself to California. The two of them had become friends, but there were innate differences in their backgrounds that made it difficult for them to become close. Agatha had little tolerance for and no desire to understand the Catholic religion. She was quite concerned that Will had converted to Catholicism, but she respected his decision and his love for Santana. Santana, for her part, could see that Agatha would never get used to the very different way of life and customs California had to offer. The woman surrounded herself with things that reminded her of home, and "home" for her would never be California. Still, she was kind and friendly toward Santana. They shared many things, particularly a deep love for their husbands, and pride in what they had accomplished.

Will interrupted Santana's musings as he announced the names of each ship—the *Annabelle Lee*, the *Geraldine*, the *California Maiden*, the *Pacific Queen*, the *Agatha Christina*, named for his brother's wife, and the *Santana Bello*, for Santana. He handed Santana a bottle of champagne, and Gerald handed one to Agatha. Only two of the six ships were docked close enough for a formal christening. The other four were anchored offshore.

Gerald led Agatha to the right, where she stood near the ship's bow. "I christen thee the *Agatha Christina*," she announced. She hit the bottle against the point of the bow, but the bottle did not break. She tried twice more, and finally champagne and glass flew in all directions, the liquid spilling down the bow. The crowd cheered, then turned their attention to Santana.

Will handed her a champagne bottle, and their eyes held for a moment in love. Santana was still amazed sometimes at how much she loved this man who had been a stranger when she married him. She took the bottle from him.

"Hit it hard," he told her.

She turned, holding out the bottle. "I christen thee *Santana Bello*," she said. She slammed the bottle as hard as she could, and champagne sprayed over her. She let out a little scream as the onlookers cheered. She smiled at Will, but the smile faded when she saw a black carriage approaching, pulled by two white horses that were driven by

a man she remembered well . . . Jesus, Hugo's driver.
Armed men rode behind the carriage, and she heard the
familiar and hated voice when Hugo shouted arrogantly at
a couple of ragged-looking men who were in his way.

His arrival created a bit of a commotion, interrupting
the final speech Will was about to give. People turned to
look, and Santana felt Will's hand tighten on her arm.
Both watched the carriage halt near the dock.

"What the hell . . ." Will muttered. He had not invited Bolivar, but the article he'd put in the paper about
the company's expansion and this event could have been
taken as an open invitation to the business community. A
man like Bolivar would use that open invitation, as an
excuse to come here and make trouble.

A woman rode in the carriage. When Bolivar disembarked, he helped her down, then led her through the
crowd.

"Why is he here?" Santana asked quietly.

Will could feel her tenseness. "To irritate us. Don't let
it get to you. We have a great day ahead of us, and he
won't be in it. We'll be through here soon."

Gerald moved closer to Will and Santana. "Who is
that?" he asked.

"The man who shot me in the back," Will answered.
"Hugo Bolivar."

"Well, well . . ." Gerald murmured.

Hugo escorted the woman closer, and Santana could
see she was perhaps a little older than Santana herself. She
was rather plain, short and thin and looking very shy at the
moment. She dressed as any wealthy Spanish woman
would, all in lace, from the lovely green satin-and-lace
dress she wore, with long sleeves of lace, to the matching
lace on her satin hat. Santana guessed she came from a rich
family, for what other kind of woman would Hugo marry,
and for what other reason? She wondered if this poor

woman had already discovered her husband's real reason for marrying her. She looked lost and unsure of herself as Hugo began introducing her to some of the businessmen present as his new wife from Los Angeles, the daughter of a very wealthy landowner there.

"That son of a bitch is using our event to draw attention to himself," Will said quietly to Gerald. "Act like it doesn't bother you, because that's exactly what he wants."

Hugo approached, his gaze raking over Santana, resting for a moment on her breasts. Then he glanced at Will and grinned. "I have come to congratulate you," he said. "And to introduce you to my new wife, Carmelita Rosanna Calderone de Bolivar. Carmelita is from Los Angeles. I was there on business when I met her."

Santana nodded to Carmelita, greeting her in Spanish and wondering how she could possibly be happy with a man like Hugo. Santana supposed Hugo had done a good job of impressing Carmelita and her family down in Los Angeles, where few people knew him; and perhaps Carmelita was just old enough that she felt she should marry before she was too old. Santana herself was almost twenty-two, and if Carmelita was her age or older, it was certainly time she married. The woman did not look happy, though, and Santana wondered if she missed her home and family, or if the real reason for the sorrow in her eyes was from knowing she had made a mistake in marrying Hugo. Santana hoped Hugo was not being as cruel to this woman as Santana suspected he could be.

"We had a grand wedding in Los Angeles," Hugo was saying to Will, keeping a hand at Carmelita's waist. "I have been there for the past month, enjoying my new wife and getting to know her family. Their gift to us was a great deal of land, so my land holdings in California are even greater now." He looked past Will to the *Santana*, then glanced at Gerald. "Ah, this must be your brother." He put out his hand, smiling and affable, as though he were some long-lost friend of Will's.

Gerald folded his arms. "Pardon me if I don't care to shake the hand of a man who shot my brother in the back."

Santana noticed the surprised look on Carmelita's face, and she wondered what lie Hugo had told his new wife about how he had gotten the scar on the side of his head. He had probably told her he'd been doing something quite valiant at the time. Then again, perhaps he didn't even care that she learned the truth. She was his wife now, and she would have to take him with all his faults.

"That is your brother's version of the story," Hugo answered.

"It is the truth!" Will said. "And everyone in San Francisco knows it, you bastard. Did you really think you could come here without your wife learning what a coward you are?"

"My wife knows that she married a man of wealth and honor," Hugo answered stiffly. "It is not her place to question anything her husband tells her."

"What possible reason could you have for coming here?" Gerald asked him. "Get the hell off this dock."

"He's here only to make Santana uncomfortable," Will said.

Hugo just grinned. "On the contrary." He met Will's piercing glare. "I came here as an honored businessman of San Francisco, to congratulate you on your new enterprise. You have done well, Will Lassater."

He held out his right hand, and Will knew he was putting on a show for the others present. Bolivar was trying to prove all was forgotten and forgiven between himself and Will Lassater, hoping it would improve his damaged relations with the business community. Will was fast becoming a power to contend with, and Bolivar knew it. He had deliberately waited until they were in the middle of things to make his grand entrance, and he had brought his new wife as a shield, knowing full well that Will would not make a scene in front of her or the other onlookers.

Still, Will refused to shake his hand, and he could see Bolivar's dark eyes film over with awakened hatred.

"Is this how you treat someone who has come here to congratulate you?" Bolivar said. "Do not insult my good intentions again, as you did when you returned the gift I sent for your first-born son."

"I will insult you anywhere, anytime, no matter who you are with," Will answered.

Their eyes held challengingly, then Bolivar said, "You are truly a vengeful, unforgiving man, Will Lassater."

Will leaned closer. "We both know who's really the vengeful one here, don't we? I'm not fooled by your act, Bolivar, and I don't think you want me to make a public announcement here that you tried to burn me out once."

"That is a lie! You have no proof that I had anything to do with the fires at your mills!"

"I don't need proof. I just trust my gut feelings when it comes to you."

Santana, fearing the two men would come to blows, was relieved when she saw Hugo take a deep breath and put on his smile again for the sake of appearances. He glanced at her, his dark eyes boring into her with a silent threat, and she realized the man still held a deep resentment toward her. The look in his eyes frightened her, and she struggled to appear unruffled, holding her chin proudly.

"You heard my husband," she said. She glanced at Carmelita, who looked ready to cry. "I am truly happy to meet you, Carmelita, but I am afraid your husband and mine have had their differences. Pardon our rudeness, but it is best if Don Bolivar leaves."

Hugo finally turned his gaze back to Will. "I will go,

but I will not forget the fact that you have insulted me one too many times. What I did at the duel was a crime of passion. I thought perhaps after all this time you could forgive and forget, and we could—"

"Cut the bullshit, Bolivar, and get going!"

It was obvious that a silent rage was building in Hugo, who began to tremble. He nodded to Agatha and Gerald, then turned and left, keeping an arm around Carmelita and greeting others with a fake smile as he escorted his wife to their carriage. "I have much other business to attend," Santana heard him telling someone. "I only had time to stop for a moment to congratulate Senor Lassater." He exchanged a few more greetings before finally boarding his carriage. He glanced again in Will's direction, looking, Santana thought, as though he would gladly shoot Will again.

"So, that's Hugo Bolivar," Gerald said as the carriage drove off.

Will slid an arm around Santana. "That's Bolivar," he answered. "So far I've managed to avoid the man. This little visit was to make an impression on the others here, not because he truly wanted to congratulate us. He's a liar and a fake, a back-shooter . . . and a man who knows nothing about forgiving and forgetting. He's the one who's still looking for revenge. He knew barging in on this affair would upset Santana and me both, and that was his real purpose for coming here."

Santana turned away, staring at the drips of champagne that still ran down the bow of the *Santana Bello.* "I feel sorry for Carmelita," she said quietly.

Will put a hand on her shoulder. "Try to put it out of your mind. We'll go greet a few of these people, then you and Agatha can go back to the house and feed the babies. Don't let that bastard spoil the rest of the day for you. It's been four years since you've had to look at those eyes, and I'll make sure this was the last time."

Those eyes. That was what bothered Santana, the awful hatred and vengeance there. Will squeezed her shoulders.

"Santana, Hugo Bolivar will never bother us again because he knows better. He only came here today to try to impress the other important people here."

Santana turned and looked at her husband. His eyes, those wonderful, comforting blue eyes, told her everything was all right. Yes, this was a wonderful day, a day they had looked forward to for so long. She must not let a brief encounter with Hugo Bolivar spoil it. That would only mean he had accomplished his intention of upsetting them. She smiled. "I am glad for the way you spoke to him and for making him leave. You are by far the better man, my husband, and he knows it. Let us go and greet our guests."

As she turned to leave the dock, she caught a glimpse of Hugo's carriage as it headed up a hill. She shivered, feeling a strange premonition that she could not name.

Sixteen

Santana sat rocking her youngest son, Dominic Hernando, in the wooden porch swing Will had built for her. The eleven-month-old boy had been born in February, a good baby, very sweet and loving, but quite an armful, another sturdy son for Will. He had finished suckling at her breast and was sleeping soundly, and Santana's arm ached from his weight. She carefully moved to one end of the swing and laid him beside her so that she could keep rocking him without holding him, using the blanket that had been around him for padding. The day had grown quite warm, and Glenn, who was four, and Ruth, now two and a half, were playing tag on the lawn beyond the *portico*.

Three lovely children, a beautiful home, a fleet of ships, and now Will had built a third sawmill even farther north, nearly to Oregon, having gained stumping rights on government-owned land. It should have been a wonderful, happy time, with so much to be thankful for, but an ugly threat loomed on the horizon, destroying that happiness for her, and leaving Will and Gerald disturbed and restless. The United States had exploded into civil war, just as Will had feared for two years since hearing about the hanging of a man named John Brown.

It was all confusing to Santana. John Brown had apparently dreamed of freeing all slaves and finding a place where they could all live together. He had attacked a federal arsenal in order to obtain weapons, and his radical idea had led to his death. News of what had happened had brought to light just how serious things were back East, and for years now they had been hearing about an ongoing civil war in Kansas, which had been admitted to the Union as a free state.

A free state. Slavery and freedom seemed to be the only topics of conversation now at the supper table. Santana could hardly believe that slavery could be as terrible as it was made out to be in a book that had fanned the flames of antislavery. It was called *Uncle Tom's Cabin*, and was written by a woman named Harriet Beecher Stowe. Santana and Will had both read the book, and while Santana had found it disturbing and hoped the country would find a way to end the practice of slavery, Will had become angry. His anger had grown as Southern states seceded from the Union, one after another. Eleven had seceded so far, and now a very real conflict was taking place, a conflict that Santana felt had no connection to California, and one in which neither Will nor Gerald needed to get involved.

She continued rocking, looking out over the vast land before her, most of it Alcala land. For most of her life this place had been far removed from the rest of the country beyond the Sierras. Perhaps if California had remained as isolated as it once had been, she could keep her precious husband from thoughts of helping preserve the Union. All this news, mingled with excitement about what was happening back east, would not filter in so easily and quickly. But an overland stage now carried mail and passengers from Sacramento to St. Louis in less than a month. Not the most comfortable ride in the world, said those who had used it, but certainly a dependable link to the rest of the States for any man who needed to get there in a hurry. The year before, the Pony Express had started carrying mail across the country in roughly ten days, and now there was a telegraph line linking California with the East, so that in a matter of hours news of the war could be sent to San Francisco.

Santana's heart tightened at the realization that it was no longer such an arduous task to "go back home," as most *Americanos* called going east. Santana had depended on the thought of a long, dangerous journey helping to keep her *gringo* husband there, in the place that had been home to him for nearly eight years now. How many times had he said himself that this was where he belonged, this was where his heart lay? Still, the rumblings of war were eating at him.

"This war isn't over slavery," Will had said two nights ago. "It's over stubborn pride and power. The Southerners are determined nobody is going to tell them what to do. Even the ones who don't think slavery is right will fight for the South anyway, as a matter of pride." He had paced half the night, smoking his pipe, getting angrier by the minute, talking about how he could not imagine any state even considering leaving the Union. He took great pride in being a citizen of the United States, and he felt this conflict should be ended swiftly. "The South deserves a good thrashing," he'd declared, "and I'd like to help give it to them. How dare they try to break up the Union, let alone embarrass this country by continuing the practice of slavery. To call ourselves the land of freedom is a mockery, and other countries know it!"

Will and Gerald had been attending meetings in Santa Rosa and San Francisco, meetings for men only, *Americanos* who wanted to discuss the war . . . men who still had family back east, or who simply felt a staunch loyalty to the Union. There had been some trouble at the mills between those who sympathized with the North and men who were from Southern states, and several brawls had taken place. In one of them a man had been stabbed to death. The man who had done it, a Southerner, had fled and could not be found. Many workers had already quit their jobs, gone east to fight. So many had left that Will was about to close one of the mills until the war was over, so that he could consolidate what men were left at the two other mills.

Santana hated the war, hated the United States for causing this strange new silence that had come between her and Will. He was so disturbed about what was happening, he had become distant. She could not understand why it mattered so much to him, and he in turn could not understand her attitude. He went to the meetings without asking if she minded, and when he came home he said little about what had gone on. He was at another meeting that day in Santa Rosa, instead of being at the mill where he belonged.

If only the war would end, Santana thought. Then they could go on with life the way it had been before the war came, happy, successful, proud parents, a close family . . . a man and woman who shared everything so intimately, including their dreams for the future. Now the future held a dark foreboding. It was one thing to worry about death or injury on the job. That was always a threat, but at least at the mills Will was experienced and knew exactly what to watch for. But war—exploding cannons, men shooting at one another, attacking with bayonets, enemies lurking behind any tree or bush; let alone the thought of her husband being two or three thousand miles away. He could be hurt, and she wouldn't be there to help him. He could die alone. . . .

Santana took a deep breath, rising and picking up little Dominic. She must not think of such things. Will would never leave her and the family, the mills, California. It was simply unthinkable. She walked out to the lawn where the other two children played and called to them to come inside for their lunch. As she turned back to the house she saw Agatha walking up the road toward her. She was carrying little William, and her other three children walked behind and beside her, thirteen-year-old James stopping at times to pick up a stone and throw it at a tree. The boy was looking more and more like his father, tall and strong. James dearly wanted to go to work at the mills, but Gerald wanted him to have two more years of tutoring first. He and Will both felt that fifteen was a good age to start learning all the things their sons would need to know so they could someday take over Lassater Mills, and to be good businessmen, they had to have proper schooling.

Santana walked back to the *portico* as Glenn ran off to greet his cousins, Ruth running behind on legs too short to keep up, her glossy black hair dancing with every step. They were happy children, unaware of the ugliness of war or the deep worries their mothers suffered. Agatha set William down, and Dora took his hand. As they came closer, Santana heard Agatha tell James to look after the children while she talked with Santana. Santana studied her sister-in-law's face and guessed she was feeling the same odd loneliness that Santana herself was experiencing, as though their husbands were already gone. Agatha came up the flower-lined pathway to the *portico*, and Santana could see she had been crying. Rocking a still-sleeping Dominic in her arms, Santana asked, "Agatha, what is it?"

The woman blinked back new tears. "I think you know." She shook her head. "It's going to happen,

Santana. Our husbands are going to go off to war, and we won't be able to stop them."

Santana stiffened. "Do not say that. Will would never leave me or the children, or the mills. He would never leave California. This is his home now."

Agatha closed her eyes and sighed. "I know how much you love Will, Santana, but there is a part of him you don't understand, because you aren't—"

She hesitated, and Santana felt the unintended hurt. "Because I am not a true *Americano*? Because I know nothing about the place from which my husband comes, or about what it is like to be a *gringo* from the land in the east?"

"Santana, I didn't mean . . ."

"I know. We are very different, Agatha, but not when it comes to how much we love our men, and how we worry what will happen. I argue with you that they will not leave only because it hurts too much to think that it could happen. I do not want to believe it until I *must* believe it." She turned. "Come inside. I will put Dominic down and have Anna bring us some tea."

Agatha followed Santana inside the sprawling home. Every inch of it, every piece of furniture, gave off the rich flavor of Spanish taste. She wondered if she would ever get over feeling like a foreigner here in California, would ever be able to call this place home. It was hard enough with Gerald here, but if he went off to war . . .

Santana disappeared down a wide red-carpeted hallway to put the baby to bed. "Come," she said when she returned. "We will sit in the rose garden outside the bedroom where Dominic sleeps so that I will hear him if he wakes. James can watch the other children."

Agatha followed her through the hallway and bedroom, on through double glass doors that led to a lovely private garden. As they walked, she admired Santana's dark beauty. Santana was taller than she, and still slender after having three children, whereas her own waist had thickened over the years. Today Santana wore her black hair slicked back into a neat bun, but often she wore it long and loose because Will liked it that way. There was a lusty provocativeness about Santana, yet also an innocence of her own beauty. She was not arrogant about it, and she was a good wife and mother. Agatha understood how Will could love her, but she would never understand how he could abandon his Protestant upbringing and turn to Catholicism. Still, it was not her business, and right now it didn't matter. At least they prayed to the same God, and she needed to talk to someone else whose faith was strong, for lately her own faith had been wavering.

Santana offered a seat beside her on a white wrought-iron loveseat. "You have been crying," she said.

Agatha sat down. "I feel so helpless, Santana. I don't like these meetings. I know Gerald's sense of loyalty and patriotism. I need him so, especially out here, but when it comes to something like this, I don't think my love or the children or the mills can hold him."

Santana stared at a yellow rosebush across the pathway. "I have the same fear. The only difference is I have my father and my brother here, and California is my home. I know you do not feel that way. For you home is Maine. That is why it is so important for you to have Gerald here." She looked at Agatha. "You feel alone here, do you not? If Gerald goes to war, you will feel abandoned."

Agatha met her eyes. "Yes. I'm sorry, but I've just never quite gotten used to being here. It's Gerald that makes it all okay."

Santana reached over to Agatha's lap and took hold of her hand. "If Will wanted to take me to Maine, I would also be afraid and feel like a foreigner in another land; but I would go because it is right for a woman to follow her husband. I am sorry you feel displaced here, but please remember that although we are very different, I am your friend. If our husbands go away to war, we will need each other. And even though this *is* my home, if Will goes away, I, too, will be very lonely. All that matters is having him with me, no matter where we live. I know you feel the same way." She rose and walked over to the yellow rosebush. Pinching off a rose, she held it to her nose to smell its sweet fragrance. "We will find a way to make them stay."

Agatha quickly wiped at a few tears with her fingers. "I don't think we can do that, Santana."

Santana felt sick inside at the thought of Will being gone for weeks, perhaps months . . . years . . . fighting in a war that, to her mind, should not be his concern. "We must not let them go," she answered rather absently, staring at the rose. She turned to face Agatha. "We must find a way to stop them."

Agatha shook her head. "I would like to be able to, Santana, but we have to remember that they are proud men, men of honor. There is nothing I want more in this world right now than for my husband to stay here with me and not get involved in that war, but if I did find a way to force him to stay, how happy would he be? Perhaps it would cause hard feelings between us. Perhaps he would only resent me for keeping him from what he feels in his heart is the right thing to do. I don't know. I just don't know."

"Honor? What is honor? I do not believe men understand the true meaning of that word. I was almost forced to marry a man I loathed because of honor. To me it is more honorable to do what is right than to make others terribly unhappy because of what you *think* is honorable. For a man to stay home and take care of his family, *that* is honor! And that is what Will and Gerald will do!"

Santana walked over and kneeled in front of Agatha. "We will keep them here, Aggie. In spite of our differences, we are both women who love our men and our children. It seems that in both our worlds, it is the man who makes the final decision about where he will live, and the woman must follow him. Our only power is in finding ways to make a man change his mind. If either one of us can do that and make one of the brothers stay, perhaps the other will not leave. We have to try."

A tear slipped down Agatha's cheek. "I have tried, but Gerald has made up his mind. I know it in the way he talks, the look in his eyes. He's going, Santana, and when he does, Will will go with him."

Santana felt as though something was pressing painfully on her heart. She rose, desperation striking every nerve end. "He won't!" she insisted. "I simply will not let him!" *I will not let him!* How was she going to stop him, though? Will was a man of determination and conviction, and that was part of what she loved about him. But if he went off to this ridiculous war, how could she ever forgive him for leaving her?

Will rode toward the home he loved, Gerald at his side, a grim look on both their faces. Neither of them wanted to do what he must do, but neither felt he had any choice.

"We have a lot of details to tend to," Will said. "We'll go up to the mill tomorrow and talk to Noel, maybe close number two up north. With two and three shut down, Noel ought to be able to handle number one. We hardly have enough men left to handle two anyway. The main mill can keep us going financially."

"That's the least of my worries," Gerald answered.

The looked at each other in mutual understanding. "We don't have any choice, Gerald," Will said.

Gerald just sighed, turning his horse and heading

toward his own home. Will rode on to his house, his heart heavy, his mind swirling with indecision, the right and wrong of it, his sense of duty. He loved his home, his babies, Santana. She would never understand this. They had already argued about it, but only in theory. This was reality.

He saw Glenn, his precious son, run toward the house when the boy saw him coming. He could hear him yelling, "Mommy! Mommy! Daddy is here!" Sometimes it was *madre* and *padre*. His children were growing up fluent in both Spanish and English. They were bright and handsome, little Ruth the image of her mother. She would be a beautiful woman someday. Would he live to see it? Was a man a fool to be a patriot? Yet again, was it right to let other men fight and die for a cause he, too, believed in?

He watched Santana come running out. The meeting had ended too late to come home the night before, so he and Gerald had waited until morning to come back. It was now nearly dark. Santana must be half-crazy with worry, Will thought. She had known this particular meeting was not just a bunch of Americans getting together to discuss the war and their responsibilities, to argue both sides. This meeting had been held by Army officers sent there specifically to recruit volunteers for the Union. It was a meeting where men would make a decision whether or not to go, and he had made his decision.

"Senor Lassater! It is good that you are back." Will's stable boy ran up beside his horse. "Let me take your horse, *patron.*"

"Thanks, Pedro." Will dismounted.

"*Patron,* your face! What happened?"

Will put a hand to his lower lip. He hadn't had a chance to look at himself, since he hadn't even bothered to shave that morning. He and Gerald had simply packed as quickly as they could to head home. Gerald had told him, though, that his left cheek was badly bruised and his lower lip was cut. "Nothing serious," he answered Pedro. "Just a little run-in with some Southern sympathizers outside the meetinghouse. Tend to my horse, will you?"

"Si, patron."

Pedro took the horse, and Will walked on to the house. He heard Santana order Louisa to take the children inside. She stood waiting as he came closer, and he could see by her face that she already knew what he had decided to do. There was something in her beautiful dark eyes that he had never seen before, terrible disappointment, a hard bitterness his gentle, loving wife had never shown. That look changed to concern when he got close enough for her to see his face.

"You're hurt," she said quietly.

"Just a little ruckus outside the meetinghouse. I'm all right." He noticed she stood stiffly, and he knew her well enough to realize she was struggling not to scream and weep. Poor, sweet Santana. Still, her father and brother were nearby. She still lived on La Estancia de Alcala, and Dominic would make sure his daughter was always taken care of.

"Were there many there?" she asked.

"Close to two hundred men."

Her eyebrows arched. "So many! Surely then there are plenty to go and fight your silly war. One more or less will make little difference."

He sighed. "It isn't a silly war, Santana. It's a tragedy for the Union. It's something that has to be ended. If we allow the South to secede and divide the United States, we can never be a great nation. United we can be one of the biggest and wealthiest nations in the world. This country is growing at a rate unknown to any other nation, and we must remain united."

He walked closer to her. "Think of it, Santana! We

are on the verge of uniting every territory from the Atlantic to the Pacific, from Canada to Mexico!"

"To what is *left* of Mexico," she reminded him. "Your United States stole all the land north of the Rio Grande that once belonged to Mexico. And you are united with the Pacific only because of more land you stole, this time from the *Californios!*"

Will felt as though she had stuck a knife in his belly. The resentment she had never shown before surprised him, though he knew she was attacking him in this new way out of fear of his leaving her. It hurt her that he would go away to fight a war she thought was not his affair, and so she would hurt him in return.

"This country is bursting at the seams, Santana. Expansion cannot be helped or stopped. At the same time such a union must be preserved. We have to live under one government and abide by the Constitution, and we cannot allow states to secede over something as horrendously wrong as slavery. This insurrection has to be stopped. Washington feels that with enough manpower, and considering the fact that the country's greatest wealth and all the industry is centered in the North, this war can be ended quickly, another six months to a year at the most. The South can't possibly manufacture what they need to keep this up, especially if we choke them off from all directions. Gerald and I have experience in handling men. Because of that we can go in as officers, which means we wouldn't be right on the front lines."

Santana slowly nodded her head. "So, you have made the final decision without talking to me first."

"We've done plenty of talking. You know how I feel. Noel can run the main mill. Our banker and accountant in San Francisco can handle that end of it. I trust Howard Paxon. I've taught you a good deal of the bookkeeping also, and you're a wise woman in handling personal expenses. Everything will be taken care of, the mill, the finances. There are plenty of men here to look after you and the children as well, and your father and brother are close." He hesitated, then added, "I'll make sure my will is in order. You and the children would always be taken care of if something happens to me."

She turned away. "It is bad enough worrying about you getting hurt at the mill, but this . . . this war . . ." She faced him again, tears in her eyes. "What difference can one man less make! Let your United States fight its war without you! Your children need you; the business needs you; *I* need you! Do not do this, *carino mio*, I beg of you. Your first duty is to your family, not to your country."

He shook his head. "You know that isn't true, Santana. There was a time when your own father and brother fought the Americans when John Fremont first intruded. Your forebears lost their lives fighting for what they thought was the right cause in their own civil wars in Mexico. A man does what he has to do in order to live with his conscience, Santana. In the long run, protecting his country is one of the most important ways a man has of protecting his family, for he's protecting their future. The stronger and more united the Union, the better for the economy, for Lassater Mills, and for the future of my children." His heart ached at the look of devastation in her eyes. "Don't you realize that the last thing I want to do is leave you and my children and go off to war? Doesn't that tell you something about how important this is to me?"

Tears began to slip down Santana's cheeks, and she closed her eyes and breathed deeply to keep her composure. Still, when she spoke, her voice was choked, her words broken with agony. "All last night I lay awake, thinking of all the things I could say . . . to make you stay. And yet I knew that none of them would do any good . . . because for men, honor means something different . . . than for a woman. I wish that I could understand this war . . . but I cannot. Still, I suppose I understand your reasons for going . . . although I am not sure I can forgive you for leaving." She wanted to run to him, to hold him and beg him to please, please stay. How could she live without her beloved? How was it that a woman could love a man so much, and also hate him the way she hated Will for going off to war?

She again fought back her tears. "When will you go?"

"I have to go to San Francisco first, talk to Howard Paxon and to our attorney. I want you to come with me, to be aware of the plans I'll be making for you and the children."

Santana studied the blue eyes that had so enchanted her seven and a half years ago, eyes that still touched her heart. She knew this was as agonizing for him as for her, but at the moment she could not sympathize with him. She wanted only to blame him. "The plans I'll be making for you and the children." It was as though he had created his own death sentence, as though he had discovered he was dying from some terrible disease. There was so much to be said, words she wanted to shout, but what was the use? Why should their parting words be ones of anger and bitterness?

"Come inside and clean up and have supper," she said, thinking what silly, simple words they were at this traumatic moment. She turned away, needing to be held but refusing to allow it.

Will followed her inside, hating himself, yet knowing he could make no other decision. He wished Santana could understand, but the woman he had married was a *Californio*, who had little interest in the United States. She would never understand the gravity of what was happening back east. He could only pray that he would make it back to his beloved California, to his precious children and to this woman who was his life . . . and that when he did come back, she would again be the warm, loving Santana he had always known.

Seventeen

Santana got up and made her way by moonlight to the patio doors. Opening them, she walked outside and listened to the night wind. An owl hooted somewhere nearby, and in spite of the distance between the roughing mill and the house, the wind was just right to catch the faint but distinct sound of the screaming band saw. She had never dreamed that sound would be almost nostalgic, but tonight it was. It had always reminded her that Will was close by. For all their married years he had stayed overnight at the mill only three nights a week, and she had hated even that.

Tomorrow he would leave, and who was to say for how long? Until now, lovemaking for them had been as natural as breathing, something neither of them could go long without. But since the day he had come home to tell her he was going off to war, she had slept in another bed, so angry and disappointed that she could think of no other way to show that anger than by denying him the very thing he probably needed the most. Why should she give pleasure to a man who was leaving her for no good reason? He knew how she felt, and had not pressed her to come to his bed.

Now, the finality of it, knowing he would be gone for a long time and that he could even be killed and never return to her . . . How could she let their last moments be spent apart, with all these hard feelings between them? Pride told her to let him suffer, not to give him the satisfaction of a moment of pleasure before he abandoned her; but another part of her ached for him, told her she could not live with herself if something happened to him and she had let him go this way.

She wore only a thin silk gown, and she folded her arms, rubbing them against the chill of the night air. She took a deep breath and swallowed back her stubbornness and determination, then walked out of the guest bedroom and into her and Will's bedroom. He was not asleep, but was standing at a window smoking his pipe. "Will?"

He turned, and in the darkness she could see the glow of his pipe. A shaft of moonlight showed that his shoulders were bare. She knew that he slept naked, knew he was standing there naked now. She did not need full light to know how wonderfully virile his body was, the scattering of soft hairs on his chest, the slender waist and muscled buttocks and thighs, the powerful shoulders and arms.

"I was about to come to you," he said quietly. "We can't leave it this way, Santana. We've hardly spoken for the last ten days, exeept out of necessity. I know how angry you are, and I'm sorry. But if you love me . . . I need to be with you tonight, to hold you, feel you against me. I need to remember everything about you, to carry that memory with me. Sometimes it's those little things that keep a man going in bad times."

Some of Santana's own anger left her at the realization that he truly hated this as much as she did. Even more, he was afraid of what he was heading into, which only showed how important this was to him, and how brave he was to do this.

She stepped closer. "I need the memories, too, *carino mio*. I will never understand this, but I will accept it because I must. And wrong as I think you are, I cannot let my beloved go away without holding him in my arms this night." She put her hands on his strong biceps, feeling the muscle there. "Without giving him his pleasure and feeling him inside of me."

She pulled her gown off and let it fall, and Will drank in the sight of her full breasts in the moonlight. As he turned to set his pipe aside, a thousand emotions exploded in him, and the part of him that did not want to go told him how easy it would be to stay. When he turned back to Santana, though, he knew this must be, no matter the right or wrong of what he was doing, no matter the pride and anger that still lay between them, no matter what his worries were about what he might be facing. This was something that simply had to be.

He lifted her and carried her to their bed. "*Siento el fuego bajo tu piel,*" he told her.

Yes, Santana thought, there was a fire under her skin, a fire that only one man had ever been able to kindle in her. No matter what happened, this man had given her six years of blissful marriage and three beautiful children. He had saved her from Hugo Bolivar's bed and a life of unhappiness. She would always have the children as a reminder of the brave man who had faced down her intended, even though he hardly knew her then, was not even sure that he loved her. He had done it out of pure decency and a sense of right and wrong, and for those same reasons, he must go away to war.

"The fire is for you, *mi vida,*" she answered. "It will always be there, smoldering deep within me, for my Will, only for him."

He met her mouth in a savage, hungry kiss, a kiss of gratefulness mixed with a terrible need to have her tonight. She answered the kiss with her own desperate desire. Both knew that this would be more than an act of love or need. It was almost symbolic, something that represented an eternal devotion, a possession of souls.

Each groaned in terrible need, his manhood quickly swollen, probing, searching for its solace in the moist warmth of her lovenest. She parted her thighs, and his hands grasped her bottom as he found his mark and pushed deep. The agony of leaving her, combined with desperate need and passionate feelings of love and devotion, made him surge wildly inside of her, circling his hips in thrusts that he knew excited her and rubbed against secret places, fanning her fire into raging flames.

Santana clung to him, tears filling her eyes as she wondered if she would ever again know this joy, feeling her beloved as one with her, planting his life deep inside her. For several minutes he moved in sweet rhythm, until finally her ecstasy climaxed in surging spasms that made her cry out his name while tears slipped down the sides of her cheeks.

Will knew how important it was that this be a wondrous memory for both of them, and he continued his thrusts, prolonging the pleasure for both of them. He raised up on his elbows, bending his head down to lick hungrily at her nipples, wanting to remember every inch of her, every curve, the feel of her full nipple against his tongue, the taste of her. Santana arched up to him in blissful surrender, grasping his arms, wanting to remember the feel of his hard body, the joy and comfort of being held by him. She had felt protected by his strength since she was only sixteen, even before he had ever held her. Just his presence was all she needed.

His life surged into her with such force, she could feel

its pulsations. She reached up and grabbed his mouth with her own, kissing him as savagely as he had first kissed her. She begged him between kisses not to stop, to stay inside of her and make love to her again, all night long, no matter how tired they both might be by morning.

Tomorrow they would go to San Francisco. Her father and Hernando would accompany them so they could escort her home. Will would board a stagecoach that would carry him through desert, over mountains, through Indian country, to that land of mystery in the east. Off to war, to shoot at other men and be shot at in return, perhaps injured, imprisoned . . . killed.

No! God would not take him from her! He would not do such a thing! Will would come back to her, her handsome, virile husband who was so healthy and full of life. He *must* come back to her!

She clung to him and felt him grow hard again, and again they made love, even more eager and needful than they had been their first night together. They moved in heated passion, the sheets quickly becoming damp and disheveled, two people wanting desperately to make the night last forever. But that was not to be. They made love twice, three times, as night moved into dawn, dawn to sunrise. When they could delay no longer they rose and bathed. Will finished packing, then spent some time with the children, trying to explain why he had to go away and that he would come back to them.

Santana felt as though she were trapped in a terrible dream, and wished she would wake up from it soon and discover none of this was real. The family buggy was packed, and after breakfast they were joined by Gerald and his family in their own buggy. Santana looked at Agatha and knew that she was suffering the same horror and unreality. She saw tears in Will's eyes when he turned to take a last look at his home.

"Visit the mill a few times, will you?" he said to her. "Keep a check with Noel, see how things are going and write me. I don't know if any of the letters will reach me, but once I find out whose command I'll be under, I'll try to get a wire or a letter to you. That will give you a location where you can send letters. With luck, the Army will find me."

"I will write," she answered. Her voice sounded far away in her own ears. She was achingly weary from a night of lovemaking that should have left her euphoric, but had instead plunged her into the deep throes of depression, for she might never share her husband that way again.

Too soon the buggies were off. They drove down to meet Dominic, Hernando, Teresa, and their children. Five men who worked as border guards for Dominic accompanied their little procession to help Dominic and Hernando watch over the women on their way back. With so many men gone off to war, all that was left were the kind of men who did not care about honor, outlaws and raiders who knew many homes were now unprotected. But there were still many Mexicans on La Estancia de Alcala who were loyal to Dominic and his family, Mexicans who cared little about the war in the East.

On the first night of the three-day journey to the city, they stayed at the home of a friend and fellow rancher. Because the entire family had to sleep in the rancher's only guest bedroom, Santana and Will could not make love. They simply slept in each other's arms, saying nothing. There was nothing left to say. The next night was the same, staying at the home of another friend. The third day they reached San Francisco, and went directly to the Wells Fargo depot. Stage runs had been increased to accommodate the almost-constant flow of men going back east. Santana thought how at one time she and her people would have been thrilled to see so many Americans leaving California, but not today.

The stagecoach arrived. Will hugged each of his children, shook Dominic's and Hernando's hands, hugged Teresa, and then Agatha, who seemed stiff and aloof. Santana knew this was killing her, that Agatha would be even more lonely than she. Gerald made the same rounds, and each man ended up hugging his wife last.

"*Te quiero muchisimo, carina mia,*" Will whispered. "*Vaya con Dios, mi vida.*"

"*Vaya con Dios,*" Santana answered, hardly able to speak the words for the lump in her throat. "*Te quiero. Te quiero, mi esposo amada.* Remember me. Remember me, and come back to me. I am afraid you will go back there and remember how much you love your homeland, and you will not come back to California." Her body jerked with a sob, and Will kissed her tears.

"How can you even consider such a thing?" he asked. "The thought of you and the children are all that will give me courage and strength in the days ahead. We will win this war, and I will come home just as fast as I can get here. Surely you know that. Pray for me. Light a candle for me."

"Each week that you are gone I will light a new candle." Santana could barely see him through her tears. She reached up and touched his face, gazed into his handsome blue eyes. "When the wind is right, I will hear the sounds of the mill, and I will picture you there, not so far away. I will pretend . . . that you will be home for supper. Every night . . . I will set a place for you at the table, and the children and I . . . will talk about their *padre*. I will not let them forget you, my beloved."

"All aboard!" the stagecoach driver shouted. The baggage man had already thrown Will's and Gerald's bags up top, and another man was securing the straps that would hold them. "We make a fast run, folks, take pride in reachin' St. Louis in less than a month. Time's a wastin'. Let's go!"

Reluctantly Will pulled away from Santana's clinging hands. Agatha had turned away, weeping bitterly, unable to watch the stagecoach leave. Gerald had already climbed inside. Will took a last look at his family, his handsome son, Glenn, whose lips were puckered from a sudden realization that this was supposed to be a sad moment. His mother was crying. Even his father was crying. What was this terrible thing that was happening?

How proud Will was of his first-born child. And then there was Ruth, two and a half now, prettier every day. She stood beside her blue-eyed brother, looking up at her father with a bewildered look in her big brown eyes. Dominic held his namesake grandson, too young to realize the gravity of the situation. The boy smiled at his father, his dark eyes dancing as he waved to him.

Will forced himself to turn away as the driver once again yelled that it was time to get on board. He climbed into the coach, his legs feeling like lead. He squeezed into a seat with two other men, facing Gerald, whose eyes showed his own agony. Will looked out the window at his beautiful wife, his children, his in-laws . . . back to his wife, thinking how he'd never dreamed when he came to California that he would find such a woman.

The driver snapped the reins, and the coach lurched and clattered away. Will watched his family until he could no longer see them for distance and dust. Then he looked up into the surrounding hills, where the magnificent redwoods had stood for thousands of years, through innumerable changes in this beautiful land. Up there somewhere were his mills, his dream . . . his home. He would come back.

SEPTEMBER 1862 . . .

Santana thought what a lovely autumn this would be if only Will would come home unharmed, but it was possible that this new baby would be all she had left of him, this precious symbol of their night of passion before he left. How fitting that God had allowed Will's seed of life to take hold and bring her their fourth child. Will would not be present for the birth, though. He did not even know he had left her with child.

In her pain she wondered if he, too, might be in pain, perhaps wounded. She had not heard from him in so long, nor had Aggie heard from Gerald. She reminded herself that as Will had explained, they were always on the move, and it was not easy to get letters sent off. She had to believe that was the only reason she'd gone so long without one. The only letter she had received so far had told her Will had been given the rank of major and would be sent to battle sites in Virginia and Maryland, where the South continued advancing in an effort to invade and take over the United States capitol.

Another contraction gripped her, and she gritted her teeth, trying not to push, since Dr. Enders had told her not to. It was not easy. The pains were deep, and her muscles seemed to be working on their own without her willing them. Oh, how she prayed this baby would be healthy! Always the pain was terrible, yet always she forgot it minutes after it was over, and she knew the baby was worth the agony. She had already decided that when she finally got another letter from Will and knew where to write him, she would not tell him about this baby. It would only worry and upset him that she'd had the child alone. She didn't want him handling any more distractions than necessary. In war, distractions and daydreaming could cost a man his life.

The pain subsided again, and she relaxed against the pillow as Louisa bathed her face with a cool cloth. Throughout her pregnancy, Santana had tried to stay happy and excited about a fourth child, but all she could think about were the reports that had been filtering back to California about how the war was going. The stories they were hearing were horrifying, the casualties horrendously high. Had Will been at the battle at a place called Bull Run in Virginia? Hernando had made it a point to go to San Francisco every ten days to pick up newspapers so they could read about what was happening, and she knew that Union forces had been defeated there. So far it seemed the South was winning more battles than the North.

Will was involved with artillery troops under the command of a General George McClellan, and according to two letters Agatha had received, Gerald was a captain, assigned to a cavalry regiment under a Colonel Burnside. That was all either she or Agatha knew. Aggie, too, was consumed with worry. She seemed to have fallen into a deep depression, hardly leaving the house since Gerald had left. If Santana wanted to see her, she had to go there, and she went often, concerned for Agatha's state of mind. She was thankful the birth of this child was getting the woman out of her house for the first time in weeks. Aggie was with her now, and preoccupation with helping with the birth had revitalized the woman somewhat.

"Just let it come now," Enders told Santana, as another pain consumed her. "You can push this time."

She breathed again in deep pants, grasping Agatha's hand. "This is going to be a . . . good one," she said between breaths. "A healthy son for Will . . . I just know it."

Agatha smiled, but there was a terrible sadness in her eyes. "I hope so, Santana."

Santana felt herself falling into the deep concentration of delivery, sinking into a world far removed from those around her. For the next several minutes she was hardly aware of anything but the pain and the fact that her baby was making its way into the world. Somewhere in the background she could hear the housemaid, Ester, scolding little Dominic, telling him he could not go into the room. Her new Chinese servant, Won Lee, added to the chastisement in her own tongue.

Another contraction forced her to push, screaming with the pain of it. She tried to think of things that would help . . . of Will coming home healthy, holding her, the feel of his strong arms around her bringing her joy and comfort and the wonderful feeling that everything was all right. The urge to push swept through her again, and suddenly there came the final release. The pain subsided to mild cramps. She heard people fussing about, heard a smack and a cry.

"You were right, Santana," she heard Agatha say. "You have a fine son. I'll clean him up for you."

A son. Juan Santos. She had already picked out the name, the name of her maternal grandfather. Will did not mind giving his children Spanish names, and so far they all looked Spanish, except for Glenn's blue eyes. Will had become Spanish at heart, although the war had reawakened his *gringo* pride and had taken him back to that other world. Surely he would not forget this world, would he? He would come home to California.

She groaned and pushed as Enders massaged her stomach to help rid her of the afterbirth. She could hear little Juan crying, and came more awake as Louisa and the doctor cleaned her up.

"Will will be surprised and happy when he finds out about this," Enders told her as he washed his hands at the washstand near the bed.

"Thank you, Dr. Enders. You have been a help to my

family for many years. You are wasting your talents here. You should go to the city and set up a practice."

Enders's smile faded. "I lost the desire for that many years ago, Santana." He picked up a towel to dry his hands. "This is as far as I go. Besides, I love my whiskey. Nobody wants a drunken physician taking care of them." He smiled fleetingly. "As a matter of fact, I'm going to have a drink right now. You're fine and so is the baby."

Santana smiled. "You've done a wonderful job delivering my babies. Did your wife have any children?"

He looked away. "No. She died while giving birth, and the child died with her." He picked up his bag. "Well, I guess with Will gone, we won't be doing this again for quite some time."

Santana could see he did not want to talk about his wife. Actually, she had never heard him talk about her. This was the first she knew of the woman dying in childbirth. She was sorry she had even asked about children. Pushing aside the fear that she, too, could die in childbirth, she thought about Enders's last remark. She felt a quick pain in her chest at the realization he was right. Until Will returned, she would not be making love. There would be no more babies.

"*Si,*" she replied. "But when he comes back . . ."

Enders grinned. "When he comes back, ten to one we'll be doing this again nine months later." He put on his hat and gave her a nod. "Congratulations, Santana. Your father and brother are outside. I'll go tell them the good news."

The doctor left, and Agatha came over with Santana's new son, placing the bundled baby in her arms. "I'll let the children come in and see their new baby brother, and mine would like to meet their new cousin."

Santana studied the boy, as dark as the rest of her

children. She kissed his velvety-soft cheek. "He is healthy? All his parts are there?"

"He is very healthy."

Santana looked up at Agatha and saw the deep agony in her eyes in spite of her smile. "I hope you're better, Aggie. You must get out more. Perhaps we could arrange a trip to San Francisco, take the children. We could stay at the house there for a few days. It would be a nice change. Would you like to do that?"

Agatha's eyes teared. "Yes, that might be nice . . . except . . . what if they come home while we're gone?"

Santana sighed. "We cannot sit here going crazy. If they come, they come. Besides, they would probably arrive in San Francisco first. Either way, I do not think it will be soon. From the news we are getting, the war will not end nearly as soon as Will and Gerald thought it might. We must be prepared for many more months apart, Aggie."

Agatha turned away, asking Louisa to leave the room for a moment. Louisa obeyed, and Agatha faced Santana again. If possible, the sorrow in her eyes had deepened. "You're so strong, Santana. This baby has made you even stronger. I wish . . . Part of the reason this has been so hard on me isn't just that I miss home and family and feel out of place here. Gerald's leaving . . ." Her voice choked, and she wrapped her arms across her breasts, blinking back tears. "It's been harder on me than I ever imagined and it's because I . . . because I refused him that last week after he said he would go. Even the night before we left to go to San Francisco . . . I wouldn't let him touch me. If he doesn't come back . . . I'll never forgive myself for that." She broke into sobs, covering her face with her hands.

Santana felt her own tears of pity rising. Thank God she had overcome her own stubborn pride that last night and had gone to Will. Now she had another beautiful son, a symbol of their final night together that she would have forever.

"I am sorry, Aggie. But I am sure Gerald understood and that he loves you very much and thinks of you every minute of every day. He will come home, and you can make it up to him then. It will be all right. God will protect them. You must have faith."

Agatha sniffled, taking a handkerchief from a pocket in her skirt. "I try. I pray day and night for him, begging God to forgive me for shunning him at a time when he needed me so. I wrote him a letter, telling him how much I love him and how sorry I am. I can only hope that he received it." She wiped at her eyes and blew her nose.

"I worry, too, wondering if Will ever receives my letters." Santana reached out to take Agatha's hand. "Do not blame yourself, Agatha. God understands, and I am sure Gerald also understands. Come to San Francisco with me. We will take the children to the parks, and you and I will go shopping, perhaps go to the theater and the opera house. It will be good to get away from here. We will go as soon as I am strong enough. Promise me you will do it."

Agatha smiled through her tears and nodded. "All right. I'll go."

"Good." Santana managed a smile too. She felt the same awful fears that Agatha did, but with Agatha's delicate mental state, she dared not show a loss of faith, dared not talk about her own fears and her aching need to see Will again. That made the waiting all the harder, for not being able to share her concerns with Agatha fully made her feel that much more alone. This trip was not just for Agatha, but for herself. She needed to get away, had been waiting only because she was carrying a baby and did not want to do anything to jeopardize her pregnancy. Now the baby had arrived, and within a month she would be strong enough to make the trip.

Yes, they would go to San Francisco. It would be good for all of them, take their minds off the terrible things they had been picturing about Will and Gerald. It would help pass a few extra days, and that was the only way to survive this . . . one day at a time.

Eighteen

Will could not help thinking how Santana had been right about this war in many ways. It seemed ridiculous that men should fight each other this way. Many of them were there just for the battle, not even sure of the reason. He hadn't lost his own conviction that this was important, but he had seen such ineptness on both sides, such huge numbers of lives lost, such agony at the medical tents, that he wondered if this all shouldn't stop. Why couldn't the leaders of both sides just get together and settle this, avoid all this bloodshed?

He was in it now, in charge of Battery E of the Pennsylvania Light Artillery. He had made a commitment, and he was a man of his word. With each battle he hoped the war would be ended, but each time that hope was dashed. The Rebels were fierce, stubborn fighters, and ending this war quickly had not been the easy task the Federals had thought it would be. Troops on both sides were made up mostly of inexperienced volunteers, which led to grave mistakes and innumerable deaths. In many cases, sheer stubbornness had given the Confederates a victory over the

Federals, many of whom had not taken this war seriously in the beginning, while the South considered it *very* serious.

Another battle was about to be joined, and Will stood waiting for orders to begin firing his cannon. It was only six A.M. and over eighty thousand Federals already stood on the eastern side of Antietam Creek near a place called Sharpsburg, Maryland, ready to surge against Confederate troops led by General Robert E. Lee. The Confederates numbered only about twenty thousand, but Will still wondered if this battle would be won. As far as he was concerned, there was no reason to be here, no reason that Lee had managed to push forward into Maryland. General McClellan had had the chance to take Richmond, victorious over General Lee in four of five attacks. Yet throughout the week-long fighting, McClellan had continually ordered his troops to withdraw. Whether he was afraid to go in and actually take the city, perhaps thinking many more Confederates than anticipated lay waiting there, Will would never know. The fact remained that they could and should have taken Richmond, and that might have ended this war.

Now here they were poised for another bloody melee. If he'd been fighting under anyone but McClellan, he would feel more confident; but he worried that even if they were victorious, McClellan would again withdraw. They had already waited too long, as far as Will was concerned. McClellan, fearful again that there were many more Rebels poised in Sharpsburg than estimated, had taken nearly two days to draw up his plan of attack, thereby losing the element of surprise and giving the Confederates time to do their own planning and to bring in more troops. If anything was going to draw this war into years rather than months, Will thought, it was hesitancy on the part of men like McClellan. Will looked at it in the same way as he would fighting one man. No hesitation in flinging the hatchet. Just get the job done.

He would like to do that now. End this war and go home . . . home to California and its gracious lifestyle, its beautiful mountains and lush valleys. Home to the giant redwoods, to his mills, San Francisco. Home to his lovely house on the hill overlooking the valley where La Estancia de Alcala lay in serenity. Home to his precious sons and daughter, and to Santana. His babies and his wife were all that kept him going, all that kept him determined to stay alive and see this through. He had been gone nine months, and it seemed like ten years. He had lost track of Gerald, and he could only pray his brother was all right.

His thoughts were interrupted by shouted orders, and finally the attack was on. Thousands of Federal infantry charged, bayonets flashing in the sun, the air filled with their shouts as they surged into a cornfield beyond which the Confederates lay waiting. At the same time Will gave the command to begin firing the cannon into the cornfield. Cannon shot ripped through the stalks, cutting them down as though one great scythe had whacked away at them, opening up the field so that the Confederates had no place to hide.

Infantry under Major General Joseph Hooker, called Fighting Joe by his men, stormed forward, slaying Rebels like rabbits. It was a pitiful sight, but Will had learned to close his heart to such things. He dared not care, not even about his own men. In this war, it was dangerous to make a friend, for any moment he might be lying next to you with a bloody hole in his head, or a leg or an arm blown off. He ordered the cannon forward as the Federals drew closer to their first target, a small Lutheran church that the Rebels used as a signaling point, waving flags from the church's tower.

Suddenly the Confederates began firing back with vehemence, and now it was Union men who were falling, by the score, by the hundreds, until suddenly the battered cornfield was thick with blood and bodies. Finally the Rebels began backing away, running for the woods beyond the church. Will noticed that the whitewashed outer walls of the church were filled with holes. His head ached from the ring of gunfire and the boom of cannon. It seemed they would reach the church, but another force of Confederates stormed toward them. He could hear men shouting "All for Texas!" and the Southern troops released a volley of shots, apparently fired by Texan sharpshooters. Again Union men fell by the hundreds, and Will and his battery were forced to head back up the hill.

From then on Will could only watch in horror, astounded at how ugly and disastrous this war had become. For four hours the battle surged first one way, then another, until thousands of bodies peppered the cornfield that lay between the two factions. The firing never ceased on either side, and the air reeked of gunpowder and blood. Mingled with the sound of gunfire were the moans and cries of men lying wounded in the cornfield. Finally the Federals reached the church, and their next target was a narrow, sunken road beyond which the Confederates had formed a line, using the road like a rifle pit. For hours the Federals tried to overrun the road, only to be driven back by furious volleys of gunfire.

Will directed his cannon at the road, but the Rebels were burrowed deep and were a difficult target. Even worse, he and his battery were targets themselves, forced to brave return cannon fire. Will lost several men and cannon when Confederate cannon balls and shrapnel exploded too close.

"They found a spot where they can shoot down the men in the road!" someone shouted at last. Federal troops charged forward, shouting victoriously. Will mounted his horse and ordered the cannon forward. A Confederate cannon shot exploded nearby, and his horse reared. Will felt a sharp pain in his right leg as he managed to leap from his horse as it fell. The animal rolled onto its right side, a bloody hole in its chest. Again Will shut off his emotions. He drew his revolver and shot the horse in the forehead to end its misery, then grabbed his gear and canteen and ran on with his men. The pain in his leg caused him to look down; a piece of shrapnel was sticking out of his calf. There was no time to think about the pain or wonder how bad the wound was. He reached down and yanked out the shrapnel, and one of his men ran up to him.

"I'll tie my neckerchief around it, sir," he offered.

Will let him tie it, then the man offered Will his horse. Will thanked him and rode forward, reaching a ridge where he ordered his battery to halt. From there the infantry was firing down on the Confederates, slaughtering them like sheep. They stormed the road then, running across dead bodies to chase more Rebels who were fleeing. It was a sickening sight, bodies piled upon bodies.

It seemed the battle was being won, but to Will's amazement McClellan again did not take advantage of the situation. He halted his forces, allowing the remaining Confederates to flee over Antietam Creek, using a stone bridge that led to Sharpsburg. It seemed to Will they should keep up the charge, but McClellan stopped the troops, saying they needed time to estimate their losses, to regroup and plan their next move.

Again the Rebels would have time to plan their own strategy, Will thought in frustration. And General Lee knew how to instill in his men a fighting spirit that made them charge into battles they knew they could not win, doing unbelievable damage in spite of being far outnumbered. They should not be allowed time to regroup.

During the lull, Will refused to let anyone tend to his wounds. Too many other men with far more serious injuries needed the doctors' care. Bodies were carried on makeshift stretchers to the little church, which was now a temporary hospital. The air was filled with cries of pain, so many that it was almost as noisy as when all the shooting was going on. It would be impossible to help them all, and many of the wounded would die where they had fallen, die from loss of blood or infection before they could get help. Will limped back and forth in front of his battery, ordering his men to reconnoiter and be prepared for another charge.

By late afternoon the orders came to take the stone bridge over the creek. Because of McClellan's hesitancy, the bridge was now strongly defended, and Will could see it would not be an easy task for Federal troops to storm across it. Orders were shouted and the assault began, and for three more hours the Confederates, in much smaller numbers, held off thousands of Federals until it simply was no longer possible. Finally the Federals surged across the bridge and pressed their way toward Sharpsburg. Victory seemed at hand, until three thousand more Confederates arrived unexpectedly, the Confederate Light Division from Virginia. Everything became confusion then, as the new arrivals were wearing blue jackets taken from captured Union troops. The Federals could not bring themselves to fire on them, not sure if they were friend or foe. Too late it became apparent that they were foe, and the Federals found their flank being smashed by fresh Confederate gunfire coming from the south. McClellan, who had earlier promised reinforcements of his own once they took Sharpsburg, decided it would not be prudent to send them in. Again a battle that should have been won was lost, and the Federals were forced to retreat over the same bridge they had fought so hard to take.

By nightfall the Federals had retreated even farther, and Will fought an urge to shoot McClellan himself. As badly as Lee's Confederates had been slashed that day, the reinforcements McClellan could have sent would have finished the job. They would have taken Sharpsburg and General Lee. It was as though McClellan had orders not to win the war, but to keep it alive instead. It was estimated that more than twelve thousand Federals were dead, wounded, or missing. Their own troops had outnumbered Lee's by more than four to one, yet they had been defeated out of pure stupidity on the part of their leaders.

Horribly wounded men were carried into every house and barn and building with four walls and a roof for miles around. Will rode for help himself, and he felt like vomiting at the sights he saw. At one house doctors' aids carried severed arms and legs outside and threw them into a pile. "So, here is your silly war, Santana," he muttered. "How I wish I was back in California with you."

He decided his wound could wait, and he found a sturdy oak tree, where he dismounted and took some paper from his gear, intending to use the light of a campfire to write Santana a letter. Minutes after leaning against the tree he fell into an exhausted sleep, dreaming of a beautiful Spanish woman with a bright smile. They sat together under a skinny lodgepole pine, enjoying the quiet of the forest.

Santana and Agatha descended the red-carpeted stairway of the theater, where they had come to watch a play. Santana clung to her father's arm, glad she had talked Dominic into coming with them to the city. Dominic did not often attend such things as the theater, and he had enjoyed the performance. In spite of the fact that Will was gone, Santana was glad to be able to spend more time with her father, who seemed to have aged faster than he should these last few years, and now appeared too frail. He had always been robust and vital, but this past year he had lost weight, although he claimed he felt just fine.

"Did you like the play, *Padre?*" she asked.

Dominic patted her hand. "It was lovely. But I had better go and call for our coach. It is past time for you to get back to the house. Little Juan will be squalling for his next feeding any time now."

Santana smiled at the pride in his eyes. Hernando and Teresa had had three more children—a daughter, Inez, and two more sons, Eduardo and Miguel. That brought the number of grandchildren for Dominic to nine, six boys and three girls. He was a proud grandfather, who doted on the children and often had the older ones come and stay with him.

"*Si,* I must get home," she answered. "I am so glad we came here. It feels good to get away and shop and dress in fine clothes and do something different."

Dominic smiled, slipping an arm around Agatha also. "And I am proud to be the escort of two such beautiful senoras. You are the loveliest women here this evening."

Agatha blushed, and Santana thought she truly did look radiant that night, dressed in pink silk, her light hair pulled up into curls, her blue eyes showing more happiness than had been there the last several months. Santana had enjoyed donning an elegant gown of her own, a melon-colored taffeta dress designed by her new servant, the surprisingly talented Won Lee. The low-cut bodice revealed her full breasts, and it was bordered with tiers of hand-embroidered ivory-colored lace.

She wished Will could see her, for she did feel beautiful, happy with the birth of Juan two months earlier. She was proud that her new gown had the same size waist as the dresses she had worn before the pregnancy. She had managed to maintain her shape, wanting to look the same for Will when he returned. Surely that would be soon, perhaps within six months. The war couldn't last any longer than that.

Dominic left them to hail their coach, and Agatha and Santana waited in the ornate lobby of the elegant theater. A huge chandelier provided light for San Francisco's elite mingling there, most of them talking about the war and how it affected California. There were not many Confederate sympathizers. Most of California's sympathy and support lay with the Union.

Santana scanned the crowd, and it was then she noticed him, Hugo Bolivar, talking with two other men. Just the sight of him brought back memories she had tried to get rid of, but could not. She looked away, but too late. Hugo had caught her eye, and she knew he would not let her leave the theater without talking to her, especially when he realized Will was not with her. He probably knew Will had gone east to join the war. The daily papers printed names of prominent citizens who had joined the cause, and last year Will's had been among them. She did not doubt that a man like Hugo, who had many acquaintances among American businessmen, kept an eye on those names.

"Let's wait outside," she told Agatha, taking her arm. Without looking she could feel Hugo approaching, like a dark cloud. She tried to make it to the double entrance-doors, but she felt a cold hand touch her arm before she reached them. She did not care to make a scene, so she forced a gracious smile as she turned to face the man she hated with passion, the man who had tried to murder her precious Will.

"Hugo," she said, acting surprised. "It has been a long time."

"Yes, hasn't it?" He glanced at Agatha. "Ah, the wife of your husband's brother, I believe. I remember you, Senora Lassater, from the day I met your husband at the docks. I had my lovely wife with me that day, if you will remember."

Agatha glanced at Santana and back to Hugo. "Yes, I remember. It is good to see you again. Don Hugo Martinez Bolivar, I believe?"

Hugo flashed a smile, showing teeth that looked almost too white. "You remembered." His dark gaze returned to Santana, raking over her, lingering on her full bosom. "How good to see you again, Santana. Married life apparently agrees with you. You are more beautiful than ever." He looked around. "And where is your husband tonight?"

Santana did not flinch, and the ugly white scar above his mutilated left ear, where no hair would ever grow again, reminded her just how much she hated this man. She was glad Will had left a permanent mark on him, and she deliberately stared at his left ear, wanting Hugo to see her pleasure at noticing it again. "Will has gone to fight for the Union, as I am sure you already know."

Hugo frowned as though concerned. "I see. The stories of that war are quite terrible, you know, thousands dead and wounded. You must be very worried. Have you heard from him?"

"Yes," Santana lied. "Will is fine, not that you truly care."

Hugo pulled at his mustache. "Oh, but I do care. I am glad to hear he is all right. But of course if you had not married a *gringo*, you would not be in such a dreadful situation, alone and abandoned by your husband."

"Will has not abandoned me. He will come home soon. His mill is still in operation, and we have four children now. He has much to come home to." She watched a look of deep envy come over Hugo's face.

"Four, is it? So, marriage agrees with you even more than I thought. I knew that you had the build for many children. Will has taken full advantage of his wife's fertility."

The remark embarrassed her, but Santana refused to

let him know it. "We have a good marriage," she answered. "And where is your own wife, Hugo? Have you any children yet?"

His smile faded, and Santana knew she had struck a nerve. "My wife is home. I am only here because I brought two new business acquaintances out on the town tonight, a little entertainment to thank them for their accounts." He folded his arms. "And no, there are no children. So far my darling Carmelita has had a difficult time conceiving."

"I am sorry to hear that," Santana told him. "I know you would like sons."

"Yes, but full-blooded Spanish children, not half-breeds. But then with California filling up so with *gringos*, I suppose it cannot be helped, can it?"

Santana knew he'd made the remark only because he was jealous that she and Will had four children. "My children are beautiful, happy, and healthy, a proud mixture of high Spanish blood and a handsome, successful American man. California is now a part of the United States. My children represent the best of both races."

"But of course. I was only commenting on how things might have been, if you and I . . . but then that is in the past, is it not? Marriage to your *gringo* apparently suits you well, and my Carmelita appreciates the honor it is to be the wife of Hugo Bolivar. She has grown even more beautiful, and we hope that she will eventually be able to bear me sons."

Santana felt a sudden, keen pity for Carmelita as she caught the familiar evil, frightening flash in Hugo's eyes. She could just imagine how he treated his poor wife for not having given him a child yet, and she did not doubt that he insisted on bedding her every night, perhaps more often than that, in order to make it happen. If eventually it became apparent she could have no children, how much worse would he treat her then? Perhaps she was not with him that night because she had bruises that he would not want others to see.

"I will light a candle for Carmelita," she said, "and pray that she becomes with child."

Hugo's eyebrows arched. "How kind of you." He looked her over again, and Santana felt as though he'd stripped her naked. "Just think what a grand family you and I would have had, Santana, many beautiful children of high Spanish blood. If only—"

"Do not speak of it," she interrupted. "It is senseless to keep talking about what might have been, Hugo. Even if Will had not come along to claim my hand, I would have found another way to avoid marrying you, even if it had meant running away." She glanced sidelong at people standing nearby. "Now, if you do not wish for me to speak louder and embarrass you in front of these others, I would like you to go back to your business friends. I do not wish for people to see us speaking when I do not have the escort of my husband."

Hugo snickered. "You are afraid people will talk?" He rubbed his chin, looking surprised, as though Santana had given him an idea he had not considered before. She regretted the remark.

"I only meant," she answered boldly, "that I do not care to be seen in the company of someone whom so many dislike. The very man who tried to murder my husband." She wanted her words to hurt and shame him, but he only grinned.

"Oh, but your own reputation is unstained, my beautiful Santana. Perhaps you are afraid that because you and I were once intended to be married, and with your husband off to war for months now, people will talk." He leaned closer. "After all, you have been a long time without a man."

Santana could not control her anger. Without thinking, she slapped Hugo, drawing the stares of others, many of whom knew who she was and certainly knew who Hugo was. Instantly she wished she had checked the urge, for the slap could be interpreted a number of ways, and people loved to gossip.

She turned to face some of the people who were staring openly. "This man insulted me," she said. "And he is a coward, who once shot my husband in the back. I will not allow him to speak rudely to me!" She grabbed Agatha's arm and whisked her outside, tears stinging her eyes, her mind whirling over whether she had done the right thing. She should have just quietly left after Hugo's remark. Now she had drawn attention to both of them. Suddenly she just wanted to go home to La Estancia de Alcala and never come back to San Francisco until Will could come with her.

"Don't let him do this to you, Santana," Agatha said. "He is the one in the wrong, and he approached you. You only spoke to him so as not to make a scene."

"And then I *did* make a scene after all," Santana answered, her tears coming then. She took a handkerchief from her handbag and dabbed at her eyes. "I hate him so much! I should have controlled myself and just left. Now people will talk."

Agatha slid an arm around her waist. "They will talk about what a devil Hugo Bolivar is. They won't talk about you."

"Santana!" Dominic called out to his daughter as his driver, Enrique, halted the elegant Alcala coach in front of the theater. Dominic climbed down. "What is it, *mi hija?*"

"Hugo." She sniffled. "He was in the lobby and he came over and spoke to me before I could get away. I answered him only to be polite, but then he insulted me."

She closed her eyes, angry with her own lack of self-control. "I slapped him, and it drew everyone's attention. I wish I had not done it."

"The bastard! I will go and—"

"No, *Padre!* Please do not make even more of a scene. Let us just go. I will tell Will about it when he comes home and he will decide what to do. Please. I just want to go."

Dominic sighed in disgust. "Come then. Let us go home."

From inside the theater lobby, Hugo watched out a window as Santana climbed into her father's coach, followed by Dominic and Agatha. He had not seen Dominic in years, and thought the man did not look well. That was good. He hoped the old man who had betrayed him was dying. Dominic had been a good friend to his father, but he had not been a friend to Hugo Bolivar, and for that Hugo never wanted another thing to do with Dominic. Perhaps once the old man was dead, he could make trouble for Hernando and La Estancia de Alcala. After all, the Alcala ranch and Rancho de Rosas shared a border several miles long. He was always looking for ways to get his revenge on both Santana and that *gringo* husband of hers. He hated them with a great passion, and he hated Dominic Alcala for turning his back on the long friendship he had shared with his father. Santana, though, may have opened a pathway for him that night so that he could find his revenge.

Fury enveloped him as he recalled his first sight of her across the theater lobby. Santana already had four children, yet she looked as slender as ever, and even more beautiful, while his own wife was apparently barren, and was gaining weight besides. He had sex with her only to try to get her pregnant, but his true pleasure came when he visited the whores. Still, there was only one woman who could have truly pleased him, and she shared her bed with a stinking *gringo*, spreading her legs for him, taking his life into her belly, giving him the pleasure and the children that should have belonged to Hugo Bolivar!

"Hugo, how about a late supper?" one of his business associates asked.

Hugo turned, putting on a smile. "Yes, of course."

The other man smiled. "That woman seemed quite a spitfire. I've heard of your reputation with women," he joked. "She wouldn't be one of them, would she?"

Hugo rubbed his cheek. Yes, this was indeed something to consider. With Santana's husband gone, it would be easy to sully her reputation, especially among the Americans, who were so ready to believe that all Spanish women were hot-blooded lovers who enjoyed men . . . all men. He would have to think carefully about this before he made any moves. He would not soon forget Will Lassater's temper, or the feel of the man's hatchet blade cutting into his forehead. This would have to be a very subtle matter, a situation where it was left to Santana to do the explaining.

"I will let you guess," he answered with a sly grin, as though suggesting the man could be right. "She is the wife of Will Lassater."

"The lumberman? Lassater Mills?"

"The same."

"Lassater and his brother went back east to join the Federals, I believe."

"*Si.* He has left his poor wife alone. I suggested that perhaps she would like the company of an old friend, but you see how she reacted. I think perhaps she was just putting on a show for others. I saw something else in her eyes."

The second man chuckled. "You're a devil, Hugo. Come on. Let's go get something to eat."

As they walked to the lobby doors, Hugo noticed a few

women of San Francisco's high society standing together, watching him and whispering. Were they also talking about Santana? It would serve her right. She had brought this on herself this time, and if he could find a way to fuel the fire, he would do it.

Nineteen

Gettysburg. Will remembered it, the fiercest fighting he had ever seen. Someone had joked to him that the entire siege had been instigated by the fact that the Confederates needed shoes. A large supply of shoes was supposedly stored in that tiny town, and when the Confederates had tried to take the town, they had run into Union troops by accident. Both sides had called for reinforcements, and the battle was on. Will's battery had been among those called in to help.

Yes, he remembered Gettysburg, and all the battles since. Bloody sieges that had left thousands dead and wounded. Gettysburg had been nearly a year ago, and the days since then had all been the same; march, try to sleep, eat wormy biscuits, fight diarreah, attack, retreat, attack, guns and cannon roaring, the earth shaking, men screaming. One battle after another, until he could no longer remember their order.

The numbers of men involved were difficult to grasp. At least sixty-five thousand Confederates at Gettysburg alone, supposedly twenty thousand more than that on the

Union side. The fighting there had lasted four days. The most heated fighting had been to claim a hill called Little Round Top. Back and forth the battle had gone, first the Rebs taking the hill, then the Yanks, then the Rebs, then the Yanks. The noise had been almost unbearable, and he'd never forget the sights of the wounded and dead.

Wounded himself in the head in whatever battle he had fought in last, Will could only piece together bit by bit how he he'd come to be marching south with several other captured Union men. Many of them were hurt much worse than he; some had died on the road and been left there. The Rebels who urged them on with gun butts and bayonets seemed to enjoy letting them know where they were going, a prison camp in Georgia called Andersonville. Will had already heard that Andersonville made going to hell seem like a vacation. He tried to think of ways to escape, but he was too weak, his mind too fuzzy, and the group of men with whom he marched was too well-guarded.

He swallowed, his tongue thick with thirst. The heat was almost unbearable, and he supposed they were already in Georgia. He didn't know how long it had been since he had wakened on a wagon amid the bodies of four other wounded men. Another prisoner, who walked beside the wagon, had told him he'd been unconscious for two days. Since then he had been herded with the others by wagon, on foot, by rail, ever southward, handed from one regiment to another as they drew closer to their destination. In some Southern towns, citizens had been allowed to get a look at them, to spit on them, throw garbage at them. Through it all, Will had moved in and out of consciousness, his head aching fiercely. Sometimes the pain made him vomit. He knew he had lost considerable weight, for his clothes hung loose on him.

He tried to think what year this was. He knew the battle at Gettysburg had taken place in July 1863. A year ago. Yes. The last battle he'd fought in had been at a place called Petersburg . . . thick forest called the Wilderness . . . May 1864. He remembered that as he'd marched his battery through the tangle of underbrush, they had walked right over the skeletal remains of men who had died there the year before, men left unburied. There was no way to know which were Union and which were Confederate.

How much longer would this war last? he wondered. The worst part about it was that he wouldn't be able to write Santana and let her know what had happened. He had at least gotten a letter off to her just before being sent to Petersburg, so he had been able to let her know he'd been at Gettysburg and had survived. But now she would have no way of knowing he was a prisoner. If she didn't hear from him for months—maybe years—she would think he was dead.

He wondered about Gerald. What had happened to his brother? He could only pray he was alive and well. Why had either one of them thought this would be a short war, or that it would be fought in the name of honor to preserve the United States? It had become a vicious dogfight, men risking life and limb out of pure stubborn pride without any idea why they were there. So many had come just for the excitement, to "kill a Yank," or "kill a Reb." Yet after soldiers on both sides were killed, a man could get closer and see the faces of the dead . . . boys, most of them, as well as men, men who were no different from any others, men with families waiting for them. Will had never seen such hatred and devastation, once-lovely and peaceful towns like Gettysburg and Petersburg turned into battered, bloody battlefields, civilians wounded and killed, pretty little farmhouses shelled to pieces.

He had done some of that shelling. His battery had performed well, and he had even been told he would get a promotion. He remembered moving forward to open his cannon on Petersburg. His men had pushed out of the Wilderness to shell a farmhouse where Rebels were holed up, then there had been an explosion near the cannon, where he'd been standing. Something had hit him in the head, and he knew now it must have been a piece of shrapnel. From that moment on, the memory of what happened had come back to him slowly.

He could remember now . . . could see the dead bodies all around him, men he had befriended, men to whom he had given orders, many of them so very young. He remembered being confused, unsure of where he was or even who he was. He had wandered off, seeking help, and had walked right into a handful of Rebels. Why they had not shot him down, he would never know. Perhaps they had seen he was staggering and wounded, no threat to them. They might also have realized by his uniform that he was an officer. Or, perhaps it had simply been a miracle of God . . . a God who might be gracious enough to keep him alive so that he could go home to Santana.

First, though, there would be Andersonville. He wished his head would clear so that he could think of a way to escape. He had to get home, get out of this mess, go back to his beloved California and his beautiful Santana and the children he loved so dearly. He should have listened to Santana, and he could only hope that when and if he made it home, she would forgive him for leaving her, that she would still love him, be waiting for him . . . that she would understand that he had thought he was doing the right thing when he left. His intentions had certainly been good, honorable; but the war itself had become dishonorable, men acting like animals.

"Keep movin' there!" someone shouted. Something hit him hard in the back, and Will grunted and stumbled forward. He wondered if he was ever again going to taste water, or if he would die of thirst along the road and be left to rot like so many others. "We're almost there, boys," his antagonist sneered. "Almost home."

Almost home. How he wished that was California, La Estancia de Alcala. Apparently "home" would be someplace far different from the peace and love he had known there. Home would be hell on earth for however long he would have to endure it. He would rather die from being crushed under a redwood than wither away and die of starvation or disease in some prison camp.

He straightened. The thought of California, those magnificent trees that stirred his blood, the beautiful woman who waited for him there, the smiling faces of his children . . . all of it brought a surge of new life and determination to him. He'd be damned if he'd let the Rebs win this one by dying in their prison camp. He would find a way to survive, and in the meantime the Union would win this war, and soon. In the past year the Union Army had won nearly every battle it had fought, and it had secured the Mississippi. Yes, the war would be over in just a few months, maybe weeks. He had to believe that. And when it ended, he would be free, free to go home to California, to Santana. He had promised her he would come back, and he was not going to break that promise.

Santana sat down on the ledge of the bay window in her father's study and took a letter from the pocket of her skirt. It was the last letter she had received from Will. She carried it with her every day, no matter what she wore or where she went. The paper was getting worn, the folds weakened and ready to tear from her opening and rereading the letter so often. Somehow, keeping it with her helped her feel close to her husband, and it reminded her that when he wrote it he was still alive.

She glanced at the doorway to the study before opening the letter again. She was anxiously waiting for Dr. Enders to come and tell her what was wrong with her father, if, indeed, he knew. Dominic had failed a great deal the last few months. He never went riding anymore, always too weak and tired, and Hernando had completely taken over running the ranch.

Lately a heavy grief had kept washing over Santana in waves that brought tears at unexpected moments. She didn't want to think that her husband could be dead, for to consider such a horror on top of the fact that she knew her father was dying . . . It was all too much to bear. Thank God her children were all healthy, little Juan twenty months old already. Twenty months, and Will did not even know the boy existed. He had been gone two and a half years, a lifetime to her, and a lifetime for fast-growing children.

Glenn was seven, and what a difference between four and a half and seven! Will would be so surprised to see how big his son was getting, and he had lost all his baby fat. Ruth was five, so bright and sweet. Little Dominic was three, a chunky, solid boy with black hair and eyes just as dark, a child who was constantly getting into mischief. It hurt Santana to realize the boy had no memory of his father, and every day she talked about him and showed all of her children pictures of Will.

She blinked back tears as she watched the soft rainfall outside. The unusually gray day matched her emotions. It had been ten years since Will Lassater had first set foot in California. . . . since that first time she saw him standing on the deck of the *Dutchess Dianna*. She was no longer the wide-eyed, curious child she had been then, but a woman. California itself had grown and changed so much in those years. San Francisco was a burgeoning city of many thousands, and the once-sleepy Spanish Territory was now a part of the United States and filling up fast with *Americanos*, in spite of the continuing war back east.

She wondered if Dr. Enders was right. He had predicted that once the war was over, California would explode on an even greater scale than in the first two years after the gold rush. He believed that the South would lose this war, and its economy would collapse. Many displaced and disillusioned Southerners would then head west. It would certainly be easier to get there now than it had been all those years ago, what with the overland stage making daily runs, and now a railroad under construction. It did not seem possible that those steel tracks could really be laid over mountains and across deserts and through Indian country, but Santana no longer doubted what could be accomplished with *gringo* money and resolve. The only reason the building of the railroad was going slowly was because Washington was too involved in the war. Many Californians believed that once the war ended, things would progress rapidly, and one day San Francisco would be linked by a transcontinental railroad to places as far east as St. Louis and Chicago.

If that was so, even greater changes would come to California, and even more people would flood into what was being called the Golden State, not just for the precious metal that lay beneath its mountains and in it streams, but for the abundant sunshine a man found there.

There was no sunshine this day, either in the sky or in Santana's heart. The rapturous happiness she had known with Will might be only a memory for the rest of her life. The things she read in the papers about the war were so startling and so difficult to comprehend, she had told Hernando to stop bringing the papers to her. Agatha still insisted on reading everything she could get her hands on, but to her the East was home. Santana could not bear reading about the casualties, the bloody battles that left ten, twenty, thirty thousand men dead or wounded. Was Will part of those statistics? And what of Gerald? Agatha had not heard from her own husband in months, but she had remained stronger than Santana had thought possible.

It was the children who kept them both going, and the constant hope that each day when they awoke, they might see their husbands walking up the road toward home. Will had been gone so long, though, that her marriage to him seemed like a dream now, a wonderful dream, of lying in the arms of a man who never really existed, a man who would probably seem like a stranger to her when he did come home.

She looked down at the letter again. Will Lassater was real. He had written this letter, touched this paper. He had been inside of her, had done wonderfully intimate things with her, and four times his life had taken hold in her and produced offspring. It was Will Lassater who had built the mill that Noel Gray had managed to keep in operation in spite of the loss of manpower, the mill that still brought in a great deal of money so that even in his absence, Will was taking care of her. The children had everything they needed, everything but the most important thing—their father.

"My dearest Santana," she read for the hundredth time.

It is now August 1863, and each day that I awaken in one piece I thank God for my life and my health. After what I witnessed at Antietam and now Gettysburg, I will never be the same man. There are times when I agree with your first opinion that this would be a useless war.

Perhaps by now you have read about Gettysburg. It could be several weeks before you get this letter, maybe even months. I just hope you do get it so that you can relieve your mind that I was not one of those many thousands who died there. But

I can tell you that whatever you are hearing about numbers of dead and the horrors of this war, it is many times worse than that, even for officers like myself. It is all too terrible to put into words. Perhaps one day, when I have come home and can bear to talk about it, I will tell you some of the things I have seen. The only way I get through every day is to think about you and my precious children constantly. Not a day goes by that I don't pray for you, hoping that all is going well there; and pray that the day will soon come when I can go back to California, to the land that I realize now more than ever is my home. I ache to wrap my arms around my Santana and hear her sweet voice, ache to see my children's faces and hear their laughter.

I love you, Santana. Always remember that, and forgive me for leaving you. I wanted to do the right thing, and I still believe that I did, but I am disappointed at the way this war has been handled, the ineptness of some of our military leaders, the way they have caused this whole thing to last far longer than it should have. If God should see fit that I am never able to return to you, please instill in the hearts of our children how much I loved them, and know in your own heart that I loved you as I have never and could never love again. You are my life, *mi esposa*, and I am determined to do all that is in my power to survive this ordeal and come home to you, to my children, to California. . . .

There was a little more, but she refolded the letter, for she knew it by heart. She put it back into her pocket and put a hand to her chest, taking a deep breath against the pain she felt there. It hit her whenever she realized that Will could already be dead and she wouldn't even know it. The ache sent shooting pains throughout her body, and she wondered if she would ever again know the happiness of their first years of marriage. Now, with her father ailing . . .

Her thoughts were interrupted when Marcus Enders came into the study. "How is he, Dr. Enders?"

The man rubbed at a several-days' growth of beard. He looked older than his years, his face puffier and his eyes redder than ever. It had taken him a while to get there that morning, and as soon as he had arrived, Santana had known he had a terrible hangover. She had ordered men to douse him with water, fill him with coffee and food, and sober him up enough to get him to the house, for all that morning her father had had a great deal of trouble breathing. She'd wanted to scream at Enders for being so undependable, but when he was sober he did good work, and he had gotten her through four births successfully. He was the only person she could turn to for help, being so far from the city, and she did feel sympathy for him, knowing the sorrow that drove him to liquor.

Enders shook his head. "Your father's condition is not good," he said, "but he's breathing better now." He stepped closer. "To the best of my knowledge, it's his heart. I think it's just gradually giving out on him. He will probably have spells when he feels better, and there is no way to predict how long he has, Santana. I wish I could be more specific, but it's just a gradual process, a few good days, more bad ones. The best thing he can do is not overexert himself. He needs rest, and he really should stay in bed from here on, although knowing Dominic, he won't do that. He's too proud to lie around waiting for death."

Santana sighed, forcing herself not to panic at the

thought of her father dying. It just did not seem possible. He had always been an energetic, robust man. "I will do what I can to keep him still and calm. I know that he worries about Will."

"We all worry about him and Gerald, Santana. I sincerely hope he comes home soon, and in one piece."

She looked back out the window at the rain. In spite of vowing not to go back to San Francisco again without Will, she had gone twice more, out of a need to keep busy and to check on Will's many holdings there. The last time she was there she had gone to a rally of Union supporters. There were men there who had seen the war close up, wounded men returned home, one with a leg missing; another an arm; one with a horrible scar on his face from a bullet wound, one eye missing and sewn shut. She wished she never had gone. "Thank you," she answered. "I know that you care."

"I like Will. He's a good man, an honest one, and brave. He's strong, Santana, and smart. He'll do all right, I'm sure. He'll come riding home any day now, I'll bet. They say this war can't last much longer. They've got the South in a rout now, and the Confederates are out of money and resources. It's only a matter of time. In the meantime, I'll do what I can to make your father comfortable and keep him alive. I know he'd like to live long enough to see Will again."

Pain swept through her heart. She knew what he meant. Dominic Alcala truly was dying, and Enders feared he might not even live long enough to see Will. Never had she felt so alone. Outside thunder rolled, and she thought how Will had written in an earlier letter that the sound of cannon and gunfire during battle was like a terrible thunder, a constant vibration that shook the earth and left a man nearly deaf for several hours afterward.

"He *will* see my husband again," she answered, needing to believe it was so. "You must be right, Dr. Enders. Such a terrible war cannot go on much longer. Surely God will end the bloodbath and bring my Will home to me." She rose from the window seat and walked closer to Enders. "I am going to the chapel now to light another candle for Will, and one for my father. Thank you for your help."

The man reddened a little, running a hand through his hair. "I wasn't much help today. I'm sorry."

Santana smiled softly for him. "You helped me deliver four healthy children, and you saved Will's life more than once. You have nothing to be sorry about. I am the one who is sorry, for being so impatient with you. I understand there is little you can do about my father's illness. Even so, I feel better knowing that you are here."

She left him, going into her bedroom and putting on a cape with a hood. When she walked past her father's bedroom, she peeked inside. He was sleeping. That was good. She walked to the other side of the house, down a hallway to a large bedroom where Louisa and Delores played with the children, using building blocks and paints to keep them busy and quiet so that they did not disturb their grandfather. Rather than cause a commotion by going inside, she quietly turned away and went to the double front doors. She stepped into the *portico*, remembering the day Will had come storming through there and into the house to drag Dominic and Hugo into her father's study, where he announced he would challenge Hugo for her hand in marriage.

There were so many good memories in this house. Surely God had not brought Will to her only to take him away at such a young age. She was only twenty-six. Will was thirty-five. She remembered how at sixteen she thought that was old, but now it did not seem so. And Will had the body, energy, and spirit of a much younger man . . . at least, he had when he left. What was he like now? Where was he? *How* was he? Not knowing was such torture, and her only solace was to pray. She put up her hood and ducked out into the rain to walk to the chapel.

*T*wenty

Will walked to the stream from which everyone at Andersonville drew his drinking and bathing water. Half the time the stream was just a trickle, so that a man could never get enough water to last even a day. With over thirty thousand men crammed into the prison camp, the water supply had gone down to almost nothing in the late-summer heat. The night before, there had been a terrific rainstorm, and the stream was swollen again, but now it was muddy.

Will dreamed of bathing in the tin tub at home with Santana. He'd gotten to the point where thoughts of the tiniest pleasures were all that kept him going—a real bath in hot water with soap; cold, fresh water to drink; a good smoke and a glass of bourbon; his children's smiles; the feel of his wife lying beside him, soft and beautiful, smelling like roses. He remained kneeling beside the stream, staring at the canteen, wondering if he would ever again know any of those things.

There were no good sights or smells at Andersonville,

only stink and ugliness and agony. The food was rotten, and there was little of it. There were no trees for shade. They sweltered under the hot Georgia sun, fought insects at night, fought insanity twenty-four hours a day. Men were crowded so tightly onto this barren piece of land that there was just enough room either to pitch a tent, using sticks, blankets, and pieces of clothing, or to dig a hole for shelter, covering it with blankets or shirts. Disease was rampant. Some men, including himself at times, spent half the day sitting on the latrine because of dysentery. Will figured any number of things caused the men to be almost constantly sick. It could be the food, the insects, the muddy water they drank. He guessed it was the water, because the long trench that had been dug for the latrine ran right alongside the very stream from which they drank, a stream that was called, ironically, Sweet Water Branch. Those in charge of the prison camp also used the stream as a garbage dump.

Living at Andersonville consisted of only a couple of choices. To make shelter and try to survive, or to give up and die, either from thirst by refusing to drink the horrid water, or from dehydration brought on by dysentery *because* of the water. There was a shortage of everything—food, clothing, medical care. Many who were brought there were already wounded, wounds that were never tended. Mosquitoes, lice, and fleas were everywhere, and at night the air literally buzzed with millions of biting insects. Will estimated that just about every fifteen minutes another man died. In the mere four months he had been there, nearly five thousand had died, buried without coffins, piled on top of other dead bodies in shallow trenches. Several times he had been assigned to burial detail, and he had learned to harden his heart against the sight.

Right now men were dying at the rate of one hundred per day, yet in spite of the thousands who died, there never seemed to be any more room. Every dead man was replaced by a new prisoner, sometimes two. It made Will wonder how it could be true that the Union was supposedly winning the war. If and when this horror finally did end, he supposed there was one man who had better make a hasty retreat, for every man at the prison camp longed to kill him. He was Captain Henry Wirz, commandant of the camp, a native of Switzerland who had served in various European armies. What was so perversely ironic was that Wirz had actually been a physician at one time in Louisiana, yet now he let wounded men suffer and die with no help. He was a cruel disciplinarian, and Will supposed his mean temper and ugly attitude came from the fact that Wirz himself had been wounded at Seven Pines in '62, leaving him with one useless arm and in constant pain. He was an angry man, whose voice everyone dreaded, and whose thick accent the men often mocked. They all hated him.

Will had often thought about escape, as had everyone, but because of the layout of the prison, it was out of the question. The entire border of the compound was enclosed by two fences, an outer stockade fence and, fifteen feet inside that one, a simple border fence made of posts and a rail. That inner fence was called the dead line. The area between the inner fence and the stockade wall was well-guarded, night and day. The minute any man even went near the dead line, he was shot without question. Some had tested it, all had died. Because the compound was situated on a high plain with no trees or shrubs behind which to hide, and no buildings to use for shelter, it was also impossible for a man to try to dig his way out. Every movement could be seen. Will had considered trying to escape when he was on burial detail, since the burial grounds were north of the stockade, outside of the compound; but again, there were simply too many armed guards for a man already weakened from starvation and sickness to try to fight or flee.

"Major Lassater!" A private by the name of Tim Sibly, a boy of only seventeen who had latched on to Will like a son, walked up to him, carrying his own canteen. "Here you are. I fell asleep." The boy leaned down to fill the canteen. "Are you all right today, Major?"

Will looked around at the mass of lean-tos and the men lying down in their meager shade. More men were lined along the latrine, sitting side by side, having long ago given up any sense of modesty. "As well as can be expected," he answered Tim.

"I shook out the blankets, sir, and I managed to swipe a couple of poles from a lean-to where two men had just died. I used them to prop up our cover blanket so there's more fresh air and light in the hole, instead of it being so damn dark and stifling when we have to pull the blanket over it for shade."

Will grinned, thinking how the boy's friendship had helped him bear this ordeal. They shared a hole in the ground, Will having decided that living under the earth was a better way to avoid insects at night. Among the prisoners there was an unspoken code of respect for each man's shelter, so that no one stole blankets or other supplies when any man left his "home" for any reason. The only time men took from another was when someone had died and no longer needed his supplies.

"Good idea," he told Tim. The boy smiled, but Will could see the fear and loneliness in his brown eyes. Tim was from Ohio, a lanky young man who talked often about his family, his mother and his two brothers and three sisters, all younger than he. His father was a farmer, and Will could tell he missed the man very much. Will enjoyed Tim's company, and they had had many long talks at night. It felt good to be able to tell someone about California,

Santana, his children, the mills. Talking about those things gave him hope that one day he would be home.

That was the greatest fear of every man there, that he might never make it back home, that this hellhole was where he would meet his inglorious death and be buried in a mass grave with hundreds of other bodies, never to make it home again, never to see his loved ones, who wouldn't even know where he was buried.

"We'd better head back," Will said, rising. He and Tim both turned as they heard the guards shouting for men to get out of the way. More prisoners were being brought in. Wirz was already at the entrance to the compound, marching stiffly back and forth.

"Let's go greet them, see who we've got," Will said to Tim. New arrivals were always a diversion, and every man in camp jumped at anything that broke up the monotony of the day.

Will and Tim headed to where the newcomers had stumbled or been pushed inside the compound. Will counted ten men, many of them with bandaged arms or legs or heads. One of them stirred a feeling of familiarity in his soul, but he wasn't sure how he might know him, since he couldn't fully see the new prisoner's face. Bandages were wrapped around the left half of his head, from under his chin and around the skull, covering his left eye, and there was an odd bulging scar across his right cheekbone, distorting his face. Still, his build, his mouth . . .

Will walked closer, until a guard shoved a rifle butt against his stomach. "That's far enough," he ordered. Will checked his anger as he waited for Wirz to perform his almost-daily routine of informing the new prisoners of the camp rules. The man strutted and swore in his thick Swedish accent, telling the new men that "If you got-dam blue-bellies even go near the det line, my men blow you to hell. You learn the rules, or you get no rations. One blanket each man. You wounded ones, long as you can walk, you got no need for a doctor. My hospital is full. Can't take no more. You all look well enough to me." He ordered his men to give each prisoner one blanket, then told the prisoners where to go to get their first day's rations.

During the several minutes that Wirz spoke, Will kept watching the man with the bandaged eye, his heart pounding with a mixture of hope and horror—hope that it was who he thought it was, horror that if it was Gerald, he had apparently received a terrible injury. He handed his canteen to Tim. "Stay here," he said.

"But, Major—"

Will ignored everyone around him, including the guard who had warned him not to go any farther. He had to know! Charging past the guard, past Wirz, he grabbed the arms of the wounded man. "Gerald?"

He knew in an instant, by the look in the man's good eye, that it was indeed his brother, but there was no chance to talk. He felt the blow to his lower back as a guard slammed his rifle butt into him. "What the hell do you think you're doin', blue-belly?"

"Who is dat man?" Wirz demanded.

"It's that Major Lassater," Will heard someone say. He dropped to his knees, the pain in his back making everything dark and confused.

"My brother . . ." he mumbled.

"Will! My God, is it you?"

Will felt Gerald's presence, but there was no time even to look up at him, to embrace him. Wirz shouted to the guards to "Teach those men a lesson," then came the blows. Will could hear Tim somewhere in the background yelling at the guards to leave him alone, but it wasn't his own beating that infuriated him. It was the fact that they must also be beating Gerald, who was already wounded and who had done nothing wrong. He covered his head and waited for the blows to stop, then heard Wirz telling the rest of the prisoners, "This is what happens when you go against the rules. Take your blankets now and make your shelters!"

Will felt men mingling around him, heard Tim's voice close by. "Major! Let me help you!"

"Gerald," Will muttered. He managed to get to his knees, his whole body in a rage of pain from blows to his back, his ribs, his stomach. He tried to focus his eyes and saw a man with a bandaged face lying beside him. He leaned over him, touching his hair, some of which was stiff with dried blood. In spite of the bandages and the ugly scar, he could see it was Gerald. "My God," he groaned, bending over and pulling the man into his arms.

"Will," Gerald whispered.

Will just held him, glad to know he was still alive. But for how long? What was the extent of his injuries? "I'll take you to my shelter," he said. "We'll be all right, Gerald. God brought you here so we could be together, and we'll get out of this place. We'll go home together, home to California, to Santana and Agatha and our children. This is a good sign. A good sign. God has let us find each other."

Men backed away, leaving the brothers alone, but Tim knelt beside Will, tears in his own eyes at the sad reunion.

"Tell . . . Aggie . . . love her . . . sorry," Gerald muttered.

Will's whole body jerked with a sob, and he raised up to look into his brother's one eye. He wiped at tears, forcing himself to ignore the pain that ate at every bone and muscle. It didn't matter where they were, or that he'd taken a beating just because he'd recognized his brother. The important thing was that Gerald was there, they were together. "You'll tell her yourself, Gerald, when we go home."

A tear slipped out of Gerald's eye. "No," he answered weakly. "Not . . . like this. I won't go home . . . like this. Half my face . . . my eye . . . gone. I can't ever . . . go home."

Will grabbed at his own ribs for a moment, taking a deep breath against the pain. "Yes, you can, Gerald. We have money. We'll get you the best surgeons to fix you up."

"No doctor . . . can fix this," Gerald answered, putting a hand to his bandages. "You haven't seen . . . haven't seen."

"All that matters is that we're both alive, Gerald. I'll take you to my shelter and we'll dig it out bigger for the three of us. This young man beside me, this is Tim Sibly. He's from Ohio. We share a shelter. We'll get you through this, Gerald, you'll see."

"I'll help him up, Major," Tim offered. "You're hurt." The boy handed Will the canteens, then slid an arm under Gerald's shoulders and helped him to his feet. "Come on, sir. From the looks of your uniform, you're a captain, huh? Looks like I'm runnin' in good company."

Will studied his brother, his own pain inconsequential compared to what had happened to Gerald. Apparently he had been shot in the face and had lost an eye. God only knew what was under those bandages, something the man didn't want Agatha ever to see. How was he going to help him? How was he going to keep in his brother the will to live and go home to his family?

So, this was where honor had brought them. This was their reward for trying to preserve the Union. He had no doubt the North would ultimately win this war, but it was obvious the ugliness and hatred would fester for a long time. He watched his brother—a man once handsome and robust, who could win any logging contest, a man who had shared Will's dream to build an empire in California—limp away, hanging on to Tim.

Will held his ribs with one hand and the canteens in the other, walking quickly to catch up with them. "We'll make it, Gerald," he said. "We're together now. We'll make it home and get Lassater Mills back on its feet. We'll be with Aggie and Santana again, and—"

Gerald stopped walking and turned to him. "Just . . . hold me, Will." The tragedy in his voice, on his face, tore at Will's heart. He dropped the canteens and put his arms around his brother, and both men wept.

Santana held her father's hand, her heart aching at the way he gasped for breath. April had brought such beautiful weather, and it had also brought the hope that soon the war would be over. Will had been gone for three and a half years, and she had not received a letter since around Christmas of '63, the one she still carried with her everywhere. Sixteen months of nothing. There was only one way to know now if her husband was alive, and that was for the war to end so that he could come home.

If only that would happen soon, for her father's sake, but even a few days now was too long to wait. Anyone could see that Dominic Chavez Alcala was dying, and in spite of the birds singing outside and the smell of roses that wafted through the window, her whole world seemed bleak. Surely God would not take both her father and her husband. It was too cruel.

"How is he?" Agatha asked as she walked into the bedroom. Santana had brought her father up to her own home so that she could be with him around the clock.

She looked up at Agatha and shook her head. "Sometimes he does not even know who I am."

Agatha sighed in sympathy. "Hernando and Teresa are here. Why don't you let them come and sit with him for a while, Santana?"

Santana looked back at her father, then leaned over to kiss his cheek.

"*Mi hija,*" he mumbled.

"*Si, padre,* it is Santana." She stroked his thick white hair away from his forehead. "Hernando is here. He and Teresa will come and sit with you for a while."

Dominic studied her, his eyes showing a little more life and sparkle than they had for the last few days. "Hernando?" He frowned. "Ah, *si,* my son. Is there . . . a problem? Did our . . . prize mare . . . drop her foal yet?"

Santana smiled. Dancer had given birth to a colt weeks ago, but he had forgotten. There was no use in explaining. "*Si, padre.* It was a fine, healthy colt. There are no problems. Hernando just wants to visit with you."

Dominic reached up and touched her cheek. "When Will . . . gets home from the mill . . . you tell him to come and see me. It has been too long . . . since I spoke with my son-in-law, no? He . . . works too hard. You get him away from the mill . . . tell him to come home."

Santana's eyes teared at this further evidence that her father's mind was going. If only Will really were up at the mill. If only it were that simple. Maybe it was best that Dominic thought that was where he was, rather than die thinking Will might also be dead, killed in a hideous, useless war. "*Si, padre,* I will tell him."

She rose and turned away. Hernando stood in the doorway, and she hurried over to him. "Oh, Hernando, sometimes he does not even know who I am. And just now, he told me to have Will come and see him when he gets home from the mill."

Hernando embraced her. "Dr. Enders said it might be like this. We can only accept it, Santana." He kissed her hair. "I just wish Will were here to help you through this."

She pulled away. "I keep telling myself it will be any

day now, and yet part of me fears it will never happen."
She wiped away her tears and left the room, walking into
the kitchen to fix herself a cup of tea.

"I wish I could do more to help," Agatha said.

Santana turned to see the woman had followed her.
She knew trying to be there for her helped Agatha deal
with her own sorrow over missing Gerald. "I know," she
answered. "Sit down at the table, Aggie. Would you like
some tea?"

"Yes, that sounds good."

"The cook and the maid are both outside with Louisa
playing with the children, so I will make it. Where are your
children?"

"They're up at the house with James. I can hardly
believe he's seventeen now. He's so anxious for Gerald to
come home so he can go to work at the mill. Sometimes he
rides up there on his own, works with Noel. He knows
that's what Gerald would want, for him to take over
if . . ."

Agatha could say no more. She put her head in her
hands. "I don't know how much longer I can stand this
waiting."

Santana stoked the coals inside the cookstove, then
added a few more chunks of coal. After setting a kettle of
water on top of the stove, she sat down across from Agatha. "It is the same for me," she said. "It is strange to
realize that in one way my father's illness is almost a blessing. Having him here has kept me busy, and has helped
keep my mind off Will and what might have happened to
him. According to the papers, every day we are closer to
the war being over. We will know soon, Aggie, I am sure."

Aggie sighed, blinking back tears. "Santana, don't you
ever get angry about it all? I mean, in spite of how much
we love them, and how much we respect their decision,

sometimes I get so angry that Gerald did this to me. I feel so abandoned. Maybe I feel that way because I'm not in Maine with my family."

"Being near my own family does not make the pain of Will's absence any easier. *Si*, I do get angry, and then I feel so guilty for it. He could be hurt, perhaps even dead, and yet some nights I lie awake hating him for going away, telling myself that whatever has happened to him, it is his fault."

Agatha toyed with the pepper shaker. "I had a dream last night that unnerved me. I dreamed about Gerald. He was running toward me, and yet he was going nowhere. He called my name and reached out for me, but try as I might, I couldn't reach him. I ran toward him, but you know how it is in dreams. You're trying to run, yet your legs won't move. Gerald kept moving farther and farther away, even though he was trying to move toward me. Finally I couldn't see him anymore. When I woke up I was drenched in sweat and I had the most awful sick feeling in my stomach. I can't shake it."

Santana reached out and touched her hand. "It was only a dream, Aggie. We are too close to the end of the war to lose hope now. Why don't you come to the chapel and pray with me? It helps my heart so much when I light another candle for Will and Gerald and my father, when I give all my fears over to the Mother Mary and—"

"Oh, no, I couldn't do that." Agatha withdrew her hand. "I do my praying at home."

Santana refused to be offended. "Aggie, I am your friend, and our God is the same God. He will not mind if you pray in a Catholic chapel with a Catholic priest. Father Lorenzo is a sweet old man who loves everyone and who will gladly listen to your troubles. Sometimes it helps just to talk to someone, let someone else join in your

prayers so that they have more power. He would understand if you do not believe in praying through the Mother
Mary. You can pray to God however you please, and Father
Lorenzo will add his prayers to yours. Just being there will
make you feel better. You will feel God's presence. I could
not have kept my faith and sanity all this time without
going there. I am going to have one of the men take me
tomorrow morning. I will take the children also, so that
they can pray for their father. Please come with me."

Agatha sniffled. "Perhaps I will, but I—I can't pray
with beads or anything like that."

"You don't have to. Just sit there and feel God's comfort. We can—"

"It's over!" they heard someone shout outside. "The
war's over! Word came by wire in San Francisco two days
ago! Hey, everybody inside! The war's over!"

Santana and Agatha both rushed outside, where a
stranger sat perched on his horse. He was answering questions already from some of the help, who had reached him
first. Louisa, Anna, Ester, and the children came running
from the backyard, and Hernando and Teresa came out of
the house behind Santana and Agatha.

"What is this?" Santana called, running up to the
man, her heart pounding with anticipation. "Are you sure?
Who are you?"

"Name's Jasper Hogan, ma'am. Me and a bunch of
others, we appointed ourselves official messengers, to ride
into the hills and gold camps and such and let people know
that the war is over. General Robert E. Lee surrendered to
General Grant at a place called Appomattox Courthouse.
I'm on my way up to the lumber mill just north of here. Is
there a road that goes right to it?"

"It belongs to my husband, Will Lassater, and his
brother, Gerald," Santana answered, smiling with excite-

ment. "I will have one of my men take you there. The man in charge is Noel Gray. He will be so happy to hear this! My husband and brother-in-law both went off to fight for the Union. Perhaps now they will be home soon."

"Yes, ma'am. Shouldn't be long now."

Did she dare truly hope that this was real? That the war was finally over? If that was true, it surely wouldn't be more than a month before Will made it back home . . . if he was still alive. She turned to Agatha, and they embraced and wept. Soon they would know. Everyone around them talked excitedly, and the children were asking questions about their father, wanting to know how soon he would be there. Santana wished she could answer that. She turned to Hernando, hugging him tightly.

"I hope he will come home soon, Santana," Hernando said. "But I'm afraid it will not be soon enough to see Father again. I think we should send for Father Lorenzo to come here and be prepared to deliver the last rites."

Santana drew away, looking up at her brother. "Oh, Hernando—"

"You know it could be any day, any moment. The priest should be here."

She closed her eyes and nodded. "I was going to the chapel tomorrow to pray, and I was going to take Agatha with me. Let me do that first. We will bring Father Lorenzo back with us."

He squeezed her hands. "Good. Teresa and I will stay here with Father until you return."

One of the ranch hands was already mounted, and she watched as he rode off with Jasper Hogan to spread the news up at the mill. The mill . . . Will's dream. Soon he and Gerald would both come home and pick up where they had left off, rebuild Lassater Mills into the empire it was becoming before they left. She had to believe that. The war was over . . . over. When her father died, she would need Will more than ever. He would come home. He would hold her again, and everything would be the way it was before he left. A little part of her told her that things could never be the same, but she would not listen.

Twenty-One

"I'm not going back, not like this."

Will leaned against the dirt wall of the hole he had shared with Tim for nearly a year now, and with Gerald for the last seven months. But this was not the Gerald he had known all his life. This man was a stranger, totally destroyed physically and emotionally. Will could hardly blame him. He felt half-crazy himself sometimes, from nightmares about the battles and horrendous suffering he had seen, and from the agony of trying to survive in this prison camp. What had sent Gerald over the edge was his wound. Shrapnel had shattered the entire left side of his face and put out his left eye. One piece had been driven all the way across his face, under his nose and into his right cheek, leaving the ugly scar there.

When he was first wounded, he had been captured and treated at a Confederate hospital, and it had been poor treatment indeed. The left side of his face was caved in and badly scarred, the eye socket sewn shut. The wound on his right cheek where the shrapnel had protruded hadn't been stitched right, resulting in the wide, puffy scar. Will knew in his own heart that if he were scarred the way Gerald was, he probably wouldn't want to go back either. How could he face Santana that way? Yet shouldn't she be given the right to see him again, to know he was alive? Wouldn't he still be responsible to take care of her and his children?

He didn't know what to say to Gerald. He had given all those arguments, but nothing worked, and he feared for his brother's mental state. It had taken weeks just for the pain of Gerald's wounds to subside, but he still suffered agonizing headaches. Although he had said nothing about suicide, Will feared that was just what his brother often contemplated.

"You have to go back, Gerald," he repeated for what seemed the thousandth time. They had had this conversation over and over, especially since the most recent newcomers all had said that the war was close to finished. In fact, there had not been any new arrivals for two weeks, a good sign.

"You know that I can't." Gerald's voice broke. "My God, why did I do this? I want to see Aggie again . . . see my children. James is seventeen now. Seventeen!" He covered his face with his hands. "Promise me . . . you'll take care of my family for me, Will."

The two men sat alone in the hole, and Will's agony was twofold. Tim had taken ill with what they figured was pneumonia. He had gotten so feverish and weak, he could no longer climb out of the hole, and guards had taken him to Andersonville's excuse of a hospital. That had been three days ago, and Will couldn't find out how he was doing. The boy had given Will the name and address of his family in Ohio, asking him to write them if he died, and begging him not to tell them how and where it had happened. He wanted Will to make something up that might help their sorrow, tell them he'd died in some glorious battle and had an honorable burial. "It would kill my mother to know I was buried in a common grave with a hundred other men," he'd told Will.

Will could only pray the boy would pull through and be able to go home. In his own weakened condition, he was having trouble keeping his own faith, especially when he looked at his beloved brother. He thanked God their parents were not alive to know about this.

"You'll be able to take care of them yourself," he said to Gerald. "When we get back, we'll find specialists who can do some repair work to your face, and when you're able to eat right and get your strength back, you'll feel better about all of this."

Gerald shook his head. "You know damn well no doctor can fix what's happened to me. I can't work, either. Mill work is dangerous enough with two good eyes. I can't do any logging or mill work with one eye."

"You can handle the book work, meet with buyers—"

"With this face? They'd be so repulsed, they wouldn't hear a thing I had to say. They'd just stare and wonder." Gerald ran a dirty hand through his hair. "The only reason I've hung on this long is because we're here in this miserable piece of hell on earth, and I figured as long as we'd found each other I'd hang on, for you, so you wouldn't have to suffer here alone. But if we're freed . . ."

Will's heart tightened at the words, words he had used before and never finished. "If we're freed, then what?" he asked. "What do you think you're going to do, Gerald? Go live like a hermit somewhere?"

"Maybe."

"And what am I supposed to tell Aggie? That you're dead? What if she finds another man and wants to remarry? It would be illegal."

"Nobody would ever know."

"Except me. I'd have to live with the lie the rest of my life. Worse than that, I'd know my brother is alive and alone. You're my *brother*, Gerald! I *love* you. We've always been close. I can't go on with life as though everything were normal and wonderful while my once-vital, intelligent, loving brother is alone and abandoned somewhere, with no one to care for him. Hell, Gerald, you might be surprised at how you're accepted by Aggie. Just to have you back will mean so much to her."

"Stop it! I'm not going to stand there and see the look on her face when she sees me for the first time. She's better off to think I'm dead, and you damn well know it. If you really love me, Will, you'll do this for me. I—I could let you know where I am. You could send me money." His voice broke again. "Please, Will. Don't ever . . . tell Aggie the truth. Promise me."

His heart aching, Will studied the shell of a man who had once been his brother. To imagine him living alone, a broken man with no one to hold him, love him . . . yet he knew what this meant to him. To love him was to let it be this way. He moved closer, put his arms around him. "I'll do whatever you want me to do," he said calmly.

Gerald wept against his shoulder. "I know I'm asking a lot. I don't know where I'll go . . . what I'll do. I don't know . . . I don't know. I'm sorry to do this to you, Will. However you look at it . . . my existence is going to make someone miserable. I can't bear for it to be Aggie and the kids."

"I know."

Will's words were almost drowned out by a sudden uproar from the thousands of men aboveground. The air was filled with shouts, whistles, even laughter, something Will had not heard in a long time. He patted Gerald's shoulder. "Stay here. I'm going to see what's happening." He hoisted himself out of the hole to see men hugging one another, giving out war whoops. He grabbed one man's arm. "What's happening?"

"They're gonna start releasing us!" the man answered. "Some of the guards told us they ain't even got enough food and supplies left for their own army, let alone us prisoners, and it looks like the war might be just about over. I got a feelin' it's already over, and they don't want us to know about it. They're probably afraid we'd riot and kill them all. I'll bet Wirz has already lit out o' here!"

Will looked around at the celebrating prisoners. He wanted to join them, but there seemed little left to celebrate, except the fact that maybe soon he could go home . . . without Gerald. The joy he had always thought he would feel when he heard the war was over was not there at all, only a heaviness in his heart. He walked back to his shelter and leaned over to tell Gerald the news.

"I don't know who will be released first," he said, "but we need to make some plans. I'm going to see if they'll let me into the hospital tent so I can tell Tim. Maybe it will help him recover to know he can go home soon." He waited for a reply, but there was none. "Gerald? Did you hear me?"

Gerald finally moved into the light, his face blotchy from weeping. "I heard you." He smiled faintly. "I'm glad, Will, for you, for Santana and the kids. You'll get the mill running full force again, won't you? Make Dad proud of Lassater Mills, make my sons and daughters rich."

Will frowned, hating the finality of his brother's words. "I still think you should come back with me, Gerald."

He shook his head. "I know what this does to you, and I'm sorry. You just remember your promise, brother to brother."

Their eyes held, and an eerie suspicion crawled through Will's gut. "Will you be all right while I go check on Tim?"

Gerald nodded. "I love you, Will."

"I love you too." He rose and walked away, heading

for the hospital tent, his mind reeling with a hundred thoughts. Going home, seeing Santana again, the work that would be involved in getting the mills back to full operation, what he was going to tell Aggie and how he was going to tell her, what to do about Gerald, how he was going to take care of him, how he was going to get his own health back to what it had once been.

He made his way through the crowd of ragged men, who looked more like walking skeletons, until he reached the hospital tent. He asked one of the guards there if he could go inside. Before, the answer had always been no, but this time the guard just shrugged. "Go ahead." Will didn't question why this time it was allowed, figuring it was because of all the celebrating in the compound. No one wanted to do anything that might start a riot. He walked inside the tent, wrinkling his nose at the smell of old blood and vomit, combined with damp, hot air.

He walked up and down the rows of cots, where men lay either groaning or quiet, most bandaged in one way or another. None of them was Tim. His heart began to beat faster with dread. Where else could he be? He searched once more, but the boy was not there. He approached a doctor who was bent over one of the patients. "Excuse me. I'm looking for someone who was brought here about three days ago," he said.

The doctor straightened. He was a gray-haired man with a wrinkled face and several days' growth of beard. His eyes were bloodshot, and he looked weary. "Describe him," he said matter-of-factly.

"Young. Only just turned eighteen. His name was Tim Sibly, and he'd come down with a painful cough that got so bad, he was even too weak to get to his feet."

"Tim Sibly. Yes, I remember. He was coughing up blood when they brought him in. He died yesterday."

The man turned around and continued wrapping the

stub of a patient's arm. Will just stared at him, wanting to kill him for telling him in such a cold, unfeeling tone that his young friend had died. The news itself stunned him. It wasn't fair! And surely it wasn't possible. Tim was so young. He had been surprisingly healthy, considering the living conditions, all the way up until the cough started. Will was sure the cause was the cold rain that had washed them out of their shelter one night, leaving all three of them shivering and wet. Somehow he and Gerald had avoided any serious sickness from it, but not Tim.

He grabbed the doctor's arm and jerked him around. "Just like that? He's dead? You're a goddamn doctor! Don't you have any feelings? Or is it just because it was a *Northerner* who died that you can tell me so flatly, without a care!"

The doctor looked down at his hand. "Don't do something that will get you shot, son. You ought to know by now that if a man is going to be a doctor in this war, he had better learn to shut off all his feelings. If I let myself care, I'd be insane by now." He pulled his arm away. "It might interest you to know that I, too, am a prisoner, a doctor from New York who served under Grant. I've been given the assignment of helping these men because the Rebs don't have enough of their own doctors to go around."

He touched Will's arm. "I'm sorry about your friend, but you should know better than to get too close to any man in this war. You must be Will Lassater."

Will blinked, still unable to believe Tim was dead. "How did you know?"

The doctor smiled sadly. "You are all Tim talked about. I was going to try to find you when he died, but I was just too busy. He was buried in one of the common graves yesterday. I'm sorry."

Their eyes held in mutual understanding, and Will

finally turned away. Tim! So young. Such a good person. He'd become almost like a son to him. Tim was going to go to California with him after the war and work at the mill. Was there anything left in this world that was right and fair?

Will made his way back to the hole in the ground that had been home for a year, determined to try again to convince Gerald to come back to California with him. Soon he could go home, yet he felt so terribly lonely. He reached the shelter and knelt beside it. "He's dead, Gerald. Tim's dead. He died yesterday. I can't believe it."

He put his head back and breathed deeply, wanting to kill someone, wishing he could get his hands on Wirz. His anger and his need for revenge for what had happened to Gerald and Tim, and for his own suffering this past year, welled up inside him until he began pounding the ground with his fists, growling like an animal rather than weeping. For several minutes he vented his sorrow and frustration, until he realized Gerald had not replied. Maybe he wasn't even down there. His head ached, and he rubbed at his temples. "Gerald? Did you hear me?" Still no reply.

He leaned over the hole, and his eyes widened at the sight of blood running along a little indentation in the floor of the shelter, pooling at a low spot. "My God!" He jumped down inside to see Gerald sitting against a wall, his wrists slashed, a pocketknife still in one hand. He had prized that pocketknife, given to him by their father, and had managed to keep it hidden from the prison guards.

"Jesus, Gerald!" Will grabbed the knife out of his hand and folded it, shoving it into the only good pocket he had left in his pants. He ripped off his own shirt and began tearing it into strips to tie around Gerald's wrists, but he already knew from the horribly pale look on his brother's face, and the blood-soaked earth, that he was already too late. He started to wrap one wrist when Gerald opened his eye.

"No," he said weakly. "Please . . . no. If you love me . . ."

Fighting tears, Will finished tying the bandage. "I won't let you die, dammit! Not my brother!"

"Please, Will. Let me be . . . with Mom and Dad. It's best this way. You won't . . . have to lie to Aggie . . . or worry about me. You will . . . have so much to do . . . when you go home. Just don't tell Aggie how I really . . . died."

"You *won't* die! You *won't!* I won't let you!" He started to wrap the other wrist, but with a last burst of strength Gerald grabbed his hand.

"It has to be this way. You know . . . it does. Let me go, Will. If you love me . . . let me go."

His eye closed and his hand dropped, and Will knew it was too late. This was what he wanted. "Gerald." He put his arms around him and pulled him against his chest, holding him there while above them men continued to celebrate what was now a sure Union victory.

Santana's memories of her father were made warmer by seeing how many people came to his funeral, so many that the little chapel at La Estancia de Alcala was overflowing and a crowd stood outside during the service. This was the way Dominic would have wanted his funeral, right there on his beloved ranch, in the quiet chapel where he had come to pray so many times over the years, spoken over by Father Lorenzo.

Birds sang outside, and it seemed so cruel to Santana that life must end, when the rest of the world continued unchanged, the everlasting redwoods still standing stalwart on the hills above. They had seen the passing of thousands. Santana felt small and insignificant, reminded of how short a human life was, and terrified that Will's life might be over already. Her mourning that day was magnified by the fact that perhaps she should also be mourning her husband's death. It had been nearly a month since they'd heard the war was over, but there had been no word from Will or Gerald.

"Life goes on," Father Lorenzo was saying. "And Dominic would want it that way. He left behind two handsome children and nine beautiful grandchildren, all sitting here this afternoon, quiet and obedient, an honor to their grandfather."

Santana hardly heard the man's words. So many thoughts occupied her mind, so much sorrow filled her heart. Nine beautiful grandchildren. Yes. Hernando's oldest, Rico, was fourteen years old now, and her own first-born was eight. Juan, the child Will had never seen, was almost three. She had always thought of herself as young, even though she was twenty-seven years old now. But on this day she felt old, for instead of being the child, she was the mother. Her parents were both gone, and she had children who looked to her as she had once looked to her own parents. Four children to raise. What a responsibility it would be for her if Will never came home. They needed their father—*she* needed their father—and she needed her own father.

Oh, the ache of it. How she would miss Dominic Chavez Alcala, who had always seemed to invincible, so strong. He had suffered so in his last days that it had been almost a relief when he died, for he was finally out of his misery. Still, she had never imagined him not being in her life, or La Estancia de Alcala going on without him. Several weeks before he died, when his mind was still sharp, he had gone over his will with her and Hernando. She and her brother would inherit the entire ranch, dividing its profits equally. Hernando would be in charge of running the vast spread, hiring and firing as he saw fit, but still required to discuss finances with Santana and keep her aware of income and expenses, consulting with her when buying or selling land or assets. If Hernando died, his half of everything would belong to his children, and the same was true if Santana died. And as long as the ranch stayed in the family, Will Lassater was to have stumping rights on the northern section for as long as Lassater Mills existed, or until the resources were used up. With as much timber as there was up there, that certainly would not happen in her or Will's lifetime.

Her father had been as generous in death as he had been in life, willing certain valuable heirlooms to each of his children. The house was Hernando's to move into if he chose. Santana would stay in the house she and Will had built from the embers of that first fire. That was her home now, and that was where she wanted Will to find her when he returned.

Yes, life went on. It would take a long time to feel the reality of Dominic's passing and realize he would no longer join the family at supper or ride out to check on new foals or accompany the family to San Francisco. He would no longer be there to give Santana advice, or to look at her the way fathers had of looking at daughters of whom they were very proud. He had long ago asked her to forgive him for almost making her marry a man she did not love and who would have been cruel to her, and she had forgiven him.

They went through the ritual of a Catholic funeral, and she prayed vigorously with her beads. When the service ended, the pallbearers carried the beautifully carved pine casket out of the chapel and to the ornate funeral wagon. The wagon would carry the casket to the family burial ground. Santana, Hernando, and Teresa and all of their children followed behind. Servants walked beside them to help watch the children, and Santana kept her face covered with a black lace veil.

At the burial ground, the crowd of mourners surrounded the burial site, and Father Lorenzo continued the service. During the service in the chapel, Santana had been so involved in her deep sorrow, she had not looked to see who had come to pay tribute to Dominic. She took a moment now to look out at the mourners through her veil, seeing friends, neighbors, business acquaintances . . .

Suddenly her heart nearly stopped beating, and she reached over and clasped Hernando's hand tightly. Hugo! Hugo Bolivar was there with his wife! Why? Surely he knew Dominic would not want him there. The audacity of it! The man caught her looking at him, and he gave her a half-smile and a nod, a look of mockery in his dark eyes. He knew she could do nothing to make him leave, for she would never create a scene at her father's funeral. And since his own father had been a close friend of Dominic's, most people would think nothing of his being there. They probably thought, after all these years, that all had been forgiven.

The man's presence made her sick. He must know that Will was not home yet, for otherwise, Hugo would not have had the courage to come there. Oh, how she hated him for doing this to her on this sacred, mournful day! Dominic had told Hugo point-blank that their friendship was over and he never wanted to see him again. Now here he was, at Dominic's funeral, putting on the appearance of a grieving friend!

The service ended, though Santana hardly heard the priest's final words. She and Hernando rose and each picked up a fistful of dirt. They threw it on top of the coffin, which was covered from one end to the other with a spray of roses cut from bushes on the ranch. Santana felt more tears coming, and she turned to Hernando, who embraced her. For a long time the two of them stood there after the rest of the crowd had departed, heading to the house to mingle and take part in the royal feast laid out for them.

"We should go join the others," Hernando finally said. "There is nothing more to do here, Santana. Let him be buried now."

"It just seems so unreal," she said, her voice hoarse from her crying. "If only Will would come home. I need him so."

"It takes time, Santana. Even though the war is ended, I'm sure he has to report somewhere to be mustered out, and there are probably thousands of men trying to get on trains and stagecoaches, trying to get home. Everything is probably a mess back there, and he might be trying to find Gerald, and Gerald trying to find Will. Don't lose hope yet."

She nodded, reaching under her veil to wipe at her eyes. "We can go to the house now, but keep Hugo away from me, please."

"Hugo!"

"I saw him . . . in the crowd."

"The bastard! He knows he has no right being here."

"Do not create a scene this day of all days. Just watch him."

Hernando nodded and led her away from the burial site. They made their way to the house, talking with old friends, sharing memories. To Santana's relief Hugo stayed away from her, and as long as he did so, Hernando left him alone. The afternoon wore on, and Santana began to feel the effects of the day's strain. When she saw that everyone seemed to be taken care of and was enjoying the food and wine, she quietly left. Louisa was in the hallway. "How are the children?" Santana asked.

"The little ones are napping. They are fine. James is watching the older ones."

"Good. I'm going to lie down for a while. I do not want to be disturbed."

"Of course." Louisa grasped her hands and squeezed them. "You rest for as long as you need to. Everyone will understand. The servants and I will see that everyone has what they need and we'll watch the children."

"Thank you, Louisa." Santana left her and walked to her old bedroom, feeling more weary by the moment. She closed the door and leaned against it, a thousand memories flooding over her, of when she'd been young and free of worries and responsibilities, the pampered daughter of a wealthy *Californio*. She removed her hat and black lace gloves and walked over to the bed. She would lie down, just for a little while, then rejoin her guests. She would be glad when the day was over and everyone left, although some had come so far that they would stay overnight before starting for home. They would have to be fed in the morning. She would have to remember to talk to Hester about that.

Later. She would take care of that later. Right now she was so weary, she couldn't bear to stay on her feet another moment. She sat down on the bed, then lay back against the pillow and shut her eyes.

In the great room Hugo stared at the hallway down which Santana had disappeared. Even though he had made a point to mingle with the rest of the crowd and make small talk, he had been watching her, waiting, thinking how vulnerable she must be, her beloved father buried that day, her *gringo* husband still not back from the war. Maybe he wasn't coming back at all. Hugo glanced at Hernando, who was lost in conversation, then he leaned close to his wife. "I am going to take a walk outside for a few minutes," he told her. "I will be right back. In spite of what happened between me and Dominic, I have many good memories of this place. I would like to go outside alone and ponder the good thoughts."

"Si, I understand," Carmelita said. She had long ago learned not to argue with her husband's wishes. "I see some women from our social circle in San Francisco. I will go and talk to them."

Hugo nodded, bending down to kiss her cheek as though he were a doting husband. Nothing, Carmelita thought, could be further from the truth. No one knew about the ugly things he did to her, how cruel he could be behind closed doors. She had learned to accept it. Perhaps if she had had children, he would be kinder to her. In public they pretended to be a happy couple, but at home she felt like a shadow of a woman, who wandered that big, cold brick house unloved and lonely. She had already had an affair with one of the gardeners out of sheer, aching loneliness, a need to be loved and held with passion and caring. If Hugo ever found out, he would most certainly kill the man, maybe her, too, but she didn't care anymore. Marrying Hugo Bolivar had been the gravest mistake of her life, and now she would spend the rest of her life paying for it. How lucky Santana was to have been saved from such a fate. She was a lovely, warm, caring woman who never could have survived being married to a man like Hugo. Carmelita knew she should be jealous of Santana's beauty, since Hugo still pined after her; but all she could feel was envy for the woman for being freed from Hugo's cold grasp.

She watched Hugo make his way through the crowd and out the door. She had no idea where he was going, and she didn't care. She walked over to join in conversation with some other women.

Hugo walked through the rose gardens outside. He well remembered where Santana's old bedroom was, and he suspected that was where she had gone. She would be alone there, and each room had glass doors that opened to its own garden. On such a warm day, those doors would be open.

In the great room, Hernando glanced around, looking for Santana. Not seeing her, he sought out Louisa and asked about her.

"She went to her bedroom to be alone for a while," Louisa said. "She needs to lie down and rest."

Hernando nodded. "I agree. Leave her alone." He looked around for Hugo, but the crowd was so heavy he could not spot him right away. Another old friend of Dominic's drew him back into conversation, and Hernando supposed Hugo had finally left.

Twenty-Two

Santana's eyes quickly closed, weariness from her loss and from worry over Will settling so deep into her bones, she wondered if she would ever be able to get back up, now that she had finally lain down. She didn't want to think about all the people beyond her room with whom she should be talking. She didn't want to think about her father being dead, or the possibility of Will never coming home. She forced herself instead to think about good things, her sweet children and how their love and their need of her had helped her get through all of this; the good memories of her own childhood and good times with her father; the way she'd felt the first time she set eyes on Will Lassater . . . and the first time he made love to her.

In only minutes she drifted off, voices fading, thoughts turning to nothing. Somewhere in the deep recesses of her mind she felt a presence, and in her dream state she imagined it was Will come home . . . come to lie beside her. Oh, how comforting that would be. She breathed deeply, allowing the dream to unfold, falling ever deeper into it, until she dreamed Will was lying on the bed. He was going to hold her. She felt the movement, and because she had fallen asleep, it took a moment for her senses to tell her that she was not dreaming, that someone really was on the bed with her, moving on top of her.

She felt a sudden alarm, and her eyes popped open. To her horror it was not Will's handsome face that she saw. Instead she looked into the evil dark eyes of Hugo Bolivar! She gasped and started to sit up to get away, but he covered her mouth and nose with a handkerchief that was damp with something that smelled strange. She tried to struggle, but her limbs grew heavy, her whole body went limp. She couldn't speak, but she could still see his face . . . his grinning face.

"At last, my sweet Santana," he said, "I shall have what should have been mine years ago. I shall possess what Will Lassater stole from me, and it will be our little secret, won't it?"

Her eyes widened in horror. Why couldn't she move? Everything felt numb, but not numb enough that she was not aware of him pushing her skirt and slips up to her waist. "One advantage," he went on, "to having friends among the lowlifes of San Francisco, my dear, is learning about the wondrous drugs that they deal with, many of them from China. Sometimes, you know, unwilling women are bought like slaves and forced into prostitution. In the beginning, they have to be given something to keep them calm, until they have been with so many men that they give up and resign themselves to their slavery." He laughed softly and again put the handkerchief to her face, until she felt dizzy and faint, her body even more numb.

"I did not know if this opportunity would come, but knowing you were still without a husband, and would be in mourning for your father, I brought a little bottle of this drug along just in case I found the chance to use it. You gave me that chance when you came in here to sleep." He grasped one of her breasts. "Now, Santana, I shall have you. You don't dare cry rape, because we were once engaged, and with your husband gone for so long, how many will think that you simply got hungry for a man and turned to your old intended, Don Hugo Martinez Bolivar? If you try to say I forced you, I will deny it. You came here to take a nap, and I went for a short stroll. And, after all, my wife is here, right out there in the other room. How could I do such a thing with my wife so close? If you try to tell others what I have done, they will think you are a crazy woman. And besides, you know what people think about rape. They always think the woman wanted it."

He pulled off her drawers, and no matter how hard she tried to force herself to move, Santana had no control. She was immobile. She could not even scream, though she felt the screams deep in her soul.

"Most of all, my dear," Hugo continued in his hateful voice, "you don't dare tell for the simple reason that Will would know, and you won't want him to know, not ever. Not only would he probably try to kill me and end up hanged if he succeeded, but he would never look at you the same way again. He would never love you the same, and he would always wonder if perhaps you were willing."

Though Santana could not see what he was doing, she was aware that he had unbuttoned his pants, that he was preparing to enter her. She closed her eyes, wishing she could close her ears as well, wishing she could just lose consciousness. But he kept on talking, and she still heard him; and she felt the painful thrust as he forced himself on her.

He kept grinning through it all, and Santana felt an ugly horror rip through every vein and bone and muscle and nerve end as she felt the sensation of his raping her.

"No one is going to come," he said, his breathing coming faster. "I bolted your door and locked the garden doors and pulled the curtains. When I am through, I will go out into the garden and reenter the house through the back. Everyone thinks you are napping, and they will not want to disturb you. You have made it all so easy, my dear."

He began moving in faster rhythm, his dark eyes glazing with sick pleasure. "But then maybe that was what you wanted," he added, his voice more strained from his own excitement. "Maybe a little part of you has always wanted this, always wondered if perhaps Hugo Bolivar might have been better in bed than Will Lassater!" His smile turned to a wicked sneer, and he gritted his teeth and kept up the horrid invasion until finally he shuddered in relief.

He breathed out a long sigh and settled on top of her, keeping his face close to hers. Santana could not stop the tears from coming then. They ran out of her eyes and into her ears while she lay there parylized from the drug he had given her. She could not even open her mouth to say anything, and the only sounds she made were little grunts and sobs that only gave him more pleasure.

"Ah, there, there," he said, wiping at her tears with his fingers. "I suppose you're weeping because now you realize you made the wrong decision. Now you realize I am the one who should share your bed. But, alas, the deed is done. You have another husband, and I have a wife, useless as she is. But there are many women in my life. You, on the other hand, think you must be true to one man. What would he think if he found out another man has been inside of you? I think you would be wise never to tell him. You can live with it the rest of your life, Santana, and be *sick* about it!" His smile was gone now, replaced by a dark, hateful glare. "You bitch! How dare you choose a *gringo* over Hugo Bolivar! How dare that *Americano* make me look like a coward, embarrass me in front of my business friends, steal my woman!" He kept his voice to a low growl, but the viciousness in it and in his eyes was horrifying. He deliberately turned his head to point out the scar from Will's hatchet. "Now Will Lassater has paid for giving me this!"

He finally moved off her, yanking her skirts back down over her legs. He buttoned his pants, then picked up her drawers and threw them on her chest. "Don't worry about the drug. It wears off in about thirty minutes. You will be fine after that." He grinned again. "Except that you will remember, for the rest of your life, that Hugo Bolivar raped you, yet you can never tell! You have no marks of force on you. You would look like a fool, and people would talk."

He leaned close again, touching her breasts while he kissed her with cold lips. "Please let me express my sorrow over your loss," he said mockingly. "And I do hope your husband returns home safely." He snickered, then turned and quietly left through the patio doors.

Santana lay trembling, still unable to move. Her head felt as though it might explode with her need to scream, to kill, but she could do nothing except lie there and contemplate what had just happened to her. The ugliness of it sank into every bone, horror raking her mind and heart. She had always known Hugo was a cruel, vengeful man, yet had never dreamed he could be capable of this kind of evil. And he was right to say that no one would believe that a man of such wealth and position would come to the funeral of his father's best friend, bringing his own wife along, and rape the dead man's daughter. Waves of nausea rolled through her at the realization he was right about all the rest of it. Even if she could prove rape, people had an opinion of women who claimed such things. There was always the vague wonder if she had asked for it or enjoyed it. She would be a marked woman, gossiped about, considered loose. The drug would leave her incapacitated long enough for Hugo to rejoin the others and mingle, looking perfectly innocent. He had planned this well, for he was also right that she could never tell Will.

Will! Hugo had just destroyed the joy she would have felt at her husband's homecoming. She would have to pretend to be happy, pretend to want her husband again, when the thought of any man touching her—even Will— repulsed her. If Will knew the truth, he would indeed go and kill Hugo and probably hang for it. He must never know. She would have to live with this for the rest of her life or risk losing her reputation, bringing shame and embarrassment on her brother and her own children . . . and risk losing Will. Even if he did not kill Hugo, his love for her would be dead. He would never look at her the same way again, never want her in the same way, never trust her. The adoring look he had always held for her would be gone.

She lay agonizing over what had happened to her, wanting to believe it had all just been a horrible nightmare. Yes, she had lain down to sleep, and because she had seen Hugo at the funeral she'd had a terrible dream about him. But as the feeling returned to her limbs and she was able to move, she realized it was all too real. Her underwear still lay on her chest. She managed to sit up, and she bent over, shivering in gasps of wretched anguish, muttering "No" over and over. This could not be true. But it was all too true.

She suddenly jumped up and ran to the washbasin, pouring water from the pitcher into the bowl. She washed herself vigorously, several times over, another hideous thought taking shape. After four children, she knew when it was the best time of the month for her to conceive, and this was one of those times. What if she became pregnant from Hugo? How would she explain a pregnancy to Will? He would think she had slept with other men while he was gone! Will was an *Americano* with a quick temper. Even after all these years, she did not know everything about *gringos*, how they dealt with a situation like this. Would he kill her? Would he take the children and leave her? She would be utterly disgraced, and she could lose everything dear to her. If she got pregnant, there would be no explaining it.

She looked down at herself, touching her stomach. Perhaps there was a way to keep from getting pregnant, or to abort what had just been done to her. Even after washing Hugo's filth from her, she still felt dirty. She must wash more. Perhaps if she took a very hot bath, she could somehow keep Hugo's life from taking hold. A hot bath and wine . . . yes, lots of wine. Maybe getting drunk would terminate a pregnancy. She had to try something, anything to ensure that what had just happened would not lead to a baby that would destroy her reputation and her marriage.

Someone knocked at the door. She just stared at it a moment, feeling removed from the world around her, as though she had fallen into a black hole.

"Santana? Are you all right?"

It was Hernando. He was supposed to have watched Hugo and made sure he stayed away from her. But then, her brother had probably been too involved talking with others. And after all, Hugo's wife was there with him. Hernando probably would never have considered that Hugo would try anything with his wife right there. And Hugo had been so clever, doing his dirty deed quickly so he would not be missed. "I—I do not feel so well," she answered. She forced her feet to move, still feeling weak and shaky from whatever drug Hugo had given her. She managed to reach the door and open it.

"Santana! You look terrible!" Hernando exclaimed. "You are so pale." He slid an arm around her. "I know Father's death was harder on you because Will is gone. I just did not realize it was quite so bad for you. Are you sick?"

She put a hand to her face. Did it show? She felt as though she had a big sign hanging around her neck that said she had been raped by Hugo Bolivar. "I . . . a little. I would like to take a hot bath. Do you think it would be a terrible thing if I did not come back out and talk to the others? I cannot face them right now. I am so tired, Hernando, and so—so depressed." She began crying again and collapsed against him.

"My poor Santana. I will get Dr. Enders."

"No! I do not need him." In spite of his usual drunken state, Enders was a very discerning man. She feared he would be able to tell just by looking into her eyes what had happened. Still, she might need him later . . . might have to bribe him into helping her abort a child. She would have to swear him to secrecy, and he would not want to do it, but maybe she could find a way to convince him.

"Santana, you're ill."

She pulled away from Hernando, loving her brother for his goodness. He was another reason she must keep this secret forever. She could not risk ruining the Chavez name. It had always held such honor.

"I will be all right, truly. Just tell Louisa to please begin bringing hot water. I will take down the tub. I just need to sit and soak for a while. It will relax me. Perhaps you could bring me some wine, some from Father's own vineyards."

"Are you sure that's all you need?"

"I am sure. Please apologize to the others for me." Already the pain of having to live with her terrible secret was tearing at her. If only she could kill Hugo! Her hatred for him was so powerful, she wondered if she would ever again be the Santana she had been only an hour ago. That hatred was made even more intense by the fact that part of her could not help blaming Will for what had happened to her. If he had not gone off to that war in the first place, abandoned her . . .

Oh, she must not blame him. It was wrong, yet she could not help an already-growing feeling of resentment. She needed him more than ever, but he was not there; and if he had never left, she would not have suffered this horror. She wondered if she could even keep her sanity now. It had been delicate enough with the loss of her father and her worry over Will. Now this ugly deed overshadowed all of that.

"Well, at least Hugo has left," Hernando said. "He and his wife just drove away, so you will not have to talk to him. He seemed sincere when he expressed his condolences to me, but I am still glad he is gone."

He raped me! Hernando, do you hear me? Hugo Bolivar was here, in my room! He gave me something so I could not move and he raped me! Right here in our father's house, on the day of his funeral!

The need to scream the words, to tell someone, sent shots of pain through her entire body, pain that seemed to gather in strength and culminate in her stomach, so that she pulled away from her brother and folded her arms around her middle. Oh, what a master at revenge Hugo was! He had gotten his revenge not only on her, but also on Dominic and Will.

"I am glad he is gone," she said, not looking at Hernando. "Please tell Louisa to help me prepare a bath. I need to sit and relax for a while in the hot water. And bring me that wine."

"*Si*, I will do what you ask." Hernando put a hand on her shoulder. "I am sure Will will come home soon, Santana. You will feel better then. In the meantime, you have me and Teresa, and the children. And Agatha has become a good friend. We are all here for you."

Santana nodded, and Hernando left. She heard the door close, and she walked to the bed, sitting down on the edge of it and bending over, breaking into bitter sobbing. She could not stop, not even when Louisa came into the room with hot water. The woman became so alarmed, she went to get Hernando and Teresa. Agatha also came, all of them fussing over her, all of them thinking that her tears were for Will and her father. At least she had that excuse, so that she did not have to explain her state of mind. She told herself she must somehow get over this. If she let it eat at her, they would begin to wonder about the real cause. She finally managed to calm herself, and Louisa prepared the bath. Once she was alone again, she gladly ripped off her clothes, clothes she decided she would burn. She could never wear them again. She had one other black dress that she could wear for going out in public.

She sank into the bath, groaning with the comfort of it, enfolded in the hot water that would perhaps wash up inside of her and keep Hugo's filth from taking hold. She poured herself some wine and drank it down quickly, then another glass, another. She washed herself over and over, wondering if it would also help to go to the chapel and pray. Should she pray for forgiveness? Had she done something wrong? Did being raped make her guilty of adultery?

More wine. More washing. She must flush Hugo Bolivar out of her body, get him off her skin, drink the wine to forget. Finally she put her head back and let her thoughts float into nothingness. She was not even aware that Louisa came back into the room to find her passed out in the tub, that she had to call for Agatha and Teresa to help get her out of the tub and dry her off. They managed to dress her in a nightgown and put her to bed, but when she awoke there, she got up and stumbled into her father's room. She could not bear to sleep in the bed where Hugo had done that ugly thing to her. She crawled into her father's bed, and she stayed for three days straight, eating little, giving no explanation as to why she would not sleep in her old room.

Everyone thought she was simply taking her father's death harder than expected. They fussed over her, all of them so kind. If only they knew, she thought. How would they feel about her then? What would they think? Would they call her a harlot?

The days slipped by, and the only thing that helped her back to reality, the only thing that forced her onto her feet and into her normal routine was the children—her precious babies, who were innocent of what had happened to her. They needed their mother, and her love for them gave her enough strength to go on. She took them home, home to the house where she had known so much happiness with Will. Perhaps there she could find some peace, find herself, pretend that nothing had happened.

Pretend. That was what life would be for her from now on. Still, the pretending would be easier if not for the fact that three more weeks slipped by . . . past the time when she should have had her monthly. The fear of pregnancy terrified her so that she could not eat. Sleep would not come, and she began plotting how she would approach Dr. Enders to ask him how she could abort the child. She had no choice. She could never explain the pregnancy to Will. She did not want to tell Enders, but what else could she do?

The day finally came when she made up her mind. She would visit Hernando, and while she was there she would find Enders and tell him what she wanted done. She could not send for him to come up to her own house, for Hernando would know she had sent for the doctor, and he would wonder why. No one must know she had seen him at all.

She dressed herself in soft blue, deciding that since she was only visiting her brother and would not be seen in public, she need not wear her mourning black. She put on a lovely little hat, needing to look pretty, continuing her display of pretended normalcy, the pretense not just for others, but for herself. Yes, she was fine now. She would show everyone that she was recovering, getting over her loss, getting back to her old self. She would talk about Will and how she expected him home any day. She would forget what had happened to her. Once she aborted the baby, she would be rid of the rape. She would put it out of her mind.

Yes, she could do that. She dressed the children and asked a hired hand to hitch the carriage. She would go and see Agatha. Maybe she would like to go visiting with her. The thought brought another little ache. She so needed to tell another woman what had happened, ask her advice, cry on her shoulder. An abortion was a horrible thing, a terrible sin for a Catholic woman; but here was something else she would have to bear alone. She could never explain this to Agatha or Teresa. She was too afraid they would not understand. If she lost their love and friendship, she truly could not bear to go on living.

No. There was no one with whom she could share this. Enders would be the only one to know, and since he was not family, it didn't matter so much what he thought. He would never tell anyone. She trusted him that much.

She gathered the children and herded them outside, preparing to climb into the carriage. Before she did so, she hesitated, her heart beginning to beat faster with new hope. Someone was riding up the roadway toward the house, someone familiar. He was mounted on one of her father's fine Palominos, and the way he rode . . .

"Will!" she whispered. Could it be? She told the driver

to watch the children for a moment, and walked down the drive that led to the house. The horse and its rider came closer. The horse stopped, then the rider kicked it into a hard run.

"Dear God. Dear God," Santana murmured. It was him. It was Will!

He reached her, and there was no time for questions, or for wondering what she would do now about the life that was growing inside her. There was time only for realizing her beloved was really there. Home! Alive! He dismounted and walked toward her on two legs, embraced her with two arms. He had not come back with some ghastly wound like the ones she had seen on some veterans in San Francisco. He was there, holding her, embracing her in those familiar arms, enfolding her in his love. Oh, how she needed this!

"Will," she cried, *"Carino mio!"* She broke into uncontrolled sobbing, and he cried right along with her.

"Santana," he whispered. "My beautiful Santana."

Twenty-Three

"I rented a carriage out of San Francisco to your father's house. I've seen Hernando. He told me about Dominic. Oh, Santana, I'm so sorry. It must have been so terrible for you, not knowing what had happened to me."

Will continued to cling to Santana, hardly able to believe that after three and a half years he was holding her again, feeling her against him, smelling her familiar scent. "What you must have suffered while I was away, raising the children alone, losing your father . . ."

Hugo Bolivar raped me, Will! What am I to do? I am no longer just yours. All Santana could do was weep and hold him. Even if she were able to tell him, which she knew she never would be, how could she do so at this special moment? How could she tell this man such a thing, when she didn't even know what he had been through himself? It was too wonderful for now that he was home, alive, in one piece. He was too happy to be there. She could not tell him such an awful thing. Perhaps, now that he was home, she could begin to erase the memory, to get back to the work of pretending it never happened—except for one thing. She could already be carrying Hugo's baby. She had been on her way to see Dr. Enders about an abortion. What was she to do now?

Somehow, though, with Will's arms around her, even that didn't matter. She heard the children coming, eight-year-old Glenn shouting _"Padre!"_

"Oh, my God, Santana, is that Glenn?" He let go of her for a moment, fresh tears in his eyes at the sight of his children. Glenn leaped into his arms, and six-year-old Ruth and four-year-old Dominic jumped up and down, neither of them remembering their father well, but realizing this was he. Santana had talked about him every single day and had kept his memory as alive as if he had only been gone a day. Little Juan, just over two and a half, hung back, staring at the stranger who was hugging his mother and siblings, not so sure about this man the others called _padre_. He frowned, pursing his lips, deciding he would not like his _padre_ right away. After all, the man was hugging his mother, and he didn't like that. He wanted all her affection to be spent only on himself.

For several minutes Will exclaimed over his children. He could hardly believe how they had changed, and realized what he had missed. With children, even a few weeks was too long to be away. They grew and changed and learned new things so quickly. He hugged each child, promising never to leave them again. Finally he noticed a small boy standing a few feet away, watching him with beautiful dark eyes and a pout. He frowned, letting go of young Dominic. "And who is this? Does he belong to one of the help?"

Santana walked over and picked the boy up, and carried him over to his father. "This is Juan Santos Lassater Chavez, your son. He is two years and nine months old, and he was born exactly nine months after you left."

A look of astonishment came into Will's eyes, and he

reached out to touch the still-frowning boy's chubby fist. "Dear God!" He glanced at Santana, then studied his son again, a new pride welling in his soul. All this time he'd had four children, not three. Here was a child he had never known, never seen as a newborn, never watched learn to walk, say his first words. He reached out for him, but the boy was reluctant to go to him.

"This is your *padre*, Juan," Santana told him gently. "It's all right. This is your father, and he loves you. He wants to hold you."

Juan just pouted more, putting his head on his mother's shoulder and wrapping his little arms around her neck. Will felt sick inside to realize he was a stranger to his own son. Santana patted Juan's bottom, feeling sorry for the look on Will's face. "He will get used to you. You have to understand he is just a baby yet, and he has never seen you before. When he sees the other children playing with you and being close to you for a few days, he will come to you too."

Will picked up Dominic again, reaching out with his other hand to touch Juan's back. "He's beautiful, Santana." He studied his wife, this woman who had waited so faithfully. She was more beautiful than he remembered, still shapely in spite of four children, still carrying that air of elegance and high-born pride. Her light blue dress made her skin look darker, creamier. Anyone who did not know her would never guess she was almost twenty-eight years old. She looked much younger, a woman who carried her years and her burdens well. Still, there was something in her eyes he had not seen before, a deep tragedy. He assumed it was because of her father's recent death and the loneliness she had suffered while he was gone. And she was too thin. She probably had not had much of an appetite since Dominic's death.

They held each other's gaze, both realizing there was

so much to talk about, so much time to make up for. Then Santana turned and began walking toward the house, Will beside her, the children running and laughing in front of them.

A plan began to form in Santana's mind, a plan to forever mask the horror that lived deep in her soul, and that would give her an explanation for the baby she feared she was already carrying. Much as she dreaded the thought of being touched by even her own husband, perhaps, if he was well enough and needed her that way . . . Yes, that could be her answer. She could say the baby was Will's. The child would most certainly be dark, but then so were their other four children. Will would think nothing of it. Rather than commit the atrocious sin of aborting a child, she could keep it and say it was Will's. Perhaps, somehow, she could learn to love it. After all, the child was innocent, was it not? How could she blame a baby for how it was conceived? Still, that was exactly what she was doing. She hated the life inside her, hated its father with even more passion than she loved her own husband and children.

Will put an arm around her shoulders. "I have so much to tell you, Santana. The war was more hideous than I could ever explain. I spent the last year in a prison camp. That's why I couldn't write you."

She stopped and looked at him, truly taking inventory of him for the first time, now that the initial shock and tears were over. So thin! He looked so much older than his thirty-seven years. He wore simple cotton pants and shirt, and she noticed he had brought with him only a small leather bag of personals. "You have suffered much," she said. "I can see it in your eyes." She wanted to hate him for leaving her, for what she had suffered from Hugo, but there was something terrible in those blue eyes, something that went deeper than the horrors he had seen in the war and what he had suffered in the prison camp. A thought suddenly struck her, and she drew in her breath. "It's Gerald, isn't it?"

Will looked away. "He's dead."

"Dear God." Santana moaned. "This will kill Agatha! I am so sorry, *carino mio!*"

Will turned to watch the children run and play. How could he tell her the truth about how his brother had died? Gerald hadn't wanted anyone to know, certainly not Agatha, not his family. "He was part of Sherman's march through Georgia," he lied. "Some sniper shot him. I, uh, I managed to find out what happened to him after I was finally freed from prison. I have the—" He hesitated, pain ripping through his insides at the memory of his brother's last moments. "I have the pocketknife our father gave him. Maybe Aggie can give it to James."

Santana wondered how much more sorrow she could withstand. They had all been so happy before Will and Gerald left. Now there were these lost years that they could never get back; Gerald would never come home; and Hugo had stolen something precious from her, a part of her that had always belonged to Will. Life could never be the same.

"You were right, Santana," he said, his voice broken. "It was a stupid, useless war. It should never have happened. If the South had not been so damn stubborn, if men could just have sat down and worked it out without all the bloodshed . . ." He sighed. "I could never begin to tell you all of it. There are no words to describe what I've seen, or the devastation the South has suffered. It will take them a lifetime to rebuild, a lifetime to get over the loss . . . and the hatred will prevail for years to come. We've saved the Union, but the price was high, and for many in the South, they will never be a part of the United States."

He removed his hat and ran a hand through his hair, thinking about Tim, poor Tim. He was glad he had at least been able to give the boy friendship and support while at the prison. Someday he would have to tell Santana about the young man who'd helped him keep his own sanity.

"Still, after what I went through at that prison," he continued, "as much as part of me has to feel sorry for what has happened, I can't help harboring a lot of hatred myself. Part of me says they deserve everything that happens to them. They deserve to suffer. They asked for this, and now they'll pay. But so many of them are just innocent citizens who never wanted this war."

Santana hoisted Juan over to one arm and put her other arm around Will. "There will be plenty of time to talk about it. For now we will just enjoy the fact that you are home and did not suffer some terrible injury. You need time to grieve for Gerald. We both need time to grieve, for your brother, for my father, for the years we have lost."

He pulled her close, wrapping his arms around both her and Juan. "I never should have left, Santana. I knew it after my first battle, but then I was in it and I had to stay. I was an officer. Men depended on me, and in spite of the ugliness of it all, I knew we had to do what we did. We couldn't let this country split up. I'll never know if it was right or wrong for me to go, but it's done now. I just wish I could have brought Gerald back with me. I feel lost without him. He was my right arm, a part of myself. It will be so hard getting started again without him."

Santana rested her head on his shoulder, breathing in his familiar scent. Will was here! Her beloved was back from that awful war. It was still hard to believe. "You will do it because it is what Gerald would have wanted. Noel has kept the mill in operation, and it will be good for you to get back to rebuilding, bigger and more successful than before. The only way to get over losing Gerald is to build Lassater Mills into the most successful logging industry in the world. You can do that, Will."

He kissed her hair. "I was afraid you would hate me for leaving."

A quick flash of resentment rushed through her at his words. Yes, there had been moments when she'd hated him for going away. After the rape, her feelings of anger and resentment had festered, hitting her for brief moments but going away again. Now Will was here, holding her again. It was easy to put aside the anger and blame. It was too wonderful to have him back again to think about the bad things. She just hoped that in time those feelings would leave her forever, that she and Will could find the joy and love they had shared before all of this.

"For now I am just glad you are home," she answered. "We can only take one day at a time, *mi esposo*. Gradually you can tell me all of it, and each day the pain of it will grow dimmer. For now it is important to let the children get to know you; and we have to find a way to tell Agatha about Gerald. It will be so terrible for her. She still feels out of place here, no matter how hard I try to make her feel at home. I think that once she finds out about Gerald, she will leave California."

They began walking toward the house again, and Will breathed in the sweet air he had missed, catching a scent of the ocean. A hawk flew overhead, heading for the pine forests higher in the hills, where the redwoods stood, ever sturdy, ever watchful over man and the way he had of making a mess of things. How he had ached to stand alone deep in the forest again, smelling the thick scent of pine, leaning against one of those monstrous trees and feeling its power, drawing from it a sense of peace, feeling closer to God and nature.

Home! He was home at last, with his precious children and the woman who was his entire reason for existing. If only Gerald could have come home with him, everything would be almost perfect again.

They reached the house, and Will took a moment to stand and look at it, the sprawling stucco home where he had known so much joy and love. "I never realized until I left just how much California had gotten into my blood," he said to Santana. "I'll never leave again, Santana. That is one promise I will keep."

Santana looked up at him, studying the blue eyes she loved so, telling herself she must not blame him or hate him. Yes, she had suffered, but so had Will. Somehow she must find a way to live with her secret horror, and even though he was a bit of a stranger to her now, she must allow a new consummation of their love—soon—so that if she was carrying a child, she could say it was Will's. She would carry the burden of the truth to her grave.

Little Juan suddenly reached out to Will, smiling. "Well!" Santana exclaimed. "I believe your son has decided to make friends."

Will grinned, taking the boy into his arms. Santana watched her husband's face light up with rapturous joy at being accepted by this son he'd never even known had existed. Yes, they would find a way to rise above the horrors they had suffered, for there was something between them that was stronger than both of them, able to conquer the bad memories and all the things that tried to destroy what they had together. That something was the love they shared, the love that had never left their hearts. She could live with her secret, as long as she had her Will by her side. Couldn't she? Part of her wanted to scream at him that she had suffered something worse than Gerald's death, worse than anything he had seen in the war, worse than that prison camp. She had been violated in a most devious, despicable way, and if Will had been there . . .

No! Look at him now with the children, hugging them all, laughing, she told herself. The children should never know, Will must never know. He was a good, loving husband and father. He was home from the war, and they would get their lives back together. Tonight, difficult as it would be for her, she would allow her husband to make love to her. They both needed it, needed to feel this reunion in the most intimate way in order to grow close again.

She followed Will and the children into the house, where Louisa and the other house servants greeted Will with exclamations of joy, Anna carrying on in Spanish about how she would have to fatten him up by cooking all his favorite dishes for him. Santana stayed close to him, touching him often, needing to reassure herself that this was real. Will was home. Somehow everything would be all right, except that Gerald was not here, would never be here. She knew how difficult it would be for Will to go on without his brother. It would be even worse for poor Agatha.

Santana slipped into bed beside her husband. After three days home, this was the first time they had slept together. For the past two nights they had stayed at Agatha's house, Santana insisting on sleeping on a cot in Agatha's bedroom. The news about Gerald had devastated her. What made it all the harder on Agatha was that there was not even a grave she could visit. It was as though her husband had walked off into the air and disappeared.

"If only I could have held him once more," she had lamented over and over. "Told him once more that I loved him, comforted him in his dying moments."

They had both assured her that Gerald most surely had known how much she loved him, that he had taken that love with him, and that one day they would be together again, in a place where there was no war, no pain.

The children had also taken the news hard, especially James, who had begun working at the mill, following in his father's footsteps. He had counted on his father coming home, and was so proud of the things he had learned, things he had meant to show Gerald. Will had spent a lot of time talking to the children, seventeen-year-old James, fifteen-year-old Suellen, eleven-year-old Dora, and six-year-old William, who barely remembered his father. William had cried almost constantly, mainly because he was distraught and confused over his mother's sorrow and the tears of his siblings.

"What a terrible three days," Santana said as she lay down beside Will. "The joy of your homecoming is overwhelmed by the news of Gerald's death."

Will pulled her close, reveling in the fact that he was truly home, lying in his own bed, his wife beside him. What a happy moment this would be if only Gerald had come back with him. Forever he would carry the secret of how his brother had really died, where he was really buried. He felt sad for James, too, who had cried when Will gave him Gerald's pocketknife.

"It's going to take all of us a long time to get over this," he said, running a hand over Santana's arm. "I wish I could erase all of this like a bad dream, Santana, but what's done is done."

Yes, she thought. *What's done is done, and Hugo Bolivar's life has taken hold inside of me. We must make love tonight,* carino mio, *so that I can say that this child was conceived out of love, and that his or her father is Will Lassater, not the horrible monster who created him.* Her emotions rose and fell in her like a mighty storm, part of her wanting her husband again in the most intimate way, to know this was real and not a dream; and part of her still hating him for leaving her, and dreading the thought of any man touching her that way. Somehow she had to rise above her fear, for she had no choice in this matter. To protect the life inside of her, protect her family's name, her husband's honor, she must do this.

"I am just glad to be alone with you for the moment," she said aloud, "to lie in your arms. So many nights I was afraid it would never be like this again. My heart aches for Agatha. How I wish she could be with Gerald this way."

"I miss him so much, Santana. I missed him when I first came out here, but that was different. I knew he would eventually come here too. Now I'll never see him again. With both my parents gone and now Gerald, the old place back in Maine sold . . . I don't know. It's like my whole past has been erased. I have no roots there now." He turned, putting his arms around her.

"Do you think Aggie will go back home?" Santana asked.

"She probably will. Her family is there." He rolled on top of Santana, holding his weight off her. It had been a long, long time since he'd given any thought to the pleasures of a woman, and losing Gerald made him feel closer to Santana. He needed her tonight, needed to know he was still a man, that the horrors of prison and the war had not destroyed him that way. "My family is here," he added. "I have no one else now. Just you and my beautiful children."

A hundred emotions rushed through Santana. An awakening of the old desire for her husband; and the stinging memory, images of Hugo hovering over her, the realization that she was no longer just Will Lassater's woman. "It . . . has been a long time, *mi esposo*."

"Much too long. I know it's been hard, Santana, all the sorrow we've known the last few days, being like strangers to each other. I want to get it all back as quickly as we can, the beautiful love we shared, the friendship, the desire. I am still Will Lassater, the man who left here three and a half years ago, the father of your children. You burned brightly in my mind through all of it. In the worst moments, when I thought I was going to die, you were there with me in spirit. I need my woman, Santana. Is it too soon for you?"

Oh, yes, it is, she thought, *in more ways than you know.* Yet even if they made love that night, when the baby was born she would have to say it had come early. There was no time to waste if she wanted to avoid any suspicion. She must force herself to bear this, and she hated Hugo even more for spoiling what once had been beautiful between her and her husband. "No, it is not too soon," she answered. "I, too, want to find what we had. I have missed you so, needed you so."

Will kissed her for the first time since he'd returned. When she'd first run to him, they had only hugged and kissed each other's cheeks, both of them feeling awkward in spite of their utter joy at seeing each other. For Will, it was time to find out if he was still a man. He feared something had changed in him, but the moment he met Santana's full lips, he knew that nothing had changed. She was still soft and beautiful. He touched her breast, feeling it through her gown and buried needs and desires burst forth with awakened glory.

Santana closed her eyes, forcing herself to remember that this was Will, her husband, the man she loved more than her own life. She wanted so much for the familiar desire to be there, and it came back to her in little spasms when he kissed her, when his strong hand caressed her breast. Somehow she had to find that part of herself that had enjoyed being a woman before Hugo ruined it all for her. She had to fight the panic and revulsion that wanted to rear their ugly heads. She must not allow it, certainly not this first crucial time, when her husband needed her so, and she needed to be able to say his life was growing in her once again.

Pretend. Yes, she must pretend. For the rest of her life

she would be pretending, lying, living with the awful secret. She felt perspiration breaking out all over her body as her husband pushed her nightgown up past her hips. Visions of another man pushing up her dress tried to make their way into her mind. No! She must not allow it! This was Will . . . Will. Her underwear came off, and his manhood was pressing against her thigh. She whispered his name, needing to say it aloud to remind herself that this was her husband and he had a right to do this.

But did he? Wasn't it his fault she was in this predicament? Oh, she wanted so much not to blame him, yet she couldn't help it. She allowed him his pleasure, feeling like a rag doll, so weary from great sorrow. The unhappiness of the last few years, especially this last month and now the last few days with Agatha, enveloped her. She could not find the passion she once had for her husband, and when he was finished she turned away from him.

Will touched her shoulder. "Santana! My God, I'm sorry. You weren't ready." He stroked her hair. "I know it's hard, but we still love each other, and that's all that matters. I didn't mean to upset you. You should have—"

"No. It's all right." She remained turned away, curling up, needing to scream at him that he had abandoned her, needing to tell him what had happened to her, loving him but also hating him. "We just need a little more time," she said.

She felt him move away from her. He stretched out on his back, saying nothing. Santana wanted to turn to him, tell him all of it, but he might not understand. He might blame her, never look at her the same way again. What hurt the most was that her passion was gone. Hugo had destroyed her womanly needs and desires. She could go on being a good mother, but she was not so sure she could be the wife Will had left behind.

Twenty-Four

Will watched Santana help Estella Joaquin tutor Glenn and Ruth. Estella had stayed on at La Estancia de Alcala after Santana married, teaching the children of the ranch hands, then tutoring Gerald and Agatha's children, and Santana's. Santana was assisting her today, and she and Estella sat with Glenn and Ruth at the huge dining table in the great room.

It was not his children's lessons that interested Will, but Santana herself, who had seemed deeply disturbed about something ever since he came home. Something was wrong, something he could not name. She was distant, distracted, nervous, evasive. He supposed it was only because he had been gone so long. They were more strangers to each other than he cared to admit, and he worried something had been lost between them that they could never get back.

She had so resented his going, and perhaps she would never quite forgive him for it. He knew he should get up to the mills and see Noel and get back to work, but he could not tear himself away from Santana. They had made love twice more in the last three days, but it was not the same. It was as though she were a different woman, not nearly as receptive and passionate as she once had been. In fact, she seemed to resent his touching her, even to resist a little.

Had something changed in him because of his malnourishment and suffering in that prison camp? Was he not the man he'd been when he left? He felt the same passion, the same needs, and although he was thinner, he had thought he was no different as a man in bed. No, it was something else, as though there was some secret in Santana's soul that she was not telling him. Perhaps she merely wanted to shout that she hated him now, would never forgive him for the lost years. Maybe she felt that if he had taken a stand not to go to war, Gerald would also have stayed in California and would still be alive. Will had certainly considered that himself. She didn't need to blame him for anything. He blamed himself plenty, especially every time he looked at Juan, whom he held on his lap now, a son he had to get to know from scratch, a little boy who still looked at him as though he were just a good friend of his mommy's, not his father.

He held a bead-counting board for the boy, watching his fat little hand as he poked at the beads and moved them back and forth. He smiled when he did so, glancing at his father proudly as though he had done something wonderful. He was a beautiful boy, his skin dark and smooth, charming dimples in his chubby cheeks. Will wished he had been present when the boy was born, and knew Santana must resent that, too.

Dominic sat on the wood floor nearby playing with building blocks. Here was another son who barely knew him. He'd only been ten months old when Will had left for the war, but at least throughout the following years he'd been old enough to understand when Santana talked to him about his father.

Still, the children would not be a problem overall. They were innocent and eager, and he knew he would gradually earn back the closeness he wanted with his sons and daughter. It was Santana who worried him. The children were unconcerned about why he had been gone. They took it for granted that it had been necessary and now he was home and everything was fine again. Santana, on the other hand, had never felt it was necessary, and everything certainly was not fine. Sometimes she was so warm, so genuinely thrilled that he was home. Sometimes the old spark and passion and deep closeness they had once had was there, but then it would vanish again, replaced by something dark and remote.

They needed to talk. Whatever was bothering her, he would get it out of her. Now. He set Juan on the floor with his bead counter and rose, but Agatha walked into the room just then. The awful sorrow in her eyes tore at Will's guts, and he wished he could do something to bring the woman happiness again. She had loved Gerald very much, and he doubted she would ever quite get over his death.

"I'm sorry to just walk in," Agatha said, "but the doors were open."

Santana rose, reaching her before Will did. She put an arm around her sister-in-law. "You know you can walk right in anytime, Aggie. We were both going to come and see you a little later. Did you get lonely?"

Agatha glanced at Will. "It isn't that so much. I need to talk alone with both of you."

Will and Santana looked at each other, both suspecting what this was about. Agatha wanted to go home. The thought stabbed painfully at Santana, for she treasured Agatha's friendship. Here was another change in her life. So many things were so different. Even though she had not been able to bring herself to tell Agatha about what Hugo had done, just her presence had brought a kind of stability to Santana's life, a sameness that she needed, a friendship she knew was there even though they did not share all their secrets.

"Come into my study," Will said to Agatha. He took her arm, and the three of them walked down the hallway to Will's study, which Santana had been careful to leave just as it had been before he left. He walked to his desk and picked up a pipe, filling it with tobacco. After he'd lit it, he said to Agatha, "You're going home, aren't you?"

Agatha looked at him sadly. "I have to, Will. I can't stay on here where I've never been truly happy, not without Gerald. It was all for him, you know."

"I know. You have parents back in Maine, two sisters, a brother."

"My parents have a huge house. We can live with them for a while, until I decide what I am going to do. With the money Gerald has coming from the mill, we'll be fine."

"I'll send you money every month," Will told her, "whatever Gerald would have gotten if he were alive. If I get the mills built back up to where they were and they grow even more, you'll be a very rich woman the rest of your life. You won't have to worry about how you'll support the children, I promise you that. You can trust me to send the money."

Agatha blinked back tears. "I know that. I'm not the least bit concerned about finances. That isn't what I came to talk about."

Will sat down in the chair behind his desk, and Agatha sat down across from him. Santana walked to a window, lost in her own thoughts, hating to see Agatha leave for more reasons than anyone knew.

"What is it you need, Aggie? Just name it," Will said. Much as he hated to see her go, he knew it was probably best for her. She had aged considerably in just these few days. Perhaps once she was back in Maine and with her family again, she would grow stronger and be better able to go on with life.

She dabbed at her eyes with a handkerchief. "It's James," she said. "He's been working up at the mill for two years now with Noel, learning the trade. He loves it, just as his father did. It's in his blood, I suppose. At any rate, he also loves California. He's met some young Mexican girl down at the main ranch, Enrique Hidalgo's daughter. She's only sixteen, but you know how young love is."

Will glanced at Santana, remembering she'd only been sixteen when he met her. She looked back at him, and for a moment all the sweetness of that time came back for them. She smiled wistfully, looking almost ready to cry. Then she looked back out the window. "*Sí*, I know how it is," she answered Agatha.

"At any rate, she's very sweet and pretty, and between her and his love of California weather and the land and the mill, he doesn't want to leave. He says it's his responsibility to go on in his father's place, learn the business from the ground up, work closely with you, and with Glenn and Dominic and Juan, too, if that is what they want. I would like him to live here with you, stay with you when he's up at the mill. I'd like your promise to be the father to him that he's lost. He may be seventeen, but he still needs a father figure, some guidance."

Will leaned back in his chair, puffing on the pipe for a moment. "Did you really think you would have to ask or coerce me into keeping him? James is a great kid. Of course he can stay with us. I'd keep every one of Gerald's children and raise them if I had to."

Agatha smiled through her tears. "Well, I supposed you would, but I wanted to be sure it's all right. Please promise you'll be very careful with his duties up at the mill.

It's such dangerous work, and young people think they're invincible, you know. They tend to take foolish chances."

"You know I'd never let anything happen to him if I can help it. He's a smart boy. I'm sure he understands the dangers."

"I just—" Agatha had to stop for a moment to find her voice. "I don't know what I'd do if I lost a child too. It will be hard enough leaving James behind . . . my firstborn. And he looks so much like Gerald. I will miss him so much. The trip home is going to be heartbreaking, but I think once I get there, things will be better, and at least I'll have my other three children with me. Do make sure to keep in touch, and remind James that he promised to write often."

Will took another puff on the pipe, then set it in an ashtray. "He'll write. I'll make sure of that. How do you intend to go back? I don't like the idea of you and the other three kids traveling alone. Let me hire someone to accompany you."

Agatha nodded. "I would appreciate that. I'll take only necessities for now, so that I can go the quickest way possible, by coach, then riverboat and train. I need you to arrange to have some other things sent by ship. I'll leave most of the furniture where it is. I won't need it, and even if I get a home of my own in Maine, I'll refurnish it. I just . . . I don't want to take much with me from California. It would only remind me of my unhappiness here. You can do whatever you want with the house, rent it, use it for a guest house." She glanced at Santana. "Santana, I hope you don't think my unhappiness here has anything to do with your beautiful California, or with you. You do understand, don't you?"

Please don't go, Aggie! "Of course I understand." Santana turned to face her. "I have always understood. I told you before that if my family were someplace else and something happened to Will, I, too, would want to be with them. You have never been truly happy here."

"What about James? Do you mind taking him in?"

Santana smiled. "Of course not. James is a wonderful boy, and with Gerald gone, Will will need his help. Besides, he is at the mill most of the time, or off wooing that young girl who has captured his eye. It is not as though he is a little boy who will need a lot of watching after."

"He still needs a mother."

Santana walked closer, kneeling in front of Agatha. "I fully understand your feelings as a mother, Aggie. I know what I would want for my own children in such a situation. I love *all* your children like my own, and I love you like a sister. I will do my best to be a mother to him however he needs me, and I will miss you so, Aggie."

She leaned up so that Agatha could embrace her. The two women hugged for several seconds, and Will felt more stabbing pains of guilt. Finally Santana pulled away and rose.

"I don't suppose we need anything in writing," Agatha said to Will, "but if you think it's necessary—anything legal, I mean . . ."

"Not on my part," Will answered. "But if you want some kind of papers drawn up about what is legally yours as far as the business—"

"No. I know how much you loved Gerald, how close you were. I've known you for many years, Will. I see no reason for legalities. Gerald's own will specified what should go to the children. All I need to know is that you have a will and legal papers filed that show that half the mill will always belong to Gerald's children."

"That was done as soon as Gerald arrived and joined in on the business."

"Fine." Agatha dabbed at her eyes once more. "I will miss you both so much, but I have to do this." She took a deep breath and stood. "I have a lot of packing to do. I'd like to leave in three days, if you'll take me to San Francisco and help me arrange the trip."

"Of course I will. We can all go, Santana, the children. We'll spend a couple of days at the house in San Francisco before you leave."

"Yes, I'd like that. Santana and I made a few trips there ourselves, just to get away."

Santana thought about Hugo, their exchanged words at the opera. She hadn't told Will about that encounter, and she never would. She hoped Agatha would say nothing, and decided she had better warn her when they were alone. She breathed a sigh of relief when Will changed the subject by telling Agatha to send James down when she got back to the house so he could have a talk with him.

"Yes, I think that's a good idea. He needs someone to talk to anyway," Agatha said. "It will be good for him to have you, and to work up at the mill, stay busy."

"Oh, I'm sure I can keep him busy," Will answered. "I've got to get busy up there myself."

Agatha turned to the door. "Thank you both, for your love and kindness and attention, for all your help, for agreeing so readily to keeping James."

"You and Gerald would have done the same thing if the tables were turned," Will said. "I have no doubt about it."

Agatha nodded. "Thank you again," she said before leaving.

Santana decided she would leave also, but Will stopped her before she could reach the door. "Santana, wait."

She turned, meeting his discerning blue eyes. Did he already know? Was it written all over her face? Did he sense it when he made love to her?

"What's wrong, Santana?" he asked bluntly. "Have

you lost some of your love for me? Do you hate me for going away? For having Juan all alone? For not being here when you lost your father?"

She frowned. "Whatever do you mean?"

Will rubbed at his eyes, sighing deeply as he leaned forward over his desk. "I'm not even sure. I only know that something is different, and I don't want it to be. Something is eating at you. Did something happen while I was gone that you aren't telling me about?" He studied her intently. "You know you can tell me anything, Santana. *Anything.*"

Not this, she agonized. *Never this!* "There is nothing to tell," she answered. "Nothing in particular happened. It is just . . . all of it . . . the lost years and all. I can't help resenting you a little for it, and I am sorry. I . . . I need time, Will. It will take a while to get back what we had before you left."

"And you will never quite forgive me for that, will you?"

She tried to hide the truth, but she knew he saw it in her eyes. No, she would never quite forgive him, but not for the reasons he thought. If he knew the truth, he would understand, but she could not tell him, and so there would always be this wall of misunderstanding between them. "I have much faith, Will. It has seen me through much heartache, and God brought you home to me. Above all the resentment, I still love you as always. I will find a way to forgive, in time."

"And in the meantime you don't want me to make love to you. I can feel it when we're intimate, Santana. You would rather I didn't touch you."

She closed her eyes, not knowing what to say. How could she explain it? She wanted so much to enjoy her husband with all the passion and joy she'd once felt when she was with him. "I did not say that."

"You don't have to." Will rose, walking over to her and grasping her shoulders. "Santana, I'm trying to understand. You need time. You'll get plenty of that for a while, because as soon as we get Agatha sent off, I'll be spending a lot of time up at the mill and with James. That will give you more healing time, more time to think, to get used to me being back. Like you said, the love is still there, for both of us. We'll get it all back someday, Santana."

She met his eyes, the blue eyes that part of her still loved so much. He was already gaining weight, returning to the Will she loved, so strong and virile . . . so gentle and understanding. Yes, he could accept and understand many things, but not the one thing she needed to share more than anything.

"I am sorry, Will. I do not understand these feelings myself. I am so thankful to God that you have come home to me and did not end up like Gerald. You are my strength, my life. It's just . . . all these changes . . . adjusting to you being home again. You yourself have not adjusted. It must be hard for you, too, after all you suffered. When I think of you at that prison, the horrible things you experienced there . . ." She embraced him, resting her head against his broad chest. "It will be all right," she told him, "just as you said."

Will wrapped his arms around her, hoping she was right. He did not believe she was telling him everything, but he also knew that whatever she was leaving out, she was not about to spill it right now. Maybe in time he would discover the whole truth behind this wall that had developed between them. "Why don't you go help Agatha pack?" he said. "It will give the two of you time to visit and be together these last few days."

"*Sí*, I will go and help Agatha," she said, pulling away. "But I will miss her so. These are such trying times."

"Yes, they are, but it will all get better Santana."

She forced a smile and nodded. "I love you, Will."

"And I love you."

Santana saw the aching loneliness in his own eyes, the almost little-boy fear that he had lost her. "I will help Estella finish the children's lessons, then go up to Agatha's."

She turned and left, and Will stared after her at the empty doorway. "What is it, Santana?" he muttered. "What is it you aren't telling me?" He clenched his fists, needing to hit something, feeling a terrible frustration that he could not even name.

*M*AY 1866 . . .

Will sat in a chair beside the bed watching Santana, who finally was resting normally. The baby had come quickly, so quickly that Santana had lain for two days in shivering shock, while Will lived with the desperate fear that she would die. They had fed the baby goat's milk, but not just because Santana was too sick to breast-feed. Dr. Enders had told Will that, unlike with her other children, Santana just was not producing the milk that she should be for this one. Her breasts were already beginning to dry, and later that day a Mexican woman from the main ranch, who had given birth three weeks earlier and was producing more milk than her baby needed, would arrive to see if the new Lassater son might take his feedings from her.

Yes, it was another son, but many things were different about this birth. Santana had never been as excited and happy about the baby as she had been about the others. The birth had been difficult and dangerous, whereas the others had all been relatively easy. Now the problem with no milk. And there was one other problem—a big one—

one Santana did not know about yet. Dr. Enders had said the boy would be mentally retarded.

Santana stirred, and Will sighed with the agony of having to tell her the news. The baby slept quietly in a bassinet beside the bed. He was a pretty little boy, dark like their other children, but his eyes were slanted, his nose too flat. Odd little flaws that, combined with the boy being unusually quiet and lifeless, Enders said were signs of retardation. He seemed healthy enough otherwise. All his parts were there, and he seemed to respond to being held. Will had held him several times already, held him and wept over feeling guilty for his condition. The only thing he could figure was that it had something to do with his own condition when he first arrived home. He had been malnourished, and for most of the previous year he'd either been sick or fighting off sickness. Had some illness lingered in his body that he'd passed on to the baby?

Santana opened her eyes and saw Will sitting there. It took her a moment to gather her thoughts and focus on him. "Will," she said weakly. She touched her stomach. "The baby . . ."

"He's lying right here beside you. You've been only half-conscious for a couple of days now." Will rose and leaned over her, kissing her cheek. All these months they had not made love nearly as often as they once would have, and for the last three months they had stopped altogether. For the first time in their marriage Santana had used the pregnancy as an excuse, but Will knew it was something more. She already blamed him for leaving her. Now he had to tell her that her baby was retarded and that it was probably his fault. The wall that had been growing between them would just get even higher. He loved her so, but he had lost her.

"He was born too fast and you went into shock," he explained, stroking her hair back from her face. "You also aren't producing milk like you should. We're bringing a woman here from the ranch to act as nursemaid, if the boy will take her milk."

Santana frowned, touching her breast, then looking at the bassinet. "The boy? It's a boy?"

Will wondered at the lack of excitement in her voice. "Yes. I haven't named him. I figured I'd let you do it. I have to tell you something, Santana, about the baby. It isn't good news."

Her eyes widened and quickly teared, and they seemed to show a strange guilt. "What? What is wrong with him?"

Will closed his own eyes for a moment, searching for the courage to say the words. "He's retarded, Santana. The doctor says we should put him away somewhere, if they have places like that in San Francisco, but that isn't my decision."

Santana covered her eyes. "Dear God! Dear God!" Was this God's justice, His punishment for Hugo's sin? But how cruel for the baby! He should not be punished for such a thing. Worse, maybe it was her fault, for hating the fetus all the while she carried it, wishing it would be born dead and she would not have to look at it and care for it the rest of her life. Oh, dear God in heaven, that was it! Her baby was suffering because of her! Maybe it was God punishing her for allowing the rape. But she hadn't. She hadn't been able to move, hadn't been able to stop him.

"It's my fault," Will said, surprising her.

She uncovered her eyes, looking at him in confusion. "What do you mean?"

"My condition, when I came home. I wasn't healthy. Maybe I picked up something in that prison camp, something that affected my health and affected the baby." He sat down in the chair again, putting his head in his hands. "It's the only thing I can think of."

Santana wanted to scream at him that it was not his

fault. The baby was not even his. She had tried so hard to think of it as Will's, but it was impossible. Now, besides keeping the secret of the rape, she had to live with this awful guilt of having hated her own baby. She had hated it so much that her body would not even produce milk. Not wanting this baby had dried her up in so many ways, her passion, her joy, her love for Will. She had to make up for that somehow.

"We cannot take him to a strange place where he will never be loved," she said. "He is . . . our son. We will love him the same as our other children, and his sister and brothers will also love him. They will help him learn and play, and with the love of this family he will live as normal a life as possible. Give him to me. I want to see my baby."

Will looked at her, and the tears in his eyes tore at her heart. Oh, it hurt so to let him think it was his fault, but it was all she could do if she wanted to keep the truth hidden. For the baby's sake, she must do that. The fact that he was retarded made him seem even more innocent and vulnerable. Now that he was born, she felt different about him. Perhaps if she just held him . . .

Will rose and leaned over the bassinet, then picked the boy up and laid him beside her. "He has some strange features. Enders says that's some of the signs. He's also extremely quiet, hardly lets out a peep. Enders says he'll probably never talk much when he's older. He knew a family with a baby like this back east. If he does learn to talk, he'll never speak well, and he'll never grow mentally beyond three or four years old. That's just his guess for now. You just have to take a day at a time and see how he progresses."

Santana turned the blanket back from the baby to see that all his parts were there. Physically, except for the slight flaws in his face, he looked normal, all his fingers and toes in place. "He is so small."

"He isn't full term. Maybe retarded babies come sooner. I don't know."

Yes, she thought, that was a good explanation. The baby opened his dark eyes and looked at her, and at first she struggled not to see Hugo Bolivar in those eyes, but that feeling quickly left her. This was her baby, her tiny son, who depended on his mother to care for him, love him. He would always be more helpless than other children, and this little piece of life was not to blame for his own existence.

"We will never send him away," she told Will as she wrapped the blanket around the baby again. "Never. He is our son, and we will love him and teach him that he is no different from other children." She looked at Will. "It is not your fault. It is *not* your fault. These things happen."

A tear slipped down his cheek. "I'm so sorry for all of it, Santana. When are you going to forgive me? When are we going to be as close as we once were?"

She pulled the baby to her breast. "Little Valioso will help us grow closer. He will need us, our love, and together we will make him know *he* is loved and accepted. You don't want to send him away, do you?"

Will smiled. "No. I want to keep him right here with us. Valioso?"

"He is precious, very special, so he will be our Valioso. Angel, precious Angel."

The baby grabbed at her gown with a tiny fist. Santana looked down at him and kissed his soft cheek. How strange that all her hatred vanished at the sight of him, the touch of him, the feel of her baby against her breast. There was only one way to get over Hugo's rape and the horror she had lived with all these months, and that was to shower this baby with all the love she could give him. To allow Will to love him as he would his own son, let him be a part of the Lassater family, a family she intended to hold together in love and not let Hugo Bolivar destroy. Yes, that would be the ultimate victory for Hugo, for this awful wall of misunderstanding between her and Will to build into something that would leave their marriage in shambles. She would not let him defeat her this way. He had almost succeeded, until she set eyes on her little Valioso, so frail and helpless and so innocent of his heritage.

"This is our baby," she told Will. "Our baby." She met Will's eyes again. "Do not ever blame yourself for this. *I* do not blame you. Please believe that. God gives us what he gives us, and we must accept it. God will see us through this, as he has seen us through so many things. We will light a candle for our baby, and we will pray for him every day and ask God to help us know how to raise him to be as normal as possible."

Will moved onto the bed beside his wife and new son, putting his arms around both of them. "Maybe you're right," he said. "I only know that I love you, Santana, more than my own life. And I love this helpless little boy and feel responsible to raise him as best I can." He leaned over and kissed Santana, still wondering deep inside if there was something she had never told him. But if pressing the issue kept her far away from him, then he would not mention it again. All that mattered was that this precious little boy was going to help them get closer. "We'll be all right, Santana, won't we?"

She could hardly see him for the tears in her eyes. "*Sí, mi esposo*, we will be all right. Do the other children know about the baby's condition?"

"They know, but I don't think they fully understand. They're just excited about having a new brother."

Santana smiled, and to her surprise she realized she wanted to smile. She was not forcing it for Will's sake. "Our children have good hearts, like their father."

Will touched her face. "Santana, we've been so far apart all these months—"

"Do not talk about it. It will not be that way anymore. *Te quiero mucho, carino mio.*" Yes, she loved him, more than ever. She had been prepared to hate this child, but the fact remained that she had carried him for nine months, and half of him belonged only to her. Her own body had given him life for nine months, and now Valioso would depend on her totally for support and love. She could not deny him those things because of his despicable father. Hugo would never know that this child was his. Everyone believed it was Will's baby, and she would love it as Will's.

Weariness set in both her and Will, for all the emotional strain they had been through over the nine months since he'd come home. They lay with their arms wrapped around each other, the baby between them making no sound. He kicked his little feet and his tiny arms flailed, one fist grabbing his father's shirt, the other a ruffle on his mother's gown.

Part Three

Twenty-Five

MAY 1869 . . .

Santana took hold of Will's hand as she disembarked their
elegant Victoria carriage. One of several servants hired by
Governor Henry Haight for this grand occasion directed
Will's driver where to park the carriage, informing him
that there was food and drink for the drivers in another
area of the grounds, where they'd wait for the governor's
party to end.

Santana breathed deeply against nervousness in attending this gala. All of San Francisco's high society would
be there. Will was among those who'd been invited to join
Governor Haight at the new capitol building in Sacramento to celebrate the completion of both the building
and the transcontinental railroad. Santana was pleased and
proud that Will had been included among the guests, but
for the past three years she had not done much socializing.
She had concentrated on devoting her time and attention
to little Valioso. He could even speak a few words now,
something no one, not even Will, had believed he would
ever do.

The son she was so sure she would hate before he was born had turned out to be a great pleasure, loving and sweet, always smiling and wanting to please. He almost never cried, and the whole family doted on him, all the other children working hard at trying to teach him things. Realizing how her precious angel had brought the family close again after Will's return made her love him all the more. She had even managed to push the memory of the boy's conception into the deep recesses of her mind, and allowed Will his sexual needs. She had learned to feign desire to such an extent that she was convinced she was healed emotionally from her rape. A year and a half ago she'd given birth to another child, a daughter named Julia Louisa.

Valioso's special needs, combined with tending another baby and Will spending so much time rebuilding his business, had provided enough distractions that the opportunity for making love did not arise as often as in those first years. Will did not complain, and Santana was satisfied that she had kept her terrible secret. She was glad to have managed a normal family life in spite of it, and even worked around Valioso's problems.

Yes, she had done a very good job of overcoming her inner turmoil and horror all by herself. She had much to be proud of. Six children for Will Lassater! Yes, Valioso was Will's son, just as much as if Will had fathered him. The two of them were close, and whenever Will was home Valioso was in his arms or on his lap. People knew better than to stare at or make fun of Will Lassater's boy, or they would answer to Will.

"Are you sure I look all right?" she asked her husband.

Will had taken her arm and was leading her toward the white pillars of the new capitol building. At her question, he stopped and turned, studying her a moment.

"Santana, you have never looked more beautiful, and I honestly mean that."

"And you have never looked more handsome, *mi esposo*."

Will had regained his powerful build, and his face was tanned, the lines of aging only making him more handsome in her eyes. Those lines had been put there by the war, and his brother's death, and years of hard work and long hours in rebuilding Lassater Mills to one of the most successful and wealthy businesses in California. She had married well when she'd wed this *gringo* with the blue eyes that still stirred her soul. She loved him for the way he had accepted her decision to keep Valioso. He had never complained about the time she spent with the boy, and he spent many hours with him himself, teaching, loving, guiding.

"I do not often see you this way," she continued, "wearing a handsome black silk suit and top hat." She put out her arm again. "I am honored to attend this party with the handsome, wealthy Will Lassater, esteemed guest of the governor."

Will grinned, leaning over to kiss her cheek. "I am the honored one, coming here with a true *Californio*, my beautiful Spanish wife. The other wives will be jealous at how trim you still are after six children. And that dress . . ."

He stopped and looked her over once more. She had had her ball gown specially made for the occasion. It was a soft peach color, Will's favorite, and the off-the-shoulder bodice came just low enough to reveal an enticing bit of her full bosom. White ruffles of Spanish lace bordered the bodice, and the dress fit her waist tightly before flaring into a cascade of ruffles in an overskirt that was fashionably looped up at the sides, revealing a long underskirt with a train at the back. The lace-frilled sleeves were short and puffed, and she wore white-silk evening gloves and carried a white-lace fan. A diamond necklace, a gift from Will on her last birthday, graced her throat, and matching diamond earrings dangled from her lobes. She wore more diamonds on her wrist, and her hair was twisted into a pile of dark curls that were decorated with diamond-studded combs.

"You'll be the most beautiful woman here," Will told her.

"I am so nervous, Will. It has been a long time since I've done anything socially, and now to have it be such a grand occasion, an invitation from the governor himself . . ." Would Hugo be there? That was her biggest fear. She had spent these years forcing back the loathsome memories, almost convincing herself that the rape had never happened. She could live with all of it as long as she never had to see Hugo Bolivar again.

"You'll be fine," Will said. "Relax and enjoy yourself, Santana. It will be good for you. You've buried yourself at home with Valioso and little Julia for three years now. You deserve some time away to enjoy yourself. We both do."

"Do you think Valioso will be all right away from us? Did you see how he looked when we left, as though he thought we were never coming back?"

Will squeezed her arm reassuringly. "Santana, he has all his brothers and sisters around him, and you know Louisa loves him like her own. He's home and safe and loved, and we'll head right back tomorrow after a well-deserved night alone together. It's been a long time since you and I were truly alone, away from that brood of kids."

He led her up the marble steps and to the entrance to the main area of the capitol building, which was being used that evening for the governor's celebration ball. Lovely violin music filled the room, where many people already milled about with drinks in their hands, their voices and the music echoing against the marble floor and walls.

A young man stopped them to ask for their invitation, then turned and called out their names as they entered.

"Mr. William Lassater of Lassater Mills, and his wife, Senora Santana Maria Chavez de Lassater."

Santana felt heat rush to her cheeks as everyone turned to watch them enter. For some reason the ugliness of what Hugo had done hit her hard as these people stared at her. Did they know? Was it written on her face? No! No, she must stop thinking such things. Of course they didn't know. She was simply the daughter of the wealthy Dominic Chavez Alcala, wife of the successful lumber baron, William Lassater. She had buried the past, and no one would ever know.

They moved through a line of greeters that included Governor Haight and his wife. Servants milled about with trays of tiny sandwiches and glasses of champagne. Prominent citizens of both San Francisco and Sacramento received Will and Santana warmly, but all the while Santana struggled with a growing panic, feelings she could not explain to Will or share with anyone.

It was easy when she was home, far removed from the public eye. At home she was surrounded by her loving, innocent children, her devoted husband, her loyal servants who were also her friends. At home she could withdraw from reality and pretend the rape had never happened. Here, though, with everyone staring . . . Why did she feel they all knew her secret? She fought an urge to run, and for Will's sake alone she smiled and pretended to be calm.

"Will!" A distinguished gray-haired man wearing a gray silk suit came up and shook Will's hand. "We did it, didn't we? A damn good investment, the railroad. You'll see that investment pay off royally from here on."

Will shook the man's hand and turned to Santana. "Dear, this is Harold Maddigan, a partner in Maddigan

Investments in San Francisco. This is the man who encouraged me to throw in on the Central Pacific. Harold, this is my wife, Santana."

Maddigan took hold of Santana's hand and squeezed lightly, his brown eyes showing obvious pleasure at the sight of her. "I am very happy to finally meet you, Senora Lassater," he said, smiling. He glanced at Will. "I've always heard you had a beautiful wife, Will, and now I see everyone was telling me the truth. Why have you been hiding her away?"

Will slipped an arm around Santana's waist. "Oh, I haven't been hiding her. I've just been busy since the war rebuilding the mills, and Santana has been busy tending to six children. The youngest is only a year and a half."

"Six!" Maddigan's gaze moved over Santana once more. "Who would ever know!" He gave Will a nudge. "You're a lucky man, Will Lassater. A successful business and a beautiful wife." He spotted another guest he needed to talk to and excused himself. Will finished his champagne and turned to set the glass on a table.

"He's right, you know," he said to Santana. "I am a lucky man." He looked around the roomful of dignitaries and their wives. "And it's just like I said. You're the most beautiful woman here." He leaned closer. "And probably the youngest."

Santana's tension eased as Will led her around, introducing her to other businessmen, who in turn introduced her to their wives. Most were friendly, but some were cool to her, and she knew it was because of her Spanish heritage. It irritated her that it had come to the point when it was her own people who felt like foreigners in California. The Americans behaved as though it had always belonged to them, and as she met the guests, her deep Spanish pride began to emerge. She felt more and more confident, not just as the wife of Will Lassater, but as an original

Californio. It was men like her father to whom these people owed their success.

Talk turned to the railroad and the prosperity it would bring to California, especially to those who had invested in the Central Pacific line. There was great concern, however, over the fact that so many Chinese had been imported to the state to help build the railroad. Now that it was finished, what was to be done with them? Some business owners claimed they would get even richer off the Chinese laborers, because they could hire them for much lower wages than American workers demanded. The trouble was, that would leave many American citizens unemployed.

Santana enjoyed listening to the men talk, but Wilma Maddigan, a plump, silver-haired woman whose dress looked painfully tight around her waist, came over and took her arm, insisting Santana join her and several other women at a table where tea and coffee were being served.

Santana left her husband's side reluctantly, deciding she must put on a good appearance for him. She noticed that all of the women at the table were American, and a few looked at her as though she didn't belong there. She held herself proudly as Mrs. Maddigan introduced her to all the women, this one the wife of a banker, another the wife of the biggest merchant in San Francisco; here the wife of the owner of several mining investments, there the wife of another banker; the wife of a druggist, a doctor's wife. All were the wives of men who had come to California to get rich.

The women did not seem concerned with business or the problems San Francisco might have with the Chinese. Their conversation consisted of gossip, discussions about social functions, clothes, jewelry, the opera, and children.

"Is it true you have *six* children?" Mrs. Maddigan asked Santana.

"Yes," she answered with obvious pride. "My oldest son is twelve now, and my baby daughter is a year and a half. I have another daughter who is nine, and three other sons. Dominic is eight, Juan is six, and our Valioso is three."

"Valioso?" Rebecca Andrews, the druggist's wife, sipped some tea. "Is that the retarded boy?"

The question struck hard, asked so pointedly and rudely. The other women seemed embarrassed, and Wilma Maddigan chided Mrs. Andrews. "Rebecca! You don't know that the rumor is even true about the Lassater boy, and even if it is—"

"It is all right, Mrs. Maddigan," Santana interrupted. The remark about her son had quickly erased her apprehension and uneasiness about joining these women. The insulting way Rebecca Andrews had asked about Valioso stirred all her feelings of motherly protection, to the point that it did not matter what anyone thought of her. It only mattered what they thought about her little boy. She turned her gaze from Rebecca to the other women.

"Valioso is simply a slow learner, but he *can* learn. We have taught him many things. He is a very loving little boy who tries hard to please his mother and father. We love him very much, and he takes special attention. That is why I have not been coming to San Francisco or here to Sacramento when Will makes his business trips. I have a special son who needs extra teaching and guidance, and when he was born I decided I would devote all of my spare time to him."

"Well, I—I didn't mean . . ."

"I know exactly what you meant, Mrs. Andrews," Santana told the woman, who had reddened with embarrassment. "You meant to imply that it is a terrible thing to have a retarded child, that we should have put him in an institution. I knew the moment my husband laid the boy in my arms that I could never do such a thing. He is my son, and he needs his mother and father much more than the average child. I have never regretted for one moment keeping him home with us. He has taught all of us about the true meaning of love and patience."

She looked pointedly at Rebecca Andrews, a woman of perhaps thirty-five. "You do not look much older than I. Do you have children?"

Mrs. Andrews raised her own chin proudly. "Yes. I have two daughters."

Santana nodded. "I would suggest, then, that it is easy to think a child like my Valioso should be put away, but unless that child is your own, a baby you nourished for nine months and who turns to his mother for protection and love after he is born, you do not know for certain what you would do in the same situation."

"Well, I suppose not," Mrs. Andrews answered. "I'm sorry if I upset you, Senora Lassater."

Santana realized she had probably overreacted to the woman's remark. She had grown to love Valioso so much more than she ever thought she could, and she felt a great responsibility to protect him from the outside world, from ridicule and scorn. Perhaps it was because she knew how evil his real father was that she wanted to shield him so thoroughly. And perhaps it was her fear that people would find out the truth that made her constantly feel she had to prove to herself and others how much she loved the boy. She told herself not to be so quick to defend in the future. These women were simply curious, as anyone would be. And as the wife of the man who ran the biggest logging business in California, she must be gracious and fit in with these women. She nodded to Rebecca Andrews. "I accept your apology, and please accept mine for perhaps being too short with you. A mother is always quick to defend her young."

The other women smiled and seemed to relax. Conversation turned to talk of all their children, their names, ages. As several couples began to dance to a lovely waltz tune, Santana noticed Will was talking to the governor. She watched proudly. He had kept every promise he had ever made to her, had worked hard to revitalize his business after returning from the war. He was building a new home for their family on another hillside, a huge two-story stucco mansion with many bedrooms for many children; and already he was talking of building a bigger home in San Francisco too. Smiling, she excused herself from the women and started toward Will. She stopped when another couple was announced.

"Don Hugo Eduardo Martinez Bolivar." The caller's voice seemed to echo too loudly against the marble floor and walls. "And his wife, Carmelita Rosanna Calderone de Bolivar."

Santana felt the blood draining from her face. Not once since that awful day had she seen Hugo again, and as long as she did not have to look at him, she felt she could live with the secret. Now here he was, one of the governor's guests. All the hatred and bitterness returned to her soul as she watched him enter, the same pompous look on his face as always. He moved through the line of greeters, and Santana told herself to be strong. She must not give a hint in front of Will just how much Hugo's presence upset her. Nor would she let Hugo see a look of horror and defeat on her face. Yes, he would love that, wouldn't he?

There! Already he had spotted her. His dark gaze lingered on her, and she met the look defiantly. She would remind him with her own eyes that she could ruin him just as easily as he could ruin her. If Will were ever to learn the truth, Hugo was a dead man. She watched Will greet Hugo with a cool nod, and she knew he was being congenial only for the governor's sake. He would not want to cause a stir at this special event. Hugo held out his hand, but Will did not take it. Hugo glanced at Santana again, and she looked right back at him, determined he would know he had not broken her or her marriage.

Other men greeted Hugo with smiles and handshakes. Oh, if only she could tell everyone in this room the truth. But she had to carry this load alone, and seeing Hugo again reawakened old resentments against Will for going away and not being there when she had needed him most.

Will saw her standing alone, and he quickly walked over and took her hand. "*Por favor, carina mia.* Don't let Hugo Bolivar spoil the first big social event you have attended in years." He whisked her onto the dance floor. "You deserve to have a good time tonight. You have given every spare minute of your time to Valioso since the day he was born. Tonight *I* want all your attention."

He whirled her about the floor, and Santana kept her eyes only on her husband. *I wish that I could tell you the truth, my love,* she thought, *just to get rid of this guilt I feel at deceiving you. But there are so many reasons you must never know, to protect your good name, and to protect our little Valioso.*

"Wouldn't these women here just faint away if you danced the *fandango* for everyone?" Will teased. "The men can't take their eyes off you, you know, and you being here with me tonight, still as beautiful as the day I married you, is my ultimate victory over Bolivar. Did you see how he looked at you? He's sick with envy."

Santana could not meet Will's eyes then. "I wish he had not come. It makes me nervous when the two of you are in the same room together."

"Bolivar is the one who should be nervous. You just relax and enjoy yourself."

The dance ended, and Will led Santana to where Harold Maddigan now stood with his wife talking to two other couples. Harold's ruddy complexion was growing redder from drinking too much champagne, and he introduced Santana to the others with great enthusiasm, obviously enamored with her beauty.

"I see our token *Californio* is here," he then said to Will. He bowed to Santana. "Please excuse the remark, Senora. I am not referring to you. The proud and honorable Spanish families of California are to be afforded our greatest respect. But men like Don Bolivar command no respect and have few friends. I am surprised the governor invited him, but as I said, he is probably a token. I am sure the governor doesn't know about the past between Don Bolivar and your husband, or he would not have invited both of them to the same occasion."

Santana felt too warm, and she opened her fan and waved it. "Yes, I would rather Don Bolivar were not present," she answered. "He once tried to shoot my husband in the back, you know."

Will kept an arm around her. "That was a lot of years ago. Most people here don't even know about it."

"I suppose not," Maddigan said, "but there are a few more like me who were already in San Francisco at the time and heard all the stories. Even before his little run-in with you over Santana, his arrogant attitude had lost him a lot of friends. I also remember something about some suspicious fires up at your mill after you married Santana. You think Bolivar had something to do with them, don't you?"

Santana felt Wilma Maddigan's eyes on her. What did a woman like Mrs. Maddigan think of two men fighting a duel over her? She managed to steal a glance around the room to see a group of women talking together and looking her way. What were they saying?

"I firmly believe Bolivar had someone set those fires," Will told Maddigan. "But I can't prove it."

"Just look at the pompous ass," Maddigan said, keeping his voice low, "greeting people with that damn cocky smile on his face. I heard he even beats his wife. You now how rumors circulate among servants, something about him being upset that the poor woman has never given him any children."

Santana watched Carmelita. It was easy to read the loneliness in her eyes, and her heart ached for the woman. She realized that in spite of what Hugo had done to her, Carmelita lived in a worse hell. Still, all the horror of her rape had returned to haunt her. She could tell by the way Hugo kept glancing at her and smiling that he knew his presence was upsetting her, and suddenly she felt removed from the others, lost in her own world of nasty secrets. The foul memory of Hugo taking her flashed into her mind with such force, she flinched.

"What's wrong, Santana?"

Will's words brought her back to reality. "What? Oh! I am just more tired than I thought."

Will turned her away from the Maddigans and the other couples. "It's Bolivar, isn't it?" he said in a low voice. "Why do you let him bother you so much after all these years? I agree I'm still angry enough to kill him if I could get away with it, but I don't let him crawl under my skin like you seem to do." Will looked at her closely, and he seemed to sense she was more shaken than he'd realized. "Is there something I should know, Santana? I've always felt there was something you weren't telling me. Does it have to do with Bolivar?"

"No," she answered, too quickly. "I mean, there is nothing to tell about *anyone*. He just still upsets me, that's all. To think I might have been his wife . . . Did you see her? Carmelita? She is not a happy woman."

"She made her choice, and you made yours."

"And the result is six beautiful children whom I miss very much."

"I know you want to go home to the children, but this is our night, Santana, and not Bolivar nor anyone else is going to spoil it."

Will led her back out to dance, and after that they spent the rest of the evening meeting other people and talking about everything from politics to the stock market. All the while Santana felt Hugo staring at her, forcing her to remember . . . remember . . .

Be strong, she told herself. *Do not let him be the victor by being faint and begging to leave early. Show him how happy you are with your husband. Let him envy Will for having six children while he has none . . . none . . .* Yes, she was the victor after all! She had her children, including a little son Hugo could never claim. He had nothing but a barren wife and an empty life.

Eventually all the guests were taken on a grand tour of the new building, then they sat down to a royal meal at one long dining table brought into the building just for the occasion. Santana smiled and chatted with deliberate enthusiasm. She was proud of how wealthy and important her husband had become, and she was determined to rub it in to Hugo, as well as to prove to him that what he had done had not broken her in the least. When everyone raised a toast to the Central Pacific, Santana felt the champagne beginning to take effect. Laughter and champagne, and the thought of her children and her husband. Yes, those things helped cover the ugliness. Those things showed Hugo he had not hurt her happiness one bit. Sitting at the same table with him, even though he was farther down, in a position where, thank God, she did not have to face him, was still the most difficult test of how much she had healed.

Dinner finished, Will took her off to dance again, and she began to feel giddy. She was winning! It was as though Hugo had never touched her at all! He was in the same room, she had faced him for the first time since her attack, and she had not crumbled. Perhaps he felt victorious knowing what he had done, but she would spoil his victory by showing him she was as happy and unruffled as if he had never touched her.

She looked up at the decorated dome that rose 247 feet above the center of the capitol building. "It is quite beautiful, isn't it?"

Will studied the graceful lines of her neck and shoulders, the way her diamond necklace sparkled against her dark skin. "Yes, very beautiful."

Santana met his eyes. Would he still love her if he knew? Would he believe she had done nothing wrong? "I love you, Will. It is growing late. I would like to go to our hotel room."

He drew her closer. "I was thinking the same thing." He stopped dancing, but held her there. "I know something is still wrong, Santana. I wish you would tell me what it is."

She met his eyes squarely. "Nothing is wrong," she lied. "I have just had too much champagne." She ran her hands along his powerful arms. "And I wish to be with my husband tonight."

"All right. I'll go hail our driver. Did you bring a shawl?"

"I left it in the carriage."

She joined Will in saying good-bye to several of the others and shaking hands with the governor and his wife, before Will left her to see about their carriage. Santana walked outside and waited, anxious to get away from Hugo's all-knowing eyes, shivering while she waited. She rubbed the backs of her arms nervously. It was then she realized it was more than the night air giving her a chill.

"Sweet dreams, Santana."

The words were spoken behind her, and she whirled to

see Hugo standing there. Her heartbeat quickened with dread. She had managed to avoid him all evening. Now he had deliberately followed her outside. "What do you want?"

"Just to say good night." He stepped closer. "I have heard you have a son who is retarded." He grinned. "How fitting. Your *gringo* husband is not so perfect after all. Perhaps the child was your punishment for having slept with another man. Have you told Will yet of your indiscretion?"

She fought the urge to scream and scratch his eyes out. He had only come out there to try to poke one last prong, she told herself. She had not behaved as he had expected, and that irritated him. "We both know the truth about that, and you must live with knowing you are a coward, and a man who will leave behind no children to bear his name!" She felt great pleasure in seeing him flinch at the words. *You do have a son, Hugo Bolivar!* she told him silently. *But you will never know it, nor will you ever know the joy he can bring to a man's heart.* "The fact that you have no sons is *your* punishment, Hugo Bolivar!"

The color in his face deepened as he came even closer. "Perhaps I should tell your husband about our little affair," he said threateningly.

"Affair? You are not such a fool, Hugo! You know he would see the truth, that he would believe me if I told him you raped me. You know what he would do to you then! You have *lost*, Hugo, in so many ways. You committed a despicable, sinful act, and God has punished you by leaving you childless. Will and I have six sons and daughters. We have something wonderful that rises above the ugliness you tried to bring me. As far as I am concerned, you never touched me!"

She turned and quickly walked away, past the huge white columns that graced the front of the building to the drive, where she waited for Will. A rage of emotions swept through her so that she could barely think straight. She had faced him alone! She had stood up to him on her own, and Will never need know about it! *Hurry, Will, hurry! Get me away from here!*

Finally the carriage appeared. She did not even wait for Will to get down from the passenger seat to help her board. She quickly climbed inside, and Will slid an arm around her. She rested her head against his shoulder, taking comfort in the safety of his presence. Tonight he would help her forget again.

Will frowned as he glanced at his wife. She seemed almost to be running from something. He looked back, but saw no one.

Twenty-Six

"Oh, Will, I had too much champagne." Santana laughed and threw back her head as Will kept an arm around her and led her into their hotel room. She struggled to remind herself to be careful what she said. She was dizzy and confused, her encounter with Hugo leaving her feeling both victorious and angry. Having to look into those eyes again, to face the man she most despised in the world, and to have to do it all alone, had stirred so many emotions she thought she could leave buried.

She wrapped her arms around Will's neck. "Make love to me, *carino mio*," she said in a sultry whisper.

Will picked her up and carried her to the bed. "I guess you *have* had too much champagne," he said. "You're acting strangely tonight, Santana." He joined her on the bed, straddling her and bracing his arms on either side of her. He wished he could understand the woman she had become, decide how she really felt about him. Ever since he'd returned from the war, he had felt the distance between them. She had said that Valioso's problems would bring them closer, and in many ways they had. But sexually, something was still wrong. First he'd felt it was simply because they had become like strangers after more than three years apart. He blamed himself for their continued problems after Valioso's birth, sure they stemmed from Santana resenting him for the boy being retarded.

She never said that she did, but the passion she'd once shown for him was never there anymore. They had both been pretending, he wanting to believe everything was fine, she acting as though she enjoyed his lovemaking. She did not respond as she once had, though, and she never came to him first. Many times she made excuses as to why they could not make love, usually something to do with tending the children.

Now, tonight, she was behaving more like the old Santana, who used to tease him with words and with her body. Maybe his idea of getting off alone with her had worked better than he thought. He stretched out beside her. "Not that I'm complaining that you want to make love." He raised up on one elbow, pushing a strand of hair back from her forehead. "Santana, you practically ran to get into the carriage. Was something wrong?"

She smiled. "I only wanted to get to our room so we could be alone. You said yourself that this was our night away from the children."

Will watched her eyes. There it was again, that look that told him she was not being totally honest. He had seen it at other times, usually when she was behaving as though she were the happiest woman alive. She was deeply troubled about something, had been for a long time, and the only reason he could come up with was that she had never quite forgiven him for leaving in the first place.

Before he left there had always been a childlike innocence and happiness in his wife's eyes. But in spite of the closeness they had achieved in working together with Valioso, there was still something missing. Each time he made love to her, he hoped to unlock the secret she held in her heart, even if it meant unleashing a terrible anger she might feel against him.

"You're right. This is our night," he answered. He met her mouth in a soft, hungry kiss, massaging her bare shoulders, then bent down to kiss her throat, the soft swell of her breasts. Whatever her reason for being more open and aggressive than she had been in years, he would not argue it. This was more like the Santana she'd been, full of passion and love and need. He so longed for the woman he had married.

Santana stretched her arms over her head and closed her eyes, relishing the feel of her husband's strong hands caressing her shoulders and breasts. She was determined to prove to herself she could truly bury what Hugo had done to her. She had faced him that night, squarely, boldly, showing him he had not destroyed her. Now she would prove at last that he had not spoiled this for her either. All these many months she'd had to simply "allow" Will his manly needs, responding as best she could, but never really enjoying her husband the way she had before he went off to war. She could not keep letting Hugo's vile act destroy what had been so beautiful and satisfying between her and Will.

She breathed deeply as Will pulled the low-cut bodice of her dress away from her breasts so that they were exposed. He tasted her nipples, and she grasped his hair as she closed her eyes, reminding herself that this was Will and it was all right. She must recapture what had been lost between them. Seeing Hugo again had dredged up so many unwanted emotions, feelings she could have kept buried if not for having to look into those eyes again. Surely making love with Will would make it go away once more.

Will had drunk a lot of champagne himself, and he moved with deliberate desire, not bothering to take off his clothes. He kissed Santana's breasts while he pushed up her skirt, then raised to his knees and pulled off her drawers. In that moment Santana opened her eyes and saw him. Hugo! This was the way Hugo had taken her, quickly and brutally, their clothes still on, jerking off her underwear to get to her. She closed her eyes again, her mind fighting the image. This was Will! Will! If only she had not drunk so much champagne. It was playing tricks on her mind. She opened her eyes once more, but she could not see Will. She could only see Hugo Bolivar leering at her, an expression of evil pleasure on his face as he forced himself inside her, stealing her dignity, destroying her purity, claiming that which she had given with such utter love and devotion only to her husband.

She could not find her voice. She lay frozen, staring. He entered her, and she gasped the word *no*. She felt the man on top of her go rigid. He thrust in quick rhythm and finished with her in seconds, as though angry. Then he pushed himself off her. She lay there wanting to scream, not understanding what was happening to her. She had been so sure she could live with what Hugo had done to her, could keep it buried, pretend it had never happened. Seeing him that night, though, had forced her to face the fact that he *had* been intimate with her, that he had stolen something so precious.

"What the hell is wrong, Santana? One minute you're begging me to make love to you, then you freeze up and practically push me away."

Was that Will's voice? For a moment she thought she was in her old bedroom. No. She was in a hotel in Sacramento with Will. This was supposed to be a special night for them, an evening alone together. What had happened?

"I . . . I'm sorry. It must be the champagne."

Will sat up and buttoned his pants. He threw his feet over the side of the bed to sit on the edge of it. "It's me, isn't it? This part of our life has never been the same since I came back. You've never forgiven me for leaving, for having Juan all alone, for giving you a retarded son—"

"No, Will, that is not so!"

"Then what is it? When I make love to you I can sense you're only pretending. All the passion that used to be there is gone. You allow me my pleasure, but that's the extent of it. You used to take your own pleasure in our lovemaking, Santana. Now I get the feeling you don't enjoy it at all. Our closeness only comes from the children. Other than that, there is something missing."

He rose from the bed, and Santana saw true anger blaze in her husband's eyes. She had seen him angry before, but never had such fierce anger been directed at her. If only she could tell him the truth! Yet that would be even more devastating than this. If he understood what she was going through . . . but how could any man understand? She could not tell him Hugo was Valioso's father. Will had shown the boy so much love and devotion. Valioso thrived on that love. If he lost it . . .

"This has been going on for almost four years, Santana! We've got to talk about it!"

She pulled a blanket over herself. "Please let me wash first."

Will cast her a look of disappointment before walking to a corner of the room, where he'd left his pipe on a small table. He said nothing as he lit it, keeping his back to her. Santana quickly got up and pulled her dress back over her breasts. She walked into a small washroom and cleaned herself, fighting a returning panic, a need to scream, to tell Will the truth. She remembered that awful day, how she'd bathed and bathed, trying to get Hugo's filth off of her. She hated feeling like that about her own husband. Her mind whirled with ways to explain her behavior. She had thought that all this time she'd been fooling him, had hoped and prayed her secret problems would not lead to this. She loved Will so, had tried to keep him satisfied without revealing how difficult it was for her to make love. She had even given him another child.

She took several deep breaths to stay in control, then went back into the room to see him standing at a window, puffing on his pipe. "I suppose you are right," she said. "When you returned from the war, we were like strangers. I could not get over the feeling that you had abandoned me and the children." It was all lies, but what else could she tell him? "You should have stayed. You had a family, a business to run. If you had not gone, perhaps Gerald also would have stayed, and he would still be alive."

The room hung silent, and Santana knew her words had hurt him deeply. She felt the lies tangling together and beginning to choke their marriage.

He sighed, turning to face her. "You were always such a loving, forgiving person, Santana. I don't understand how you can be this way after all this time. I thought we were doing okay, but tonight, the look on your face . . ." Though they stood across the room from each other, she could see the anger still burning in his eyes. It tore her heart to pieces. "Is there someone else?"

The question devastated her, and her eyes widened in shock. "Someone else! Another man? How could you think such a thing? You know that every spare moment of my time has been spent on Valioso! You know that I am incapable of cheating on my husband!"

Will looked away. "I know you haven't seen anyone since I got home, but I was gone for a long time, Santana. I've been telling myself for four years now that things would get better, but they haven't. We don't make love nearly as often as we did before. You used to come to me, but now you never do. And the way you looked at me just now . . . You don't enjoy my lovemaking anymore. You simply force yourself to endure it. You've been pretending for a long time, and *I've* been pretending there was nothing wrong. Tonight it was just more obvious. The way you behaved at first, I thought this would finally be different." He met her eyes again. "*Is* there someone else? Or should I say *was* there someone else?"

"Never." She raised her chin defiantly. "I have always loved only you, *mi esposo*. It hurts my heart that you would think such a thing."

He set down his pipe and walked across the room to stand close to her. "And it hurts *my* heart to realize you no longer enjoy my lovemaking! What happened, Santana? It's like I came home to a different woman. How could you love me so passionately before I left, and be so different when I returned? All this time I've tried to brush it off, pretend everything was fine. I thought in time things would get back to normal, but it isn't happening."

A tear slipped down her cheek. "I—I cannot explain it," she said, feeling helpless. It seemed she was going to lose him either way. If she told him the truth, or if she allowed this terrible misunderstanding to remain between them, she would lose him. It was simply a matter of deciding which was less painful for him, and which most protected Valioso. That left her no choice at all. She looked away from him. "I am sorry, Will. When you were gone, the children became my whole world. I felt so abandoned, as though you had deserted us. I felt if you truly loved us, you never would have gone. I am sorry, *carino mio*. My trust in your total devotion to us was ruined when you left for a war I never understood, for a country to which I will never feel any allegiance."

Will straightened, and Santana could feel his tension and anger. "Do you still love me, Santana?"

She met his eyes, aching at the hurt she saw there.

"Yes, *mi esposo*, I do love you. There has never been another."

Will wanted to believe her. But if it wasn't another man who'd come between them, what was it? He had lost her, and he wasn't sure exactly how. He supposed it was a combination of situations that had snowballed into something he could not control, and that frustrated him deeply. He was a man who had been in control of every aspect of his life . . . until the war. Here was another casualty, and he was helpless to know what to do about it.

"Go to sleep, Santana." He turned away, tucking his shirt into his pants.

"What are you going to do?"

"I'm going out for a while. I need a drink. We'll head home first light. I know you want to get back to the children."

"Do not blame them, Will. They are innocent."

He thought the remark a little strange. "I would never blame my children for anything. I only blame myself."

Santana did not know what to say. His pain was her pain, but she had to let it be this way. "Do you still love me, Will?"

Will pulled on his suit jacket, then faced her, studied her lovely face, one that belied her thirty-one years. She was still perfection, and any man would want her. He wanted to believe there had been no other, but he could not forget a remark Noel had made to him not long after he'd returned from the war. He'd never told her about it because he'd brushed it off as a vicious rumor, but some of the workers at the mill had been saying they'd heard Santana had an affair with someone in San Francisco while he was gone. Noel didn't know when or how the rumor had started, but he didn't believe it, and he had set the other men straight. Will himself had been so glad to be back in one piece from the war, so glad to see his family and get back to normal living, that he could not face the rumor. He had buried it deep . . . until now. He still didn't want to believe it, but what else was he to think, the way she had been behaving?

"I still love you," he answered. "I just wish you would tell me the truth, Santana. That's all I care about. Until I feel you're being totally honest, we can't get our lives back to where they once were."

He turned and walked out, and Santana stared after him. She wanted to run to him, to explain, but turned and walked to the bed instead, feeling weary and beaten. If only she could admit to all of it. If only she could turn to her husband for the strength she needed to carry this burden. But she had to protect Will from killing Hugo; and she had to protect Valioso from the ridicule he would receive from others, perhaps even from his own family, if they knew how he'd been conceived and who his real father was. The boy would be an outcast. She could not let that happen, even if it meant losing Will. She stretched out on the bed and wept, sobbing until her sides ached. Finally she fell asleep.

It was very late when Will came back. Santana woke when she heard him enter the room. She waited for him to speak, but he said nothing as he undressed. He did not even ask why she had not undressed herself. He pulled back the covers and climbed into his side of the bed, and Santana could smell tobacco smoke and liquor on him, as well as the faint scent of a cheap perfume.

The drive home was nearly silent. Santana watched the soft roll of hills that led home, remembering the time when Will had risked his life to save her from being abducted along a road like this one. California was more settled now, not so lawless, although Will and Enrique Hidalgo, who had driven their carriage to Sacramento and back, did carry weapons.

So much had changed in California. The railroad was there now, and Americans flowed in from the East in such numbers, she wondered if there was anyone left beyond the Sierras and the Rockies. San Francisco seemed to be the gathering point for all newcomers. It had grown from merely about eight hundred residents before the gold rush, to a population of nearly one hundred thousand. It was a city of contrasts, with so many Chinese that they were forming their own little section in the city called Chinatown. There were other poor neighborhoods, and there was still a red-light district, although city authorities were trying to clean it out, as well as bring law and order along Pacific Avenue and Kearny Street, the infamous docks area where Will had met Noel . . . and where Santana had first set eyes on him.

Yes, much had changed since then. San Francisco now had many theaters and wonderful shops, opera houses, museums, parks, fine hotels, and the fancy homes of the rich on Nob Hill. Montgomery Street was the center of business, and Will had offices there, his wealth managed by accountants she didn't even know. He had come a long way in the fifteen years since he'd first arrived in California, and Lassater Mills was still growing.

She wished things could be the way they'd been then, with not so many new people flocking to California, when life was quieter, less complicated, her father still alive. She missed him so, and no one understood that she had never been able to mourn her father's death properly.

If only Will had killed Hugo the day of the duel. Then he would have been out of their lives forever. If Will knew the truth of what Hugo had done, he would probably never forgive himself for not planting that hatchet in Hugo's skull. But the past was past, and there was no undoing what Hugo had done.

They left Enrique off at the main ranch, where they talked for a while with Hernando and Teresa, pretending that all was well. Will drove the carriage himself then, heading up the road that led through quiet forest toward home. Soon they would move into the bigger house they were building, a home that she would furnish and decorate to her heart's content, with plenty of room for all the children . . . one big, happy family. That was what they were supposed to be. The mansion that was being built in San Francisco was Will's dream home, and it would be at least two years before it was completed. The interior halls, doors, banisters, fireplace moldings, nearly every inch of the interior would be made of beautifully carved primavera wood from South America. The door windows and several other windows would be of stained glass. She had agreed to it because Will wanted one house that was styled more like a home he would have had if he were in New England.

Yes, these should have been the happiest years of their marriage—six children, beautiful new homes, a thriving business. If not for the war, Gerald's death, Hugo's violation . . . She studied the countryside, remembering when she and Will used to ride over hills like this, young, in love, simply happy to be together.

Will headed the carriage to the left, and she realized where he was going . . . to her special place. They neared the clearing and there it was, her forever tree, the faithful lodgepole pine where she used to come to be alone. It was here that she and Will had talked all those years ago. It had been a long time since she'd been here. Will halted the fine black horse that pulled the carriage and climbed down. He came to where she sat and he leaned against a wheel, meeting her eyes.

It was cool, and he wore a cotton jacket and a felt hat.

She liked him in a hat. He was even more handsome that way. She only wished that the love and passion she used to see in his eyes were still there, but now she saw only hurt. She had been so determined not to let Hugo destroy the love she had shared with this man, but a part of her had died with Hugo's attack, and she had not been able to bring it back to life. It made her sick to realize Hugo's plan to destroy her from the inside out was working. Something important had been lost the night before, and she saw no way to explain to Will why it had happened. She must protect the love he felt for Valioso, and she must protect the boy himself, who loved his father with such innocent trust.

The children were all she had now, and it was as though Will had read her thoughts when he spoke.

"I've been thinking," he said. "You've got the children. I have my business."

Santana waited, her stomach hurting at the coldness in his voice.

"I came out here to build Lassater Mills into something much bigger than my father ever dreamed of," he continued. "I intend to do just that. I've let things slow me down and take my attention away from all that. From now on, I'm going to put every waking moment into the business. I haven't done some things I've wanted to do, simply because I felt it would take too much time away from my family . . . and from you. Now it seems it doesn't matter so much to you anymore. Something was lost between us when I went off to war, and that's my fault. I've tried to get it back, but apparently it hasn't worked, and now you're burdened with Valioso, also because of the war."

"I do not think of Valioso as a burden. He is a joy. I have told you over and over that I do not blame you for his affliction, Will."

Will turned away, removing his hat to run a hand

through his hair before putting the hat back on. "You say you don't, but your actions don't match your words. Maybe you do still love me, Santana. I know that I still love you. But we need to step back a little, each of us turn to other things for a while.

"I want you to know that for the next few months, maybe years, I'm going to work closely with James and also bring Glenn in on the business. I want to expand even more. There are millions of acres of virgin timber up in Oregon and Washington, around Puget Sound, up around Astoria, Gray's Harbor, Coos Bay. I'm going to expand our line of ships, build two businesses, lumber and shipping. I know I can do it. Noel runs some of the mills practically single-handedly now, and I've got other good men. James is learning to the point that he can take over a couple of mills on his own, and someday I'd like to teach Glenn the shipping end of it. That's less dangerous than working at the mills."

He stopped to take his pipe from his pocket, then retrieved a small, flat can of tobacco from another pocket and began stuffing the pipe.

"What are you trying to tell me, Will?"

"I'm trying to tell you that I won't be around a lot for a while. You said the children became your whole world when I was away. You're a wonderful mother, Santana. You go ahead and devote all your time to the children, especially Valioso. Teach him everything you can. Give them all schooling, teach them to ride, give them your love. I'll teach my sons the business as each of them gets old enough.

"Our new home is nearly complete. Between furnishing and decorating it, and tending the children, you'll be plenty busy. You won't miss me much while I'm traveling. I'll have to be in San Francisco a lot, as well as travel up to Washington and Oregon. We'll each do what needs doing and stop trying so hard with each other. I'm tired of pretending."

Santana felt numb. How could the love and passion she had once felt for her husband have come to this terrible estrangement? There was a time when she never would have thought it possible, yet she could do nothing to stop it, because she did not know how to deal with her own inner turmoil. "I understand," she answered quietly. "And you must understand that I love you, as much as ever. Please tell me that you do not believe there was ever another man."

Will lit the pipe and puffed on it for a minute. "I'm not sure what to believe. I only know you were a different woman when I came back. I didn't notice it at first because I was just so damn glad to be home. Then Valioso was born and you got pregnant again, and I was trying to rebuild . . . I just never stopped to face reality until last night, and the reality is something has been lost between us. I hope somehow we can get it back, but right now I'm too angry inside, too guilty, too hurt, and too confused."

Hugo raped me! She wanted to scream the words, to help him understand, but she could not make herself speak them. "Maybe you are right. Maybe we do need time apart," she said at last. "Maybe we tried too hard when you came back. I buried my own resentment because I was happy you were home and alive."

Thunder rolled in the distance, and Will looked up at the sky. "We'd better get home." He finally met her eyes again. "I'm going to have Noel move his family into Gerald's old house. It's a fine home and shouldn't be sitting there empty, and Noel's wife deserves to live in a nice place. His two oldest boys work at the mills now, but there's still an eleven-year-old daughter and a nine-year-old boy. Bernice will be good company for you, and the two youngest children can join ours in lessons with Estella."

He told her everything with a note of finality, as though she had no say in this decision he had made. Santana knew he was in no mood to argue, and after hurting him as she had last night, she was not about to try. She did not want him to be gone even more. She needed him. But she would let him go, only because it was easier than trying to explain. Will climbed back into the driver's seat and got the horse into motion again. He held the reins in one hand and his pipe in the other.

"With James, Noel, Derek, and Noel's sons, I can expand and have dependable people managing every mill," he told her. "Captain Eastman is still with me. I'll work with him in expanding our shipping line, build some warehouses. By the way, I'm giving Bolivar a run for his money. I've taken away some of his warehousing business already." He puffed on the pipe. "I'm going to outdo all of them, Santana. Gerald would have liked that, Gerald and my father both, and it will mean being able to send even more money back to Agatha. I'll make up for all of it, Santana, for hurting you, for Gerald's death, for Valioso's affliction. And I'll keep the promise I made my father to build Lassater Mills into something much greater than it ever was back east."

I only want you here with me, Will. "You are a man of dreams, *mi esposo*. Whatever you set out to do, you always succeed."

Except that I destroyed the one thing most important to me, Will thought. Time. Yes, that was all they needed. Time away from each other. He could not bear being close to her and feeling this cold distance between them. He would bury himself in his work, and maybe somehow, after a while, they would find each other again. He said nothing more as he headed home, where the children all ran out to

greet them. Yes, they had this, sons and daughters. This
would hold them together until they could recapture the
love and trust they had once shared.

He watched Santana climb down and greet each child
—Glenn, Ruth, Dominic, Juan, little Julia, who was held
by Ruth. Then came Valioso, drooling slightly, his slanted
eyes full of joy at seeing his mother again. Will's own heart
ached as he watched the boy, and guilt tore at his insides.
He climbed down, and all six children attacked him with
hugs and smiles. He picked Valioso up and carried him
inside.

Santana watched her children follow their father into
the house, watched Valioso hug Will around the neck. She
knew that if losing Will personally would save the love he
felt for Valioso, then that was how it would have to be.
Seeing the light in the boy's eyes whenever he was with
the man he believed to be his father made her able to bear
the burden of her loneliness.

Twenty-Seven

Will raised a bottle of bourbon and shouted with the other men who were rooting for James. "You can do it, James! Your father was never beat!"

James's face was beet-red. He strained and grunted, lips curled, teeth clenched, his brawny arm glowing with sweat. Sven Erickson was considered the strongest man of the woods, able to lift logs no other man would consider trying to lift. He could saw faster, chop faster, climb faster than any other logger, and this day, at the annual loggers' picnic Will held for his men, the big Swede, who was seven years older than James, had won nearly every contest Will had devised.

The wrist wrestling had been going on all day, with eliminations bringing it down to this final duel between twenty-three-year-old James Lassater, the boss's nephew, and Sven Erickson, the pride of the woods. The original Lassater mill was still the biggest of the seven lumber mills Will now owned, with eighty men working round the clock to keep the lumber flowing out to the rest of the world seven days a week. A small city now existed at the site, with saloons, stores, a barbershop, a school, a livery, even a church. It was a noisy place, with some families living in small homes and cabins, but populated mostly by rough single men who took pride in their virility.

This contest was important. Although Noel now managed the entire operation there at the original mill, Will intended to put James in charge of the cutting crews. Defeating Sven would earn him a great deal of respect from the other men, most of whom were older and did not always take orders easily from someone as young as James.

Will felt emotion stab him as he watched the boy, who was a replica of Gerald, including Gerald's powerful build. Will preferred to remember his brother that way. He had managed to bury the memory of how Gerald had looked when he'd arrived at the prison camp, even more emaciated the day he'd killed himself. That was not the Gerald he'd known and loved. He was glad James had stayed behind when Agatha returned to Maine. The way he'd turned out, it was like having Gerald with him again.

"Now! Now!" he shouted. The crowd of men was going wild, all of them holding up fists full of money they had bet on either James or Sven. James had Sven's arm headed downward, but the boy was literally screaming with the effort. "You can do it, James! You can do it!"

Will had won many such contests himself, and he knew that wrist wrestling was as much technique as it was strength. He had taught James some of that technique, and combined with the Lassater stubbornness he'd inherited, James could beat a man like Sven if he set his mind to it.

At last it was done. James pushed Sven's hand far enough to touch the pine table that had been set up outside for the contest. Those who had bet on James roared and cheered, then began collecting money from others.

James sat exhausted, still panting, his head down on the table. Sven slapped him on the shoulder.

"We'll do it again, boy, when I haven't already been chopping and sawing all day in other contests. You caught me when I was already tired out from competing all day."

"Come on, no excuses, Sven!" one of the men shouted. "The boy beat you fair and square."

Will watched carefully, knowing how quickly a good-natured game could turn into an ugly brawl among such men. Sven was an easygoing man, though, who was not conceited about his strength as some of the others were.

"All right. All right. He beat me fair and square." Sven put out his hand. "Come on, boy, let's shake on it. We'll do it again next year."

James raised his head, then slowly rose, rubbing his arm. "I don't know if I want to try you again," he answered. "You just about killed me, Sven."

The big Swede laughed as they shook hands, and Sven looked at Will, giving him a wink. "Them boys up at the logging site will show him some respect now, won't they, boss?" he said.

Will raised his bottle to the man, suspecting Sven might have decided to let up a little at the end, knowing how important this was to James. "That they will," he answered.

The rest of the men surrounded James, congratulating him, pounding him on the back. Will felt lucky to have the kind of crew he had. They were mostly rough and uneducated, but they respected him. He had worked hard to earn that respect, paying his men well, providing the best food and facilities possible. He tried to be fair in how each man was treated, allowed drinking and gambling and even allowed prostitutes at the mill sites, as long as none of those things interfered with the men's work.

He wished he could do more to make their jobs safe,

but that was all but impossible. On average, a man was lost to death every month, more to injuries. But these men knew the dangers of this work, and they did it anyway. It was something that got into a man's blood. No matter how big he got and how much he traveled, Will needed this, to come to the logging sites and mingle with the men, visit the cutting crews, even do a little cutting himself once in a while.

He shook hands with some of the men, drank down some bourbon, even kissed a few of the prostitutes who mingled with the crowd. The bawdy women were a mixture of American, Mexican, and Chinese, most of them not very pretty, but their eagerness made Will long for the time when Santana had been that way toward him. For two years he had been gone more than he'd been home, and when he was home, he and Santana slept apart. They were like strangers more than ever, even more than when he'd first returned from the war, and he could hardly stand to think of it. How could he love someone so much and find it so hard to tell her anymore?

He had been tempted to find some pleasure, to ease his needs, with Elaine Ramirez, a young prostitute who was the talk of the camp. She was beautiful and Spanish, and she reminded him of Santana in so many ways. She was not Santana, though, and Santana was the only woman he really wanted. He slugged down more bourbon, hoping to dull the pain of wanting her. Until Santana Maria Chavez de Lassater came to him in true desire again, he would not bed her.

"I am proud of you, James," he said aloud, putting an arm around the young man's shoulders. "Let's go over to Higby's saloon and celebrate. I'm leaving tomorrow for the mill up at Oregon. Time to make the rounds, so to speak. They're having their annual celebration next week."

"I wish I could go with you, Uncle Will." James

walked to the saloon with him across a muddy, open area. "But you've given me a lot of responsibility now. I'll do a good job for you."

"I know you will. Someday you'll be a full partner, James, just like your father was. He sure would have been proud of you today."

"Do you really think so? Sometimes I miss him so much, Uncle Will."

"I know. So do I."

James stopped walking before they went into the saloon. "I need to ask if you care if I get married."

Will's eyebrows arched in surprise. "Well, I'd say it's about time. You've been seeing the Hidalgo girl for five or six years now."

James grinned. "Juanita was only fourteen when I started seeing her. Her parents have been very firm about her waiting until she had all her schooling. She'll be twenty in two months. We will marry then. I finally have her parents' permission."

Will smiled. "I know how stubborn the Spanish can be about allowing their daughters to marry, even ordinary folk, like Juanita's father and mother. It was even worse for me, with Santana being so highborn and promised to another Spaniard. Her father was not thrilled that an American wanted to marry his daughter."

James laughed. "I remember Father reading us letters about it. I wish I could have seen you in that duel with Hugo Bolivar. It's become a real romantic tale over the years."

Will felt new pain at the words. Romantic. Yes, that was how it had been once for him and Santana . . . passion, romance, a fiery need for each other. "And probably exaggerated," he said aloud.

"I don't think so. I just hope Juanita and I can have as

good a marriage and as fine a brood of children as you and Santana have."

And I hope you are much happier over the years, Will thought. "Just don't ever leave your wife and go off to war, James," he told the boy. "It can hurt you in many ways, even if you come back alive."

"I'll never leave Juanita," James said. "I saw what Father's leaving did to my mother."

Will nodded, wishing he could share his own heartache, but he kept it to himself. "Don't get married until I get back, will you?"

James laughed again. "Then don't take too long."

Will studied the boy's blue eyes, seeing Gerald before him. He pressed his shoulder. "I'll be back within a month. I'm taking Glenn with me. He's fourteen now. Time for him to start learning the ropes."

They entered the saloon, which was packed with men who grabbed James and began congratulating him. There was no more chance for them to talk. Will decided to try to find Noel and go over some business with him, but when he turned, Elaine was standing before him, her sultry beauty almost startling him.

"Stay and drink with me, Senor Lassater." Her eyes moved over him hungrily, and her full breasts swelled above her low-cut dress. "Here in the camp, you are like the other men, only more handsome than most. Sometimes a man needs something more than his wife, no? I would be proud to please *el jefe.*"

Will allowed himself the pleasure of drinking in the sight of her full breasts, so exposed that he was sure the only thing her dress covered was the nipples. "I may be *el jefe* for these men, but not of you women," he answered with a grin, meeting her eyes. He saw the desire there, the fierce passion he used to see in Santana's eyes. Yes, it would be so easy, but in spite of the distance between him and

Santana, he knew there would be even less hope of their finding each other again if she learned he was up there sleeping with the whores.

He took a few bills out of his pants pocket and stuck them into the bodice of Elaine's dress, enjoying the feel of her breasts against his hand. He let it linger there while he spoke. "Maybe another time."

She took a deep breath, so that his hand was squeezed between her breasts and the front of her dress. "I will be here."

Will slowly removed his hand, wondering if he was a fool to continue this loyalty to Santana when she seemed not to want him anymore. He left the saloon, knowing he had to get away from Elaine quickly or do something he would always regret.

Outside, he breathed in the pine-scented air, fighting manly urges buried too long, needs the bourbon had aroused. He headed for a building used by Noel for business and paperwork, knowing that in spite of everyone having the day off, his faithful friend would be there working. He would talk with Noel for a while, then go home and see the children before leaving for Oregon. That was the only way he could handle the wreck his personal life had become, by continuing this conquest of the business world.

No other mill owner, and few businessmen of other professions, came close to what he had achieved, and he was still growing, in spite of the recession San Francisco was currently suffering. With the railroad completed and few new gold discoveries being made, unemployment was a major problem. A general unrest could be felt in the city, and officials worried there could be riots against the Chinese. The mansion he was building there was nearly completed, but because of the unrest in San Francisco, only servants lived there. He had advised Santana to keep the children away from the city until things had settled.

At least the financial problems of the area had not affected his own business. Demand for his lumber came from other parts of the country and all over the world, and Lassater Mills continued to thrive. He had even heard that Bolivar was having financial difficulties, which pleased him greatly. He decided that when he got home from Oregon, he would have to do some investigating. Perhaps he could secretly buy out some of Bolivar's holdings.

Thoughts of Hugo Bolivar always brought back memories of those early years, when he'd won Santana, and held Bolivar's life in his hands. Maybe he should have killed him, but he had taken much more pleasure in defeating the man in other ways. After the fire at the mill, Bolivar hadn't caused any trouble. He'd apparently taken seriously Will's threat to kill him all those years ago. It pleased Will to see the look of envy in the man's eyes whenever Bolivar saw him with Santana, and now it was possible he could ruin him financially. Revenge was indeed sweet.

Now, if only he could recapture the Santana he had married, everything would be perfect. Elaine's offer burned at his insides, but the memory of how it once had been with another Spanish woman burned much hotter. Elaine was not Santana. There was no other Santana.

Santana stood with five of her six children at the grave of Father Lorenzo, wishing Will and Glenn were there too. They were in Oregon, though, unaware that the faithful priest of the Alcala family had died. Hernando and Teresa and their five children were there, as well as most of the hired help of La Estancia de Alcala. Hernando had sent for a priest from Sacramento for the funeral, and Father Lorenzo had been buried in the family plot, alongside Dominic and Rosa.

A canvas canopy had been erected over the grave site to protect the mourners from a steady rain, and thunder rolled in the distant hills. Santana had never felt more alone. Father Lorenzo had been her friend since childhood, and his death seemed to represent the death of her innocent youth. She should have gone to him after Hugo's attack. Maybe if she had at least told Father Lorenzo, he could have helped her pray about it and find a way to overcome the emotional damage the man had done to her. Perhaps she could have found a way to remain close to Will.

Now it was too late. Father Lorenzo was the only person she would have considered telling about her ordeal, but she had never found the courage. Now, there was no one left to turn to. She must find a way out of the mess she had made of her marriage on her own. She could not let the gap between her and Will continue to widen. It was hurting not only them, but the children. She knew in her heart that Will still loved her, that he was suffering his own loneliness, and it was not his fault. How could she blame him for something he knew nothing about? How could she keep turning him away without any explanation, making him feel it was his fault, making him believe she could not forgive him for leaving her, allowing him to blame himself for Valioso?

Valioso, five years old now, clung to her hand and stared at the grave, his face contorted into a constant grin, his stunted intellect making it impossible for him to comprehend death and agony. He lived in a world of his own, where there was nothing but Mother and Father, love and peace, a joy for life that the average person, even a child, did not experience. He saw only good, understood only laughter and happiness, thrived on love. He could not in a million years understand a man like the one who had fathered him, nor comprehend that there were any problems between his mother and father.

More and more Santana missed Will. More and more

she was coming to believe that he'd been right. It had been better for her to distance herself from him, to refrain from sex for these two years. Will had inadvertently given her time to heal, something she had not had a chance to do.

As she had healed, she'd begun wondering if her husband had turned to someone else, the prostitutes at the camps, or perhaps had found some other woman, a respectable one, with whom he had fallen in love. It was such thoughts that stirred something deep inside that she had left buried for five years, since the day of her father's funeral. The woman in her that only Will had touched was trying to wake up, longing for her husband, feeling a seering jealousy at the thought of some other woman in her husband's life . . . in his bed. She vowed that when Will returned from Oregon, she would try to talk to him, find a way to get close to him again. They could not go on like this, but she knew she would have to make the first move. She had hurt him deeply the night of the governor's ball. He would never seek her out again. She would have to go to him. She had to let go of the ugly recent past and resurrect memories of those first years with Will, remember the passion and desire her handsome *gringo* had stirred in her soul.

It was all still there somewhere, waiting to be reawakened. She closed her eyes when the presiding priest asked everyone to join him in prayer, but she did not hear his words. Instead, she prayed inwardly to Father Lorenzo, to the Mother Mary, asking for help in finding her way back to her husband. Surely God had brought them together, had meant for her to love and marry Will Lassater. If so, he would also find a way for her to overcome this one stumbling block. Surely their love was stronger than anything that came against it. That love had produced five beautiful children they would share forever . . . and it was strong enough that Will loved a sixth child he thought was his.

Will was a good man with a big heart, and if he could accept and love Valioso, surely he could forgive her for hurting him as she had.

She hoped she had not waited too long, that she had not lost his love forever. She had almost gone to him the night before he left for Oregon, but she had decided to wait, only because he would be leaving the next morning, and they had so much to talk about. There had not been enough time. She was still determined not to tell him the truth about Valioso, but she would find a way around it. Perhaps through prayer, God would bring her an answer.

The service ended, and Santana, her brother, and the others made the sign of the cross, taking one last moment for a final farewell. Santana then hustled the children into a covered carriage that would take them back to the main house, where Hernando and Teresa now lived. She could bear going there as long as she stayed away from her old bedroom. The room had been completely redecorated, with frills and a canopy bed. It belonged to Hernando's oldest daughter, seventeen-year-old Rosa Maria. She was a beautiful young woman, and she reminded Santana of the enthusiasm and love for life she'd had at that age.

The carriage bounced over the pathway that led from the graveyard to the house. Thirty-three. She was thirty-three years old now. Will was forty-two. Maybe it was too late for both of them, after all. Still, Will was as virile and strong and solid as when she'd first met him, even more handsome with a touch of gray at the temples, set against a deeply tanned face, lines of wisdom around his blue eyes. She had managed to stay trim, but there was a little gray in her own hair, and her face was not perfect and free of age lines, as it had been at sixteen.

She noticed Noel Gray's horse tied in front of the house and wondered what he was doing there, but there was no time to give it much thought. She hurried the children into the house out of the rain. Teresa had planned to serve food and drink to all the ranch help who had attended the funeral, and the huge dining table was covered with an assortment of edibles. As the children stared hungrily at all the food, Santana took their shawls and cloaks.

"You must behave," she reminded them, wishing Glenn were there. She had grown accustomed to her oldest son helping her with the rest of the children, but Will thought it was time for Glenn to learn logging. It worried her, having her son in that kind of danger, but she knew Will would watch out for him, and she knew how important it was to him to have his sons come into the business. She missed Glenn, who had grown into a dashing young man. His blue eyes, set against the dark skin of his face, evoked a masculine sensuality that had all the girls talking. He was the perfect blending of her Spanish blood and Will's American looks.

Valioso grabbed her skirt. "Pick up, Mommy," he said.

"Not right now, Valioso. Mommy has to help Aunt Teresa serve the guests. You stay with Ruth. She will get you something to eat, and you must be very careful not to spill your food or lose it out of your mouth." She paid no heed to the stares of some of the help as they came inside. She had grown accustomed to people staring at Valioso. Most of these men and women knew he was retarded and accepted it, yet still they could not help gawking. She knew they did not mean to be rude.

"Senora Santana." Santana turned to see Hilda, Hernando's housekeeper, standing beside her. "Senor Gray is here to speak with you. He says it is very urgent. It is about your husband."

Santana gently pushed Valioso toward Ruth. "Where is he?"

"He is in the study."

Santana frowned, her heart beginning to pound with dread. There were so many deaths and accidents at the mills, but she had grown accustomed to the dangers, and Will was seldom around the actual work anymore. Surely this had nothing to do with such a problem. Besides, Will knew how to watch out for himself. Perhaps it was something else. He had gone to Oregon by ship. Dear God! Had the ship sunk? But that would also involve Glenn. She would not want to go on living if something happened to her son. No! It couldn't be that. Perhaps Will had simply sent a messenger to tell her he would be in Oregon longer than he thought. It had already been a month. He was supposed to come home soon.

She put a hand to her stomach and took a deep breath before entering the study. The look in Noel's eyes brought a knot of pain to her insides. "Noel! What is wrong?"

The man rose from a chair to face her, tragedy in his eyes. "It's Will. A messenger arrived at camp this morning. We have a ship waiting to take you to Oregon as soon as you can get to it. I'll accompany you to camp and on down to the shore where you can board."

Santana's eyes widened with horror. "What has happened? What about Glenn?"

"Glenn is fine. Will saved his life, but apparently in doing so he might lose his own. There was an accident up at one of the new mills. They were trying out a new chute they'd built to get the logs down from high country. A log flew off and headed right for Will and Glenn. Will managed to push Glenn out of the way, but the log tumbled right into Will, broke a lot of bones. He's in a hospital up in Eugene. Your son is with him, but all Will does is groan your name. If you want to see him before he . . . Well, I just hope he lives long enough that you can talk to him." There were tears in his eyes. "I'm sorry, Santana."

Santana shivered, turning away in shock. Was this

how her prayers would be answered, for her husband to die before she could make amends? Will! Not Will! Not her strong, handsome husband! God could not be doing this to her!

"Go and get my brother, please. Send him in here. I have to make plans for the children, especially Valioso."

"Sure."

Noel left, and Santana sank into a chair. All the hurt she had caused the man she loved so dearly welled up in her soul and burst forth in deep sobs of regret. He had to live. She must be given the chance to make up for the lost years. Surely God would allow her that. "Will," she sobbed. "Please do not die. I cannot live without you!"

Twenty-Eight

Santana clung to her hat with one hand and held on to a leather grip with the other as the coach that carried her from the coast to Eugene bounced and swayed over the rough dirt road. She looked at the man and woman in the seat across from her, who were also hanging on for their lives.

"Don't worry. It isn't too much farther," the man told her. "We've made this trip many times. The wife's got relatives in San Francisco."

Santana nodded. She didn't like making small talk. All she wanted was to get to Will, and she had prayed all the way there that he would not die before she could see him again. That he would not die at all. So many things to make up for. So much time lost.

This was the only route people could take from the coast to Eugene, and the thought of Will being carted over this road in his injured condition gave her the shivers. At least, according to what the man who'd brought her to Oregon had told her, Will had already been about halfway inland when the accident happened. He didn't have to ride as far as she was.

"You've been awfully quiet since we boarded," the woman said to her. "What is your name? What's your reason for coming to Oregon? We're Mr. and Mrs. Webster. My husband owns a feed supply in Eugene."

Santana answered only to be polite. "I am Dona Santana Chavez de Lassater. My husband is Will Lassater. He owns Lassater Mills. Perhaps you have heard of him."

Mrs. Webster's eyebrows arched, and she quickly scanned Santana, as though she were surprised that someone like Will Lassater would marry a Spanish woman. Or perhaps the woman was simply impressed that Santana was married to someone of such wealth. Santana was in no mood to care what the woman was thinking.

"Oh, yes!" Mrs. Webster said. "Your husband has opened several mills in Oregon. Are you here to meet him at one of them?"

Santana glanced out the window, but saw nothing except thick forest. It was no wonder Will had wanted to start new mills here. He could log several varieties of trees that could not be found in California, and thus expand on the types of wood he sold, meeting all the different lumber needs worldwide. She felt the old excitement she'd once felt when Will used to talk about logging, remembering the day she and her father went to visit the mill to see how it all worked, remembering the screaming saw, remembering Will taking her off alone to tell her she shouldn't marry Hugo . . . remembering a kiss.

"No," she finally answered. "He was badly hurt in an accident at one of the mills not far from Eugene. He is in a hospital there." *Oh, Will, please do not die! Please forgive me for everything!*

"I'm terribly sorry. We didn't know," Mr. Webster said. "I hope he'll be all right."

"Thank you," Santana replied. She should never have let what Hugo had done destroy all those things she and

Will used to share. What if she was too late? What if Will was already dead? How could she bear the guilt of making him so unhappy these last two years? Actually, it had been five. He had sensed the change in her soon after he had come home from the war, and he'd blamed it all on himself these last five years.

Finally she could see signs of civilization. The trees were thinning, and she glimpsed buildings and homes in a valley below. "I see a river," she said.

"That's the Willamette," Mr. Webster told her. "Runs all the way down from the Columbia up at our northern border."

"I see." It struck Santana how little she knew about places other than California. In spite of all of Will's traveling, this was the first time in her thirty-three years that she had ever left her homeland. She'd been too wrapped up in the children to travel with Will to the new logging sites; and she had never cared to travel east to that mysterious United States from which her husband came. Will had been to so many places, coming to California first by ship, traveling back east in the war, moving through the southern states during the war, coming all the way back to California again. He'd been all up and down the coast, and she had remained on her father's ranch, devoting all her time and attention to her children, never leaving the land that was in her blood.

"We're almost to the stage station," Mr. Webster said as they entered Eugene. He pointed out various streets, told her where his feed store was, but she did not pay much attention. All she could think about was how she was going to tell the children if their father died. She had tried not to alarm them too deeply, but even Valioso had sensed something was terribly wrong. He'd lost his smile, something very rare for him, and he had clung to her as though terrified. It had not been easy to leave him. He had come to depend on her totally, almost never letting her out of his sight except when he slept. He knew that if his mother was going away, it was something very important, maybe something bad.

She felt sorry for James, too. Up at the mill he had embraced her before she left, tears in his eyes. If Will died, it would be so very hard on James, after losing his own father. Will had become Gerald's replacement, and James loved him just as much. He had told her to tell Will he would put off his marriage to Juanita Hidalgo until Will was well and able to come to the wedding. She prayed that day would come.

The coach finally halted in front of the stage station, and Santana waited impatiently for the driver to hand down her carpetbag. She had not brought much, caring only about getting packed quickly so she could get there as fast as possible. She asked for directions to the hospital, then removed her shawl before heading up the street. Along the coast it had been cool and foggy, but it was almost July, and inland it was much warmer. Still, perhaps she just felt too warm because she was so nervous over what she would find. Poor Glenn. If his father died while he was up here alone with him, the boy would be devastated. *Oh, please, God, let him still be alive!* She half ran to the small white wooden building three blocks away. She hurried inside, stopping at a desk where a young woman in a plain black dress with a stiff white collar sat looking at some papers.

"I am the wife of Will Lassater," she said. "Please, is my husband still here? Is he still alive?"

The woman looked up at her, sympathy in her eyes, and for a moment Santana felt as though someone had plunged a knife into her stomach. "I'm so sorry about what happened, Mrs. Lassater, and so glad you finally made it here. I think the thought of needing to see you again is all that kept him going at first, and it was long enough that it's quite possible he will live. He seems to be starting to mend."

Santana dropped her carpetbag, feeling almost faint with relief. She closed her eyes and grabbed hold of the edge of the desk. She'd been so sure the woman was going to tell her Will had died. "Thank God," she said, a sudden sob making her gasp. The woman hurried out from behind the desk and put an arm around her.

"Are you all right, Mrs. Lassater?"

Santana nodded. "Yes. I just need a moment to compose myself before—"

"Mother!" Glenn came out of one of the rooms. "I thought I heard your voice!" For the last two years her oldest son had seldom hugged her, saying he was getting too old for such things; but now he ran to her and embraced her. "I'm so glad you're finally here. Dad's been asking and asking for you." The boy began to cry. "It was so terrible, Mother. I didn't know . . . what to do except just stay with him. The log rolled over him . . . broke so many bones. One arm bone came right through the skin and he got a bad infection from it, but that's better now." He pulled away. "He's been in so much pain I can hardly stand to watch, but I've stayed right with him." He wiped at his tears. "He asks for you constantly."

Santana looked him over. So thin and tired he looked! "I am proud of how you have stayed by his side and looked after him." She kissed his cheek. "Take me to him, Glenn. He will be all right now. I am sure of it."

"He saved my life. He pushed me out of the way."

Oh, how she loved Will Lassater! Of course he would do something like that. She suddenly felt free of all the horror she had lived with these past six years. None of it mattered now. All that mattered was that Will was still alive, and God was going to give them a chance to recapture all that they had lost. "Your father would give his life for any of his children," she answered. She looked Glenn over again. "You were not hurt at all?"

"Just my leg a little. The log glanced off it, but not enough to break anything. Just a bruise. Come on. Dad will be so happy to see you. The doctor isn't here right now, but he'll be back soon. He can tell you about his injuries."

Santana told herself to be strong as she followed her son into the room where Will lay. "I'll leave you and Dad alone for a while," Glenn said. He left the room and closed the door, and Santana forced back an urge to run when she finally saw Will—splints, casts, bandages everywhere, even a bandage around his head. "Will!" She hurried to his bedside and leaned close, gently taking hold of one hand. "Will, *carino mio!*"

It had been a long time since Will had heard his wife address him that way. Was she really there? He opened his eyes to see Santana bending close. He studied her dark eyes, still so beautiful, and he could imagine that if she took her hair out of the tight bun she wore it in, let it fall loose and long, she would look hardly any different from the young Santana who had stolen his heart. What was that in her eyes? Something different. Something he had not seen in such a long, long time. Love. More than that. Passion, forgiveness. "Santana," he muttered. "Don't . . . leave . . ."

"I am not leaving until you can leave with me, my love." Her eyes brimmed with tears. "Oh, Will, you must live . . . for me . . . for the children. They want their father to come home, and I want my husband to come home, home to California and La Estancia de Alcala and the big redwoods and the Palominos, and . . ." She stopped when a sob caught in her throat, and she knelt beside the bed, resting her elbows on the edge of it. "Come home to *me*, Will. I love you so! I need you. I want you home. I am so sorry for all the heartache I have caused you. I was wrong, so wrong! Please believe me when I tell you that none of it was your fault. I never should have blamed you for going off to war. It was something in your heart that you had to do. Please get well and come home to us, Will."

Will continued to study her eyes. Yes, there was something different there. "I had to see you once more . . . tell you I'm sorry . . . I stayed away like I did . . . tell you I love you, Santana. You're still my beautiful Santana . . . my wife . . . the only woman I want. I never turned to any other woman. I needed to tell you that before I—"

"Do not talk of dying!" Santana felt the old fiesty stubbornness that had given her the courage years ago to defy her father's and Hugo's wishes and fall in love with her handsome *gringo*. It rose again in her soul, this time for a different reason. She leaned closer, fire in her eyes. "You are not going to die, Will Lassater! You have six children who need their father. You have not finished teaching Glenn and James all that they need to know, and one day it will be Dominic and Juan who will need your guidance. You are an important man who is needed to run a logging empire. It is much too soon for you to die. You are only forty-two years old, and you are one of the strongest men among those who run your mills. Would any of them give up so easily? I think not! Would Gerald want you to give up?"

She stood up, folding her arms and looking down at her husband with authority. "You are going to get well, and I am going to stay right here until you are healed enough that we can take you home. While you recover there, you will have time with the children. You have hardly seen them these last two years. They miss their father. Valioso asks about you all the time." She could not help the tears that trickled down her cheeks, and her voice grew softer. "And your wife needs you . . . in every way. *Te quiero mucho, mi esposo*. I had decided before you were hurt that I want you back in every way, if you still want your wife in the way you once wanted her."

For the first time since the accident, Will felt a desire to hang on, not just long enough to see his wife again, but for good. He had no idea what had changed, or why. It didn't matter. The woman he saw now was the Santana he had married, full of fire and pride . . . and desire.

"If I had to go through all this . . . to get you back . . . then it was worth it," he mumbled.

Santana shook her head. "No, my beloved, you did not have to go through this. I had made up my mind when you first left for Oregon." She knelt beside the bed again, grasping his hand. "I love you so, Will. All the way here . . . I was so afraid I would be too late. You must get well. You must come home."

Will managed enough strength to squeeze her hand lightly. "All these years I managed to keep from getting hurt. Now when all I'm doing is going around inspecting sites . . . this happens." Tears formed in his own eyes. "*Te quiero*, Santana. Now that you're here . . . I feel better. It's going to take months . . . but I want to mend at home. As soon as the doctor says I can be moved . . . I want to go home . . . to La Estancia de Alcala. I miss the children. But most of all . . . I've missed you . . . the Santana I married."

Santana kissed his hand, such a strong hand, yet he'd been so gentle with her that first time. It had been so beautiful . . . not ugly like with Hugo. She would never again compare the two experiences, or allow what Hugo had done to turn something so wonderful with her husband into something hideous. This was Will, and he was a good man who loved his wife and had patiently waited through something most men angrily would have refused to allow. He could have forced himself on her, taken his husbandly rights, but he had left her alone. Because of that she was a whole woman again. "The Santana you married is right here, Will. And she will never leave you or deny you again."

Will felt a wave of new energy sweep through him. By God, she was right. He *wasn't* ready to die! Not if there was a chance his family life could get back to what it once was. He had survived the war and prison camp, and he would survive this, as long as Santana was at his side. "Santana," he murmured. "I've never known . . . such pain."

She leaned close and kissed his cheek. "Think of the forest, *mi amor*, the peace and beauty you find there, the strength you draw from the giant redwoods, the smell of pine and fresh-cut wood, the feel of the bark against your hand, the quiet of the forest where you can walk with God. When you are well, we will walk in the forest together, just the two of us. We will lay a blanket on a bed of pine needles and we will make love with only the birds and the deer to see us. Think of that, *carino mio*, and before you know it, it will be so."

A tear slipped out of his eye and down the side of his face. She remembered and understood the things that gave him strength. "I would like that," he answered, his voice growing weaker. "Making love to you . . . alone in the forest. Are you sure . . . that's what you want, Santana?"

"Si, mi amor, it is what I want. I have never been more sure."

"I wish . . . that I could hold you."

"You will hold me again, when you are well, and it will come sooner than you think. The children and I will help you."

He managed a faint smile, in spite of more tears

running from his eyes. "I miss them, Santana. I miss Valioso . . . the way he smiles at me."

With those words she knew keeping the truth from him had been worth it, for the love Will felt for an innocent child who deserved that love. She had borne her secret alone, and now she could live with it. Never again would she let it rob her of the treasures of life and happiness.

"Children! Children! You must quiet down and be little ladies and gentlemen," Santana scolded. "Someone is at the door. It could be another business friend of your father's." She walked down the carpeted hallway of their mansion on Nob Hill, deciding to answer the door herself rather than call the maid all the way from an upstairs bedroom.

She liked this San Francisco home better than she'd thought she would when Will had first started building it. But she had not been happy then. Now this home was filled with love and laughter. All the children were there, the younger ones playing hide-and-seek in the hall and parlor and library. She called to Glenn, who was in the study with his father. Santana had pushed Will there in his wheelchair so that he could do some paperwork. He could not push himself around in the chair yet because his arms were still not fully healed.

"Glenn, come out here and get your brothers and sisters involved in something less noisy, please. Take them in the library and let them work on puzzles. And Ruth, you should be practicing your piano."

They did not obey immediately, but rather gathered around her to see who was at the door. As soon as Will had been well enough to travel, they had come to San Francisco. He had not been healed enough to continue the three-day journey to the ranch, and he had decided to stay here until he could walk. There were better doctors in San Francisco, and he was close to his offices. His managers and accountants could come to the house for meetings. Santana had sent for the children to join them, and they had been thrilled to come to San Francisco. It was an adventure for them. Soon they would all go home together, where Will would heal fully.

It had been four months since the accident, and Will was getting stronger every day. She was eager for the day when he would be well enough for them to do the one thing they both needed to consummate the new love they had found. She was ready to be a woman again, Will Lassater's woman.

Santana opened the door, and quickly her smile left her. Her heartbeat quickened at the sight of Hugo Bolivar standing on the porch with papers in his hand and anger in his dark eyes. "What—"

"I wish to speak with your husband!" he demanded.

Santana put a hand on Valioso's shoulder as the boy leaned against her leg, grasping her skirt. The rest of the children stared, and Glenn, old enough to understand the hatred and rivalry between this man and his father, stepped forward. "What do you want with my dad?"

"That is our business!"

Santana stiffened with pride and defense, quickly regaining her composure and wits. She was pleased to realize she could face Hugo without the horror and dread he had always brought her before. "This is our oldest son, Glenn, and he knows a great deal about his father's business," she said sternly. "You will not speak to him as though he were hired help. And Will is still not well. Perhaps you do not know about—"

"Of course I know," Hugo interrupted. "The whole town knows about your poor, dear husband." He sneered.

"But his injuries have not stopped him from robbing me behind my back!"

Santana frowned. "I do not understand—"

"Your brother now owns Rancho de Rosas! And don't tell me you didn't know about it!"

"But I didn't—"

"It was purchased by an anonymous buyer. If I had known it was your husband . . ."

"You said Hernando bought it."

Hugo stepped closer. "Your brother is not devious enough to have done this on his own. Hernando is simpleminded and too honest for his own good. Will Lassater did this! I want to speak to him!"

Santana kept a hand on Valioso's shoulder, worrying Hugo intended to say something that would spoil everything she had worked so hard to protect. She stepped back, holding Hugo's gaze defiantly. "Show Don Bolivar to your father's study," she told Glenn.

Glenn glared a warning at Hugo. "Follow me."

Hugo walked past Santana, and she realized he had aged considerably since she'd seen him at the governor's ball more than two years ago. He seemed to be shrinking and was much thinner. Will had mentioned that he'd heard Hugo had overinvested and overspent, and now that San Francisco was in a financial slump, Hugo was losing money. The thought pleased her, and apparently Will had done something to take advantage of the situation, but he had not told her about it. She told Ruth to take the children to the library and followed Glenn into the study.

When she reached it, Hugo was already raging at Will, who sat in his wheelchair behind his desk. He was watching Hugo with satisfied humor in his eyes as the man carried on about being deceived, threatening to sue Will.

"You put Rancho de Rosas up for sale," Will said calmly when Hugo finally stopped to take a breath. "I made an anonymous offer through my lawyers, a fair price, and you accepted. You needed the money and it was a legitimate sale, after which I put the ranch in Hernando's name. Now La Estancia de Alcala is doubled in size, and Hernando's and my descendants will be wealthy for years to come. I have no doubt that in the end, the most valuable asset in California won't be its minerals and forests. It will be the land, and Dominic Chavez Alcala's descendants will own plenty of it. You made a mistake selling that land, Hugo, and you've just realized it; but all your ranting and raving won't get it back for you. I also know the gold mine you owned has played out. Seems to me like you've made some bad investments and poor decisions all the way around." He put his pipe to his lips and gave it a couple of puffs, then leaned back and grinned. "If you have anything else to sell, I'm listening."

Santana stood behind Hugo, but she could feel his rage. "You stinking *gringo* bastard!" he shouted. "I would not knowingly sell you a clod of dirt!"

Will shrugged. "Then get out of my house. I am certainly not going to give Rancho de Rosas back to you, and since you have no other business to conduct with me, you have no reason to be here. And I'll thank you to watch your language in front of my wife and son."

Hugo stiffened. "Your wife?" He turned and looked at Santana, and her heart seemed to move into her throat. She held his gaze squarely, though. Surely he would not say anything. How would he ever explain it? He knew Will would never believe she had willingly allowed Hugo to violate her, and at the moment he was already embarrassed at how Will had taken advantage of him. He had raped her solely to destroy her from the inside. The problem was, he had failed, and he knew it. It frustrated and disappointed him, and Santana felt a rush of victory at the look in his eyes. He was caught. He could say nothing, and as long as what he had done had not ruined her life and marriage, then he could not enjoy the revenge he had planned.

He looked back at Will. "Your wife deserves no respect from me. She was once promised to me and she broke that promise and brought dishonor to the Chavez Alcala name. She married a *gringo*, and her children are half-breeds, one of them a worthless retard!"

Glenn moved in front of the man, his fists clenched. He was shorter than Hugo, but gaining his father's burly build. "You shut up and get out of our house," he told the man, teeth gritted. "I'd never ordinarily hit an old man, but I'm sure tempted!"

"It's all right, Glenn," Will said. "Your mother and I know Don Bolivar is just puffing smoke, trying to make up for the things he's lost through his own ignorance and bad reputation. He's a lonely, childless old man who thought money was all that was important in life, and now he's losing that too. He's masking his own hurt by trying to hurt others."

Hugo glared at him. "I wish my bullet had found your spine!" he growled. "And someday you will learn that the worst decision you ever made was to let me live that day!"

He looked at Santana, and she knew he expected his words to cut hard, but she did not flinch.

"You have nothing left to threaten me with, Hugo," Will said. "Get out."

Hugo turned back to Will. "You have stolen everything from me."

"I stole nothing from you. Everything you've lost, you lost from your own ignorance. As for Santana, she fell in love. Being promised to you was an arrangement made by two people from the old world, and I suspect that if Santana's father had known the kind of man you would become, he never would have made that promise, no matter what your father did for him. You're just damn lucky

I'm in this wheelchair, or I'd take you out on the front lawn and make you pay for your remarks about my wife and Valioso. Now get the hell out of my sight before I let Glenn light into you!"

Hugo stood with clenched fists. Santana waited in strained silence, half expecting him to blurt it out. *I bedded your wife, Will Lassater, while you were off fighting your gringo war.* But he knew it was useless. He looked her over scathingly, but Santana no longer felt the shame and guilt such a look had once caused. She felt, instead, a surprising peace.

Hugo walked out without another word, and Glenn followed. "I'll make sure he leaves," he told his father.

Santana folded her arms, giving her husband a scolding look. "You didn't tell me about buying Rancho de Rosas."

"I intended to. I only signed it over to Hernando yesterday. I told your brother a long time ago that if I could ever find a way to get my hands on Bolivar's land, I'd grab it up. I've had my lawyers watching his estate for a long time. He's losing money and assets fast. He's a wicked, lonely, spiteful old man who's going broke, and I'm enjoying watching it happen. Don't let his words hurt you."

She walked around the desk and knelt in front of him. "As long as I have you, nothing he can do could hurt me. I know that now. I used to be afraid of him, but today I saw what you saw, a lonely old man who is nothing. He is of no significance."

Will smiled, reaching out to touch her face. "To hell with Hugo Bolivar. Let's not even talk about him. I'm proud of how you've managed here, bringing the kids, taking care of me, playing hostess to important men you've had to entertain while I'm healing, letting them use our home like an office. Things will calm down and I'll be getting out of this chair soon. We'll go home then, find some peace . . . find each other. I can't wait until I'm healed enough to be able to make love to you, Santana."

She reached up, and he met her lips. *Yes, to hell with Hugo Bolivar,* she thought. *We have won, Will.*

Valioso ran into the room then, holding a piece of paper with crayon scribbling on it. "For Daddy," he said, the ever-present smile on his face. He came around the desk, oblivious to his father and mother kissing, and proudly handed the paper to his father.

Will saw the love in the boy's eyes, and smiled when he took the paper. "This is beautiful, Valioso. Thank you."

Valioso laughed, throwing back his head, always excited to please.

Santana turned away at seeing the guilt her husband still felt for Valioso, a guilt he did not deserve, but could not be helped. Thank God Hugo had not blurted out the truth in his anger, and thank God the man did not consider that Valioso could be his own son. She rose and walked to a window that faced the street. She saw Hugo talking to a neighbor. He was mounted on a fine black horse, sitting straight, arrogant as ever. To have faced him and felt nothing was a wonderful experience.

He finally rode off, and she raised her chin and breathed deeply. *Go, Hugo. Go away and never come back. You are done. Finished! My husband will never know the truth.*

Twenty-Nine

Santana watched her children open their Christmas presents. She had not even dressed yet, but had only pulled on a robe. None of the children had dressed either, too excited about Christmas to take the time. This was a day to be lazy and enjoy the family.

She could not imagine a more wonderful Christmas, with so much for which to be thankful. Will was fully recovered, although he would always walk with a slight limp from one knee never healing right. He could not bend it completely, but it seemed a minor problem considering the fact that he could have died. The healing had taken six months, but doctors in San Francisco considered that speedy and remarkable, and they attributed the recovery to his excellent physical condition at the time of the accident. He was a strong man, and determined . . . determined to get well so that he could again be a husband to her.

They were home, back at their new house at La Estancia de Alcala, now one of the biggest spreads in northern California, thanks to the purchase of Rancho de Rosas.

Hernando had been overwhelmed by what Will had done, and Santana was proud of how well her brother was managing the enormous ranch. Dominic would have been proud too.

She watched as Will sat on the floor playing with Valioso and the puppy they had given the boy for Christmas. Valioso was in heaven. He loved being with his father, and he was thrilled with the puppy, which eagerly licked the boy's face. Valioso threw back his head and laughed, something he always did when he was especially pleased. Saliva trickled out of the side of his mouth when he got so excited, and Will took a handkerchief from his pants pocket and gently wiped it away.

Again Santana felt the stabbing pain of her husband's suffering over the boy, but the glow on Valioso's face was worth the price she was paying and causing Will to pay for the secret she had to keep. Valioso carried the puppy over to her and plopped it in her lap, and Santana laughed as it began busily licking at her neck, its tail wagging with joy. She took pleasure in the feel of its soft belly and its thick black fur. She handed it back to Valioso.

"Bring it here, Valioso!" nine-year-old Juan told his brother. "We'll all play with it."

Valioso ran to his siblings, who had finished opening their presents, and the children began teasing and darting at the puppy, making it chase them. Soon the room was filled with screams and laughter. Will and Santana watched for a few minutes, before Will took hold of her hand and tugged, making her get up. He pulled her into his arms, rubbing her back. "This is one of the best Christmases I can remember," he said.

She looked into his blue eyes, taking great pleasure in feeling again the stirrings of her youth, the old desire, the longing to mate with this man she loved so. They had not made love yet since the accident, and she had not said anything, afraid he was not ready. Now, though, she saw a sparkle in his eyes that she used to see so many years ago . . . before the war. . . .

"This is a wonderful Christmas," she said. "I am glad we came back here for it. San Francisco is an adventure for the children, but they are happiest here, especially Valioso."

Will sighed and kept an arm around her. "Come to my study and drink a little wine with me, Santana. A Christmas toast to each other someplace quiet." He led her out of the great room and down the hallway. "We had to get out of the city, you know, what with the threat of riots. Men without jobs are beginning to blame it all on the Chinese laborers. There have been a lot of scuffles and some raids and beatings. I have a feeling it's going to get worse before it gets better, and I feel sorry for the Chinese, who really aren't to blame. They're good workers, sober and dependable, and we're the ones who brought them over here to work on the railroad. Be that as it may, I don't think San Francisco is a good place for the family right now."

"I agree." They walked into the study, and Will closed the door, quietly slipping a bolt to lock it without Santana noticing. "I also am worried about the drought," she continued. "It frightened me when we read about the Chicago fire two months ago, the terrible loss of property and lives. It made me want to get out of the city. If you had been well enough, I would have left then, but I wanted you to be near the doctors. Our own Dr. Enders is a good man, but he is getting old."

Will walked to a cabinet and took out a bottle of wine, made from grapes grown on La Estancia de Alcala. He poured a little into two glasses he took down from a shelf. He kept drinks and glasses handy for visits from business acquaintances, but this morning he wanted to share a quiet drink with his wife. "I'm worried about the drought, too, but not in the city. I'm worried about the mills. The forests are tinder-dry." He walked over and handed her a glass. "But we aren't going to let it spoil this very special day, are we?"

"No," she answered. She took the glass, and they each sipped the sweet red wine. "Not just because it is Christmas. Every day is special now that you are well again, *carino mio*."

Will took a second drink of wine before setting his glass aside. "I'm more recovered than you think," he said with a grin. He ran a hand along her arm while she sipped more wine herself. "Well enough to want my woman."

Santana frowned. "Will Lassater! We cannot just go to our bedroom in the middle of the morning. What would we tell the children?"

He took her wineglass away and set it down. "The older ones wouldn't need an explanation, but it doesn't matter, because we aren't going to the bedroom. I locked the door to the study."

She glanced at the door, then looked back at her grinning husband. *"Here?"*

He pulled her close. "Watching you this morning, how beautiful you look . . . I don't want to wait until tonight, and like you said, it would be awkward to go to our bedroom. Hell, you're still wearing your nightgown and robe. It gives you an excuse to go upstairs and wash when we're through."

"Will . . ."

"I told Glenn earlier that if we disappeared for a while, he should keep the children busy and make them leave us alone."

"You told *Glenn?*"

"He's old enough to understand."

"Will, I will be embarrassed to death to face him at the breakfast table!"

He untied her feathered satin robe and pulled it open to study her breasts, pleased to see her nipples aroused to hard peaks beneath the satin cloth. "Just act natural." He lost his smile, touching her cheek with the back of his hand while he pulled her close with his other arm. "I have waited a long time for this, Santana."

She felt the power in his arm and was aroused by her husband's strength and desire. Her eyes teared. "Too long, my beloved, and I am so sorry." She let the robe fall to the floor, and her heart beat so hard it almost hurt. She wanted him! She felt no reservations, saw no repulsive visions. She saw only her husband's beautiful blue eyes, knew only that she wanted to please this man, and to take her own pleasure in return. It was a final victory for her, for nothing from the past rose up to interfere with this wonderful desire and passion she was feeling. "Are you sure you are well enough?"

He slipped his fingers under the straps of her gown and pulled them off her shoulders. "There is only one way to find out."

Santana shivered with want as she dropped her arms so that he could slide the gown off them. It fell to the floor, leaving her standing there wearing only a pair of lacy drawers and her slippers. "I hope . . ." She swallowed, suddenly feeling like an inexperienced virgin. "I hope my body still pleases you." Her nipples tingled as Will studied them while he removed his smoking jacket and threw it aside.

"You are as beautiful as you were when I married you, and you know it. Still slender in the right places and round where it matters." He removed the silk pajama bottoms he'd worn under the smoking jacket, and Santana faced one last challenge by dropping her eyes to gaze at her husband's manhood, large, hard, eager to find its way into her lovenest. It did not frighten her as she thought it might.

Instead, a burning need to feel him inside her caused her to throw her arms around his neck and meet his mouth in a fiery kiss.

Her eagerness was all Will needed to know that he had back the Santana he had married. He groaned with the want of her. He slid his hands inside her drawers, grasping her firm bottom while he kissed her suggestively. She responded with whimpers of desire, running her tongue between his lips, pushing herself against his hardness.

"God, I want you so, Santana," he said between kisses, his voice husky.

"And I want you, *mi esposo*," she whispered, "as I have never wanted you." She threw back her head as he kissed her neck, her shoulders, bent down to taste a taut nipple with eagerness, as though it were a succulent fruit. She groaned his name when he moved farther down, kissing her belly, the crevice between her thigh, and her most private place, a place she had never given willingly to any man but Will Lassater. She sank to the thick Oriental rug that decorated the floor of the study, allowing her husband free rein with her body.

Santana floated into ecstasy from a combination of the magical things Will could do to her, and the wonderful joy of realizing she was free of the past and could enjoy this as a full woman again. She wrapped her fingers into his hair and rocked herself against him. It had been so long since she'd enjoyed this, in only seconds she gasped in a shuddering climax that left her wanting to scream for him to fill her as only he could. She had to force herself to be still because of the children, and she knew it was the same for Will, whose eyes were glazed with desire when he raised up to meet her gaze.

Neither said a word as he reached for her and pulled her up, leading her to a leather couch that had a blanket spread over it. She lay back on it, closing her eyes when

Will moved between her legs. He came down to meet her mouth and pushed his throbbing hardness inside her, and her scream of satisfaction was muffled against his kiss. He moved in quick rhythm, a man who had gone too long without his woman. He was so swollen, it almost hurt, but Santana took erotic pleasure in the pain. This was Will, and he had waited patiently for this for so long. Other men might have been untrue, and she could not blame him if he had turned to another, but she trusted that he belonged only to her. He was the most wonderful, forgiving man a woman could want, and she would never deny him again.

Too quickly his life surged into her. But within the space of a breath, his shaft grew hard again, and he continued the rhythm as though there had been no break at all. Eagerly they clung to each other, bodies heated and damp, mouths meeting in fiery, hungry kisses. She dug her nails into his shoulders, ran her hands along his arms to revel in the strong muscles there. No, Will Lassater was certainly not ready to die. He was alive and well, and as much man as he ever was.

He pounded into her, a man on fire mating with a woman ready to consume that fire and help him calm the flames. She responded by arching up to greet each thrust, secretly celebrating her own freedom, freedom to be a woman again, freedom from the past and the secret she would carry to her grave. This was Will, her beloved Will! They belonged to each other again in every way.

Santana clung to him desperately, so happy he was alive and in her arms. She ran her hands over his body, wanting to feel every muscle, the hairs on his chest, his face, his nose, his thick hair. She trailed her fingers down to his buttocks, pressing with his every thrust as though to push him deeper. He raised to his knees, lifting her hips, and finished in a last wild surge of desire, his eyes glazed and determined, as though he would conquer whatever it was that had kept her from him for so long.

And you have conquered those fears, my love, she thought. *At last I belong only to you again.* She closed her eyes and gasped when his life surged into her once more. She could not control the tears, tears of relief and joy. She reached around his neck and pulled him down to her, and he kissed her.

"I love you, Santana," he whispered.

"And I love you, *mi vida,*" she answered. "We are one again, in body and in spirit. Nothing will ever come between us again."

"Never." He kissed her cheek. "Never."

He took an afghan from the back of the couch and pulled it over them, then made love to her again, gently, slowly, able to take his time now, so they relished every inch of each other, sharing a strong bond that had never really left them. He was still her brave and handsome *gringo*, and she was still his exotic Spanish wife, the forbidden young girl for whom he had been willing to die.

Santana awoke with a start. The house was dark, yet there seemed to be a soft glow outside the window. She heard a rumble in the distance. Rain. Finally they would get some rain, but it wasn't raining yet. She got up and put on her robe, then jumped when a bolt of lightning caused a loud pop not far away. It was followed by a clap of thunder that literally shook the house.

One of the children started crying, and Santana hurried into the hallway. The crying was coming from four-year-old Julia's room. She hurried there, realizing the child had been frightened by the thunder. When she went inside, she saw the strange glow again, and now that she was more awake, she realized what it might be. Her heart seemed to climb into her throat as she ran to the window to look outside.

Fire! The entire forest north of the house was in flames. She quickly picked Julia up in her arms, telling herself to stay calm for the sake of the children. "Hush, Julia. It's all right. Mama's here."

"Santana! Santana, where are you?"

Will must have awakened and seen the fire. "Here!" She ran out of Julia's room. "Will, the forest is on fire!"

"I saw it!" Will was buttoning a pair of pants. "Wake the rest of the children. I'll get Valioso and wake the help." He grabbed a lantern that hung lit in the hallway. "Take this with you. I'll get one for myself."

"Where will we go, Will? What will we do?"

"Just gather everybody at the front garden! There may not be time to hitch a wagon. We'll have to make a run for the valley. Maybe we can reach the pond below the hill!" He left her then, and for one frantic moment Santana wondered if there was something she should try to save. No. There was no time to save anything but the children.

"Mommy! Mommy! I'm scared!" Julia cried.

"You mustn't be. *Madre* and *Padre* are right here. Be a brave little girl now, won't you?" She set Julia down but kept hold of her hand, calling for Ruth as she hurried to Juan's room. She knew a forest fire could spread over acres in minutes, jumping from treetop to treetop. Outside the lightning continued to rip through the sky, casting quick, bright, eerie light inside the house that made everything more confusing.

Ruth ran out into the hallway. "Mama! What is it?"

"Forest fire! We have to gather the children in the front garden. Your father went to get Valioso. Help me wake the rest of the children. We must all stay together! I'll get Juan. Go and get Dominic!"

Glenn came running down the hall. "Where's Dad?"

"He went to get Valioso. You and Ruth get Dominic and meet me and your father in the front garden." Santana hurried into Juan's room, keeping a tight hold of Julia's hand. She woke Juan and hurried him into the hallway. Downstairs Anna, Ester, and Louisa were yelling "Fire!" Louisa headed up the stairs to find Santana, who met her halfway. "Go to the front garden!" she ordered.

Ester began screaming and crying, carrying on that her husband was probably trapped up at the mill. The cook, Anna Martinez, told the woman to calm down for the sake of the children and get to the front garden. The house was glowing now, and a rush of flames suddenly exploded through a back window. Santana clung tightly to Julia and Juan, looking back to see Glenn and Ruth hurrying down the stairs with Dominic. She quickly counted. Five. All five. Will had gone for Valioso. She felt a rush of panic at the realization that she had not seen Will or Valioso since Will had said he would get the boy. Valioso's room was just on the other side of hers and Will's, so they would always be close to him.

"Get to the garden!" she ordered Ruth and Glenn.

They all ran down the stairs, past an already-burning kitchen. Santana told herself she must not worry about the fact that her beautiful new home was burning. The tile roof had not kept the fire away as Will had hoped. Instead, it had blasted right in through the windows, like an orange monster come to consume them. They all raced to the front of the house, and Santana did not have to hold up her lantern to count heads. The fire was so close, it lit up the sky, and the air was stifling hot. She quickly looked around. Everyone was there, even all the help . . . everyone but Will and Valioso.

"Where is your father?" Santana asked as she looked

around, her heart pounding. "Will!" she screamed. "Will! Valioso!"

"I'll go back and try to find them!" Glenn told her.

"No! More of the house is burning now. It is too dangerous! Your father would want you to stay with us. He knows the forest and fires. He knows what to do!"

The tops of trees beyond them suddenly exploded in flames, and embers spilled down everywhere. The children screamed as some of them landed in hair and on clothes, burning them. "Glenn, stay with us!" Santana demanded. "Help me get the children to the pond! We cannot stay here and wait!"

She picked up Julia. Glenn took hold of Dominic and Juan, and Ruth took Juan's other hand. "Run! We must run!" Santana shouted, the fire roaring all around them now. Wearing only nightclothes, all of them barefoot, they dashed down the drive, Louisa running behind the children to be sure they stayed together. Santana told herself to concentrate only on matters at hand, but she could not help being frightened for Will and Valioso. Would her husband die trying to save a child who was not even his own? Yet she knew he would risk his life for any child, even if it was the son of a man who worked for him. That was his nature.

And Valioso! He was so sweet, so innocent, and it was only because of him that she had been able to bear those black years after Hugo's rape. She could see his ever-present smile, feel his little arms around her neck. She could not imagine now that any parent would put such a child in a horrid hospital for the insane, to rot away unloved. She had never regretted for one day keeping the son she'd been so sure she would hate.

Her lungs ached from running while breathing the furnace-hot air, and she could feel fire on her heels as she raced for the pond nearly a half-mile below the hill. It had never seemed so far away. She ignored the stones and sticks that cut into the bottoms of her feet. There was no time to worry about her or anyone else's injuries, for a much worse injury would be deadly burns if they did not reach the water.

The forest all around them now was a raging inferno, the fire creating its own rush of wind that made it spread even faster. Finally they made it to the pond, and Santana ordered everyone to get into the water and wet themselves down. "Glenn! Ruth! Make sure the younger ones do not go out where it is too deep!"

They all huddled in the water, the children crying and whimpering, Ester sobbing that her husband was up at the mill, which had also surely burned. Santana dunked herself and little Julia, who screamed in protest, but it was the only way to protect themselves from falling embers. She held the little girl close as she looked up the hill. Both their first home and their brand-new home were engulfed in flames. To the right she could see Gerald's home also burning. It was then she saw others heading for the pond. "Bernice!" she called out to Noel Gray's wife. "Here! The pond!"

Bernice Gray, panting and crying, reached the water with her thirteen-year-old daughter, Mary, and eleven-year-old son, Johnny. The Grays' two oldest sons, Tommy and Mark, worked at the mill with their father. Santana wondered about James, prayed he was all right. She would not want to have to write Agatha and tell her her son was dead. Or that Will and Valioso . . .

No! It could not be! But where were they? Her chest ached so, she thought her heart might stop beating.

"Oh, thank God we made it!" Bernice said. The heavyset woman plunged into the water, clinging to Mary and Johnny. "Oh, Santana, the mill! My husband and sons!"

Santana waded over to the woman, keeping an arm tightly around Julia as she reached out to touch Bernice's shoulder. "We can only pray for them."

Bernice sniffed back tears. "Are you all right? Are all the children here?"

Santana looked toward the house again, feeling sick at the sight of her home in flames. She prayed the fire would not spread to the ranch below and burn out Hernando and his family. "All but Will and Valioso," she answered. "Will went to get him, and I have not seen them since." She struggled against an urge to scream and scream, just as loudly and for as long as she could. Where were they? Where were her husband and son?

Finally she saw the figure of a man walking toward them. The bright orange light behind him made it impossible to see his face, but Santana recognized her husband's shape, the broad shoulders and slender hips. She handed Julia to Glenn and told him to stay put, then waded out of the pond. "Will!" she called. "Hurry!"

Why was he going so slowly? He could be burned! She ran to him, grabbing his arm, and in the glow of the fires she could see his eyes. She felt as though her blood had left her, and she thought she might faint. His eyes! Such tragedy there! His face and clothes were black from smoke, and there were burns all over his bare arms and shoulders. Tears began to stream down his face, making salty pathways through the soot.

"I couldn't find him," he said. "He must have run away, confused by the shouting and the flames. He wasn't . . . in his room. I searched and searched until the fire . . . forced me out. I couldn't find him, Santana. I couldn't find Valioso."

They stood staring at each other, suddenly oblivious to

the roar of flames all around them. Santana looked up at the house to see the roof beginning to cave in.

Valioso! Everything went black then. She felt herself falling, felt Will catch her. He picked her up in his arms, and as he carried her back to the pond, she could feel him shaking with grief.

Thirty

The mill was spared. The fire had started from lightning just south of the mill, and it was blown away from the mill by a north wind that carried the flames farther south, blackening and destroying everything before it, including Will and Santana's homes, Noel's home, all the outbuildings. Several prize Palominos were lost, Will's ranch hands unable to take the time to get them out of the barn. The fire had simply come too fast to save anything at all, and the only thing that had rescued Hernando's house and the other buildings at the main ranch was freshly plowed grape vineyards and vegetable fields between the fire and the ranch. The wide expanse of dirt acted as a breaker, cutting off the flames.

The facts that Noel and James and Ester's husband were fine, the mill intact, their other five children unharmed except for a few superficial burns, were all that buffered the pain in Will and Santana's hearts. Little Valioso's body had been found amid the ashes of their home, and from his position when Will and Glenn found him, it appeared he had taken his puppy into a playroom, where he had hidden in a closet because of the thunder and lightning, perhaps before the fire ever reached the house. Why he hadn't responded when Will had called for him, no one would ever know. Always wanting to please, it was possible he'd been afraid he had done something wrong by hiding in the closet. His puppy was found dead not far from his body.

Such sorrow was hard enough for any woman, but the guilt Santana felt over not having wanted Valioso in the beginning made her own grief more unbearable. She had loved him so, had tried these five and a half years to make up for hating the unborn fetus, yet now that did not seem to count. She could not help feeling she was being punished for her sin. Besides that, she suffered even more guilt for the horrible grief Will was bearing. Not only did he feel Valioso's retarded condition was his fault, now he felt responsible for the boy's death. He had collapsed to his knees at the child's grave, sobbing that he should have found him, should have saved him.

Since the funeral, they had again grown apart, this time because of Will. Santana needed her husband's strength more than ever, but the strength to carry on had to come from inside herself. Will withdrew into a quiet shell, hardly speaking to her or the children. While Bernice and her two children had moved into Hernando's guest house, Will and Santana and their five children stayed at Hernando's, bunching up to share rooms with Hernando and Teresa's children. Santana slept in a room with Ruth and sixteen-year-old Inez. Julia shared her old bedroom with Rosa Maria. Will and Glen stayed with twenty-year-old Rico, and Dominic and Juan stayed with eleven-year-old Eduardo.

Santana suspected Will was glad for the sleeping arrangements. It gave him an excuse not to sleep with his wife, which meant there was no chance to be alone with her. She knew it was because he thought she surely blamed him for Valioso's death, just as he had once thought she blamed him for the boy's condition. Her own grief was all but unendurable, but she knew Will suffered a different kind of grief. It had been even worse for him because he had seen the boy's body. He had not allowed Santana to see the child or the dog, but they had been buried together in the same coffin.

The children were also grief-stricken, and it was their need of her that kept Santana going through the black days that followed the fire. Will was away most of the time, throwing himself into helping clean up, making plans to rebuild, visiting the mill, doing everything he could to stay busy and not think about the loss. Santana suffered alone, and so did Will.

For eight weeks they drifted apart, each lost in a grief much greater than just losing a child, a grief made worse by guilt. Both lost weight, both found it difficult to sleep. Santana was plagued with dreams, a recurrence of nightmares about Hugo, flashes of memories about Valioso, his smile, his hugs. He had become so much a part of her everyday life, she hardly knew what to do without him. Everywhere she turned she saw him, for he had followed her around like a shadow for five years. It seemed unreal that he could be gone, and constantly she expected him suddenly to appear and run to her, throw back his head and laugh with that innocent joy that was always in his eyes.

One night she awoke again with a start. It had become a regular experience for her, to sleep a couple of hours and then jump awake, taking a moment to sort dream from reality, to realize what had happened was all too true. Valioso was dead. Her little boy was gone, and her only consolation was that he'd had his puppy with him, and that in life he had been a happy child, oblivious to his own shortcomings.

She sat up. Yes, that was something Will must understand. Why should he blame himself for Valioso's condition when the boy had suffered not at all from it? Valioso had been a very happy child. Perhaps God had taken him home so that he would not suffer more as a grown man. Then again, perhaps the boy had just been a gift to help her bear those first few years. Now the gift was gone. Was that a sign that she should take the final step and tell Will the truth? With Valioso dead, there was no reason to keep the secret any longer. She had thought she could bear it, had suffered with it only because of the boy. Now she was not so sure she could carry it to her grave, nor could she let Will keep suffering. She had wrestled with her conscience for so many years, and it was finally wearing her down. Valioso's death had loosed all of the despair and guilt, and she could no longer fight to keep something inside that desperately needed to be released.

She rose from the bed, achingly weary from so many nights of lost sleep. She pulled on her robe and walked out into the hallway. She needed to think. Perhaps fresh air would clear her head. She walked to the end of the hall and out into a garden. A soft breeze drifted from the north, and even after all these weeks, it still carried the smell of smoke and burned brush and pine. She shivered at the memory of that awful night, the memory of the look in Will's eyes when he stumbled to the pond, covered with burns. Crickets sang, and an owl hooted somewhere nearby . . . and her ears caught another sound, a strange choking sound. She frowned, making her way by moonlight toward the sound, realizing as she drew closer that it was someone crying.

Her heart felt shattered; it could be no one else but Will. She walked around a cluster of rosebushes and saw him kneeling at a bench as though praying. He was still dressed in denim pants and a calico shirt. Had he been

awake all night? She knew that many nights he did not
sleep at all. She hesitated, wanting to go to him, yet afraid
of embarrassing him in what must be a very private moment for him. She could not leave him there alone, however. He tried to be so strong, a proud man who felt he had
failed his son. She stepped closer. "Will?"

He sniffled and looked up at her, then quickly rose,
wiping at his eyes with his shirtsleeve. "Go away,
Santana."

"No. We are each grieving alone, when we should be
sharing our grief, and we each carry a guilt over Valioso's
death, except that you have no reason to suffer any kind of
guilt at all."

He breathed deeply to regain his control, then ran a
hand through his hair and turned away. "What do you
mean? What do you have to feel guilty about? I'm the one
who was sick and caused his condition. I'm the one who
failed to save him from the fire."

Santana closed her eyes and clasped her hands, praying for courage, praying that what she must tell him would
not mean losing him forever. "Will, Valioso was a happy
boy. He was not aware there was anything wrong with him.
There is no reason to feel guilty for his condition. I think
he was happier than most normal children. And maybe it
is best that God took him while he was still young and
oblivious to the hurt others could cause him."

Will sat down on the bench. "Maybe. That doesn't
help how I feel about it." He looked up at her. "What did
you mean about suffering your own guilt? You were a wonderful mother to him."

Santana studied his face, wondering if soon she would
see nothing but hatred in his eyes. "I did not want him.
Before he was born I hated the life that I carried. After he
was born, I realized that no matter how he was conceived,
he was an innocent baby who needed our love. I loved him

as much or more than our other children, and I have spent the last five and a half years trying to make up for how I felt about him before he was born."

Will frowned. "What the hell are you talking about? Did you hate me that much right after the war, that you'd hate the child I gave you?"

Santana closed her eyes, tingling all over with dread. She could not let this continue. "Valioso . . ." She paused. "Valioso was not your child."

She opened her eyes, watching him. There it was, the look she'd dreaded. He stared at her in disbelief, shock, doubt, the horror of the truth sinking in. "What?"

She swallowed. "Valioso's father was Hugo Bolivar. Now that Valioso is dead, I cannot allow you to spend the rest of your life feeling guilty."

Will just stared at her, slowly rising, his gaze moving over her as though he did not know her. "What the devil are you talking about?"

Santana shivered at the look in his eyes, now changing from shock to anger. "The reason it was so hard for me to forgive you when you came back from the war was not just that you had left us. It was because you were not here to protect me. If you had not gone away, I would never have suffered the horror that I suffered. Hugo Bolivar raped me."

There. It was said. Why had it suddenly been so easy to tell him? Perhaps because he deserved to know . . . and because she had to say it or go crazy. Will's eyes widened in disbelief. "What in God's name . . . When? Where?"

Why did she feel so calm? She actually felt stronger saying it. It was as though a great weight were being lifted from her shoulders. "The day of my father's funeral," she answered. "That is how evil and sick with vengeance Hugo Bolivar is. He knew that you were still away. He used the funeral as an excuse to come to the ranch. He even had his wife with him." She folded her arms across her chest at the memory. "I was so upset over losing my father, and not hearing from you, thinking you, too, might be dead. I felt so weary. I went to my old room to lie down, and I fell asleep there."

She turned away, unable to bear the way he was looking at her. Would he blame her? Hate her? "I awoke to Hugo Bolivar hovering over me. He knows our house well, saw me go to my room. He apparently snuck in through a patio door while I slept. He . . . put a handkerchief over my nose and mouth. It was wet with something that had a strange smell. He told me it was some kind of drug he'd learned about from the criminals in San Francisco. Whatever it was, it left me helpless. I could not move. I was paralyzed, yet conscious, and that was exactly what he wanted. He wanted me to know what he was doing to me.

"He laughed and said that I belonged to him at last. He said I dared not tell you, because you would hate me, divorce me. It would bring shame to me and my family. People would not believe it if I cried rape. He would only say I was willing, a woman who had been without her husband for too long, a woman hungry for a man. Because I was once engaged to him, he said people would believe I had turned to him out of need, and because of the way he raped me, there were no marks, no sign that I had been forced. He wanted me to suffer with the secret for the rest of my life. I could do nothing but lie there, staring at those . . . evil dark eyes of his . . . watching him smile while he . . . took me."

Her voice choked on the last words, and she breathed deeply to stay in control. "Afterward . . . I could only lie there for nearly an hour before I was able to move again. I asked Louisa to fix me a bath so that I could wash away his filth. I hoped that the hot water, a lot of wine . . . would make it all go away. If it was not Hugo's seed that made Valioso retarded, perhaps it was my own fault, for drinking too much wine that night, sitting in that hot water hoping that the combination would abort any life Hugo might have put into me." She covered her face, gasping in a sob.

"My God, Santana!" Will exclaimed. "Why didn't you tell me?"

She shook her head, taking a moment to gather her strength. "By the time you came home . . . I already knew I was with child. I was even thinking of having Dr. Enders abort it, in spite of what a sin that would have been. And then . . . you came home . . . and I realized that if we made love soon enough, I could say it was yours and spare the risk of dying from an abortion, and spare spending my afterlife in purgatory . . . spare my family the shame of it if it was discovered. I did not tell you because you had been through so much yourself in the war. How could I tell you such a thing when you first came home? You were not well, and the joy I saw in your eyes at being home again . . . I could not spoil that.

"Besides, I was afraid you would try to kill Hugo and end up in prison yourself. I was afraid of what I would see in your eyes. Hugo told me you would not believe me, that because you had been gone so long, you would think I had slept with other men, that all American men thought Spanish women were hungry for men. He even said he was going to spread the rumor that I had done just that."

Will felt as if a knife had been plunged into his heart. So, that was how the rumors had started. Hugo Bolivar.

"As it turns out," Santana went on, "you later suspected another man. My heart broke when you asked if there had been another." She turned and faced him. "Oh, yes, there *had* been another! An evil, twisted man who left me with a secret that sometimes made me vomit! At the time it happened, I was afraid, vulnerable, lonely. My fa-

ther had just died. I believed the things Hugo told me, and
I was afraid of losing your love . . . except that I almost
lost it anyway, because I could not help blaming you for all
of it. Yet I loved you so, *carino mio*.

"For those next months I hated the life that was growing inside of me, hated the man who had planted it there.
But when Valioso was born, I knew I could not blame him
for the sins of his father. He was an innocent child, and I
did not want him to suffer. He deserved to be loved, to
know the kind of love that I knew you were capable of
giving him. I could not deny him that. I did not want you
to hate him, or make me give him away to a hospital. I was
afraid that if you knew the truth, you would not want him
anywhere near you. And I was afraid you would try to kill
Hugo. I kept the secret to protect both you and Valioso.
Now that Valioso is . . . dead, it no longer is important
to protect him, except to protect his memory and the love
his brothers and sisters had for him. I would never want
them to know. I only tell you because I can no longer bear
to see you suffer over a child fathered by Hugo Bolivar."

She waited, and for the next few minutes there was
only the sound of crickets, and the vision of Will standing
there, frozen in place, his eyes unreadable. Finally he
turned away, shivering. "So," he said quietly, "that explains the way you behaved, the reason you avoided me in
bed, never came to me willingly. It explains so many
things."

"*Si*. It took me many years to want you as a woman
again, even though I loved you as much as ever. When you
first came home I allowed you your husbandly rights, but
for me it was almost unbearable because of the memory
Hugo left me with. Finally, the night of the governor's ball,
I—I opened my eyes, and I saw Hugo. That was why you
saw a look on my face that told you I did not want you. I

did not know how to explain it except to let you believe I had not forgiven you because of the war.

"Please know that I have always loved and wanted only you, *carino mio*. I would never, never willingly give myself to another man. I know now that Hugo never touched me at all, because in my heart, you are the only man who has touched my soul, the only man I have given myself to out of passion and love."

An aching hurt showed in his eyes. "You should have told me. I'm not a man to blame a woman for something like that, or to blame a child for its parent's faults. I could have helped you through all of it. I wouldn't have hated Valioso."

"Wouldn't you? Just think about how much you hate Hugo. I could not let you think of that man every time you looked at Valioso. And I could not take the risk that you would lose that temper of yours and go and kill Hugo for what he did to me. I can only pray that now you will realize that would be a useless thing to do. Valioso is dead. I managed to overcome the terrible thing Hugo did to me. You and I found each other again, and I learned to be a whole woman. Hugo is a withering old man who is losing his fortune. God is punishing him in his own way. We do not need to do it."

"Don't we?" Hatred fired in Will's eyes, and she could feel his rage. His hands curled into fists, and his jaw flexed. "The day of your father's *funeral*? His wife just out in the other room? You're lying there worn out from worry and grief, and he comes in your room and visits something like that on you?" He turned away. "Sweet Jesus! He's more of a monster than I thought. Why didn't I kill him the day of the duel? Why didn't I *kill* him!"

"Will, I need you now more than I ever have in my life. I can hardly bear this grief over Valioso. Please do not add to that grief by doing something foolish that could cost you prison or your life. These are not the old days. You cannot go and take your own revenge. There are laws—"

"There are laws against rape!"

She stepped closer. She was never sure how to reason with Will when he was this angry. "It has been over six years. It would be impossible to prove now, and it would only bring me and the children great shame. Please, Will, let it go. Let it go! I only told you because with Valioso dead, you had a right to know, and the secret was eating at my insides so that I could no longer bear to carry it." Tears filled her eyes. "Please, Will, do not do something foolish." He started to walk away. "Where are you going?"

"For a ride. I have to think."

"It is still dark!"

"I'll be all right. Hell, it's almost morning anyway."

"Will!"

He walked off into the darkness, and Santana could not be sure what he would do. She sat down on the bench and wept, her tears a mixture of fear and relief. She could only pray that she would not regret what she had done.

Santana moved through the morning in a daze, helping Teresa with getting the children their breakfast. Estella came to the house to give the children lessons. She had been teaching at the ranch the night of the fire, and because her home had been on the south side of the plowed fields, it had been spared.

Santana was glad for the lessons. They kept the children occupied. She was too worried about Will to handle the noise and activity that morning. She walked outside and up a small hill to the family burial ground. A new grave was there now, beside her parents' and Father Lorenzo's. Oh, how she ached to hold her little boy again, to see that ever-present smile. She prayed he died from smoke long before the flames reached him.

She knelt beside the grave, touching some wilted flowers that lay on top of it. "My sweet Valioso," she whispered. "Mama loves you, but you are in a better place now, and you are loved much more than I could ever love you. Forgive me for not wanting you. How could I have known you would bring me so much joy, that you would be the very thing I needed to help me survive?"

She heard a horse approaching, and looking up, saw Will riding over the hill. He noticed her at the grave and turned the horse to head in her direction. How wonderful her husband looked perched on a fine Palomino. He was forty-three now, but strong and handsome as ever, the lines of aging only making him look wiser, more manly. His sandy hair was still thick, his eyes still so blue. But what did she see in those eyes now? She was not sure.

He rode close to the burial plot, then reined the horse to a stop and dismounted. He kept hold of the reins as he walked over to her, a determined look on his face. "We're going to see Bolivar."

Santana knew that tone in his voice. There was no arguing his decision. She swallowed, not sure what he meant to do. "Why?"

Will drew in his breath in an effort to control his anger. "Because you deserve to face the son of a bitch and let him know you've told me the truth, that he didn't accomplish a thing by doing what he did, except to commit a sin he'll have to live with the rest of his life. To embarrass him in front of his wife. He's got to know he didn't hurt us at all, and I want to see him shake in his high black boots when he finds out I know the truth!"

"You—you won't hurt him?"

"I don't know yet what I'll do."

Santana turned away. "I think he already knows you have won. You bought Rancho de Rosas out from under him. You are growing more wealthy every day, while he is losing everything."

"I don't care. I want to face him on this. I want him to realize that I know."

Santana swallowed, shivering at the thought of finally facing Hugo with Will at her side, the truth out in the open. It would be a pleasure in a way, but she feared what Will might do. "I do not think it is fair for his wife to know. I am sure she has suffered enough over the years just being married to the man and being unable to give him children. I do not wish to add this burden to her heart."

"Fine. We'll ask to see him alone."

Santana faced him. "*Gracias*. We will go then." She watched his eyes, seeing the hurt there, the guilt . . . and was that love?

"I'm sorry, Santana, for what you suffered. I have more to say to you, but I want to do this first. We can't begin to heal the wounds until we look the enemy in the face and show him he can't defeat us."

She nodded. "If that is what you want, *mi esposo*, then we will go."

Will glanced at Valioso's grave. "I loved him like my own, you know. As far as I'm concerned, he *was* mine. I won't shame Valioso's memory by letting Bolivar know he was the father. Valioso was too sweet and good for anyone ever to know he came from the seed of a man like Hugo Bolivar." He looked at her again. "I don't want anyone to know, not even Bolivar. *I* am Valioso's father."

Santana smiled. "*Si, carino mio*. And you were a good father. He loved you, and you loved him, and that is why I could never tell you the truth."

Will shook his head. "You're a lot stronger than I ever gave you credit for." He turned away. "We'll leave today. We'll tell the others it's a business trip." He mounted up and rode off, and Santana knew there would be no talking this out between them until he had done what he felt he must do. Her stomach rolled at the thought of facing Hugo, but at least Will would be at her side. "God help us all," she whispered.

Thirty-One

Santana waited nervously beside Will, both of them standing at the front door of the stone mansion Santana had hated when she was young. She thanked God that Will had come along and saved her from having to live here all these years, in this cold, heartless home in the city. Will raised the knocker and banged it a second time, and finally a butler opened the door, peering out at them. He was not anyone Santana recognized.

"We are here to see Hugo Bolivar," Will said with a note of authority. "Tell him Will Lassater and Dona Santana Chavez de Lassater are here."

The butler stepped aside to let them in. "Don Bolivar is quite ill, sir," the man said. "I will check with Senora Bolivar to see if he can receive guests."

He left them to climb a circular staircase that led to the rooms above, and Will looked around the two-story-high foyer. It had marble floors, and a grand chandelier hung from above. He thought how he could build a home much finer even than this one for Santana, but she would have none of it. She wanted her simple stucco home, just like the one that had burned. It had been bigger and fancier than their old house, but still warm and homey. This place seemed to fit its owner—cold, overbearing.

Every time he thought about what Bolivar had done, he wanted to crush the man's skull. If only he had killed him in the first place! What a horrible, unspeakable thing he had done to Santana, and for her to have held such a thing inside all these years, thinking to spare everyone but herself, only showed how strong she was, how important her family was to her.

He should have guessed. He *had* guessed. There had been another man, just as he'd suspected, but it had been a horrible nightmare for her, something that had left her unable to be a woman again in the fullest sense for years afterward. He ached to make love to her, just to reclaim her for himself, to remind himself who this woman belonged to. But first they had to face Bolivar. She had to reach this last hurdle and rid herself of this man and the memory forever.

Poor Valioso, so innocent of all of this. Now he understood why Santana had put so much time and energy and love into the boy, not just because of his condition, but because she needed to soothe her own conscience over not wanting him. What woman *would* want the child of such a dastardly deed? God worked in strange ways, and he did not doubt that Valioso's problems had been a blessing in disguise, something that touched Santana's heart and made it possible for her to love him in spite of his beginnings. The child had given her a reason to keep going, had kept her busy and preoccupied during those years of healing. Now it was Will who had to heal, from his own guilt for not being home when his wife needed him most, guilt for not killing Hugo Bolivar when he'd had the right and the chance.

He glanced down at Santana, and he could feel her

trepidation. He had demanded they do this, and she had not argued, even though it had to be the hardest thing she had ever done. She needed his strength and comfort, but for these last three days on their journey to the city, he had been too full of anger to give her what she needed. Maybe when this was over . . .

He saw Carmelita coming down the stairway, and he was startled to see that although she was younger than Santana, her hair was already graying heavily. It was no wonder, he thought, having to live with a man like Bolivar. God only knew the hell the woman had been through. She wore a plain dark blue taffeta dress, and her hair was drawn into a pile on top of her head. She wore no earrings, no jewelry of any kind except a wedding band, and her eyes showed a deep sorrow.

Santana's own pity for the woman was mixed with a great relief that she had never had to walk in Carmelita Bolivar's shoes. She seemed to be a proud woman, and Santana well knew how difficult Hugo could make life for such a woman, who probably had thought she was marrying a charming, wealthy Spanish gentleman. Her religious beliefs would prevent her from ever leaving her husband, so she had lived with her personal hell all these years.

"Senor Lassater. Dona Chavez de Lassater," she greeted them stoically, her eyes revealing her indignity at their presence. "I am well aware that you have no good feelings for my husband. Why would you pay your respects now that he is dying?"

"Dying?" Will frowned. "We didn't know."

"The doctor says it is a cancer. It is all through his body. When it reaches his brain, he will die, which the doctor says will be in only a few days. He is suffering great pain, and often he begs me or the doctors to shoot him and end it."

A proper death for such a devil, Will thought. "Can he speak? Would he know us?"

"Si," Carmelita answered. "But what possible business could you have with him now?"

"It's personal," Will answered. "We would like to see him alone."

"Will, maybe we should just leave," Santana said.

"No." He kept his eyes on Carmelita, suspecting she realized this involved a wrong her scoundrel of a husband had committed. *"Por favor,* Senora Bolivar, this is a matter of great importance to me and my wife. It could even be important to Hugo, since he is dying. There are certain things a man must get in order before he dies."

Carmelita studied his eyes, turned her gaze to Santana. She saw a deep agony in the other woman and had no doubt that Santana had known her own horror at Hugo's hands at one time or another. As a wife who had made promises to her husband in marriage, she felt a duty to protect him. In her heart, though, she could not help thinking he deserved to die as he was dying, God forgive her. And she did not doubt that Will and Santana Lassater deserved to have whatever last say they had come there to say. She looked back at Will. "I will show you to his room."

She turned and walked across the marble floor to the staircase, and Will took Santana's arm and followed. Carmelita said nothing until they reached a doorway, where already they could hear Hugo groaning in agony. Carmelita turned to them. "You will barely recognize him. He weighs less than a hundred pounds."

Santana's eyes widened in shock. Only three months ago Hugo had stormed into their home in San Francisco, ranting and railing about Will buying Rancho de Rosas.

"I know that you have been buying some of Hugo's property," Carmelita added, looking at Will. "When he dies, I will sell all that is left to pay off debts and go home to Los Angeles. San Francisco is not a pleasant or safe place to be right now. There has been rioting and unrest, and this city has never been home to me. If you are interested in buying whatever Hugo has left, come and talk with me after he is gone."

Will felt sweet revenge at the words. Yes, he would gladly buy up anything Hugo Bolivar had left, own every last piece of property and commercial enterprises the arrogant man had once owned. He nodded to Carmelita. "I'll be glad to help you out. I'm sure you'll take comfort in being able to go back home."

"*Si*. I miss my family and southern California."

Santana thought how much like herself Carmelita was, a true *Californio* who felt a special loyalty to home, to the land where she had been raised. Even though she was still in California, coming to San Francisco was like leaving home. "*Gracias*," she said to Carmelita.

The woman met her eyes, and Santana saw her grief, a grief not for Hugo, but for herself. "You are a lucky woman to have found a man like Senor Lassater. I read about the fire, your son. I extend my deepest sympathy, but remind you that at least you had him for a while, and you have five other children in whom to take comfort. I have never known such a blessing. Perhaps if I at least had had children, life would have been more bearable. I would have known some joy."

She turned and left them. Santana looked up at Will, who kept hold of her arm and led her into the room where Hugo lay in a large bed, looking shriveled and old, his cheeks sunken, his black hair thin and lusterless. His head moved back and forth as he groaned in agony, and it took a moment for him to realize Santana and Will were standing there. Seeing him that way, every last bit of horror that lingered deep in Santana's soul over what he had done to her vanished. Hugo Bolivar was being properly punished by God.

He looked stunned to see her there, and shame and anger filled his dark eyes, eyes that used to make her shiver, but were now glassy and yellow-looking, the fire gone out of them. "Go . . . away," he whispered.

Santana didn't move. "My husband knows what you did to me," she said. "He would gladly kill you, but it is obvious God is doing that for him. I only came to tell you that your plan to destroy me did not work, Hugo. Will knows everything. I told him that you raped me. You said that if he ever knew, he would leave me, but here he is, at my side. We have a love that is much stronger than anything you ever could have done to us. I want you to know before you die that our love is stronger than ever, that you did not succeed in your effort to ruin that love. You can die knowing that you committed a terrible sin. You can die wondering if you will be sent to purgatory for what you have done. I am sure you committed many other sins. The journey to heaven, if you ever make it, will be long and slow for you, Hugo Bolivar."

The man groaned and shuddered, putting a hand over his eyes. "Go away!" he said in a stronger voice. He moaned in pain, then took his hand away, looking wide-eyed at Will. "No! Wait!" He reached out to Will. "Kill me! It is what . . . you have always wanted . . . to do. Kill me, Will Lassater. The doctors . . . my wife . . . they would never tell. I am already dying. You would only . . . be putting me out of . . . my misery. Kill me! Enjoy the vengeance . . . you have always wanted."

Will shook his head. "Your suffering is much more pleasurable to me," he answered. "I suggest you get a priest up here and confess to all the things you have done wrong, unless you choose to burn in hell." He squeezed Santana's arm and led her toward the door.

"Wait! Wait!" Hugo tried to sit up, still reaching out to them. "Kill me! You . . . have your chance. Please. Please end this pain!" He fell back to his pillow, and Will kept walking, hurrying Santana to the door and down the stairs, where Carmelita waited. Santana stopped before the woman, and they shared a look that told it all. Santana took hold of Carmelita's hands.

"I am sorry you never had children," she told her. "I hope you find peace in going back home."

Carmelita nodded, her eyes misty. "It does not matter that I am childless." She glanced up the stairway toward Hugo's room. His cries of pain could be heard through the open door. "I am not so sure that I would want a child fathered by Hugo Bolivar. Perhaps God would have punished him for his cruelty by making all of his children deformed . . . or retarded."

Santana gasped and let go of Carmelita's hands. Will grasped her arm, holding it tightly in his own shock. She knew! Hugo's wife knew about Valioso!

"How—"

"I am not a fool," Carmelita interrupted Santana. "I know my husband. It was only a guess about your son, but I see in your eyes that I was right. Do not worry. I never told a soul, and Hugo never suspected, fool that he is. I commend your strength, Dona Lassater, and your valor in keeping the boy and loving him." She looked from Santana to Will. "Go in peace now. It is done."

She turned away and went back upstairs. Santana looked at Will. "My God, she knew!" she whispered.

"She's a strong, wise woman, much like you, and I have just gained an even greater respect for the pride and honor of your race, Santana. Let's go home."

Santana closed her eyes and took a moment to let it all sink in. It was over now, and she wondered how she had let a worthless man like Hugo Bolivar nearly destroy her marriage and her own will to live. He was nothing now, a near-penniless, shriveled, dying old man who would go to his grave with the burden of his sins in life.

She rested her head against Will's chest, and his strong arms came around her. She thanked God for bringing this man into her life, for his ability to forgive and understand, his capacity to love above and beyond the ordinary man. "*Te quiero, mi esposo*," she told him.

Will kissed her hair. "Everything will be all right now, Santana."

The carriage rolled over gentle hills, and Will and Santana watched the countryside, each lost in his and her own thoughts. Santana waited for Will to speak, unsure what he was thinking or feeling. He had said little since seeing Hugo. They had left San Francisco only an hour later, and they had spent the last two nights at the homes of friends who lived along the way, rather than sleep in the open. The area between San Francisco and the ranch was still unpopulated and lonely, with no inns along the way. Although they had a driver along and there was more law in California now, Will still carried a rifle and a handgun when they made this trip. The two places they stopped, Will spent the night smoking and talking with the man of the house about the fire, always avoiding the subject of Valioso; and Santana talked with the woman about nothing *but* Valioso, often breaking into tears.

It seemed Will was deliberately avoiding her, and now that things were cleared up with Hugo, that confused Santana. At the homes of those who hosted them, they slept apart, Will on the couch, Santana sharing a room with one of the children. As they rode together in the carriage, Will made small talk about business, rebuilding, spoke with the driver, Enrique Hidalgo, about James marrying Enrique's daughter, Juanita. He went on about how he hoped to lumber out some of the burned trees before the wood became too brittle, wondering how he was going to clean up the useless wood. He said Santana would probably have to supervise most of the rebuilding of their home, as he had too much to do in other areas.

They finally reached the main ranch, where Will dismissed Enrique and took the reins himself. He asked Santana to get in the front seat with him, and she obeyed. "There's something I want to do before we see the children," he told her. He snapped the reins and headed away from the house, toward their own spread, taking a road through many acres of plowed fields, then veering left at the little road that led to the spot that had been Santana's favorite hideaway when she was young. The carriage clattered and bounced over the old dirt road that now led through burned-out forest. It broke Santana's heart to see it, especially to think that her faithful lodgepole pine tree was surely also destroyed. When Will finally reached the clearing where it stood, though, she gasped in surprise. There it was, skinny, scraggly, but green and alive, untouched by the conflagration that had consumed everything around it.

Will drew the carriage to a halt and pushed on the brake, then sat there quietly a minute. "I wanted you to see that tree," he finally said. "I don't know how it was spared, but it was, and to me it's a symbol of our love, able to withstand anything that comes against it, something that will last forever, just like you told me all those years ago." He rested his elbows on his knees. "I haven't said much since we left San Francisco, but riding with Enrique, then staying with other people, the circumstances just weren't right. I thought maybe if we came here before we went home . . ." He sighed. "I let you down in the worst way a husband can. If I had been here . . ."

"If you had been here, Valioso would never have existed, and I would not have known his special love," she interrupted. "We have faced the evil that almost destroyed us, and we have seen that it is nothing but a defeated man who is dying."

Will looked around, then wrapped the reins around a peg and climbed down. He reached up for Santana, and she took his hand and also climbed out of the carriage. Their eyes held in a new understanding, and Santana saw the apology in his.

"No more blame, Will, for either of us. Our greatest sin was only to love so much that we did things that hurt each other, when we were trying to protect each other. We know now that everything we did was out of love. We made mistakes, but we cannot go back and change any of it. We can only go forward."

He studied her dark eyes, touched her cheek with the back of his hand. "Of all the treasure I have accumulated since coming to California, you are the most valuable," he said softly. "You are more beautiful than the land, stronger than the redwoods, gentle as the sea. It will take us some time to get over Valioso, but we will find our way again, and the love will still be there." He took her hand. "I want to show you something." He led her to an area of burned trees and grass, close to her favorite tree, then had her kneel down with him. "Look at this. I found it the day I went riding alone after you told me about Bolivar and Valioso."

He pointed to a little sprig of a tree that was poking up through the charred soil. "This is what made me see how like that lodgepole pine our love is. The lodgepole is stubborn and persistent. Its cones are tightly closed, but they pop open under extreme heat, and it's one of the first trees to sprout again after a fire. This one probably came from a cone from your favorite tree." He fingered some of the black grass around the new little tree. "From these ashes a new forest will grow, Santana, and from the ashes of our past we can grow too. It struck me that this fire sort of represented burning away our past, the unhappy memories. You kept your heart and emotions closed to me for all those years. Now that you've opened up to me, like the pinecone, your grief and shame can be released, and our love will grow again, just as trees like this keep the forest alive and growing forever."

Santana's eyes teared at the beautiful words. Yes, it was so true! She felt like a new woman, except for the sudden hurt she felt every time it hit her that Valioso was gone. She looked down at the sprig of tree, touched it lightly. "This makes me think of Valioso," she said. "It is comforting to think that this is his spirit, come back to life to be with us. He loved walking with me in the forest."

Will blinked, unable to speak for a moment. Finally he nodded. "It's strange. I thought the same thing when I saw this little tree . . . that Valioso . . ." Again he could not speak. Finally he stood up and wiped at his eyes, taking a deep breath. "Santana, what I've learned . . . about Valioso . . . it doesn't change how I feel about him. I want you to know that. I loved him, and he . . . loved me. I'll always think of him as my own."

"I know, *carino mio.*" Santana walked around the little tree and put her arms around his waist, resting her head against his chest. "Let's put a little fence around the tree so that nothing happens to it."

"I'll do it today." Will wrapped his arms around her shoulders. "You have told me so many times that I am your strength, but I don't think you realize that I also need you, Santana, that your own strength has kept me going through bad times, through the war, the prison camp, Gerald's death, all my hard work building Lassater Mills, the accident that nearly killed me. All those times all I had to do was think about you, and I found a way to keep going."

Santana looked up at him, and their eyes held. In the next moment his mouth found hers, and she felt the possessive passion in his kiss, knew he was aching at the thought of another man touching his wife. Yet surely he knew she had never belonged to anyone but Will Lassater, her handsome *gringo*, her *Americano*. He crushed her against him, and she was taken back to that first time they talked here in this same place. It seemed a lifetime ago. Thank God Will had come into her life.

"*Te quiero*," she said softly, resting her head on his shoulder.

"*Te quiero*," Will answered, kissing her hair.

They stood there holding each other for a very long time, and an unseen little boy watched, still smiling.

ABOUT THE AUTHOR

An award-winning romance writer, ROSANNE BITTNER has been acclaimed for both her thrilling love stories and the true-to-the-past authenticity of her novels. Specializing in the history of the American Indians and the early settlers, her books span the West from Canada to Mexico, Missouri to California, and are based on Rosanne's visits to almost every setting chosen for her novels, extensive research, and membership in the Western Outlaw-Lawman History Association, the Oregon-California Trails Association, the Council on America's Military Past, and the Nebraska State Historical Society.

She has won awards for best Indian novel and Best Western Series from *Romantic Times* and is a Silver Pen, Golden Certificate, and Golden Pen Award winner from *Affaire de Coeur*. She has also won several Reader's Choice awards and is a member of Romance Writers of America.

Rosanne and her husband have two grown sons and live on twenty-nine wooded acres in a small town in southwest Michigan. She welcomes comments from her readers, who may write to her at 6013 North Coloma Road, Coloma, MI 49038-9309. If you send her a stamped, self-addressed #10 (legal size) envelope, she will send you her latest newsletter and tell you of her other novels and her forthcoming books.